The Female
INVI WRIGHT

Editing by: Amy McNulty

COMPLETED WORKS
by Invi Wright

***

STANDALONE
The Nanny

Aine

Lord of Dread

THE FEMALE SERIES
The Female

Her Males

Their War

Chev's Mate

Queens (coming 2025)

THE CURSED KINGDOMS SERIES
The Cursed Kingdom

The Shattered Kingdom (coming 2025)

TRIGGER WARNINGS CAN BE FOUND ON:
inviwright.com

THANK YOU

***

The largest thank you possible to my husband. You gave me the confidence and support to pursue writing, and none of this would be possible without you.

Also, to my Patreon subscribers: Inesha Thompson, Patience Isch, Kamira Evans, Kimberly Belbot, Brianna Kathleen, Emily Anne, Sharon Hartsoe, Bhavini, Ashleigh Drew, Maria Anderson, Verity K., Vanessa Turpin, Michell Wilson, Gigielle, Lone Hornbech Bünger, Dakota Lane, Lora Beth Farmer, Andi Shields, Alicia Salmon. Your support is the sole reason I'm able to do this, and I can't properly convey in words just how much you mean to me. I hope you enjoy this story!

Chapter One

CHARLOTTE

MY FINGERS ARE bloody, but that's nothing new.

I grab my hangnail with my teeth and rip, the pain barely registering. There's a slight metallic taste as I remove my finger from my mouth and flip to the next page in my book, eager to see what happens next.

Not that I don't already know.

I've read this book too many times to count, and I could recite it from memory alone.

My chest expands as my lungs fill with oxygen, and I hold my breath for a long minute before letting out a silent exhale. I squint to read my book's printed words, my reading light losing charge and growing dim. I tap the side, hoping it'll brighten, but it doesn't work.

Frowning, I bring the book closer to my face instead. This is better.

I work through three more paragraphs before realizing I haven't digested a single word. *Damn.* I return to the top of the page.

It's impossible to focus with the rats scampering within the walls and the stomping feet above my head.

My dad's guests have heavy footfalls. Having people in our home is terrifying, but it would look suspicious if my dad never welcomed guests.

He works with these men, and it's been a while since they last saw my mom. It's not often that ordinary men get to look at a female, and it's considered rude of my dad to keep her hidden. I think that's bullshit.

Mom was lucky to have been purchased back when women were scarce but still relatively attainable. Dad had good timing, buying her only months before the Seekers took over the auctions and prices for women skyrocketed.

Now females, at least young ones, are practically nonexistent. Whenever one is unlucky enough to be born, they're taken immediately from the hospital to a holding facility. They'll never know their parents, and they'll be forced to live there until they're of age to be sold.

Mom's adamant there are many children like me, born at home and hidden without the Seekers' knowledge, but I'm not so sure about that.

Things have gotten especially bad in the past twenty years. The price of women is so high that men are often forced to pool their money together to afford one. I saw a news segment on a woman who'd been sold to a group of twenty-seven men just last week.

The horror is unimaginable, and it makes me wish my parents had handed me over when I was born and things were better. Now, I risk being sold to many instead of just one.

A particularly large bang has me jumping in my chair, my blood running cold until I hear the unmistakable sound of Dad's laughter filtering down through the floorboards.

My hideaway doesn't do much to block out noise. It's both a

blessing and a curse. I can hear everything happening outside my small, underground hole, but that means so can everybody outside it.

We've padded the floor and walls with cheap carpet to help prevent any noises from seeping out, and I've made a chair out of pillows so it's not too uncomfortable.

Turning to the left, I deflate as I peer at the numbers on my small digital clock. It'll probably be a few more hours before Dad's guests leave. My back is already hurting, and I stretch it out before returning to my book. I've reached a steamy scene, and I contemplate masturbating to pass the time.

I about died of embarrassment when I found the worn romance novels lining my shelf only days after my twentieth birthday. They must be almost a hundred years old, probably written shortly before the female decline began. No books, especially romance ones, have been published in recent years.

The pages are yellow, and the cover is so faded it's nearly impossible to make out the image of the shirtless man that covers it. Still, I knew what they were the moment I saw them.

They were paired with a note from my mom telling me that just because I may not be able to experience sex doesn't mean I shouldn't be aware of it or enjoy it.

She's never asked me about the books or acknowledged their existence, but I'm sure she and my dad have noticed how weathered the pages have grown over the years.

I decide against touching myself and close my book just as another loud bang shakes the floor above me. What the fuck are they doing up there? They're dropping things every ten seconds.

A small smile spreads across my lips as I realize my parents are probably tipsy. They seldom drink nowadays, but I enjoy it when they let themselves have a good time.

Their constant stress is aging them quickly, my father balding while my mother goes gray. They don't seem to appreciate my old people jokes, their concern about what will happen to me when they die almost always ruining the fun.

I've long since come to accept that I'll spend most of my adult life in this house, and despite what they may wish, I'll be forced to turn myself in when they die. My only other option is to stay here and wait to be discovered by the scavengers who would undoubtedly break when they heard the house was abandoned.

I just need my parents to survive until I'm no longer fertile. Women unable to get pregnant aren't sold, and they're allowed to live out their remaining years in secure facilities.

My back still hurts despite my stretching, and I set my book on the ground before grabbing my discarded headphones. I've read this book too many times, and it's growing stale.

Watching videos on my phone is risky, but I should be safe if I wear my earbuds and keep the volume low.

Dad assured me tonight's guests are human like us, so they shouldn't be able to hear any light noises from me. It's only when stronger species come over that things get risky. Humans are at the bottom of the food chain, and our senses are nothing compared to most others.

My heartbeat could be enough to give me away.

Grabbing my phone, I plug in my earphones and navigate to the news. I keep the buds out of my ears and turn the volume down before selecting the live feed. It takes a minute to load, but once it does, I click the volume up a couple of notches to ensure the audio is coming through the wires and not blaring out of the phone.

Once I'm sure it's safe, I pick up the buds and slide the right one in my ear, purposefully keeping the left out in case the phone becomes disconnected and the audio source switches.

It's better to be safe than sorry.

I shift my focus to the news segment. Two over-polished

human men chat mindlessly about the disputes between the demons and ogres, laughing as they place bets on who they think will come out on top. There are quiet rumblings that the demons have begun to produce females again, and the ogres are demanding a census be taken.

The demons are refusing, specifically the Wraths, and now everybody else is growing suspicious of their numbers.

I'm not sure if I believe it, though.

I can't let myself believe it.

It took me a long time to accept that this is the life I'm destined to live, and I can't let myself get my hopes up. Female birth rates aren't going to improve, and the outlook of my life isn't going to change.

I grab a granola bar as the conversation between the men switches to the topic of humans. We've been relatively good about staying out of the public eye recently, and most everybody lost interest after our last known female was born ten or so years ago.

It's disappointing that everything nowadays is about the capture and cost of women. My books suggest that we used to care about arts and culture, but that's no longer seen as important.

Now you are either male or female, purchaser or purchasee. Nothing else matters.

At least for the humans, I suppose. I don't know much about the other species.

The men on the screen grow excited as they disclose the capture of over fifty human women. My jaw goes slack as they speak the haunting words, and my snack is long forgotten as it drops to the floor.

Over fifty?

They show footage of women being dragged and pulled from a giant underground hideaway, all crying and screaming as the Seekers force them into large, armored vans.

The reporters explain that they're being taken to the last remaining human facility and are scheduled to be sold next month. They joke about traveling here to buy one themselves, claiming this to be the largest find in over forty years.

The Seekers rarely come to the human realm, and the women became too comfortable. They felt a foolish sense of security and traveled out of their hideaways. It was a stupid mistake.

The men laugh and explain that the women would peek outside and expose their faces to the sun, and they praise the Seekers for being able to catch them with just that.

My blood runs cold with each word, fearful that I, too, will be caught like the rest of these women. I'm more careful on a lousy day than they appeared to be on a good one, but occasionally, I have ventured close to an open window, and I even took a step into the sun once.

The Seekers don't share the details surrounding their technology, but I know enough to fear ever stepping on open land. They know everything that happens outside.

My stomach roils as I pull out my earbud and turn off my phone. I can't watch any more of this. Not when I'm hiding in my hole waiting for men to leave my home.

A capture this large is going to put too much attention on us. If I had to guess, I'd say the humans will spend the next five or so years under careful watch. I'll need to be extra cautious.

Despite the loud stomping from upstairs, I force myself to close my eyes and keep my cries silent. I wish I were one of the happy women in the books I read about.

I wish I were my mother.

She's married to a good man. My dad doesn't treat her like she's some sought-after property to be purchased and paraded around. He'd rather die than hurt my mom or me, but I fear that men like him don't exist anymore.

If I'm lucky, I'll be purchased by a man wealthy enough that the offers from his peers won't tempt him. I'll be fortunate not to be passed around by hundreds of grabby, desperate men.

Men like the ones upstairs who invited themselves to our house so they could leer at my mother.

Disgusting, dirty men.

Chapter Two

CHARLOTTE

MOM PUSHES HER thin gray hair out of her face before smacking Dad's arm, her movements quick and decisive.

He snorts and pivots away in a sad attempt to avoid her half-hearted attack. It's been a few hours since their guests left, but the effects of the alcohol they drank still seem to be coursing through their veins.

Their laughter quiets as Mom rises from the couch and begins gathering my dinner dishes. I didn't get to eat with them like I usually do, but there were plenty of leftovers for me to munch on.

"Thanks, Mom!" I beam, offering her a toothy grin as she takes my plate.

I can tell both she and Dad feel guilty about me having spent all evening in my hideout, and no amount of assurances on my end seem to be helping. It's not the first time I've had to hide down there, and I'm sure it won't be the last.

It's a part of life, and I accept that.

Dad turns to me as Mom wanders into the kitchen, his brows pulled tight and lips pursed. I take a moment to look him over, noting the deepening lines that stretch across his forehead and the slight sagging of his cheeks. It feels like he's aging before my very eyes, the healthy young man I still think him to be a painful contradiction to the one that sits here now.

If it weren't for our matching brown hair and prominent noses, I doubt anybody would be able to tell we're father and daughter.

"Come here," he says.

Throwing out his arms, he gestures for me to squeeze into the small space between him and the edge of the couch. He does this every time he has guests over, and as sweet as it is, the news of the human captures has me too on edge to pretend to enjoy it.

Dad lets out a low grunt as I plop beside him and throw my legs over his thighs. I lean against the sofa's armrest as I get comfortable, my cheeks heating as I take in my dad's pained expression.

I'm not a child anymore, and his body isn't exactly equipped to take the impact of a full-grown adult's legs dropping onto his lap.

"Sorry," I mutter.

Dad forces out a laugh as he grabs my shins, his hands warm and comforting.

"Don't be," he says, giving my leg an affectionate pat.

As always, he takes a few moments to collect himself and set the mood for the conversation I've had with him hundreds of times. We both know I don't need to hear this, but it's more for his benefit than mine.

He's always so filled with guilt after having guests over.

The sounds of my mother messing around in the kitchen fill the silence between us, her quiet humming a comforting background noise.

"It's important that you know I don't think of your mother as property. I don't enjoy showing her off like that and would never"—he pauses and turns to make eye contact with me, his solemn expression showing how much he needs me to believe his words— "*never* let anybody touch or hurt her. I love you both more than anything else in this world."

I nod, my lips twitching upward as I acknowledge his confession. I've never doubted this, and if I ever did, I'm sure it was squashed between the ages of five and fifteen when he repeated these words nearly every week.

My lips purse as we progress to the next part of the conversation, and my body tenses as I wait. Dad's reaction is the same as mine, his fingers wrapping around my shin like he's afraid I'm about to disappear into thin air.

I suppose, in his mind, that's a genuine possibility.

"If you are ever taken from us, I want you to know that no matter what happens, you're not property. You are your own person, and you deserve nothing less than to be treated that way," he says, his voice thickening as he continues. "Say it."

I lick my dry lips before repeating his words.

"I am my own person, and I deserve nothing less than to be treated that way," I say, trying and failing to ignore his intense gaze on the side of my head.

If I were truly my own person, I wouldn't be forced to spend my entire life in hiding.

"Dammit, Dave," Mom huffs, walking back into the room. She's carrying a tray of tea. "I told you to stop making Charlie do this. She's a grown woman, and she doesn't need to be sitting on her father's lap repeating self-assurances."

I laugh, shrugging slightly as Dad moves to give me more room on the couch. He grumbles something quietly in response, but he's smart enough to keep his retort low so Mom doesn't hear it.

She's understandably in an irritable mood after having guests over, her patience run thin after spending all evening being leered at by my father's co-workers. I don't blame her, and if anything, I commend her for her ability to stay so composed.

"Let me help," I mutter, reaching forward and grabbing the tea tray.

I politely ignore the tremor of her hand as I set it on the table and ready their drinks. Dad takes his with sugar, always has, but Mom's easy and drinks it black. They both give thankful smiles as I hand them their cups, and I throw some sugar in mine before leaning back against the couch.

"We should discuss the repercussions of yesterday's capture," I say. I'm sure they've heard about it.

They watch the news with an even closer eye than I do.

Neither of them respond to my statement, their reluctance to talk about what happened last night incredibly frustrating. It's crucial we're all on the same page with these things.

I watch through narrowed eyes as they exchange hesitant glances, their body language almost immediately giving away that there's something they're hiding from me. I bite my lip while waiting for them to fess up, my teeth absentmindedly gnawing at the skin.

"What is it?" I finally ask when neither takes the initiative to speak up.

Mom's the one who gives in first, a pained sigh slipping from her lips as she runs her fingers through her thin hair. She avoids looking at me and stares at the front door, her anxiety visible in every action.

"Your father's co-workers mentioned something pretty concerning," she admits. "There are rumors that the Seekers have been given permission to begin house raids."

I gulp. "House raids?"

If it's anything like it sounds, we're in deep shit. The only thing that's allowed me to remain hidden this long is that Seekers aren't allowed in our homes without proof of an unregistered female. The human government enacted a law prohibiting raids after they accidentally killed a young boy a few years before I was born.

I clear my throat. "Seekers aren't allowed to enter our house without evidence of an unregistered female. That's the law."

Mom stares at her drink as she shakes her head, the trembling of her shoulders a telltale sign that she's beginning to cry. What does she mean, *no*? Is the government changing its stance? That surely would've been mentioned by the news reporters.

The atmosphere in the room is uncomfortable at best, and we fall silent as we lose ourselves in our thoughts. It doesn't take an expert to understand what this means, and the knowledge that it's only a matter of days before I'm captured has us all at a loss for words.

Humans have never been given much attention. Most species find our short lifespans and weaker bodies unappealing. They don't want to risk ruining their bloodline with us, but recent declines have made them desperate.

Fifty females is a lot, and if the Seekers shift their focus to the human realm, they'll be able to examine our homes within an unnervingly short period of time. We don't have the means to fight back. Especially not now.

I'm sure they'll struggle to find the deep underground facilities I've heard are hidden around the world, but their scanners will be able to pick up that there are three bodies in this house instead of the expected two. My hideaway isn't deep enough to fool them.

"What are we going to do?" I whisper.

Mom releases a loud sob, and Dad says nothing as he wraps his arms around my waist and pulls me into his chest. I know he expects me to cry, they both do, but I only feel numb. I've spent my entire life waiting for the other shoe to drop.

"You should turn me in," I say.

The Seekers will kill Dad if they find me, the punishment for hiding a female severe. If they hand me over, they'll still be punished, but it will be manageable. There will be no death, and Dad will likely still be allowed to maintain ownership of Mom.

She's beyond the age of childbearing, so it's not as if another can buy her. I'm willing to bet there are millions of horny men who would do so gleefully, but the human government has restricted the sale of women who can't procreate.

It's only allowed when the female has the possibility of getting pregnant.

"Absolutely not," Dad whispers into my hair, his voice shaky. "That isn't an option we're willing to consider. There's always the possibility they won't come."

I open my mouth to argue, but I change direction and shut it as I take in my father's expression. His lips are set in a firm line, his eyes hard and shrouded in warning. No amount of reasoning will change his mind, at least not tonight.

The conversation goes stale as Mom continues crying and Dad refuses to listen to my suggestions. It's taking everything within me not to scream in frustration as the night goes on, my anger reaching an all-time high by the time I give up and head to bed.

I eye the hidden latch that leads to my hideout as I move about my bedroom, debating whether or not I should sleep down there for the next couple of weeks. It realistically wouldn't be of any use. If the Seekers scan our home, they'll be able to find me even if I'm hidden.

I turn away from the latch and crawl into bed.

Fear prevents me from turning off my lamp, and I stare at the ceiling while waiting for sleep to find me. I don't know when the Seekers will come, but I'm willing to bet it won't take long if the rumors about the house raids are true.

The Seekers are known for their efficiency. I give it a week at most.

Despite the exhaustion I feel throughout my body, I can't fall asleep. Instead, I try to imagine what my life will be like when I'm inevitably captured. I'll be held at the human facility until somebody, or multiple people, purchases me during the next auction. Given the current demand, I doubt it will take long.

Humans are genetically compatible with most other species, so just about anybody will be able to buy me. I only hope it'll be by somebody who resembles my kind. I'd rather die than be purchased by an orc or goblin. Their grayish-green skin, hunched frames, and disproportionate heads aren't exactly what I'm looking for in a partner. The mere thought of having to push the giant head of an orc baby out of my body is enough to make me cry, and that's not even taking into account the rumors of orcs' harsh treatment toward females.

The house grows silent as my parents finally head to bed.

I could always sneak out while they're sleeping. I estimate I could get a few miles away before being spotted, and it would be impossible to know exactly what house I'd come from.

They could DNA test me to determine who my parents are, but I doubt they would go through the hassle. At least, I hope they wouldn't.

A loud bang has me jolting out of bed, my mind flying in a thousand different directions as I stumble toward my hideaway. My mother's scream is earsplitting as I trip over my bed sheets, my movements jerky and panicked as I sprint to the small trap door.

My bedroom door bursts open, and I scream as my hair is grabbed from behind. My feet fly out from underneath me as my legs take longer to process that my upper body has been restrained.

I throw my elbow back in an attempt to hit the person who's wrapped his arm around my waist, the attack proving ineffective as I'm dragged from my room.

The Seekers are here.

My kicking and screaming appear to make no difference as I'm forced down the small hallway and into the living room. Mom's already there, and my eyes dart over the blood that trails from her hairline to her cheek.

I look behind her, taking in the face of the man restraining her arms. He looks vaguely human, but the bulge of large teeth behind his shut lips and his flat nose informs me he's anything but. His muscles flex as Mom fights against his hold.

He seems annoyed by her struggling, but his eyes light up as he notices me being pulled into the room. Mom continues to fight, but she hasn't seen me yet.

I follow Mom's line of sight as I'm dragged toward the shattered front door, and my legs give out as I notice where she's looking. Dad lies face-down on the floor, his unmoving body signaling that he's either knocked out or dead.

Given the pain in my mother's screams, I'd say dead.

Time seems to slow as I'm ripped from my house, the pain from the man's grip fading and the sound of Mom's screams disappearing until all that's left is the blood pumping in my ears. I'm disconnected, viewing everything as if watching through a television screen.

Mom pries herself free and lunges for Dad. She notices me at the last minute and pivots, but she only takes a few steps before being grabbed again. This time, the man forces her onto the floor.

She'll be taken to a facility, but there's no rush to get her there.

Their goal was to grab me, and as I'm thrown into the back of a vehicle, that goal has been achieved.

I'm barely able to register that this is the last time I'm ever going to see my house or parents as the van starts to pull away, the men sitting in the front chatting excitedly amongst themselves.

They'll be heavily rewarded for capturing a female.

This will make their careers.

It's impossible to block out the crying from the women around me, their quiet sniffles and occasional sobs hard to ignore in the otherwise silent room.

They've all been captured tonight, just as I have, and more are added with each passing hour. I knew the Seekers would move quickly, but I didn't anticipate this level of speed. I thought I had a few days.

Their swiftness is suspicious, though, and I'm beginning to think this has been planned. The human government probably approved the raids long ago and waited until there was a breakthrough capture to allow the Seekers to launch their attack.

It's a good plan.

Nobody will know their homes were going to be broken into and torn apart either way, and those who approved the raids can wash their hands of all responsibility.

My head throbs as I look around the room, eyeing the women sitting around me. I've never been around anybody but my parents before, and I'm surprised by the sheer number of females it seems were also in hiding.

I always believed I was alone in my struggle.

A few women are sleeping on the hard floor, exhaustion pulling them under. I'm jealous of their ability to sleep when our world is crumbling. Instead, I sit rigid on a small stone bench with three others. These benches line the room, only separated by the worn-down wooden door the Seekers are bringing us in through and a nicer, well-kept one that has yet to be opened.

We watch silently as more and more females are brought in and tossed onto the ground like unwanted toys.

My heart breaks every time a little girl is added, her wide, terrified eyes confused as she tries to make sense of what's happening. Most are old enough to understand they're a hunted gender, but occasionally, there's one too young to comprehend even that.

Somebody will usually swoop in and help out, cradling the young female in her arms until she falls asleep or lowers her sobs into quiet sniffles.

Nobody here looks older than their mid-thirties, confirming my assumption that the Seekers are only collecting the women they aim to sell. I was hoping that wouldn't be the case and my mom would be brought in, but I'm losing hope.

I'll never see her again.

I'll never see either of my parents again. My father is likely lying dead on the living room floor, and he'll remain there until he rots into the floorboards.

He was a good man who deserves a burial, but because he was hiding a female, he'll be seen as a traitor. Nobody will honor him, not even the men who came for dinner.

The room grows silent when the nicer, well-kept wooden door opens and a man enters. He looks human, short and wide with thin, white hair. He holds a clipboard, but says nothing.

He takes his sweet time looking us over before pulling a pen out of his pocket. I hold my breath as he jots down a few notes and points to the five women closest to him.

"Come with me," he orders.

For a long moment, there's nothing, but then they follow him out of the room. It's not like we have any other options, and causing trouble will only make things more challenging. What feels like only minutes later, he returns and calls for a few more women to follow him.

Nobody returns, and I hope it means we're being moved to more comfortable rooms.

We'll probably be added to the auction the men on the news spoke about yesterday and, in one month, be sold to the highest bidder.

I turn toward the children with a low sigh.

Except them. They'll remain here until they're old enough to be sold. It changes from species to species, but the human government doesn't approve the purchasing of women until they're well into adulthood—usually in their early twenties.

They say it's because they care for us, but we all know they just want extra time to mold us into docile, rule-obeying women. Females who don't scream and fight go for a higher price.

One of the younger girls begins to wail as she wakes from sleep, her tiny hands curling into fists as she rubs at her cheeks and pushes back her unruly dark hair. She's wearing footy pajamas, and I can't help but imagine what her night looked like.

Did her parents know what was going to happen? I wonder if they gave her extra sweets and cuddled with her until she fell asleep in their arms. Or maybe they put her to bed as they do every night, probably having to wrestle with her as she complained about not being tired.

Either way, she's here now.

The man with the clipboard returns, and my heart pounds as he points a stubby finger in my direction. He calls for four other women to join me, but I pay them no mind.

My hands shake as I walk to the door, blood rushing through my ears and blocking out all other sounds. Unable to resist, I turn and look over the room one last time.

I'm met with expressions of pity.

I'm sure I looked at the women who left before me the same way.

The man clears his throat, and I follow him into the facility.

The fluorescent lighting in the hallway is intense, and I blink a few times as my eyes adjust. The sterile, white walls make everything feel brighter than it really is. I've seen images of this facility before, but I quickly realize it's nothing compared to actually being inside it.

There's no personality or attempts to comfort in here. Everything is made to be efficient and cheap, which I suppose makes sense. Ultimately, we're objects to be sold, and there's no point in wasting money to keep us happy.

Despite my father's constant claims that I'm not property, this building makes me feel exactly that.

The man leads us down a long hallway before turning right. His pace is fast, and our pattering bare feet are loud as they echo off the walls. My skin breaks out in a cold sweat, and I hug my arms to my chest as he slows and comes to a halt.

We copy him, waiting nervously for further instructions.

"We need to get some information from all of you," he says, pointing at the doors lining the corridor to our left.

One is open, and I peek inside to see what I'm dealing with. The room is small, containing only a desk and two chairs. Like everything else in this building, the walls and furniture are a crisp, unnerving white.

"One person per room. Somebody will be in shortly to speak with you. You'll get a physical once you're finished, and then be brought to your rooms."

He's loud, but he hardly seems to care or notice. Where is everybody else? I expected to see at least one other employee walking about.

Maybe they're busy with the females who have already been

brought in.

"Any questions?"

He's met with silence. That's becoming a common theme here.

He doesn't wait to see if we follow his instructions before he spins on his heel and heads back down the hallway from which we came. We all turn and watch him leave, our attention on him unwavering until he's entirely out of sight.

It feels cocky of him to leave without ensuring we aren't going to try to run, but it just shows how locked down they must keep this facility. There's absolutely no worry in their minds that any of us will escape.

Besides, there would be no place to go even if we did. A woman on the street will surely be noticed, and I'm willing to bet the men I'd encounter on the street will be no better than the ones here.

I make eye contact with the other women, waiting to see who goes first. A tall brunette dressed in what I assume to be her father's or brother's clothing eventually enters one of the rooms. Her actions are catalysts for the rest of us.

My feet carry me to the room with the open door, and I sit in the chair farthest from the door. Crossing my legs and intertwining my fingers on my lap, I will the thundering of my heart to settle as I wait.

What information do they need from me? And what kind of physical do they intend to conduct? I've never seen a doctor, but I'm pretty sure I'm healthy. Nothing hurts.

Several minutes pass before a young man with a clipboard enters the room. He looks human, which is comforting, and his short stature and thin limbs give me the confidence that I could take him down should he try to harm me.

"Good morning," he says. "I'm John, and I'm here to collect

some basic information from you."

He sits in the chair opposite me, barely glancing in my direction as he pulls a pen from his pocket. My jaw clenches as he clicks the pen with a tired sigh, his expression flat.

"Your name?" he asks.

I blink, debating whether or not I should answer him and, if I do, whether I should tell him the truth or lie. I suppose the only point of lying would be to protect my family, but it doesn't matter much when my mom has been captured and my dad is dead.

"Charlotte Myers," I say, deciding it would be too hard to remember a fake name.

John hums, writing it down.

"Age?"

"Twenty-five."

He hums again, the noise quickly earning a spot at the top of the list of things I hate.

"Species?" he continues.

"Human."

He raises his eyes from the paper and looks me over with a slight frown. Why has my answer shocked him?

"Full human?"

"Yes."

He nods but says nothing further. Instead, he begins to make note of my features. My nose crinkles as he labels my hair a mousy brown, and I purse my lips when he follows that up by describing my looks as adequate.

He could at least fill that in when I'm not here to see it.

"Can you read?"

"Yes."

"How educated are you? Your best estimation is all we need."

"I was taught the basics of the core subjects," I admit, my cheeks reddening.

My parents did the best they could, but they weren't highly educated themselves, and we stopped schooling once they became unsure of how to do the work. We tried educational workbooks, but there were only so many a couple of childbearing age could buy before rousing suspicion of an unregistered female.

"Great, we're almost done," John assures me. "Number of sexual partners?"

"Zero."

Considering I've been in hiding my entire life, I can't imagine how he'd expect an answer other than that.

John hardly looks surprised as he writes that down. I hate him, but I'm glad he isn't leering at me. This interaction feels nothing short of clinical, which isn't what I expected.

"Are you aware of what sex is?" he asks. "We offer a health class for the females who don't. It's a fairly basic course. If you understand the mechanics, you probably don't need it."

I contemplate the offer.

"I know what it is," I eventually say.

I've read enough romance novels to understand what happens between a man and a woman. The last thing I want is to attend a class and be reminded of what I'll be forced to endure in a month.

John turns the page of the form.

"Sexual orientation?"

I shrug, not understanding why it matters.

He continues to stare, not accepting that as an answer, and I resist the urge to say something snarky.

"I'm attracted to men."

At least, I assume so. I haven't exactly been around any, but I enjoy the look of the ones on the covers of my books.

"Any allergies?"

I shake my head.

John writes everything down, his handwriting nearly

impossible to read. I want to rip the pen out of his hand and jab it into his eye, but I refrain.

"There are men available to you during your time here," he says. "Some women find it empowering to have sex with someone of their choosing before being sold. It lowers your price, but we figure it's the least we can do. If you'd like that at any point, reach out to your handlers and they'll help you through that process."

Handlers.

My lips twitch, disgust rolling through me at how casually he speaks about all of this. I suppose it's easy not to care when it's not your life and freedom being ripped out from underneath you.

John doesn't wait for my response as he signs the bottom of the form and stands from his chair. He shoves his pen into his shirt pocket before handing me the slip of paper. I don't want to take it, but I do.

"You'll find the clinic down the hall and to the left," he says, opening the door and pointing in the direction I'm to go. "They'll take this sheet from you before beginning your exam."

I nod, refusing to let any tears fall.

He gives a few more instructions before leaving, but I'm too numb to pay them much attention. John's footfalls are loud as they echo down the hallway, and I wait until I can no longer hear them before standing. I stare at the paper in my hands, feeling its weight before running my thumb over the ridges the tip of his pen made.

I want to go home.

Chapter Three

CHARLOTTE

I POKE AT my food as Erica gushes about her experience with Ben, her words hushed as she shares all the dirty details of their late-night tryst. She pushes back her deep red bangs, the hair almost always curling into her bright green eyes. I think she's one of the prettiest girls here, and I'm sure Ben was happy when she chose him.

Not wanting to embarrass myself, I laugh with the rest of the women before taking another bite of my bland sandwich.

Today's the day of the auction, and most of the women here have taken up the offering of a man at this point. Some have even chosen to take multiple. Erica was one of the few remaining women holding out, but it appears she decided to go for it at the last minute. I don't blame her.

We've been playing ignorant to the future we all know waits for us, but I can tell it's felt by the tense muscles and furrowed eyebrows whenever conversation stops. We can pretend all we want, but the truth weighs heavily on our minds.

"I was so incredibly nervous," Erica admits, flourishing under the attention of the other females. "But he was honestly so attentive to what pleased me. I can see why they keep these men around."

The women surrounding us giggle, and most nod along in agreement. I almost feel silly for not accepting the offer, and I hope I won't regret it when I'm sold. I doubt the men who purchase me will wait long before pumping me full of their children.

Given the commotion and tense bodies of the guards standing along the wall, I assume buyers have already begun to arrive. I imagine that beyond the stillness in this room, the facility is in chaos. Everything needs to be perfect for our buyers.

The intricate details of what happens during the auctions are kept quiet and out of the news, but I've heard rumors that they can be extreme.

Some women here have gone as far as to say that females are often made to lie on their backs and expose their bodies to the room, but I'm holding out hope that's untrue.

The human government is known to have stricter laws regarding the treatment and purchasing of women, and I'd like to believe they wouldn't allow us to be forced into such vulnerable positions.

To my surprise, the men here have been relatively respectful. I anticipated being treated like an animal, expecting men to order me around with greedy grins, but that's not been the experience.

Some men even seem to feel pity, offering up information and sneaking in small luxuries for us to indulge in. I've gotten more chocolate this past month than in my twenty-five years leading up to this. Our guards will likely never be able to afford a female, and they're desperate to do whatever they can to earn the affection of one in the short amount of time they have with us.

Either that or they're hoping to flatter a female enough that she picks him to share her bed. It's probably the latter.

I turn, watching a few guards chat amongst themselves. If I'm going to take up the offering of a sexual experience, this is my last opportunity.

I suck my cheeks into my mouth and bite idly at the skin as I mull it over, going back and forth as I debate what I want to do. It might be nice to have that choice over my body, but it also feels like admitting defeat.

With a sigh, I shift my focus back to the table. As foolish as it may be, I'd like to hold out hope that the man—or *men*, I suppose—who purchases me will love me as my father did my mother. Giving myself away feels like giving up on that dream, and I'm just not ready to do that.

Some of the women here have told me I'll probably be more expensive because I'm a full human. They say men like humans because we're weaker and less likely to fight back. It's no secret we don't hold the same abilities or strength as the other species.

"I heard the king of Wrath is coming today," Erica says, capturing the attention of the now-silent table.

My hands still at that information, my fingertips digging into the soft bread of my sandwich until they tear through. Wrath is the most notorious of the demon kingdoms, and the things I've heard about its king are unfathomable.

That explains the nervous energy shared between the guards.

The Seekers brought in a total of seventy-two females during their raids, and I'm sure the news has spread far and wide. It's the largest capture in over fifty years, and I wouldn't be surprised to hear that many powerful men have come to view us.

"That's wonderful," The woman across from me, Leslie, sneers. "Can't wait."

The sarcasm in her voice is thick, and I agree to her sentiment with a jerky nod. Some poor female is about to go home with the ruler of the most feared demon kingdom. I feel bad for her.

"I'm glad I don't have to worry about that," she continues. "Demons hate my kind."

Leslie is quiet about her bloodline, but it's clear she's human mixed with some sort of fairy. Her pointed ears and tall stature give her away.

I chuckle, faking humor in a desperate attempt to hide my nerves. I'm sure anybody who looks hard enough will notice my shaking hands or tapping feet, both clear signs of the anxiety that flows through every pore of my body.

The ringing of the announcement bell quiets us, the entire room stilling until a pin drop can be heard.

One of the men—Anthony, I believe his name is—clears his throat and steps to the front of the room. He's human, short with dark hair and blue eyes, and he fidgets as he looks over our frightened faces. If I didn't know any better, I'd say he almost appears a bit sad, but I refuse to acknowledge that.

"The auction begins in under an hour, and it's time for you to shower and ready yourselves," he announces. "Remain unclothed when you finish."

Nobody moves. I take a moment to wrap my mind around his order. Why does he want us to remain unclothed? The auction horror stories I've overheard these past few weeks flash through my mind, and I set my mangled sandwich on my plate.

I've lost my appetite.

"Now!" Anthony's voice rises to a shout.

A part of me wishes we'd rebel, seizing the last opportunity we have to fight for our freedom. I want to, but there's no point. There's no real freedom left for us.

A few females stand and leave. Their actions spur a few more to follow, and before I know it, we're all silently complying with the orders. The guards may keep them hidden, but they carry weapons. We wouldn't get far even if we tried to fight back.

I join the crowd of women heading to the communal showers. It took me a long time to get used to them, but now it hardly fazes me. I don't love the guards who stand inside and stare, but at the end of the day, there isn't any point in getting upset about something I can't control.

When I step inside the large room, I strip and search the rows of shower heads until I find one that's unoccupied. Small barrier walls separate each shower area, but they go no higher than my waist and offer no privacy. They only serve as a ledge on which to set our soap bars.

Quiet, nervous chatter fills the room as I mindlessly scrub off today's grime. The always-on mentality has run me thin, and I can see its effects in my lack of appetite and shrinking fat deposits. I'm practically a skeleton.

I doubt I'll ever experience the happiness I felt at home with my parents.

The only upside I can find is that there'll be no more what-ifs. No more worrying about what will happen if and when I'm captured and sold. I'll finally have my answers.

The women on either side of me hide their cries in the shower water, sticking their faces under the spray and letting their mouths open in silent wails. I feel their pain. It penetrates every inch of my body until I fear I'm nothing more than it.

My father would have cursed me for even thinking it, but I've decided I'll end my life if the man or men who buy me are cruel. It's not a decision I've made lightly, but I refuse to spend the rest of my life in pain.

I will not be owned, and if that means dying to preserve my dignity, so be it.

The guards order us to hurry, their eyes raking across our bare forms as they take one final look at our bodies. I resist the urge to cover myself as I leave my stall and am ushered into the hallway with the other women.

I stare at the ground and follow the feet in front of me, more than a little humiliated as I'm paraded naked in front of the guards. They lead us to a large waiting room just outside the auditorium where I assume the auction is to take place.

A part of me breaks as I cross the threshold of the room. My body moves forward, but a chunk of my soul remains behind. Everybody finds a bench to sit on or a wall to lean against, and I follow suit and head to a small seat left open between two pointed-eared, black-haired women I haven't had the opportunity to speak with during my time here.

They offer closed-lip smiles as I approach, and I respond with one of my own. Now's not the time for pleasantries and chatter.

Besides the occasional sniffle, the room is silent, the atmosphere so thick, it feels suffocating. We wait patiently as women pour in, each still wet from their showers. They cover their bodies in a sad attempt for modesty, tiny goosebumps pebbling up along their skin as it's exposed to the cold air.

Anthony enters only once we've all settled, his attention cast downward at the clipboard in his arms. I want to break that fucking clipboard.

"Andrea Laurent, you're up first," he says. "Come with me."

I turn toward Andrea, watching her face pale. She and I have become close, well, as close as you can become when stuck in a place like this. She's fully human like me, and with her large chest and giant brown eyes, I have a feeling she'll be sold at a high price.

She remains frozen as we all turn toward her and wait to see what she does. I can't imagine how horrifying it must be to go first, to be the first piece of meat offered to the vultures who sit waiting.

Eventually, she manages to stand on shaky legs, the muscles quivering beneath her weight as she approaches Anthony. He seems to take pity as he curls a hand around her elbow and leads her from the room.

She keeps her face toward the ground as she exits, and the door slams shut behind them. A strained undercurrent of emotion flows through the room as we are again enveloped in silence.

I look at the women I've come to know these past few weeks, my mind replaying every fact and tidbit of information they've shared with me. I'd go as far as to say that some of them have become friends, and it hurts to know I'll never see them again.

They're going to be sold and used for the remainder of their lives. Just like me.

Anthony returns a few minutes later with a noticeable pep in his step. Despite his attempts to hide it, it's impossible not to notice how he straightens his spine and fights back a smile.

I resist the urge to lunge at him as he glances at his clipboard and calls another name.

As before, all eyes turn to the poor woman in question, everybody watching as she stands and leaves.

This continues over and over, with Anthony returning every few minutes to escort another woman to the auditorium. At some point, he stops trying to hide his excitement, and the wide grin on his face makes me want to vomit.

We must be selling at a price he's quite satisfied with. Yay for him.

"Charlotte Myers."

All eyes turn to me.

I want to be angry about the lack of privacy I'm given in this scary moment, but I don't hold any resentment.

Sucking in a slow breath, I urge my legs not to fail as I stand and follow him out of the room. The corridor is empty and free of guards, and my bare feet patter loudly against the cold floor.

Anthony leads me toward the auditorium door.

I wonder what it'll look like in there. Will it resemble the torture chamber I fear, or will it be a regular room? Will it hold tens, hundreds, or thousands of bloodthirsty men?

My questions are answered as Anthony opens the door and ushers me inside. The room is pitch black, with one singular spotlight shining on a small stage. There are miniature glowing lights along the floor that lead to the spotlight, and I follow it, knowing it's expected for me to stand underneath it.

I don't love that the darkness of the room prevents me from seeing, and I especially don't like that standing under the light further blinds me.

I can feel eyes on me as I climb the few steps to the platform. Shame warms my face as the men look at my naked flesh, murmurs breaking out throughout the room. I wonder if they can see the tears streaming down my cheeks and dripping onto my collarbones.

If they do, I doubt they care. This is fun for them—the worst day of my life considered the opportunity of a lifetime for them.

Chapter Four

SILAS

GRAY LEANS FORWARD, resting his elbows on his knees as another girl is brought into the auditorium. His black eyes casually scan over her, and he shoves a piece of his dark wavy hair out of his face to better see. I look around the room, bored, before turning back to Gray.

He's fidgeting, the incubus unable to sit still for longer than a few minutes at a time. We've been here for almost an hour now, and he's reaching his limit.

I'm hardly surprised when he turns toward Aziel.

The Wrath pretends not to notice, but I see his hands clench into tight fists by his sides. I'm glad I chose to sit behind them.

The girl steps on the stage. Her hair's so long it touches her hips, and she hides behind it as she covers her narrow chest and midsection with her arms. She's too tall to be fully human, and two sharp fangs peek through her lips.

Gray's nostrils flare as he tries to smell for any excitement or arousal seeping off Aziel. We both know he won't find any, and I'm honestly not sure why he keeps searching. Aziel may be leading this current endeavor, but his decision to purchase a female is solely for Gray's benefit.

After Gray went into one of his rare incubus feeding frenzies, attacking us in our sleep, Aziel gave in and agreed to purchase him a female. He claims it's to keep Gray out of our dreams, but I'm fairly certain he was going to do it regardless.

Despite his callous attitude, he has a soft spot for Gray.

Aziel shifts and pivots away from Gray, avoiding acknowledging the man's intense stare. I can tell he's growing frustrated with the incubi's actions, and I don't blame him. Neither of us anticipated Gray taking this long to pick a female.

I expected him to buy the first one that came on stage.

Gray's always been vocal in his desire for a female companion, and I'm sure he would've gotten one long ago if Aziel hadn't been so stubborn.

The girl on the stage is sold, and almost immediately she's ushered out of the room and replaced with another. This one's shorter with thick hips and red hair, and she looks almost entirely human.

Her body convulses as she sobs, and I hold back a wince as her fate filters through my mind. She's not going to live a happy life, and the group of ogres who buy her this evening will ensure that.

Aziel turns to me as I view her fate, his expression alone giving away that he's in my head.

I hate when he does this. He knows better than to enter the mind of a fate, and being the king of Wrath isn't enough to prevent him from getting lost in my head. I'd have to search for him, and it would be a waste of time.

Gray continues to stare at Aziel, and I hold back a smile as the Wrath snaps. He moves quickly, grabbing Gray's chin and directing it toward the stage.

"Stop staring at me," he huffs.

Gray's responding smirk doesn't go unnoticed. He enjoys riling Aziel up, especially when it results in Aziel touching him. The incubus loves attention, and he seems to think all touch is good touch.

Cheers so loud that we can hear them through the thick walls of our private viewing room capture my attention as a horde of ogres purchases the girl on stage. I feel pity as tears bubble up and spill over her cheeks, her body visibly shaking as she's ushered out of the room.

"Fuck this," Aziel snaps, finally losing his patience.

He rolls up his sleeves and stands, his intentions to leave clear as Gray frantically grabs his arm and tries to pull him back into his seat.

"Oh, come on," Gray whines. "Is it so bad I want to pick a female all three of us enjoy?"

I have no intention of using his female, but I don't bother trying to correct him. Gray doesn't listen even when I try, often pretending he can't hear me or pointing out my arousal whenever the topic is brought up. He fails to understand that just because the thought of a woman underneath me is enticing doesn't mean I plan to act on it.

I had my fill long before the female decline, and I'm not interested in forcing one to be with me now.

"You're acting like a child and wasting my time," Aziel sneers. He jerks a chin in my direction. "Good luck getting Silas to buy you a female."

Gray clenches his jaw and straightens his spine when compared to a child. Calling him that was a low blow. Aziel knows the incubus is sensitive about our age difference.

Gray is rapidly approaching his second century, and while that may seem old for many of the weaker species with short lifespans, it's nothing for a demon. Aziel is just about to hit his sixth, and even that is seen as young by some. Myself included.

Uninterested in Aziel and Gray's arguing, I turn back to the stage just as another woman comes stumbling in. Her frightened expression matches the faces of all the others sold before her, but I know immediately she's the one we're taking.

My inability to see her fate, and the pain I feel when I try, is all the confirmation I need. Her future is intertwined with mine and, by extension, Aziel and Gray.

"All right, all right! I'm sorry," Gray says, trying to diffuse the situation.

He's pushed Aziel too far, though, and when it becomes clear Aziel isn't going to relent, Gray gestures to the girl on the podium.

"I'll take her," he says.

He hasn't even looked at her, but I doubt it matters. He's an incubus, and he'll find himself satisfied with anybody.

I scan the female, unhappy with her small and fearful posture. I miss the time when women stood with pride and confidence. That doesn't exist anymore, and it's hard to enjoy the company of a being that's terrified of you.

I must admit I like her brown eyes and wild hair, though, both uncommon features among the demons but not too far off from our black hair and black eyes. I was worried Gray would pick a female with brighter looks, one with blonde hair and light eyes, but I feel it's better to find one who will not stick out too much when beside us.

We draw enough attention, and the last thing I want is a fairy-looking creature that attracts even more.

Aziel's tense stance relaxes at Gray's apology, his frown softening as he turns to evaluate the girl. His expression gives away nothing, but Gray's sly smile is enough for me to know hints of arousal must be seeping from him.

It seems I'm not the only one pleased with the female's

appearance.

The woman shuffles uncomfortably, shifting her weight from foot to foot as she stares into the crowd. Her pupils expand as her eyes attempt to adjust to the dark room, but I can tell she still can't see by how she looks at nothing with purpose.

Clasping my hands, I tilt my head to the side as I try to determine her species. Most females here are human hybrids, but I can't determine what this one is mixed with. I hope it's something strong, but the fact that I'm unable to tell has me fearing it's probably not.

Leave it to Gray to choose the weakest female here.

The seller moves behind her after giving us a moment to look. In respect, I try to keep my eyes above her collarbone, but in a brief moment of weakness, my gaze drops to her breasts before darting back up.

Gray fucking giggles as he spins toward me. I hate how excited he is over the fact that Aziel and I enjoy the sight of the woman he's chosen. We've made it clear we have no interest in intimacy with a purchased female, and his refusal to accept it is frustrating.

The seller calls out her name and age, his grin growing as he declares her a full human.

That particular piece of information has me wincing, and any arousal I may have felt shrivels. Being surrounded by three powerful demons is a lot for even the strongest of species, and even though Aziel and I have no intentions of using Gray's human, she'll still live in our home.

The power that seeps from us will tire and drain her, forcing her body to submit as a defense mechanism. It's only a matter of time before she's a shell of a person.

With Gray using her daily, I give it mere weeks.

I debate speaking up to request we choose another,

specifically one mixed with a more robust species, but it won't do any good.

I cannot change fate, and this is hers.

Being one of the last fates is hard, and I must take my duty seriously to avoid the same ending as the others of my kind. Aziel has managed to protect me from those who seek to end the fated lineage, but should I step out of line, I doubt even he would have the power to save me.

Most demons hate me, fearful of what I know and the power I've gained with age. I've been around for a long time, and in the thousand years I've existed, they've been unable to kill me. It infuriates them.

Now I'm protected by the King of Wrath, which only furthers their anger.

The men in the crowd grow rowdy as the seller states the human's virginal status and high likelihood of birthing twins. She looks shocked as he says this, making me wonder how much of her health profile has been disclosed to her.

Only humans can produce two children in the womb, and the fact that she has good odds will make her expensive.

Immediately, bids are put into the small tablets the auction house provided us. Gray hardly even looks at the amount of money he's offering up as he snatches the remote from Aziel's hand and jabs his finger against the screen.

Aziel doesn't seem to care. He could probably buy the entire lot without making a dent in his pocket.

As annoyed as I am, I'm happy this female won't be bought by a horde. The odds aren't good for most women, and she's lucky to be purchased by us. She'll only be expected to serve one man, and Gray's possessive nature will keep her from being shared.

His inability to fit in with his own kind is what led him to us in the first place, his desperation for close relationships odd for an incubus. His den practically tore him apart when he was a teenager and came home with a female, his family laughing and mocking as he claimed her as his own.

Denying his brothers and sisters the opportunity to have her was considered a slap in the face. Incubi share—jealousy not an emotion they typically feel. Gray doesn't speak much about what happened that day, but he left the horde without her and has never returned.

"You're aware the female you purchase will be your responsibility?" Aziel asks. "It'll be on you to ensure she's fed and kept happy. I don't want some fearful, meek being scurrying around our home for the next sixty years."

Gray scoffs. "Of course. I know how to care for a woman."

"You know how to *fuck* a woman. That doesn't mean you know how to care for one."

Gray pulls his gaze from the tablet and meets Aziel's cold stare. Both refuse to back down, which isn't a surprise.

"Gray isn't a child," I say, drawing their attention. "The human will be properly cared for."

The tension continues to build, and I direct my following words toward Gray. "And you'll hold up your end of the bargain and stop feeding on Aziel. No more sneaking into his dreams."

Gray nods, annoyed, before returning to the device.

It takes a minute for the bidding to slow and another for Aziel to realize everyone has dropped out and Gray is bidding against himself. He takes the tablet back with an annoyed exhale. Gray only smiles, happy that his waste of money has earned a reaction.

I shake my head, finding them entertaining as the seller calls Aziel the winner. A few men turn to look through the transparent wall of our viewing room, their anger visible as they realize who they just lost to.

Gray's new female continues to peer around, her legs shaky

as the seller steps forward and helps her off the podium. She flinches when he grabs her elbow, but she otherwise doesn't react.

Aziel and I stand to leave as the female is escorted out. Gray will be handling her delivery, and I need to get back to work.

"Have you seen her fate?" Aziel asks.

I shake my head, silently admitting to the ties she'll have with me. "She's a full human," I say after a moment of silence.

Aziel nods, lifting his hand to pinch the bridge of his nose. We didn't come here today for such a weak female, and I know he shares the same reservations as me. Our presence will exhaust her, and Gray's use will kill her.

We've seen it happen before, and it seldom takes humans long to succumb to our species' darkness.

"It's only a matter of time before Gray grows bored and sells her," Aziel says.

I shrug, unsure about that.

"You once said that about us, that he would grow tired and return to his den," I remind him gently. "That was, what, a hundred and seventy years ago?"

Aziel sucks on his teeth, his anger permeating the air before he tenses and teleports back to Wrath. I run a hand through my hair, annoyed by his rude departure, before following.

What have we gotten ourselves into?

Chapter Five

CHARLOTTE

I DON'T THINK my lungs are working.

My chest heaves as I'm led out of the auditorium, an overwhelming feeling of suffocation spreading through my body. Objectively, I know I'm getting the oxygen I need to survive, but my brain isn't getting the memo and is forcing me to hyperventilate as I make my way down the hallway.

That wasn't as awful as some warned it would be, but I know this experience will stay with me forever. Every second I was forced to stand under that light felt like hours, and the sounds of excitement that emerged from the darkness were horrifying.

How many men were there, their eyes raking over my bare flesh as they decided whether or not I was worth their money? I could see dim screens light up as Anthony read my information, but I refused to let myself count them.

The number seemed to grow once he said I have good odds for twins, and I hope my shock wasn't too evident. Did my parents know? It almost guarantees that whoever bought me has breeding in mind.

I'm uninterested in knowing how many men tried to purchase

me today, and I'd rather die than hear how much I was sold for. I wasn't in there for as long as the women who went in before me, and I hope that means something good.

Either that or I'm desperately reading into things that have no meaning. It's probably the latter.

It usually is.

I continue struggling to breathe as I follow Anthony down the hallway and into a room I've never been in. He beams as he gestures for me to enter, and it takes everything in me not to lash out and attack him.

Dirty fucking man.

He made us believe he was, at least to some extent, on our side. His pitiful glances and occasional encouragement were all a facade. I curse myself for not recognizing it earlier, but seeing the joy currently spread across his face shows the truth.

He only ever saw us as paychecks.

I enter the room with a defeated sigh. Fighting him will only make things harder for me.

"Somebody will be by shortly to groom you," he says before shutting the door.

The unmistakable sound of a lock clicking into place follows, but I hardly find myself surprised. It's not the first time I've been locked in a room, and I'm sure it won't be the last. Being in this facility has taken a lot from me, my hopes for freedom first and foremost.

All the women called into the auction before me are here, most currently being groomed. Some lie on beds receiving full-body waxes, and a few are getting their hair cut.

I recoil as I spot a woman in the corner getting her head shaved, and with a heavy heart, I realize it's Erica. She was gleefully sharing her experience with Ben just an hour ago, and now she's sobbing quietly as that same man shaves her head.

I'm surprised whoever purchased her requested this, and I hope it was the only demand they made.

A loud cry distracts me, and I turn to see some blonde I've only spoken to a few times receive a wax. The male grooming her presses his hand to her tender skin after removing a large chunk of her pubic hair, and he waits for her cry to die down before adding more hot wax to her body.

Other than the occasional pained grunt, the room is silent.

Well, mostly.

The groomers don't seem to have the same reservations and chat loudly amongst themselves as if this were a regular, everyday occurrence.

I move to stand along the back wall. A few other females are also waiting their turns, and I nod in silent greeting as I join them.

My hands clench into tight fists as a woman spreads her legs for a waxer, her face contorted in pain as he applies hot wax to her inner thigh. I can't even begin to imagine how painful that must be, and I hope the men who purchased me don't desire the same level of softness from my skin.

My dad never required such things from my mom, and in turn, I've never been expected or encouraged to shave. I prefer it that way, finding it unnecessary to rid myself of the hair my body naturally produces.

When the locked door opens, I turn, expecting to see another female or groomer step inside. Instead, one of the human guards comes wandering in, his lips pursed as he scans the room. He lingers on Erica, not even bothering to hide his staring, before shifting to one of the women lying on their backs getting waxed.

I hate how he leers at her, but nobody says anything about it.

We never do.

His eyes finally land on me, and my pulse begins to race as I drop my head and pretend not to notice. I'm not sure what he's doing here, but I have no interest in getting involved. I hold my breath as his booted feet approach my bare toes, and I continue staring at the ground as he lifts one of his tattooed arms and grabs my bicep.

Once more, my lungs feel inefficient as I'm ripped from my spot and pulled roughly toward the door. I lick my lips nervously as I follow him into the hallway, pausing as he stops to lock the door behind me.

"Your males have decided to forego the grooming," he says.

He doesn't wait for my response before leading me down the hallway, his pace fast and hurried. My arms cross protectively over my chest as I rush behind him, my skin sweaty despite the cool chill in the building.

I hoped I'd be given something to wear before being introduced to my buyers. Did they specifically request I be brought to them naked?

Do they plan to take me right away?

Anthony claimed I have a high likelihood of birthing twins, and I'm sure whoever purchased me is intrigued by that. Two children mean more opportunities for a female, and that's all people care about nowadays.

I won't be surprised if they take me before we even leave the building, and I dig my fingertips into my arms at the thought.

Refusing to cry, I hold my head high as I'm led to the exit. The guard scans his keycard to unlock the door before leading me outside.

Despite how I feel, I straighten my spine and stand tall. My father told me I need to appear strong. He said men will respect me more if I do. I've never believed it, but I'm desperate enough to try.

There's a car waiting by the door, its deep black color blending in with the night sky. I didn't even realize it was nighttime, and the moon casts little glow.

It fits how I feel. Dim and dark.

I hear a car door slamming shut before spotting the driver rushing around the front. He barely spares me a glance as he opens the back door and gestures for me to enter.

I've mindlessly followed all the orders I've been given since being captured, but this is where I hesitate. Are my buyers in there? The vehicle is small, but I estimate four or five humans could fit inside. Will they take me in the backseat?

Are they even human?

My pulse races as I think over the possibilities. I'd love to be bought by an elf or shifter, but I know that's wishful thinking. I'd never get so lucky as to be paired with a blessed breed.

The driver clears his throat when I make no attempt to enter the vehicle, the noise startling. I look around the parking lot and debate running. This is my last opportunity to do so.

I could hide underground and survive off canned food and rats.

The guard grabs the back of my neck as if sensing my thoughts, his grip painful as he shoves my head down and pushes me toward the car.

I hiss as I'm forced forward, but the noise is cut short as I stumble into a hard chest that most definitely wasn't there a second ago. The guard behind me lets out a pained moan, and I stare at the torso of the man standing between me and the car as the guard's hand is forcibly removed from my neck.

"I don't believe you're in a position to be touching what's mine."

The voice is low, and my body reacts to it in a way it most definitely shouldn't. I hug my arms tighter around myself in horror. I like it. I like his voice so much I want to bathe in it. What the fuck is wrong with me?

I look up.

He's beautiful, easily the most beautiful man I've ever seen.

He's tall, and his black hair and black eyes immediately give him away to be a demon. There are many different kinds, but given my body's unwanted reaction to him, he must be an incubus.

An incubus purchased me.

His gaze remains on the guard behind me, and I step to the side. I don't want to get caught between them, especially not as I watch him twist the guard's wrist.

He continues until it snaps with a sickening crack.

The guard screams.

It's horrific, and I stare at the ground as I slip into the back seat of the car. There's no point in running away—not from a demon.

The door shuts behind me, and the incubus smiles as he walks around the car and climbs in beside me. I've read that demons thrive off chaos and pain, and I don't want to excite him with mine.

My fingers dig into the flesh of my sides as I try to ignore the scent of the incubus. It saturates the air surrounding me, urging me to crawl closer and beg. I refuse.

The incubus clears his throat, his nostrils flaring.

A second later, to my complete relief, he pulls back on the lust he's emitting. "My apologies," he says. His voice is like honey, so thick and gravely I want to hear it every second of every day. "I haven't had to soften my scent in many years, and the thought to do so slipped my mind."

He reaches for the hem of his shirt and tugs it up over his head. I knew this was a possibility, but I still can't hide my dread as I stare at his bare, muscular torso.

"Breathe," he says, no doubt sensing my line of thought. "I'm giving this to you to wear, unless you'd prefer to walk around naked. I'm not going to complain if that's the case."

I blink, my hand visibly shaking as I accept the shirt he holds in my direction. He watches as I put it on.

The fabric covers me to mid-thigh, which is better than nothing.

His scent clings to the shirt, but I do my best to ignore it as I hide underneath the black fabric. I don't expect him to hold his scent back for long, and I mentally prepare myself to remain strong when he stops.

"What's your name?" he asks.

I clear my throat so it doesn't croak and show my fear. I'm pretty sure demons can smell pheromones, the species able to detect emotion through scent, but I'd like to preserve what little dignity I have left and try to hide it.

"Charlie," I say before thinking better of it and shaking my head. "Charlotte."

The shortened version of my name feels special, and I don't want the memory of it tainted by this male.

Besides, I'm not Charlie anymore.

That woman disappeared in the weeks I was forced to live in the facility, and I can only imagine how much further I will stray now that I've been purchased. I'd give anything to go back in time and be with my parents again, and I curse myself for all the thoughts I once had about turning myself in.

"Charlie," he says, speaking the word slowly.

I grimace as he uses my nickname, internally cursing myself for having offered it up. That was a stupid thing for me to do.

"I'm Gray," he continues, ignoring my discomfort as he grabs my wrist and brings my hand to his mouth.

I cringe as he kisses the center of my palm, and I draw in a deep breath when he releases me a second later. My body continues to betray me, and I feel nothing short of humiliated as the corners of his lips twitch.

"I'm assuming you've gathered that I'm a demon by now," he says, waiting for me to nod before continuing. "We'll use a portal to get home."

Why? I thought demons could teleport. Gray watches me silently before reaching for my hand again. I snatch it away, not wanting him to touch me.

"Do you have any questions?" he asks after another few seconds of tense silence.

I try not to look too surprised.

We were told it's best to remain quiet until the men who purchase us state their rules and expectations. It's the best way to avoid angering them and getting off on the wrong foot. While I may not know much about demons, I do know they have a notorious reputation for a reason. I doubt this man would think twice before killing me. He didn't when it came to snapping the guard's wrist.

"What do you want from me?" I ask.

Gray blinks. He's a sex demon. We both know what he wants.

"What rules do you have for me?" I try instead.

Gray seems pleased as he dips his chin in a subtle nod. He purses his lips, drawing my attention to them. They're full, and I can't stop staring as I subconsciously lick mine in response.

"I have no rules for you. Aziel and Silas might, but I don't," he says. "You can do whatever you want to me."

The sexual innuendo doesn't go unnoticed.

"Who are Aziel and Silas?" I ask, pretty sure I already know the answer.

He confirms my suspicions as he explains them to be his brothers. My heart falls as I realize I will be serving three incubi, maybe even more. While I don't know much about that particular type of demon, they're notorious for passing around and sharing their females.

"I think you'll like our home," Gray assures me, his abs flexing as he glances at my bare legs.

His shirt manages to cover most of my thighs, but there's still more leg showing than I'd like. I nervously tug on the hem, desperate to cover myself as much as possible. It's a silly attempt, considering he's seen everything already and very literally owns me, but I do it nonetheless.

"You'll like Silas. He's quiet like you," Gray continues, politely ignoring my trembling hands. "Both he and Aziel claim not to want a female, but I could tell they liked you."

Two incubi claiming not to want a female? I doubt it.

Gray sighs when I don't respond, his frustration growing as he struggles to communicate with me.

"If I'm honest, I thought you'd be more fun," he mutters.

My horror grows, and I do my best to hide it as I clear my throat and glance at the divider between the driver and us. I suppose that confirms it. I'm to serve three demons, acting as a fun object for them until they grow bored and kill me.

I'll die before I let that happen.

––––––––

Does Gray usually stare this much?

His gaze is intense and uncomfortable, but I do my best to avoid it as I look out the car window. Most buildings we pass are rundown and overgrown with weeds, but we occasionally travel through a few neighborhoods that still look occupied.

It never occurred to me just how barren the human realm has become, making me wonder how it must've looked before the female decline. I've seen images, but I'm sure they're nothing compared to the real thing.

I pick at the skin of my fingers and bounce my knee in a sad attempt to self-soothe, but it doesn't work. I somehow believed I'd feel relieved after being bought, that the pain of the unknown would vanish into thin air and there'd be no more worrying.

I also hoped I'd be purchased by a kind man like my mom had been. Now I realize how foolish that was.

I have so many questions, but nobody to ask. Gray may have said he has no rules, but I don't believe that. Males always have rules, and I'll be damned if I get tricked into believing otherwise.

"Are you aware I'm an incubus?"

"Yes."

That was made clear the moment I smelled him. Even if it weren't for the unwanted arousal he makes me feel, I'm sure I would've been able to figure it out by his looks. Demons are distinct, and while most are conventionally attractive to humans, this man screams sex. His every movement is fluid and graceful, and he carries himself with a level of confidence I didn't realize existed.

"And you know incubi can't use their lust to claim a virgin?" he continues, reaching for me before changing his mind and retreating.

I fiddle with the hem of his shirt. I've never heard anything about this, but that doesn't surprise me. Demons aren't exactly known to be forthcoming about their shortfalls. Unless he's lying.

Would he lie about that? I don't see why.

Gray groans when I shake my head.

"I need you to use your words," he says, shoving his hair out of his face.

The wavy strand falls right back in front of his eye, and I resist the urge to smile when he frowns and blows it away. Instead, I hide my trembling hands underneath my thighs, not liking how transparent my body makes my feelings.

"I didn't know that," I say.

Gray cracks a smile. "It's not exactly a common topic of conversation. I'm sharing this so you feel more comfortable around me. I'll only be able to feed off your dreams until you give me permission for more."

I try not to let my anger show as I nod. He will be sorely disappointed if he thinks I'll ever give him permission for more. The only men I want are the ones who live in my romance novels, and, unfortunately for me, they aren't real.

Assuming he's telling the truth, he'll have limitations as long as I remain a virgin. I intend to stay one. The moment I lose that, he'll be free to take me as he pleases, using me until I'm addicted to his touch and unable to have a free thought that doesn't revolve around him and his lust.

I can't do anything about the dreams.

Gray clears his throat. "Aziel and Silas don't have the same limitations since they aren't incubi, but they would never do anything you don't want."

What? I was under the impression they were all incubi. He called the other two his brothers, and sex demons tend to live in small hordes.

"Are they demons?" I ask, finally meeting his gaze.

He smiles when I look at him, his sharp canines catching the light filtering through the window. I try not to pay any attention to them, but his lingering scent still pulls at me, and I find myself staring at his mouth for several moments longer than appropriate.

Gray's an attractive man with full lips and large, dark eyes. I suppose it makes sense, given he's made to be seductive, but even that knowledge does nothing to deter me as I lower my gaze even further. He's shirtless, and I gulp as he leans back and clasps his hands behind his head. The action brings attention to his shoulders and biceps, the muscles distracting.

Demons are larger than humans, and this man is no different. He's probably about six and a half feet tall, and he carries a decent amount of muscle. My pulse races as I imagine how it would feel to have him on me, and I hate myself for every dirty thought that follows.

"It's sexy." He laughs, breaking me from my daze. "Watching you lust over me but not being able to do anything about it. It's a foreplay I'm most definitely going to enjoy."

My cheeks warm as shame courses through me. My father is probably rolling in his grave seeing this, watching me lust over the incubus who bought me. Gray may seem friendly enough, but I'm sure it's all a ploy to get me to give myself to him. Once my virginity is lost and he no longer needs that approval, I'm sure his true colors will come out.

"To answer your earlier question, yes," Gray says. "Silas is a fate, and Aziel is a Wrath."

I stare wide-eyed at him. It makes sense that a few Wrath demons would be at the auction considering their king was in attendance, but I didn't anticipate being purchased by one.

My anxiety worsens as I try to recall everything I've ever learned about fates and Wraths.

Fates are almost extinct and are rarely discussed in the media. I know they're hunted because of their abilities and often tortured for the information they can see, but that's about it.

My mouth is dry as I work up the courage to speak. "A Wrath?"

I *would* get stuck with the worst of the demons. Just my fucking luck.

Gray shrugs. "Aziel isn't as bad as you think."

"And a fate?"

"Yes, and I think you two will get along. He was quite intrigued by you, as was Aziel." Gray wears a smirk I don't want to know the reason for.

He continues to grin as the car slows to a stop. Gray exits and walks around the front, his steps slow and steady. I contemplate running again, but judging by how quickly he moved when the guard grabbed my neck, I have a feeling I wouldn't get far.

Instead, I tug at the hem of my borrowed shirt as he opens my door and extends a hand.

I pause, hesitating, before reaching out and accepting it. The skin-to-skin contact affects me immediately, my muscles clenching as my need for him blooms.

He releases an audible groan as he tightens his grip on my hand, his eyes rolling back and head lowering as he inhales my scent. As much as I know I should feel disgusted by it, I find myself aroused, my body warming as I meet his gaze.

I want him to touch me.

"Fuck, Charlie." Gray pins me against the car, his hips pressing against mine. I don't notice the chill that meets my bare legs. "You're not going to make this easy for me, are you? You're still so affected even with my scent suffocated."

Nodding mindlessly, I let out a gasp as he grabs my waist, his palms covering the bone as his fingers dig into the flesh. My nerves feel on fire as he squeezes me, his body heat warming me through his shirt. I inhale, breathing in his scent.

It's so good. I want to bury myself in his skin and live there forever.

"You smell so fucking sweet," he moans, squeezing me one last time before stepping away.

I want to cry as he releases me, overcome with agony when his skin no longer touches mine.

Gray's chest expands as he sucks in a deep breath, his jaw slack as he works his head from side to side. Eventually, he clears his throat and spins around, giving his back to me as he gestures to the building the driver brought us to.

It stands alone, with nothing but trees surrounding it on either side, and honestly doesn't look like anything special. There are many portals in the human realm, most of them used by the weaker species who cannot teleport, and I assume this is one of them.

Several guards I somehow managed not to notice until now are in front of the doors, their backs stiff and posture tense. Their grotesque, uneven faces signal them to be nightmares.

We're far enough away that I struggle to make out all the details, but what I can see at this distance makes me shiver. Their bodies look unnaturally long and thin beneath their dark cloaks, their faces hollow and broken.

An overwhelming urge to cry settles over me the longer I look, my shoulders hunching forward as defeat and despair fill my bones.

"Keep your eyes lowered," Gray instructs, cupping the back of my head and easing it down. "You don't want to look at a nightmare."

I stare at my shoes, relieved as some of the anguish dissipates. While I may not know Gray very well, I'll trust him just this once.

A warm hand settles on my back, urging me forward. My movements are clunky, and I clench my hands into fists as the effects of Gray's lust wear off and I'm forced to face what I just did.

Is this what the rest of my life is going to look like? Overwhelming desperation and arousal followed immediately by crippling regret and self-loathing?

Gray fists the back of my shirt to stop me from walking as we reach the nightmares.

"What's your business?" The crackling voice sends shivers down my spine.

The closest thing I can think to compare it to is nails on a chalkboard, high-pitched and blood-curdling. My toes curl against the ground as I hold back a physical response. Gray mindlessly rubs my back, his attempt at comfort doing nothing to help my reaction to the nightmares.

"I'm taking Aziel's female home," Gray says, sounding eerily calm around these horrors. "I'm sure you've heard about the human auction tonight."

I suppose I should be glad I wasn't purchased by a nightmare.

The man who questioned Gray hums, sounding displeased.

"Why didn't you teleport? Rumor on the block says Aziel is sharing his power with you."

Gray stiffens but remains quiet as the man begins to laugh.

"Is Daddy punishing you?" he continues, mocking Gray in a way that has me on edge.

I was under the impression Gray was powerful, and, as frightening as that may be, I was hoping it meant he would keep me to himself. What happens when others of his kind demand to use me? He'll be in no position to say *no* if he's weak.

And what does he mean by *Aziel's female*? I thought it was Gray who purchased me. He said I'm to serve him, not Aziel or Silas, so I don't understand why he'd say I belong to the other man.

Am I some gift? A present from one demon to another? I want to vomit.

Gray tightens his hold on the back of my shirt, his fist closing around the fabric and forcing it to stretch against my front.

"That's a good question!" he chirps. "Would you like me to bring Daddy here for you to ask yourself? I'm sure the king of Wrath would love to meet the man who denied his female entrance into his kingdom."

Silence follows Gray's words, and a second later, he's nudging me forward. I'm too horrified to notice. The king of

Wrath? There's no way.

No.

Gray taps my back again, a quiet order to walk slipping from his lips when I don't immediately move. I stumble, my mind running a thousand miles a minute as Gray leads me into the building and toward the giant portal in the center of the room. It looks inconspicuous, like a large doorway leading into a darkened room, but I know it's anything but.

"I'm assuming you've never gone through a portal?" Gray asks.

I shake my head.

"Well, I won't lie and say it'll be a great experience. It's better than me teleporting you, though. You'll probably feel a bit sick, definitely dizzy, but I'll be here to keep you on your feet." He strokes my back again.

I hate how comforting the action is, and I find solace in knowing it's his scent making me feel that way. I'm not going crazy. His lust would do that to anybody, and once there's distance between us, I'll feel normal again.

Gray doesn't rush me, his movements slow as he lets me take the lead. I approach the portal, but I pause before stepping through. Turning, I peer out the front doors of the building, desperate for one last look at the world I consider home. I'll never see this again.

Chapter Six

CHARLOTTE

MY STOMACH CHURNS the moment my body materializes in the demon realm. I gag and slap my hands over my lips as I stumble forward. The ground hardens beneath my feet, the feeling of it only worsening my discombobulation as I bend over and heave.

Gray's grabbing my torso a second later, his grip preventing me from toppling headfirst into the cement. I flail in my panic, and he wraps his arms around me as I struggle to regain my balance and find spatial awareness.

This is the worst thing that's ever happened to me—and that's saying something.

I go limp after emptying the contents of my stomach, the side of my head smacking against Gray's ribcage as I hold on to him for dear life. He doesn't say anything as I fail to collect myself, and he holds me silently as I squeeze my eyes shut and pant.

After a couple of seconds, I find the strength to open my eyes, forcing myself to unclench despite still feeling like the world is spinning around me. The moment my eyes are opened, though, I wish for them to be closed again.

I'm met with the sight of Gray's ruined shoes, my sick having landed all over them and his pants.

Shit.

"It's fine. One pair of shoes is hardly going to upset me," he says, probably feeling my body tense as I stare at what I've done.

He tightens his grip as I try to twist out of his arms, my hands releasing his biceps before pushing him away. Gray lets me go before he seems to change his mind and grabs me once more.

"We might as well rip the bandage off. I'm going to teleport you now. It shouldn't be too bad," he says just as everything begins to spin again.

The pressure in my skull reaches an all-time high as I lose control of my neck muscles and my head lolls forward. I can feel my vision tunneling as the ground disappears from underneath me again, my consciousness fading as Gray teleports me.

"Fuck, I'm so sorry," he says, wiping the wetness on my cheeks as I blink away the momentary loss of awareness. "I didn't realize how weak you are, and I thought it'd be best to get the travel over with quickly. I should've waited another minute or two for you to adjust."

I groan, his words going in one ear and out the other as I try to make sense of what's happening. My stomach roils as I look around, but it's hard to focus when Gray's face is only inches from mine. He looks worried, his eyebrows pulled tightly together and lips pursed.

I blink slowly as I become aware of my back on the ground, and I turn my head to the side to confirm my thoughts. Am I lying down? Did I fall? I'm not sure.

Gray straightens as I come to, his expression of concern remaining as he watches me push myself up on shaky elbows. We're in the middle of a large entryway, with tall ceilings and a wide corridor leading into what I'm sure is some grand estate.

I frown, and an intense shock of pain radiates down my tailbone as I sit up. I suppose that answers my question about whether or not I fell. Shifting my weight off my butt, I flip onto my knees before taking a moment to catch my breath.

The power filling this room is suffocating, the intensity of it overwhelming my dazed mind and weighing me down like a blanket. I assume it's a mixture of Gray's and that of the two other males he lives with. It feels like being caught in a smoke-filled room, and every inch of my body is on high alert. I hate it.

I continue slowly working my way up, desperate to stand on my own feet. The last thing I want is to get caught on my back when meeting the elusive Silas and Aziel. Gray might not be able to take my innocence against my will, but that limitation does not affect the other two.

My knees are wobbly when I finally stand and put my weight on them, and Gray reaches out to stabilize me. When I'm steady, he doesn't remove his hands as I wish he would, and I try my best to ignore the immediate lust that overtakes my body at the physical contact.

He sucks in a deep breath as his grip on me tightens, but thankfully, he says nothing about it. I don't think I could live through the humiliation of having him comment on my constant unwanted arousal.

Gulping, I wrap my arms around my waist in a self-hug and look around the room, my eyes widening as I take notice of the moving figures all along the walls. The tall, black blobs are smoky, fast, and nearly impossible to get a good look at.

They must be demons, too. Their inability to take physical forms comforts me slightly, but I still find myself instinctively stepping toward Gray.

He chuckles, his gaze traveling toward the dark figures. "Those are our shadows. They work here and shouldn't bother you. They know you're off limits."

My feet move on their own accord as Gray guides me through the entryway he teleported us into. He leads me into a giant open room, one that looks like a larger version of my living room back home. The only difference is there's no television in here and the furniture seems uncomfortable.

"This is our sitting room. We don't spend any time in here," Gray explains. "I'll show you to your bedroom and give you time to settle before dinner. I'm sure you're eager to relax."

I nod. Despite my earlier reservations, Gray doesn't seem so bad. If this continues, I'll consider myself lucky.

Gray falls silent as he leads me down a maze of hallways, each identical to the last until we reach a stairwell.

"All our bedrooms are located upstairs," he says, turning to watch my reaction. I offer him none. "You shouldn't encounter too many shadows up there."

That's good to know. We ascend, and the stairwell opens to a circular loft with small hallways darting off in every direction.

"That's Aziel's corridor," Gray says, pointing down the hallway to the left of the stairs. He then points to the one across from us. "This is Silas's."

Both are bland and scarcely decorated, and I make a mental note never to go down either.

There are two more hallways, and Gray leads us down the one next to Silas's.

"Your room is next to mine," he says.

I don't like that, but I know better than to complain. At least I'm getting my own room. There are stories of females who were forced to share with the men who bought them.

I can't imagine how awful it must be to share a bed with an incubus.

The last thing I want is to wake in the middle of the night with arousal slickened between my thighs and an urge to crawl over him. I've heard horror stories of women doing exactly that, becoming dependent and addicted to their incubus males.

As much as I'd like to think I'm different and unique, I know I'm not. He's going to ruin me just as his kind is notorious for doing.

Gray's hallway is dark, but I can still make out every door we pass.

"This is a cleaning closet," he says as we pass the first one. "And you're better off not knowing about this one," he continues, pointing to the second door. It has a lock, and I stare at the metal before nodding.

His mysterious tone piques my interest, but I don't question it as he leads me forward another couple of feet and stops at the third door.

"This room is yours." He reaches around me and pushes it open.

I hesitate, scared of what will happen when we're alone in a bedroom, before stepping inside. Gray follows, and I hold my breath as I look around.

The room is larger than I expected, with a king-sized bed sitting directly across from the door and a vanity and dresser along the left wall. It's well-furnished, but the lack of personal items makes it look bare. My bedroom back at home was full of trinkets and small items I collected over the years.

Gray's heat spreads across my back as he wraps an arm around my waist and pulls me against his bare chest. I refuse to be distracted by it as I eye the red silk sheets on the bed. I bet they would feel soft against my skin as he presses my face into the mattress.

The hand on my hip tightens as he buries his face in my neck and breathes in my scent, a loud groan seeping from his throat as he smells me. Instinctively, I tilt my head to the side so he has better access.

No.

It takes everything in me to pull away. *Stupid Charlie.* Gray is an incubus, a creature desperate for sex and willing to take whatever action necessary to get it. I need to fight harder against his lust.

Gray clears his throat.

"You can try to fight it all you want, but it's only a matter of time before you're begging me to take you," he teases, his playful tone a drastic contradiction to his terrifying words.

"The door next to the dresser is a closet," he explains, pointing to the cracked-open door along the far left wall. "I'll buy you all the clothing you need." That's good to hear. I was worried I'd be forced to walk around in only his shirt. "The door on the right is a bathroom. It connects to both our bedrooms."

I take a small step forward and graze my fingertips over the red silky comforter. It's softer than anything I've ever felt, and as I push down on the mattress, I'm glad to note it's comfortable. The bed I was given at the facility was as hard as a rock, leaving me with agonizing back pain each morning.

"You're taking her to bed already?"

I spin toward the new voice, my eyes landing immediately on the two men standing in the doorway. They tilt their heads to the side in an oddly similar manner as they look me over, their expressions unreadable.

They both look like Gray, with black eyes, black hair, and muscular frames that could tear me apart in seconds. The one on the left is slightly taller, his head just clearing the doorway, and he expresses outward disgust at the sight of me.

It's not a good sign, and my pulse races as he fixes his rolled-up sleeves and exchanges silent communication with the demon on the right. That one doesn't look nearly as angry, and he cocks his head to the side as he regards me.

I assume this one's the fate. Something about his knowing stare gives it away.

His expression shifts into a scowl, and I step toward Gray.

This must be Aziel and Silas. The two men exude too much power to be anybody else. My head lowers to my chest in submission, my knees clanging together as I nervously tug at the hem of my shirt.

"I wasn't going to fuck her," Gray argues, wrapping his arm around my shoulders.

I stumble slightly as he pulls me into his side, my feet uncoordinated, but Gray quickly absorbs the impact and steadies me.

"I can't help that my female wants me," he gloats.

I'm sure my cheeks are beet-red, and if I weren't so out of my element, I'd argue that I don't want him. I'd explain it's his lust that turns me on, and if I could stop my body from reacting to him as it does, I would in a heartbeat.

I don't *want* to want him, and I hate every second my body refuses to get the memo.

Of course, though, I would never say that.

The last thing I need is for him to decide he doesn't like me and sell me to another. Demons aren't my species of choice for a sexual partner, but there's much worse out there. It's known that demons are spiteful, and I wouldn't put it past Gray to sell me to a nightmare if I made him angry. Assuming he doesn't kill me instead.

Gray gestures toward the two men.

"This is Aziel and Silas," he says by way of introduction.

"Aziel," the taller one on the left says, gesturing to himself.

The one on the right is quick to chime in. "Silas."

Both Aziel and Silas are making no effort to hold back the power that pours from them. It has me feeling exhausted, my mind unable to focus on anything as I look between the two in panic.

Silas says nothing and steps back as Aziel moves farther into the room.

"Why is she wearing your shirt?" Aziel asks.

Gray shrugs. "Why does it matter?"

Unless Gray was already muting his power when I got in the car, he's the weakest of the three. I'm not too familiar with demon biology, but I know their age correlates with their strength, which determines their status.

They get stronger as they get older, and that strength earns them more respect.

"Have you fucked her yet?" Aziel asks, cutting to the chase. "She doesn't smell like you."

I gulp, refusing to let myself cry in front of these men.

I knew this would happen, and acting all surprised isn't going to help me. Dad said I need to appear strong, and that's precisely what I'm going to do. I may be at a disadvantage here, but I won't let them see me break.

"I'm only going to be feeding on her dreams for the time being," Gray says.

Silas quirks a brow, amusement briefly flashing over his features before he hides it away. Aziel, on the other hand, seems to be seething, his face contorting into a scowl and his hands clenching.

"No, you're going to fuck her now."

I stare wide-eyed at the two arguing men, panic-stricken as Aziel insists Gray take me. I'm sure they can all hear my fluttering heart and choppy breathing from where I stand, but they ignore it.

Despite this entire conversation being about me, they're pretending I'm not even here.

Do I have no say in this? The thought fills me with horror, and I instinctively step back. Gray's hand slides down my arm before dropping and hanging limply by his side. I take his easy release of me as a good sign and move back another step.

"I am not going to fuck her," Gray says.

Aziel blinks, making no attempt to hide his frustration. "What was the point of buying you a female if you have no intentions to use her?"

Silas steps forward and drops a hand on Aziel's shoulder.

"Aziel, give her time to adjust," he says.

It's good to know that Silas is the most level-headed of the three. Everything about him screams authority. It's intense, and I wonder if he's the one in charge. I assumed it would be Aziel, considering he's the royal, but maybe I was wrong. I don't know enough about fates, and I'm not sure where they stand in the social hierarchy.

"I won't be one of those men who abuse their female just because I can." Gray sounds more confident now that Silas has chosen his side in this argument.

I'm grateful for it.

Aziel looks infuriated, his lips flattening into a straight line as he looks between Gray and me. My body tenses as I wait for his response, scared he will continue pushing the issue.

I'd do well not to trust him.

"You made a promise. I don't want you feeding from me," he says.

Gray shrugs and looks back at me before leveling his stare with Aziel once more.

"She's a virgin. I promised I wouldn't use my lust."

Aziel laughs. "That's never stopped you before. You love fucking virgins."

I try to hide my shock, but I know I've failed when Aziel snaps his gaze to me and laughs once more. Was Gray lying to me? It sure sounds that way.

My fingers continue to fiddle with the hem of the shirt I'm wearing, worrying the fabric between my fingertips as their argument continues to unfold.

"I'm only going to feed off her dreams, and that's that," Gray finally says.

Aziel clenches his jaw. "You'll starve."

"I'll be fine," Gray snaps. "Besides, I doubt it will even go that far. She's desperate for it."

All eyes turn to me. My bottom lip trembles, the stress of today getting the best of me as my eyes grow wet. I don't want to be some pawn for Gray, and I don't want to be here.

I'd kill to be with my family again, even if that means I spend the rest of my life in hiding. These men are going to be the death of me, intentionally or not.

Gray drops the argument as he notices my silent crying, his cold expression softening.

Aziel turns to Silas and mumbles something I can't hear before leaving. The room feels lighter with him gone, and muscles I didn't even realize were tensed relax. Silas and Gray's proximity still has me on edge, though, and I watch the two of them through narrowed eyes.

Gray moves toward me, but he pauses as I scurry backward. The back of my legs meets the edge of the bed, preventing me from moving farther. I feel like a lamb being led to the slaughter.

"You don't need to be so afraid," Gray promises.

I don't believe a word that comes out of his mouth. I can already tell he'll never love or respect me as my father did my mother, and because of that, I'll never not be afraid of him.

Men who treat women like property are dangerous.

Gray huffs and runs a hand through his hair. His fingers catch in his messy curls, and he flinches as he tries to remove his hand.

I step to the side, moving around the bed as Gray takes another step closer. He frowns and glances at Silas one last time before leaving the room altogether. Instead of going through the door we came in, he storms through the bathroom and into his connecting room.

My attention shifts to Silas. He hasn't moved, his body still lingering in the doorway.

I don't know what I expected a fate to look like, but he fits the bill. His face seems to hold a thousand answers to questions I don't even know I have, and he watches everything around him with nerve-wracking intensity.

His throat bobs as he swallows, and I clasp my hands together as he leans his shoulder against the doorway.

"Despite what I'm sure you think, nobody's going to force themselves on you," he says, looking down the hallway I know leads to the stairs.

My lips twitch. I'm glad somebody seems to be on my side. I don't know what it is, but Silas doesn't give the same terrifying energy as the others. I think it's his disinterest in me, his attention curious but not sexual.

Aziel, and especially Gray, look at me like I'm prey and they're the predator waiting for the perfect opportunity to strike. I bet they'd go straight for the throat, sinking their teeth into my jugular while their claws rip open my underbelly.

Silas looks at me like I'm a person—admittedly one who annoys him, but a person nonetheless.

"Aziel has never had sex," he says, "and he can't without creating a life bond. The royal Wrath lineage is too strong, and the fates gave him that weakness when he was born. It'll keep him away from you. Gray pushes boundaries, but he won't do anything you truly don't want. If he grows too hungry, I'll see to it that he gets fed from a different source."

Despite my doubts, I find myself relaxing. I suppose Silas could be lying, but I fail to see what he'd get out of that.

I still don't know how I feel about Gray or if I believe he won't use me when he gets hungry. He bought me to feed him, and it would be a waste of money. I'd be stupid not to recognize that.

Silas looks around my room. He hums as he evaluates it, his eyes lingering on the closet before moving to the bathroom door.

"Lock the door to Gray's bedroom when you're in the bathroom," he says. "If you're going to masturbate, don't do it in there. He'll be able to smell you from that distance."

I flinch, uncomfortable with the topic of masturbation.

He continues. "You're free to move around the house, but I'd recommend you stay out of Aziel's wing. I won't sit here and threaten you to stay away from mine, but I'd prefer if you did."

I nod, glad to finally be getting some helpful advice.

Silas is quickly becoming my favorite.

"We have no intentions of sharing you, and visitors will be told you're off limits. Should anybody ask, though, you're to say you belong to Aziel. If it gets out that you're Gray's, he'll be expected to share you with the other lust demons."

I gulp. "If Aziel is a virgin, why would he need a female?" My voice shakes.

Silas pushes off the wall and clears his throat. "He can't have sex with you, but that doesn't mean you can't theoretically pleasure him in other ways."

This is information overload.

"You look tired. Get some sleep. Gray will send somebody to wake you for dinner." Silas turns and leaves without another word.

I don't move, my body frozen as I wait to ensure he's not coming back. I count to ten before working up the courage to step forward and close my door. The hinges are silent, but I still move slowly to prevent it from making a noise as it shuts.

My hand shakes as I switch the lock.

I'm sure if they wanted to enter, they could do so with ease, but I'll take whatever false sense of security I can get.

Spinning, I rush toward my bathroom door and do the same thing, shutting it with a quiet click before locking myself in.

My heart feels like it's pounding out of my chest as I press my back to the door and catch my breath. If I'd been asked five minutes ago what I wanted, I would've said it was to be left alone, but now that I am, I want nothing more than to have the distraction back.

I struggle to wrap my mind around what's happening as I search the room, ripping open drawers in a desperate attempt to find something of use. I don't know what I'm looking for, but in my crazed state, I convince myself I'll know when I find it.

The place is entirely bare, the entire room void of any personal belongings. Not so much as a speck of dust is to be found, making me wonder if this furniture is new. There's no way somebody would take the time to clean the tight corners inside the dresser drawers or the tiny screws inside the vanity stool.

Still, I search through every drawer and crevice in the room before sinking onto the bed. I eye the bathroom door, debating whether or not I should snoop around in there, but I decide against it. I don't know if Gray is inside his room right now, and I don't want to risk him catching me searching through his personal belongings.

I doubt he'd be pleased.

Lying back on the mattress, I sink into the soft sheets and stare at the ceiling. The beginnings of a headache are already building inside my head, the dull pain radiating from my temples toward my eye sockets.

I rub my forehead, grimacing as I massage the skin. Gray's

shirt rides up my legs at the action, exposing the tops of my thighs. I completely forgot I was wearing only his shirt, and I wonder when I'll be given my own clothes.

I'd like to have some bottoms, something to put more space between the incubus and me.

The distance gives me a clearer mind, and I wince as I recall our previous interactions. I practically threw myself at him on multiple occasions. It's no wonder he called me desperate.

He might have hidden his lust today, but I doubt that will last for long. I shiver at the mere thought of being trapped by my addiction to him. It's only a matter of time.

I allow my eyes to slip shut as my thoughts travel to Aziel. He's hard to read, but given how he spoke to Gray, I know he's one to stay away from.

My headache continues to grow as I rest my head on my pillow. It won't kill me to get a few hours of sleep. I hardly got any last night, my anxiety about the auction too high to find rest. Now that I finally have a moment to decompress, I feel that exhaustion creeping up on me.

Besides, I need my energy if I'm expected to join the three of them for dinner.

Being around them is draining, and I don't know how long I'll be able to manage it. I'm still overwhelmed even when they pull back on the power their bodies naturally emit. It sticks to their clothing and lingers in the air.

I hope it only feels this intense because I've never been around it. Humans don't emit power the way demons do, and maybe this is something I just need some time to grow familiar with.

My eyes grow heavy. The thought of falling asleep feels scary, but it's not something I can put off forever.

Gray's probably going to sneak into my dreams as he's mentioned multiple times now, but there isn't anything I can do about it. I rarely remember my dreams, and I soothe myself with the knowledge that even if he does make an appearance, I won't remember.

I curl into a ball on top of the covers and shove my face into my pillow.

There's nothing I can do.

Chapter Seven

CHARLOTTE

MY BACK ARCHES as warm hands slide up my thighs. I keep my eyes shut and focus on the calloused fingers as they move inward and grab a handful of my flesh.

I'm sitting on a lap, my back pressed against a chest and my hands holding the wrists of the man behind me. Despite my iron grip, I make no effort to stop him, the feeling of his skin on mine too good to put an end to.

I think I'd die if he removed himself from me.

He squeezes my thighs and groans before spreading my legs. I adjust for him, moving my thighs to rest on either side of his. My eyes ache from how hard I'm clenching them shut, and my teeth bury into my bottom lip as I hold back a moan.

My mind is hazy with lust as the hard body shifts below me, a low chuckle emerging from the man when I shiver. His hand continues upward. The arousal I'm feeling is unlike any other, and to think I believed my romance books were as good as it got. They don't even compare.

Lips press against the side of my neck as the man continues his teasing, his fingers leaving desperation in their wake.

"Open your eyes," he whispers.

His tongue meets my neck before he digs his teeth into the flesh and sucks my skin into his mouth. It's borderline painful, but he releases me and grazes his lips over the spot in apology.

It takes every bit of willpower I have to open my eyes. They feel stiff and the sudden light burns, but I hardly notice as I look around. I'm at the head of a table in a room I've never been in, and Aziel and Silas are sitting on either side of me.

Aziel is to the left, his chair pushed out a few inches from the table so he can face me directly. Silas sits on the right and adjusts his positioning to mirror Aziel.

What's going on?

I turn to see who's behind me, my pulse racing when I lock eyes with Gray. He smiles, his black eyes never leaving mine as he hooks his fingers into my underwear and pulls them to the side. I have half a mind to be embarrassed about this, but the emotion doesn't come.

"Watch them," he says, pressing another kiss to my neck before grabbing my chin and turning me toward Aziel and Silas. "See how turned on they are at the sight of you?"

Are they? I lower my gaze, gulping as Silas reaches into the waistband of his pants. Everything feels weird, but these men are so distracting that it's impossible to think too much about it.

Gray continues to touch me, his voice low as he urges me to watch the other two men pleasure themselves. I do, and I arch further into the incubus's fingers as the scene plays out in front of me. It feels good, too good, and when my eyes roll back and my muscles tense, there's nothing I can do to stop it.

Fuck.

I rip open my eyes and shoot up in bed, gasping and clutching at my chest as an orgasm tears through me. What the fuck? Collapsing on the mattress, I take a few seconds to steady my breathing and figure out what just happened.

This was Gray's doing. He forced his way into my dreams just as he promised. I thought it wouldn't be real, that I'd wake with no recollection and live in blissful ignorance.

Instead, I woke up mid-orgasm with humiliation filling every pore of my body. My jaw clenches shut as I adjust my shirt, pulling it back down my legs. It must have ridden up in my sleep.

Did Gray choose everything that happened in my dream? Why were Silas and Aziel in it? Was it really them, or just dream versions of them? Something moving draws my attention, and I snap my head toward the shadow that lurks just beyond the open bedroom door I swore I closed and locked. Glancing to my left, my shoulders slump as I realize the bathroom door has also been opened.

Is this Gray's way of telling me my privacy will never truly be mine? That he controls my physical life as much as my unconscious one? He didn't need to open doors to do that. I'm already aware.

"Dinner's ready." The shadow speaks quietly, his voice surprisingly deep.

I nod, too exhausted to argue. My feet shake as I push myself off the bed, but I ignore the sensation and follow the shadow out of the room. He leads me down the stairs and through a maze of hallways before finally stepping to the side and gesturing for me to walk through the next doorway alone.

Aziel and Silas don't so much as spare me a glance as I enter the dining room, their faces buried in the devices in their hands. As much as the stronger species love to mock and belittle humans, almost all have adopted some aspect of our technology.

I refuse to look at Gray as I slip inside and sit in the chair farthest from the three. This room is identical to my dream, and the men are even sitting in the same spots. Gray is at the head of the table, smirking, with Aziel on his left and Silas on his right.

It confirms that Gray was behind my dream. There goes the last bit of hope that it was all a figment of my imagination.

Matching the rest of the estate, the dining room looks grand and expensive, with vaulted ceilings and dark décor. The brass chandelier above the long, wooden table somehow manages to light the room up enough that I don't feel like somebody is going to jump out of the shadows and capture me.

These three men live in luxury, which I suppose I should be grateful for. Men who live in such abundance don't often feel the need to share their females, and if I'm lucky, they might even purchase another and take some of the pressure off me.

I continue to avoid Gray's stare as I cross my hands over my lap and look at the food on the table. Dishes I don't recognize sit on display, the scent making my mouth water, but I remain still and wait for somebody else to make the first move.

Silas finally looks up from his phone, and he makes eye contact with me as he shoves it into his pocket. A sly smirk plays on his lips, and I don't trust it.

"You're looking better," he says, capturing Aziel's attention. "There's more color to your cheeks."

Aziel mumbles a quiet agreement while Gray bursts into laughter. I cringe at the sudden noise, my pulse racing as I try to figure out why he's laughing. It's probably about me, but I hope it doesn't have anything to do with the dreams he subjected me to.

"That's because of me!" he says, slamming his hands on the table before bringing them together in a joyous clap. "We fed each other real good this afternoon."

I lower my chin to my chest as he shouts this. It was foolish to think he'd keep what had happened between us a secret. I should've known better than to expect such privacy from a demon, let alone an incubus.

It's his nature to boast about his conquests, proudly sharing with anybody who'll listen.

"She had way more lust to offer than I thought she would. Our female has been unsatisfied for a long time now." His words slur as he stands and begins to fill his plate.

He seems almost drunk as he continues to boast about my ability to feed him, his voice loud and jarring in the otherwise quiet room. I have to admit he looks better, his sharp cheekbones slightly more filled out and his black eyes holding a spark that wasn't there before.

I suppose he must have been hungry.

Aziel raises a brow while Gray shares his approval of me, his excitement probably revolving around the selfish fact that Gray won't need to feed off him anymore. Silas grabs his plate and begins to fill it once Gray is done scooping his food, his expression flat as he listens to the ramblings of the incubus.

Gray rises and saunters toward me, his movements fast and confident as he grabs my empty plate. His smile grows as he replaces it with the one he already filled, and he gestures toward it in a silent invitation for me to begin eating.

I don't, and I remain as stiff as a board while he bends and plants a wet kiss on my forehead. The physical contact fills me with need, my body's reaction disgusting.

"I don't know why you sat so far away," he mumbles.

My pulse races as he reaches for the back of my chair and drags it toward his. He's clearly unhappy with the purposeful distance I put between us, and I resist the urge to argue as he slots me next to him at the head of the table.

Silas wordlessly leans over and grabs my forgotten plate, his chest grazing the top of the table as he stretches over the two empty seats that were between us. I lick my lips, but I still don't speak as he places the plate in front of me.

I've lost my appetite.

Did Gray already tell them what happened in my dream? Did he say I desire them? It would be a lie if he did. I don't want any of these men.

Aziel pulls out his phone and reads over a message I now know is from Silas, a smirk playing on his lips as he turns to Gray. I'd pay good money to know what that message says.

"I presume this means you won't be sneaking into my dreams any longer?" he asks.

Gray shrugs, and Aziel's smile falls.

"I mean, I don't need to," Gray starts, "but our female wants all of us, and it might be fun to pull *you* into *her* dreams." He sounds hopeful, and I refrain from showing any outward disgust.

Aziel's gaze briefly slides to me, his eyes trailing over my face before lowering to my body. I can feel Silas doing the same, his gaze practically burning my skin.

"I'll be passing on that invitation," Aziel eventually says, grimacing as if the mere thought disgusts him.

I refuse to be offended when Silas chuckles and politely declines the offer as well, and I remind myself I don't want them to want me anyway. Gray continues to try to persuade them as they begin to eat, his desperation to pawn me off more than a little frustrating.

I begin shoveling food into my mouth, hoping I'll be excused once I'm finished. Being forced to sit here while I'm so openly humiliated isn't exactly fun, and I struggle to hold back tears as I shove the burning-hot food down my throat.

The food is good, but I'm not in the right state of mind to enjoy it.

Aziel interrupts Gray's rambling. "I'd appreciate it if you refrained from crying."

Continuing to stare at the plate in front of me, I nod and beg my tears to reabsorb into my eyes. The demons can probably smell the saltiness. Tears continue to streak down my cheek despite my attempts to stop them, dripping quietly onto my plate.

Aziel stands and leaves the now-silent room with a loud sigh, his footfalls echoing off the floor until they disappear altogether.

They're going to sell me if I can't get my emotions under control. I tighten my grip on my fork. I'm merely a pet to these men, and unless I want to be placed in an even worse situation, I need to get my shit together.

Gray puts what I think is supposed to be a comforting hand on my thigh as the tense silence in the room grows, the noise only broken when Silas sighs and leans back in his chair.

"Ignore Gray," he says. "We've all fallen prey to him at some point. It truly isn't anything to be ashamed of."

Gray huffs. "She knows it's nothing to be ashamed of."

Silas blinks and cocks his head to the side, confusion written all over his face. "Are you stupid?" he asks. "Why do you think she's sitting here crying? Not everybody enjoys having the details of their first sexual experience thrown around the dinner table. Especially when it apparently involved the other people present."

Gray's posture deflates, and a second later, he removes his hand from my thigh and returns to his food. The atmosphere is practically unbearable as I wait to be excused.

Will Gray take the initiative himself, or am I expected to ask to leave? I don't want to offend or anger him, and the fear of doing either renders me silent as I work to clear my plate. Gray gave me more food than I can possibly ingest, but I still shove down as much as I physically can.

"Do you like the food?" Gray asks, his voice lacking the excitement it held when I first arrived for dinner.

I nod.

As Gray opens his mouth to respond, I realize I can't feel their power. My head snaps up, and I look at Silas to confirm his suffocating smell is gone. Nothing is coming from him or Gray, and when Aziel was here, nothing was seeping from him either.

Did Gray ask them to hide it? I'm surprised they'd do such a thing for me. I doubt I would've been able to sit through this meal if I'd also had to experience the crushing weight of their power. Objectively, I know their power suppression is probably a one-time thing, but I can't help but hope it stays.

I play with the food on my plate as my stomach grows full, my frown deepening as I think about how lively and exciting family dinners used to be. Dad was an excellent cook, always whipping up something delicious while Mom and I watched. I loved helping him when I was younger, and we'd pretend to be contestants on a baking show.

Even when his arthritis grew painful and he struggled to move around the kitchen as he once did, he still insisted on making most of our meals.

"Why are you so sad?" Gray asks, pulling me from my thoughts.

I shrug, unsure how much I should share with him. Will he grow angry if I talk about my family and home? I can't think of a good reason why he would, but I don't want to take the risk.

"Tell me why you're unhappy. I can smell your pain," he continues, his sharp tone earning a snort from Silas.

The fate seems to grow tired of the conversation as he stands and leaves, his half-eaten plate long forgotten as he exits the room. I watch him go, my heart pounding.

I don't like being alone with Gray.

"I was thinking about my family," I admit.

I expect Gray to question me further, but instead, he hums and orders me to finish eating. I force a couple more bites of food down my throat, pretty sure my stomach is about to explode.

"I'm finished." I set my fork on my plate and peer up at him.

He's already looking at me, his eyes wide with interest as his gaze flickers all along my face. He's just so pretty with his full lips and sharp jaw and dark eyelashes.

I want him to kiss me.

He leans in.

"Do you want me to kiss you?" he asks.

I nod. I want it so badly.

Gray gives me what I need, closing the distance between us and pressing his lips against mine. This is my first kiss, and I let my eyes shut as a quiet moan emerges from my throat. He feels so good.

He takes control, slipping his tongue between my parted lips. I can't help but imagine how amazing it would feel on other parts of my body, and I shiver as he grabs my waist and pulls me onto his lap.

His lips find their way to my neck, and he bites at the skin as he did in my dream, the action acting as a shock to my brain and sending me scurrying off.

Fucking incubus.

He watches with a lazy smile as I throw myself onto the floor and scramble to my feet, my cheeks reddening in shame at how easily I fell into his lure. I remind myself that I hate him as he stands and gestures for me to follow.

"I'll take you back to your room," he says, still smiling. "I won't be interrupting your sleep tonight."

I don't know whether or not to believe his promise. While he doesn't exactly seem the type to outwardly lie, that doesn't mean he's keen on speaking only the truth.

My bare feet patter quietly against the floor as I trail behind him, my thoughts rushing a million miles a minute as we reach my room and he steps to the side and gestures for me to enter. I turn to see if he plans to follow, but he offers only a wink before reaching in and shutting the door.

I stare at the wood before spinning to face my bed, my eyes widening as I notice the large television on top of the dresser and the small pile of clothing on the bed.

Yes. Holding my breath, I step forward to get a closer look at the clothes I've been given. The material is soft, and I realize they're pajama bottoms when I unfold them. Glancing around to ensure nobody is inside the room lurking at me, I bring them to my nose and inhale.

This belongs to Silas, the earthy scent identical to his. My body tenses as I do the same with the next piece of clothing, surprised to realize they're Gray's. The next item is again Silas's, and the one after that is Aziel's. Did somebody go through their rooms and steal all their soft pajamas? Was this done with their permission?

I hope so.

If not, then I hope they have enough clothing that they don't notice. I pull off Gray's shirt and slip on the thick sweatpants and a long-sleeved shirt.

I'm practically drowning in the fabric, but I can't bring myself to care as I turn the television to a human news channel and crawl into bed.

I'm ready to wake up and realize this has all been some awful dream.

Chapter Eight

GRAY

CHARLIE'S LIGHT SNORES make their way to my ears as I peek into her room. She's buried beneath layers of blankets, her entire body hidden except for a tuft of messy brown hair resting on her pillow.

She's had a long day, and I'm glad she's getting some sleep.

I'm also happy to see she's using the TV I had the shadows bring in during dinner. The pamphlet I received from the auction house appears to have been accurate in its claim that humans enjoy watching it.

I'm not personally a huge fan, but I see the appeal.

A human news channel I've never seen before is on, and the men on the screen chat about some drama that holds no meaning.

Those males know nothing of what's happening in our realms. They latch to the tiny crumbs we give them, obsessing over arguments and restrictions that have no importance to us.

I rest my shoulder against the doorframe and continue looking around Charlie's room. It's bare. Besides the few articles of clothing I managed to scrounge from our rooms, she has nothing.

That's probably why she was so sad at dinner. It makes sense she'd be missing her family and belongings, and I hate that I didn't think of supplying her with those comforts before bringing her here.

Silas would have remembered. The realization makes me angry, and my jealousy worsens as I remember how kindly he spoke to her when they were alone earlier. I should've been the one to explain those things.

I'm failing my female and she hasn't even been here an entire day.

Does she think I'm a lousy caretaker?

Incubi aren't known for our paternal instincts, our interests typically revolving more around pleasure and desire. I've never had to care for a female, and I hope this one will be patient while I learn.

Charlie lets out a particularly loud snort before rolling over, her face emerging from the blankets as she turns toward me. I admire her upturned nose and the light smattering of freckles across her cheeks before retreating into my bathroom and closing her bedroom door.

She locked them when she took her nap earlier, and I'm taking it as a good sign that she didn't do it again. I'm unsure what changed her mind, but the optimistic side of me wants to believe it's because she knows nobody here will hurt her.

She trusts me already.

I hold back a smile as I step up to the bathroom mirror and look at myself. My cheeks have filled out since feeding off her, making me look better than I have in weeks. It's shocking how much lust she was able to share with me through just her dreams.

The idea of eventually getting to feed off her in real life has me holding back a groan. She's the perfect female, and I know Aziel and Silas will grow to appreciate her as well. It's obvious they're both attracted to her, and despite their best attempts at hiding it, I could smell their arousal when I told them about Charlie's dream.

Aziel's too old to be continuing to hold out on taking a bonded mate, and Silas is growing angsty with each passing year. We're all desperate for some genuine intimacy. That's exactly what Charlie can provide.

Silas and Aziel think she's to be nothing more than a short-term fling, something to keep me busy for a while, but I'm ready to settle down and I'm hoping they come to feel the same way once they've grown comfortable with having Charlie around.

I bite my bottom lip and turn away from the mirror as I feel my want for Charlie growing. I'm still hungry, and it's hard to resist the urge to seep into her bedroom or dreams.

Fighting the impulse to do those things is hard. I promised I'd stay out of her mind tonight, and I'll be damned if I turn back on my word. She needs to trust me. I made a mistake in telling her I couldn't have her unless she consented. I'd only meant to make her more comfortable around me because I *won't* take her until she consents.

I hadn't expected Aziel to reveal the truth so quickly.

I step into my bedroom and wander toward the small desk in the corner. The auction house gave me so much paperwork and documentation on Charlie, and I skim over the pages until I find the information about her home and family.

This will be the perfect thing to cheer her up.

Forcing my body to relax, I summon all my strength and teleport to her home. I'm not as strong as Aziel and Silas, and my muscles ache at the effort it takes to move myself. It's going to be worth it, though.

A second later, I'm standing in Charlie's living room.

I'm unable to get my bearings right away, my mind discombobulated as I stand in a space I've never been in before. I don't need my eyes to know there's a decomposing corpse in here, though, the smell of rotting flesh overwhelmingly potent.

I look around until I spot the body in question. Some man lies on his stomach in the center of the room, his arm outstretched and face buried into the yellowed carpet. He's wearing pajamas, but it's hard to tell much beyond that.

He's been here for a while, his body already beginning to liquify into the floor below. This must be Charlie's father. The Seekers don't take kindly to men who hide their daughters, and I wouldn't put it past them to have left him here to rot.

I reach up and pinch the bridge of my nose, angry they left my female's father here. She'll be crushed when I share the bad news with her. A small part of me debates not saying anything, but as I turn and look over the photos hung on the walls, I know I can't do that.

I'd want to know if I were her.

What's the human tradition for death? I purse my lips as I try to recall it, and I feel my shoulders round as I remember the burials. This would be so much easier if I could burn him as the demons do.

Fuck. Humans burn their dead, too, don't they? I'm not quite sure, but I'm confident they bury.

I'll work on him later.

Stepping over the man's body, I turn and head down the narrow hallway leading to the bedrooms. The first door on the left is open, and I take one look at the floral curtains and gray bedsheets before continuing my journey.

I may not know Charlie very well, but I sure know there's no way she'd decorate her space so poorly.

I pass a small bathroom before reaching the last, cracked open door. My eyes widen as I peek inside and scan the messy chaos. It's safe to say Charlie's a bit of a hoarder. She's done an excellent job keeping the space relatively clean, but the clutter is unreal.

It'll take me all night to bring this junk back home.

My chest expands as I suck in a deep breath. I'm going to be exhausted once this night is over. Aziel is going to kill me for using all my energy, but it's for a good cause.

I'm doing it for our female.

An open shelter door is built into the ground, and I peer into it before wrinkling my nose and kicking it shut. It reeks of fear, and I have no interest in knowing what's inside.

This must have been where Charlie hid.

The door blends in with the floor when it's shut, and there's a rug pushed to the side that must have lived over it to hide the few subtle seams. *Smart.*

I move to the other side of her room and open her bedroom window to let some fresh air in. Her dad's decay has permeated throughout the entire house. Heading to her closet, I dig through it until I find two large suitcases.

They're old and dusty, probably having sat here since before she was born, but they'll do. I plop both on the bed and begin packing anything of Charlie's that looks important. She has a lot of items, and I find myself struggling to understand why she has the things she has. I can't think of any use for the small, rubber squeaky duck on her dresser, but I pack it anyway.

She can throw out whatever she doesn't want.

It doesn't take long to fill the suitcases, and I rock back on my heels as I zip them up and travel back home.

It takes a moment for my bedroom to materialize around me, but once it does, I'm dumping the contents onto the floor and teleporting back. I'll store her things in my room while she's sleeping and move them into hers tomorrow morning.

It should put her in high spirits and show I'm not such a bad guy.

Rolling my shoulders, I give myself a moment to adjust before repeating the process. It grows tiring quickly, and when I return for the fourth time, I need to sit down.

My hands shake where they rest on the mattress, and I stare at them in anger. A demon my age should be able to make these trips with ease, and the fact that I can't is more than a little frustrating.

If it weren't for the constant state of starvation I've forced myself to endure these past hundred-something years I've been with Silas and Aziel, I'd be stronger. Aziel feeds me well when I'm able to sneak into his dreams, but he gets so mad that I only try to enter in dire situations.

A better incubus would've taken what he needed and grown strong. I know my kind shames me for my disinterest in using my lust as they do. It's not as if I haven't tried, but I always leave feeling dirty.

I'd go to the succubi if I could, but they don't want to sully themselves with an incubus they think is damaged. God forbid my nontraditional values rub off on them.

My hands continue to shake, and I clench them into fists as I realize I'm not going to be able to make it home. I can hardly stand at the moment, let alone pack another bag, bury her father, and travel back.

I tuck away my pride and seek out Aziel.

Humiliation warms my cheeks as I reach through the bond I forced between us. It's easy enough to find him, and I hope he doesn't push me away as I coax our bond and poke at him, begging for entry.

I thought feeding from him and igniting the bonding curse the fates gave him was such an exciting thing at first. I—a young, untrained incubus—somehow managed to compel the mind of one of the strongest beings in existence and tie his life to mine.

We didn't even have sex, and I never laid a finger on him. It shouldn't have triggered his curse, but I think the fates intervened and made it happen. I've tried asking Silas, but he won't speak about it.

Still, it was exhilarating to have that source of power, and it made me untouchable.

While I still pride myself on bringing Aziel to his knees, asking him to share his power through the bond is shameful. He's told me before that he's happy to do it, but I've always refused.

It's one thing when I sneak into his dreams to feed, but having to beg him for it like a child is humiliating. The incubus in me is more than happy to feed on him through sex, but to take a handout is apparently where I draw the line.

Aziel pushes against our bond before opening, his endless reserve of power there for my taking. My eyes roll back as I brush against it, the desire to fill myself to the brim overwhelming.

I'm sure it would hardly affect him if I did. My age prohibits how much power I can physically hold, and it's nothing compared to what Aziel has stored inside him. He probably wouldn't stop me if I tried to fill myself, and if anything, he would encourage my greed and shove his power into me until I was drunk off it.

Still, I resist.

He won't be getting the satisfaction of feeding me like an infant, and I'll be damned if I allow him to think this is going to be a regular thing. I'm doing this one time and one time only, and only for my female.

If I grow hungry in the future, I'll slip into his dreams like the good incubus I am.

My mouth opens in a silent moan as I begin to absorb Aziel's power, pleasure coursing through me as I fill myself with him. The bond between us pulses at the connection, and despite my body screaming at me to take more, I sever it once I have enough to see me through one more travel.

Aziel tries to reach out as I end our connection, his soul brushing against mine and begging me to open so he can give more. I push him away with a huff, annoyed he's making such a big deal out of this.

If he tries to have a conversation about this when I get back, I'm going to punch him in the throat. If he dares tell Silas, it will be his precious testicles that meet my fist.

Pushing up off Charlie's bed, I storm around her home, pulling all the pictures off the walls and counters. There are so many of them, and it looks like each one that includes her also has a copy with her missing. They must've switched them out whenever they had company.

That's so sad.

I only take the ones she's in before heading into the small bathroom and grabbing all the beauty products that hold her scent. Shoving everything in the suitcases, I zip them up before returning to the body in the living room.

My muscles ache, and an unbearable headache is already beginning to form behind my eyes as I head to the backyard in search of a shovel. I worry Charlie will be mad at me for burying him before she has the opportunity to say goodbye, but considering her dad is pretty much jelly at this point, I'm willing to take the risk.

She doesn't need to see this.

There's a small shed in the far corner of the yard, and I march up to it before ripping open the door and locking eyes with the tool I desire. Grabbing the shovel, I turn and evaluate the yard for the best spot.

There's a small garden near the back door that looks like it was well-loved at one point, and with a shrug, I head over and begin digging. My exhaustion makes the task harder than it should be, but after an hour, I've gotten something decent enough to fit a full-grown man in.

My nose crinkles as I head inside to grab him, and I hold my breath as I drag him by his shoes through the back door and into the hole I've created. He fits perfectly, and with a triumphant smile, I begin to cover him with dirt.

"The afterlife your kind believes in doesn't exist, but I'll honor the human tradition for Charlie and speak a few words to your corpse," I say to the man's bloated, unrecognizable face.

"Who you were is unknown to me, but from the images around the house and the love your daughter holds for you, I assume you were a good man. I don't know what happened to your wife, but I promise I'll take good care of your daughter. She'll see a life that is full and lacks nothing."

My vision funnels as I continue to shovel him in. I should've taken more from Aziel. A small part of me debates reaching for him again, but I refuse. If I need to spend the night here and sneak into some random human's dream, then so be it.

I blink and shake my head before continuing with my words to Charlie's father.

"Two other demons and I have purchased Charlie. We have no interest in harming her, and she won't be forced to bear us any children," I promise, even though I know he can't hear me.

I look around, trying to think of something else to say. Each shovel of dirt I drop on the corpse helps to cover his scent, and my mind clears as the smell of pain weakens. It pours from him, and I'm willing to bet it took him a while to succumb to his injuries and die.

Unconscious men don't feel pain, and I can tell he was in a lot of it.

"I will lie and tell her your death was quick," I continue.

After a few more minutes of shoveling, Charlie's father has vanished underneath the dirt and I'm patting down the loose bits on top. It looks good, if I do say so myself.

I drop the shovel and drag myself back into Charlie's bedroom. My shoulder smacks painfully against the doorway as I barrel inside, but I hardly notice as I grab the suitcases and force myself to teleport home.

The transition is excruciating, feeling more like I'm walking through lava than the usual warm heat. I'm burning from the inside as I reach my bedroom, but I manage to make it back in one piece.

I bet I'm looking more like a nightmare than an incubus right about now.

Dropping the bags to the ground, I take a few steps toward my bed and collapse face-first onto the mattress. My lungs feel like they're on fire each time I inhale, the organs expanding painfully until I'm pretty sure I'm about to die.

This is the worst I've felt in over a hundred years, and if I weren't such a goddamn gentleman, I'd be balls-deep in my female right now. I contemplate traveling to one of the demon brothels for a quick fuck, but I don't have the strength to make it there.

I'll be stuck between dimensions until either Silas or Aziel takes pity and fishes me out.

Again.

Blinking slowly, I let my eyes fall shut before allowing my mind to expand and search the house for a body to feed from. The shadows don't offer enough to fill me, but they'll give just enough that I can travel to the nearest brothel in one piece.

I hate going to them, especially when Silas and Aziel are nearby and can feed me just fine, but I'm hesitant to make them angry when Charlie's still so new here. I don't want them retaliating by harming her.

It takes every bit of willpower I have to slide past Charlie's bedroom. I can practically taste her sweet, sleeping mind. It would be so easy to slip inside and feed on her. She was so receptive to my touch earlier, desperate to please me and the others.

I bet I could pull just enough from her to have me back on my feet. I'd still be hungry, but I'd be functioning.

Silas's mind calls to me as I seep through the hallways, his body strong and ripe for the taking. There's a danger that comes with slipping into a fate's mind, though, and the last thing I want is to get trapped in the fated world. You can only access it through a fate, and they would tear me apart the first chance they got.

I move toward Aziel. It's clear by the softness of his mind that he's sleeping, and the temptation is too much to resist. He's gotten better at telling when it's me controlling his dreams, but I occasionally get away with it. The bond between us makes it easy, unintentionally forcing his body to welcome my intrusions.

I inch closer to him. He would taste so good. He always does.

Making up my mind, I travel into his bedroom and slip into his consciousness. There's almost no resistance.

Aziel dreams about his father, but I look away as I'm exposed to something I know he wouldn't want me to see. Flinching at the noise, I manipulate his mind and move him into his office.

It takes Aziel a moment to adjust to the change of scenery, confusion flashing through his eyes as his mind creates a storyline around the shift. With a dulled sigh, he straightens up and begins to sort through the papers on his desk, his gaze filtering over the pages as he gets to work.

I resist the urge to laugh. Aziel has never been one for creativity, and I suppose I shouldn't be too surprised he's chosen to do paperwork even in his dream state.

He should be glad I'm here to spice it up.

I turn toward the door just as Charlie comes rushing through it. I'm unhappy with how long it takes me to conjure her, and I hope my slower reactions don't ruin this.

Aziel looks surprised as she comes barreling inside, her footfalls loud as she stomps to the front of his desk. He sets his paperwork down and plasters a look of calm on his face, but I hear how hard his pulse is racing.

"I didn't know you were back," Charlie pouts, crossing her arms over her chest. I've put her in a lowcut, short red dress, and I bounce on my heels when Aziel's eyes dart to her chest. He's taking the bait.

Aziel quirks a brow, clearly not understanding what she's talking about.

"I never left," he says, reining in his scent.

My lips twitch, happy he's attempting to bring my female comfort. I was worried he'd refuse to suppress his power around her, but he only let out some minor grumbling before pulling it in when I asked.

He's got a soft spot for my human.

Charlie scoffs, her foot tapping impatiently against the ground. "Why didn't you come and find me when you got back?"

Aziel shakes his head, his confusion growing as he tries to understand what's happening. His dream state tends to make him slow, but this is extreme even for him.

I make Charlie cry. Thick tears well in her waterline as her bottom lip begins to tremble. Aziel has never been smooth around women, and crying makes him especially nervous.

"I—" he starts, pausing to lick his lips as Charlie sniffles and wipes her cheeks. "I don't know."

His eyes go comically wide as she stomps around his desk, and he remains frozen as she pushes back his chair and climbs on his lap.

I watch with mild interest as Aziel's mind catches up to his body, his heart hammering as he tries to push her away. What he fails to realize is that I'm in control here and she won't be moving until I'm fed.

I kick up her crying, turning her soundless tears into loud sobs. Aziel freezes again, his hands going still where they push against her thighs.

"Why don't you want to have sex with me?" Charlie asks, shoving at his chest.

A small part of me almost feels guilty as Aziel fumbles around trying to comfort her, his hands moving to her shoulders before sliding up to hold her cheeks. He wipes her tears with his thumbs and shakes his head in response to her accusations.

"No, no, don't say that. You're beautiful," he assures her. "I just can't touch you."

Charlie frowns, grabbing his wrists and moving his hands to her breasts. Aziel gulps as she presses him against her, the sweet scent of his arousal filling the air. I hold back a moan as I feel it seeping into me, and I have Charlie lower her hands to his hips.

"You're touching me now, aren't you?" She moans, her fingertips sliding under the hem of his shirt and brushing against his bare skin.

Aziel's hips twitch as she continues her teasing, his resolve cracking as she grinds herself against him.

"Please," she whispers, leaning in so her lips graze his ear. "I want you to make me feel good."

His arousal tastes divine as he pulls down the thin straps of Charlie's dress, exposing her chest to the air. He moans as he explores her body, stroking her skin with excitement.

"We shouldn't be doing this," he admits, his voice hoarse. "You can't touch me."

Charlie hums, reaching for his zipper. "I don't care. I love you."

Aziel recoils, his expression shifting into one of disgust. He knows. Fuck.

He makes no effort to push her back as he turns and looks for me, his eyes narrowing as they meet mine. It's next to impossible to spot an incubus by accident in a dream, but if you know what you're looking for, it's hard for us to stay hidden.

He knows me well enough to search in the dark, hazy corners of his mind.

I summon ropes to wrap around his wrists and ankles when he moves to stand. Aziel grunts as I tie him down, his look of betrayal growing.

"Fuck you," he snaps.

I shrug, smirking despite the pain that still courses through every inch of my body.

"I'm in charge here," I remind him, tightening the straps for dramatic effect.

There's a burst of energy as Aziel releases the full extent of his power, the silent threat heard loud and clear. He could easily break through the straps if he wanted. My shoulders roll forward as I remove the bonds, but I also take the clothing from Charlie and Aziel in a last-ditch effort to seduce him. I'm so hungry.

All I want him to do is cum.

Aziel turns away from me as he takes notice of his now-naked state, his arousal spiking as Charlie rubs her bare body against his. She moans, her movements timid in the way I know they'd be in real life.

She's submissive. Aziel will love her.

His jaw clenches as she touches him, his breath choppy as he grabs her hips and sets her on his desk. He's on his feet the moment she's out of his lap, his body distanced from hers as he settles his glare on me once more.

I hang my head in defeat as he holds her at arm's length, my body practically curling in on itself as I realize I wasted the last bits of my energy on this failed seduction attempt. I should've just gone to one of the shadows.

They'd never send me away, and if anything, they'd feel honored I chose them.

Aziel looks me over, his eyes lingering on my face and hands. They're shaking again, and I hide them behind my back so he can't see. He's going to be mad that I let myself get this far. He always is.

"You fed through our bond tonight," he says.

I nod. I don't want to talk about it. What I did is shameful enough as it is, and the last thing I want is to hear Aziel's condescending assurances that I'm welcome to his reserves whenever I want. I'm a grown man, and I refuse to let myself become a whore to a stronger demon, as so many of my kind love to do.

"What happened?" he asks.

I shrug, waving in the general direction of Charlie's room.

"My female misses her family and home. I was bringing her belongings here," I explain, happy to prove I'm a good caretaker.

Aziel sighs. I can feel him trying to share with me through the bond again, but I reject it. I don't want to feed that way.

"Take it, Gray."

I shake my head, refusing. The silence between us is tense as Aziel waits for me to change my mind, his anger growing when I resist. The wooden desk cracks as he slams his fists down on it, his eyes flashing to Charlie when she jolts.

He looks over her bare form, his attention lingering on the space where her thighs meet. I made sure she was nice and wet when she was grinding herself against him, and that moisture has not faded during our argument.

Aziel brings his hands to her thighs and steps between them, and I grow immediately giddy. He's going to do it.

"You've created her for me, yeah?" he asks. "This isn't her soul in my dream?"

I grunt, offended he thinks I'd pull her into his dream. "I'd never trick you into bonding yourself to anybody, Aziel," I snap. "Of course she's not real."

Aziel hesitates, shooting me one last sharp look before huffing and taking hold of his soft length. I'm annoyed he thinks so little of me, and I have Charlie remain still instead of seducing him as the women I create usually do.

Not that she needs to, though. Despite Aziel's attitude, I can tell he's attracted to her. Her naked body alone is enough to get him going. Within seconds, Aziel is urging her to lie back on the desk and lining himself up. I lick my lips and moan as he sinks inside, filling her with one hard thrust.

Knowing he's under no expectations to make this pleasurable for her, he wastes no time beginning to thrust, his hips smacking into the backs of her thighs as he hooks her ankles around his shoulders.

He rams into her so hard, he'd break her pelvis if she were real, and I wince as I make her moan and beg him for more.

If he ever does try to touch her in real life, I'll have to teach him to be gentle. The only women he's ever had experience with are the ones I create for him, and luckily for him, he can't bring them any harm.

Aziel grunts as he uses Charlie, rutting into her quickly and trying to reach his completion as soon as possible. I fall to my knees as I breathe in the lust he emits, soaking it up with greedy moans. It's so good.

Wanting to draw this out for myself, I have Charlie beg him to slow down.

"Please, I want to cum." Her voice rings into the room. "I want you to make love to me."

Aziel curses, a nasty expletive thrown in my direction as he slows. Charlie gasps in response to the new tempo, her voice hoarse as she encourages Aziel to enjoy this new pace.

I continue to breathe in his lust, overwhelmed by the intensity as it heals my sore body.

"You feel so fucking good." Aziel moans, quickening again as his orgasm approaches.

His fingers curl around her waist. He's close. I can feel his orgasm building inside him as if it were my own.

I know she's not real, but I can't help but love the sight of her and Aziel together. I want us all to be together, and that starts with Aziel and Silas accepting her as their female. They'll demand I get rid of her if I tell them my hopes, but it's only a matter of time before it's their hope as well.

I want more than just a female I feed from. I want her to be our bonded mate.

Aziel throws his head back as he spills inside her, his body pulsating with delicious power I eagerly soak up. *Fuck.*

His forehead is damp as he pulls himself away from Charlie. There's an insecurity in his eye when he turns to me, the emotion shocking. Aziel is never insecure.

"Would she have enjoyed that as much as this one?" he asks.

I try to keep the surprise out of my expression as I take in what he's just asked. He's never cared before.

"Probably not," I admit. "You were too rough, and you made no attempts to please her."

Aziel hums before shrugging and stepping away. He looks me up and down as he evaluates my current state, a quiet grunt emerging from his throat as he determines I'm up to his health standards.

With a tense nod, he turns back to Charlie and shoos her off his desk. I have half a mind to ask him if he'd like me to teach him how to please her, but I don't want to push my luck. Instead, I have her vanish into the shadows of his dream.

I'm going to take it as a good sign he's taken it upon himself to worry about her enjoyment of their sex. He'll probably pretend this never happened tomorrow morning and yell at me for sneaking into his dream, but I don't think he hates it as much as he says.

He's always so soft and kind in here, but the moment he's back in the real world, he's cold. From the short memories I've seen of him and his father, I understand why he feels the need to maintain that callous facade.

"It's time for you to leave, Gray." Aziel sits in his chair and returns to his dream paperwork.

I hesitate momentarily, opening my mouth to apologize before scoffing and slipping back into my body. It wouldn't hurt him to thank me every once in a while.

Chapter Nine

CHARLOTTE

MY STEPS ARE silent as I tiptoe through the estate, sneaking from room to room before the demons wake up. I've always hated my inability to sleep in, but for once, I'm grateful my body wakes me before the sun rises.

It gives me time to explore.

Craning my neck around the doorway, I'm met with the sight of a large, bustling kitchen. It's surprisingly modern, the sleek design a far cry from the almost medieval décor that exists everywhere else in this place.

Shadows glide around the room, their hazy bodies paying me no attention as they ready breakfast. At least, I hope they aren't paying attention. It's hard to make out any details on their bodies, let alone figure out where they're looking.

I watch with interest for another long moment before forcing myself to turn away and continue my exploration. If they're cooking breakfast, I assume that means the demons are expected to wake soon. I want to be back in my room before that happens.

I'm unsure if I'll be given jobs or chores to fill my days, but I hope Gray takes it upon himself to inform me of anything I'm expected to do before I get into trouble.

A small part of me debates seeking him out to ask when he wakes up, but the thought of willingly putting myself in his vicinity seems silly. I can't control myself around him, so trying to avoid him as much as possible would be best.

The last thing I want is to get sucked into his enticing pull and launch myself at him, as I've done multiple times. Each incident leaves me embarrassed and ashamed, and I'd like to prevent that from happening.

Tiptoeing past the kitchen entrance, I move through the dining room before stumbling upon another long hallway. This place is larger than I initially thought, and I make a mental note to draw myself a map when I return to my room.

I glance around the newly discovered corridor before stepping onto the red rug running down its center. A sideboard sits along the left wall with what I assume are expensive vases on top, and I tentatively walk past and peer into the wide entryway opposite it.

Oh.

I gulp, shocked to see so many floor-to-ceiling bookshelves. Inching closer, I lean inside and peek down the first aisle. The shelves appear to run around the entire perimeter of the room, and four rows run down the center.

I'm careful not to touch anything as I enter and explore the first aisle on the left, my eyes darting along the spines of the books. There must be thousands in here, and each one looks incredibly old.

Most are written in a language I've never seen before, probably the native tongue of the demons. Almost all places have switched to using the universal language these past hundred or so years, but I'm not surprised my *owners* haven't gotten the memo.

They probably think they're too good to read in anything other than the demon language.

Even if they speak the universal one.

Careful to keep quiet, I round the first aisle and make my way down the second before repeating the process with the shelves on the right side of the room.

It takes everything in me not to reach out and touch the spines of the books. I've always been a big fan of reading, but the only material my parents ever provided were old paperbacks with covers that had worn off long before they'd come into my possession.

These beauties look priceless, most hardcover and detailed with intricate designs. I wonder how they'd feel in my hands and if they're as heavy as they look.

I round the last shelf and come to an abrupt halt as I notice the large form in the farthest corner of the room. My heart pounds as I lower my chin and look at the demon, my mouth running dry at the sight of Silas watching me from an oversized leather chair.

He doesn't look angry, which I take as a good sign, and he sets his book down as I give him my full attention. I hope he can't hear my heart racing as I internally panic at having been caught snooping.

Is he going to punish me for entering this room? Will he have Gray do it for him?

"Are you looking for anything specific?" he asks.

I shake my head and shift uncomfortably.

Silas quirks a brow before letting out a low hum. I shouldn't have gone exploring before checking to see if somebody was in here first. It was careless, and I know better than that.

At least it's not Aziel or Gray I've stumbled upon.

Silas is holding back his power, as he was yesterday during dinner, which I take as another good sign. It makes it much easier to be around him. My cheeks warm at the thought of him keeping it away for my comfort, but I quickly push that idea to the back of my mind.

I'm reading into this way more than I should be.

Silas clears his throat. "Do you like to read?"

I nod. "Yes, I enjoy it." The audible shake in my voice makes me wince.

Silas politely ignores my nervousness as he sets his book on the small table to his left. My clammy hands clench into fists as he gestures for me to sit in the empty chair opposite his, and I hesitate before stepping forward and lowering myself into the seat.

There's also a tiny couch tucked away in the reading corner, but it's closer to Silas and I want to keep my distance.

"What language do you read?" he asks.

My face reddens, embarrassment making me flush. "I speak and understand the universal language, but I only know how to read human."

Silas frowns and shifts in his seat. He crosses his right ankle over his thigh, creating a triangle with his legs. "I was under the impression most people in the human realm were taught universal. You speak it well."

I shrug, lowering my gaze to my lap. My fingers pick anxiously at the hem of my oversized pajama shirt, and with an internal scream, I realize I just so happen to be wearing the one belonging to him. Thankfully, he hasn't seemed to notice, and if he has, he's been kind enough not to comment on it.

"I didn't have the opportunity for a formal education," I admit, shrugging. "The only learning books my parents could find for me were ones written in human."

Silas hums. "Would you like to learn? I'm sure Gray would be more than happy to hire you a tutor."

I open my mouth to decline before clicking my jaw shut. It would be nice to get an education, and it would give me something to do during the day.

I'm still unsure if Gray expects me to help around the house, but given the number of shadows I see slinking around, I assume my assistance isn't needed.

The corner of Silas's lip turns upward as he watches my reaction.

My cheeks flush under his watchful eye, and I try to keep my thoughts far from anything remotely soft. I don't know what kind of relationship he has with Gray, and the last thing I want is to anger the incubus by giving him the impression I'm getting too close to his friend.

I clear my throat and let my eyes roam over the tall bookshelves. "Most of these are in a language I've never seen before. Is it demon?"

In an attempt to hide my shaking hands, I shove them underneath my thighs. Silas watches the action before standing, and I shrink as he towers over me.

"Yes, most of these were written before the adoption of the universal language," he says, gesturing for me to stand. "Come, follow me."

Trying not to appear too scared, I raise my chin and stand. This is the first time I've ever stood so close to him, and I note with fear that I only come to his chest. Are all demons this tall?

His movements are smooth and full of confidence as he leads me down the aisle on our left. I follow closely behind, almost bumping into his back when he abruptly stops at a shelf in the far corner of the room.

I eye him as he steps aside, my attention lingering on his friendly smile before turning toward the bookshelf he's brought us to.

I'm sure my shock is visible as I scan the spines, my excitement rising as I realize they're all in the human language. I must have missed these earlier. There seems to be a rich mix of genres here, and I bounce slightly as I notice some more exciting-sounding titles.

"Most of the books here are mine," he says, "and you're more than welcome to take and read whatever you please. If there are any you'd like that aren't here, just let me know and I'll purchase them for you. Or you can ask Gray."

I nod, already knowing I will not be asking him to buy me anything.

Despite my apprehension, I force myself to look up at Silas. He's been kind to me so far, and if there's anybody to whom I feel I can ask my questions, it's him.

"What's my role in the house?" I ask.

Silas looks confused. "I'm not following."

I grimace, looking for different wording. "What are the expectations of me here? What does Gray want from me?"

Silas sighs, his chest deflating as he lets out a long exhale.

"Gray's odd for an incubus," he says. "He wants a relationship, somebody he can give his affections to. He has no interest in hurting you, but he *will* need to feed. That doesn't always have to be penetrative sex, but that's a conversation you're better off having with him." His dark eyes narrow as he acknowledges Gray's need to feed. "Gray will see to it that you're kept happy here."

I nod, grateful for the explanation despite the fear it brings about.

"And Aziel? He doesn't seem to like me very much."

Silas laughs, the deep noise erupting from his chest. My pulse picks up at its suddenness, but I quickly calm down. It's just a laugh. Laughs aren't bad.

"Aziel doesn't like anybody," he admits. "Don't worry about him. Despite his cold attitude, he'd never do anything to upset Gray, including harming you."

Silas patiently waits for my next question. I hesitate before speaking again, worried he'll find me annoying, but as I take in his relaxed posture, I gather the courage to continue my interrogation.

"What am I supposed to do all day?"

Silas shrugs, gesturing to the books. "You can read if you want. I don't believe Gray has any jobs he wishes for you to do. As I mentioned earlier, you can ask him to find you a tutor if that's something you'd find enjoyable. We have many educated shadows in our employment, and I'm sure we could find one who'd be more than happy to teach you. I imagine being chosen to educate our female would be considered an honor for many demons."

Silas falls silent when I don't respond, and a sly smirk spreads across his lips before he bends down. I remain frozen as he brings his face toward mine, my pulse racing as I feel his breath fan across my face. Is he going to kiss me?

He's an attractive man, and his kind personality is incredibly comforting. A small part of me wishes he'd purchased me instead of Gray. I imagine I'd have a happy life if I were Silas's female.

I try not to let my disappointment show when Silas brings his mouth to my ear.

"Would you like me to let you in on a little secret?" he asks. He doesn't give me time to answer before continuing. "Incubi are desperate to please, and Gray is no exception. Find a way to make that work in your favor."

He straightens back up and smooths out his shirt as if his little comment never happened. I'm not sure if he meant it to sound as sexual as I interpreted it, but I refuse to humiliate myself further by asking for clarification.

I remain frozen, Silas's attitude making me feel emotions I'm nowhere near ready to try to sift through. He seems to take pity and steps away, but I notice the way the corners of his lips twitch upward. He finds this humorous.

"Why don't you go ask Gray about the tutor? I can tell you're excited by the idea." He gestures toward the door.

I mindlessly nod, admittedly happy about the possibility of getting a proper education. It's always been something I wished I had. The idea of having to ask Gray makes me a bit wary, but I tell myself I can't live in the shadows forever.

I'm going to have to speak to him at some point.

With one last hidden glance at Silas, I leave.

This place feels almost too good to be true, and I find myself antsy as I wait for some bomb to drop. There's no way I've gotten lucky enough to be purchased by a group of men who genuinely have no intentions of harming or breeding me.

Despite their friendly attitudes, I know it's just a matter of time.

As much as I'd love to have a tutor as Silas suggested, the thought of seeking out Gray and asking him feels overwhelming. It wouldn't surprise me if he demanded something in return for his favor, and the last thing I want is to be indebted to him.

I push my hair out of my face and release a shaky breath as I walk through the dining room and past the kitchen doors. The shadows are still here, all working in comfortable silence as they ready breakfast.

Peeking around the corner, I make sure the hallway leading to the stairs is empty before hurrying toward them. My earlier assumption that the three demons would still be sleeping was wrong, and I'd like to get back to my room before running into anybody else.

I move quickly, but I come to a hard stop when Aziel's voice echoes through the large doorway that leads to the sitting room. I eye the distance between the sitting room entrance and the stairwell just past it.

There's no way I'll be able to make it there without crossing him. Internally cursing, I straighten my back and drop my chin as I press against the wall and continue forward.

Hopefully, he won't even notice me.

His voice grows louder, and my footsteps speed up in response. *Keep your head down and be quiet.* I stumble over my feet as he comes barreling around the corner, but I regain my balance quickly and slide closer to the wall.

Aziel pauses as he notices me, the frown on his lips deepening as he pulls his phone away from his ear and hangs up on whomever he's speaking to. I stare at the ground as he approaches, still holding on to my childish hope that he'll continue walking and leave me alone.

It's not until he's cornering me that I realize how foolish that thought was. I'm his intended target, and the realization has me pressing myself further against the wall. Why does he hate me so much? He's the one who bought me.

I make myself appear as small as possible as he grabs my shoulders and pushes me into the wall. My back arches, and a quiet hiss slips from my lips at the sharp pain, but I continue to hold my ground.

His power is suffocating as he invades my personal space, and its intensity makes me desperate to drop to my knees.

I stiffen as he bends down, his face burying into my hair before he inhales, smelling me. Is he upset I didn't shower? The stronger species tend to have more powerful senses, but I didn't think they would be so intense.

Aziel's fingers continue to dig painfully into the muscles of my shoulders as he lowers his face to my neck and smells me once more. I stare at the stairs, desperate to leave.

"Charlotte." Aziel grunts as he pulls his face away from my

neck and straightens back up. His hands loosen slightly where they hold me, but he maintains a firm grip to keep me in place. "I bought you for one simple reason. Do you know what that is?"

I gulp, struggling to keep a straight mind when his power seeps out of him like this. Why is he so angry? What have I done? *What has Gray done?*

"I'm sorry," I apologize.

Aziel snarls. "You're to feed the fucking incubus. You're to keep him *out* of my dreams."

I was purchased to be a steady source of food for Gray, and when he said he'd stay out of my dreams last night, I was beyond relieved. As I stare at Aziel's heaving chest, I realize that didn't mean he would go without.

I'm willing to bet that he fed from Aziel again. It would explain the demon's current anger.

"I didn't know," I plead, not caring how transparently fearful I am. If being weak is what's going to keep me alive, then I'll be the most helpless female the demon has ever seen.

Aziel laughs and releases me.

"You're going to fuck Gray today," he spits out, his words holding no emotion and leaving no room for argument.

My bottom lip trembles, the action seeming to anger Aziel further as he pushes me into the wall again. I wince as my shoulder blades slam against the plaster.

I wonder if Silas would defend me if I could somehow make it back to him. Probably not. He's stuck up for me a few times, but I doubt he'd argue with Aziel on this—especially if my assumption that Gray snuck into Aziel's dreams last night is accurate.

I was purchased for the sole purpose of feeding Gray, and I know that's what's most important to them. They don't see me as a real person. I'm nothing more than a means to an end.

There's no time to react as Aziel releases my right shoulder and grabs my chin, his fingertips digging into my cheek as he forces me to look at him. I stare at his nose, unable to work up the courage to meet his eye.

"I expect you to have welcomed him into your bed by lunch. If the scent of your fucking" —Aziel pauses and leans forward to smell me again— "*purity* is still lingering, you'll be spending a week in an incubi den until you're begging us to take you back."

Despite my attempts to contain them, large tears build in my eyes and spill down my cheeks. I clench my jaw shut as I nod. I knew better than to think these men were genuine in their promises not to hurt me.

I'm grateful at least one of them is letting their true colors show early. It's better to learn now than be lulled into a false sense of security and crushed later.

Aziel steps back, and he lets out a quiet sigh as he takes a moment to look me over. His eyebrows pull together and his mouth relaxes before all traces of softness vanish and he walks away.

I watch, frozen, as he heads through the doorway leading to the dining room. The second he's out of view, I slam my hands over my mouth to muffle my panting. My knees threaten to give out as the adrenaline drains from my body, leaving me exhausted.

His power lingers in the room, making me fear it'll be stuck to my clothing. If I didn't know any better, I'd say he was purposefully forcing it out around me, but I'm not familiar enough with him or his species to know what it naturally feels like.

I shake my head in disbelief before letting out a dry laugh and wiping my cheeks. Crying isn't going to get me anywhere. Leaning against the wall, I take a moment to collect myself and recite my father's words. I am nobody's property. They can scare and hurt me, but they can't steal my self-respect.

They can't take that from me.

I push off the wall. My knowledge of incubi dens is limited, but from what I do know, giving myself to Gray will be the lesser of two evils.

The dens are notorious for overfeeding and draining their females until they're weak shells of their former selves. From the hushed whispers I've overheard throughout the years, they're known to use up their women in mere days and are frequent customers of the auctions.

I'm unwilling to take the risk of being sent there.

My mouth goes dry as I hurry up the stairs and rush toward Gray's bedroom. Pushing away all my fears, I force my mind to go blank as I halt outside his bedroom door.

There's a lot of clattering in there, loud bangs followed by the bathroom door slamming shut a few seconds later. Not wanting to put this off any longer, I knock.

The noises come to an abrupt stop, and I bite at the inside of my cheek as I wait for Gray to open the door.

He does so quickly.

Gray leans against the doorway and smirks down at me. My face flushes as I take in his unclothed state, my pulse quickening as I unintentionally give him a quick onceover. Besides a pair of absurdly tight black underwear, his body is bare.

Knowing my job is to seduce him, I allow myself another moment to admire his frame. He looks how I imagined him to, with long limbs and strong muscles that make my thighs clench.

When he flexes, I force myself to look away and glance into the bedroom behind him. It's at least twice the size of mine, covered in dark, muted colors and featuring a bed that could easily fit six people.

I assume that's the exact purpose of it, and I wouldn't be surprised to learn he's filled it to the brim on many occasions.

"Charlie," he says, stepping aside so I can enter. "Where'd you wander off to this morning?"

I purse my lips before forcing out an excuse. "I wanted to look around before everybody got up. I didn't think my absence would be noticed."

I'm opting to be truthful, but only because he'd probably be able to sense if I lied.

Gray hums, thankfully not appearing upset over my exploring.

"I'm surprised you've come to my room," he continues. "I thought it would be the other way around."

I shrug, remaining quiet. Should I tell him Aziel sent me here to sleep with him? He might stay true to his word and refuse to have me, and I don't want to take that risk. Aziel is clearly in charge here, and as much as I'd like to believe Gray is genuine in his promises to keep me safe, I have no trust in the Wrath king.

Gray doesn't seem to notice my sour mood as I approach him, his smile only growing as I tentatively place my hands on his waist. He stills, and I feel his lust slip out in response. I wonder if touch makes it harder for him to hold it in.

I slide my hands up the sides of his abdomen, hoping to lure out more.

My goal is to get so overwhelmed by it that I start to want what's about to happen between us. Clenching my jaw, I lean forward and inhale his scent as more begins to spill out of him.

It immediately begins to take effect, intense arousal building inside of me. Gray looks confused by my actions, his eyebrows pulling together before he cups my cheeks.

"Are you okay?" he asks.

I nod, plastering a wide grin on my face.

"Yes. I've been thinking a lot about the dream you gave me yesterday," I say, internally cringing at how desperate that makes me sound.

Gray rubs my cheeks with his thumbs before lowering his hands to my shoulders. I hold back a wince as they land on the spot where Aziel grabbed me earlier. I'm most definitely going to be bruised.

Shrugging his hands off my arms, I dig my fingers into the muscles on his sides and urge him to walk back into his room. Trying to emulate the scenes I've read about in my books, I lead him to his bed and push him onto his mattress.

Gray chuckles as he lies down, his arms darting out to grab my waist and pull me on top. I breathe in more of his lust and feel my muscles relax as I straddle him. His underwear does little to hide his body's reaction to me, and I stare at the bulge before settling myself on top of it.

He moans and rolls his hips, further pressing himself against me.

Before I can register what he's doing, I'm pushed to the side and placed on my back. I stare up at him, my mind hazy as I crane my neck and bury my face into his chest to better breathe in his intoxicating scent.

Gray pulls back, his eyes narrowing before he bends and kisses my collarbone.

"You're an awful liar, Charlie," he whispers. "Why are you trying to feed me?"

Gray trails his lips from my collarbone to my neck. It feels good, and I tilt my head back as my mind goes blank. He's so distracting, his mere presence intoxicating. Every cell of my body is receptive and desperate for him. Gasping, I watch through my eyelashes as he pulls back and licks his lips. I want them on me again.

"*Charlie*," he sings, teasing me. "You need to learn how to see past my lust."

I blink before moaning as he lowers his head and licks my

throat. My back arches, the feeling amazing. His lust fills my lungs, the smell of it everything I've ever wanted.

It's so good.

"Why are you trying to feed me?" he repeats, grabbing my thighs and pulling them open so he can slide his hips between them.

"Fuck," I gasp.

Gray grinds against me, his hardened length pressing against my clit through the material of our clothing. I groan, eager for more. If this is what feeding him will feel like, it may not end up being as bad as I initially thought.

I'll hate myself later, but it feels incredible at the moment.

Gray's sigh is laced with disappointment when he pulls away, and I wince as I look into his black eyes. Shouldn't he be happy I'm feeding him?

"Answer me, Charlie."

I don't want this to stop, and I wrap my arms around his neck to prevent him from pulling away any further. He laughs at the attempt before grabbing my wrists and pushing my hands into the mattress next to my head.

This position is excellent, and I crane my neck to breathe in more of him. His lust isn't as intense as it was when I first met him, but it's still seeping out. I'm willing to bet intimacy makes it harder for him to hide it away.

He presses another kiss to the corner of my lips before disconnecting his hips from mine and hovering over me. Unhappy with the distance, I raise my pelvis until it connects with his. Gray's eyes roll back before he shakes his head and hardens his expression.

The sight of his disappointment makes me want to cry.

"Do you want me to fuck you?" he asks, tilting his head to the side. "Think hard before you answer."

Groaning, I nod. I want nothing more than that.

Gray frowns and tuts, his fingers tightening around my wrists. Why does he think I wouldn't want him to fuck me? I want whatever he's willing to give.

I'd let him kill me if it meant I could feel his hands on my body.

Gray watches me, his eyes trailing all over my face before he rolls to the side. The departure makes me cry, and I let a loud whine slip from my lips before I grab his chest and try to throw myself on top of him. He grunts as my knee makes contact with his manhood, but he quickly forgets about it as he dodges my attack and climbs off the bed.

"Charlie, relax," he coos as my bottom lip trembles. "Give yourself a few seconds to calm down. I've accidentally gotten you high."

I don't pay attention to what he's saying as he walks to the bathroom door. He drops his head against the wooden surface, his hands clenching and unclenching by his sides. It looks like he's having a hard time, and I prop myself up on my elbows before sitting on the edge of his bed.

"You're so fucking tempting," he moans, spinning to face me.

My pulse begins to slow. The distance helps me see past his lust, and my cheeks warm as the shame of my actions hits me.

What the fuck did I just do?

"Do you feel better?" he asks.

"Yes."

Lowering my attention to the floor, I stare at it as I slide off his bed. Despite my regret, I still need him to take me. Aziel will send me away if he doesn't. I hope I haven't ruined my chance, but I think it should be easy to convince him.

Saying *no* goes against everything Gray is.

I shift my weight from foot to foot before tentatively

approaching Gray. His eyes narrow as I close the distance between us, but he makes no attempt to stop me.

"Why are you trying to feed me?" he asks again.

I shrug, not wanting to answer. Will he turn me away if I tell him it's because of Aziel's threats? I know he won't believe it's because I genuinely want him.

My jaw clenches as I think of an excuse.

"I just want to get it over with," I say.

Gray shakes his head, his expression unreadable. It takes everything in me not to recoil when he tucks a piece of hair behind my ear. It's cute, but I won't be swayed by it. That's something I thought only happened in the books I read.

"You're lying," he whispers.

Why does he even care? I was bought to feed him, so I don't understand why he's being so hesitant about it. He's an incubus, for fuck's sake. Sex should be as natural to him as breathing.

Gray frowns when I don't immediately respond, his expression mirroring mine. His eyes slip shut as he leans forward and sniffs my head as Aziel did earlier, but thankfully, unlike his counterpart, he doesn't follow up the action with a painful shove.

"Did Aziel say something to you?"

I shrug, not answering his question. Gray watches my reaction closely, his shoulders dropping as he grabs my waist and pulls me into his chest. I tense as he wraps his arms around my body, uncomfortable with the intimacy.

I'm trying to get fucked, not hugged.

"I suspect you're not going to share with me what he said, but I can promise you it wasn't the truth. He's not going to hurt you," Gray says. "Despite your very persuasive attempt, I won't touch you until you want it."

Zero part of me believes him, but I won't argue. Aziel gave me until lunch to take Gray to bed, and I'll try again later. There's no way I'm going to an incubi den.

Gray rubs my back before stepping away. I lean into him as he disconnects himself, my eyes fluttering shut as I breathe in his lust one more time. Why's he making this so complicated? I was under the impression he'd happily take me to his bed.

Gray changes the subject. "I have something to show you!"

He seems excited as he gestures to the bathroom door, and I look between him and it in question. Did he stock it with feminine products or something? Gray's smirk widens as he pulls the door open, and he hurries through it into my connecting bedroom.

I follow, cautious. What did he do?

Gray spins, his attention zeroed in on my face as I step into my room and look around. I freeze, every muscle in my body growing tense when I spot the trinkets on my dresser. My eyes grow comically wide when I look up and notice the photo frames hung on the wall above it.

How did Gray get these?

"I brought all your things here," Gray proudly says. "You're a bit of a packrat."

I snort, the reaction unintentional. Dad loved to call me the same thing, and he usually followed his insult by demanding I clean my room.

My smile falls.

I look back at the family photos Gray hung up. Dad's smiling in all of them, and I walk closer to better see my favorite one. It was taken a few years ago, and I look over the thin lines on his forehead before sliding to where his arms wrap around Mom and me.

He was so scared to have these photos taken, worried they'd fall into the wrong hands and expose my existence. It took my mother and me months to convince him we'd keep them safely tucked away from prying eyes.

I never thought I'd get the opportunity to see them again—or any of my things, for that matter.

Gray's footsteps are quiet as he walks over, and I listen as he comes to a halt directly behind me. He remains silent as he watches me examine the photos.

"My parents?" I ask.

A pained sigh reaches my ears before hands are placed on my shoulders.

"I don't know about your mother, but your father…" Gray pauses and tucks another piece of hair behind my ear. His fingers linger, stroking my ear before he returns his hand to my shoulder. "He's been buried in the human tradition."

My bottom lip quivers. I've known deep down that my father has been dead this entire time. His body was so still, and the blood below him was too great to result from a minor injury.

"Did you bury him?"

The Seekers would never have taken the time to do so. God forbid they show any respect toward the lives they steal.

It's possible one of Dad's co-workers stopped by to say goodbye, but I doubt they'd care enough to bury him. If anything, they were probably enraged after learning he had been hiding a female for the past twenty-five years.

Gray clears his throat. "I did."

I remain silent, too lost in thought to respond.

"Does that make you upset? I didn't think you'd want him left in the house," he continues. "He's buried in the garden." Gray rubs gentle circles into the bruised skin on my shoulders.

I mindlessly nod. Dad loved his garden. Without thinking, I turn and throw my arms around Gray's waist.

He returns the hug immediately, squeezing me tightly against his bare chest. I remind myself not to get distracted by the feeling of his hard flesh pressing against my cheek or the lingering lust from my attempts to seduce him earlier.

Gray kisses the top of my head. "I swear I'm not the bad guy you think me to be."

I squeeze, unsure how I feel about him. I don't believe he's as kind and genuine as he wants me to think, but I'm willing to admit he might not be as bad as I initially thought.

He's offering me a better life than most females are granted, and it seems genuine enough. If it weren't for Aziel's threats, I imagine I could potentially find myself happy here.

Gray gives me another tight squeeze before nudging me toward my bed. My pulse races as the backs of my thighs make contact with the mattress. Is he going to take me now? I know it needs to happen, but I'd like time to decompress before getting into action.

"Relax, Charlie," Gray says, urging me to sit. "I'm going to go talk to Aziel. You can stay up here for as long as you want, and I'll return in a bit to check on you."

What's he going to talk to Aziel about? I hope not me.

Gray looks me over, his eyebrows furrowed and lips tight, before turning and leaving. I stare at my door for a long while, waiting patiently for him to return and tell me this is all some elaborate trick and I'm a fool for falling for it.

When he doesn't, I flop onto my back and look around. I used to pride myself on being able to contain my emotions, but these past few days have broken that mental resolve.

I can't believe Gray brought my things here. Standing, I walk to my dresser and begin to sift through everything.

Each trinket sends me into a downward spiral of painful memories, but I enjoy it nonetheless. These are the last pieces of my family I have.

I wonder if Gray can find my mom. I know asking him to buy her would be too much, especially since she probably isn't even eligible for sale, but I'd be content just knowing she's safe.

She's the only family I have left.

My hands shake as I begin to move my things around the room. I feel like a fraud as I find homes for my items. It's wrong for me to be getting so comfortable, especially when I know they'll be sending me away soon.

Aziel is probably telling Gray right now that he must get rid of me—that either I feed him or I am sent away. I doubt Gray will be able to change Aziel's decision on the incubi den, and I hope he'll let me feed him instead.

I'd much rather do that.

Chapter Ten

SILAS

AZIEL STORMS INTO the library with a loud groan, his posture stiff and his hands clenched into tight fists by his sides. He looks pissed, but that's nothing new.

Thirty minutes. All I want is thirty minutes of uninterrupted silence. I knew it was too much to ask for.

"Can I help you?" I ask, mildly intrigued as Aziel throws himself onto the couch.

What's got him in such a mood? Aziel has never been much of a morning person, but this is extreme even for him.

He leans forward and rips my book out of my hand before throwing it against the wall on the opposite side of the room. *What the fuck?* The pages scatter and fall to the ground in a heap, and I grind my teeth to stop myself from throwing *him* against the wall.

Given the overwhelming scent of arousal and Gray that pours off him, I'd guess the incubus snuck his way into his dreams last night. I lean back in my chair, not the least bit surprised. Gray picked a nervous, virginal human.

Charlie isn't going to be offering herself for a long time, and Gray's much too patient. It will be a while before she lets him feed from her, and Gray still needs sustenance until then.

"Tell me what you know," Aziel orders.

I shake my head, unwilling to share anything with him. I like Gray's female. She's tense and reeks of fear most of the time, but I can tell she's going to make Gray happy. I haven't seen him this excited in years, and I'll be damned if I give Aziel the information he needs to justify ruining that.

Telling him I can't see anything about Charlie's fate will only worsen his anger. He probably assumes I was exaggerating when I said it at the auction house, and I have no intention of telling him just how serious I was. He's going to be stuck with her for a while.

"You know I can't tell you anything," I say, standing and forcing my face into his neck.

He recoils, but not before I catch a whiff of Charlie's fear. It's embedded in his skin, and a wave of anger erupts from me. I knew I should've escorted her back to her room.

"What did you do?"

The laugh that bubbles up out of Aziel's chest is dark, and I struggle to hold back my snide remarks about its resemblance to the laugh his father used to have. As much as he claims to hate the man, he sure is turning more into him with each passing day.

The Aziel I met all those hundreds of years ago was determined to be different. He didn't experience such enjoyment from hurting others. The man standing before me now is a replica of his father. He's losing himself.

"Aziel," I repeat when he doesn't answer.

He shoves me away, and I step back but hold my ground. He's in for a rude awakening if he thinks Gray and I will let him batter Charlie around without repercussions.

We are his only family, and as much as he pretends he doesn't need us, he'd be devastated if we left. Hurting her will cause Gray to do precisely that, and as much as I love Aziel, I'm uninterested in standing beside a man so easily overcome by his wrath.

"Oh, fuck off," Aziel snaps. I watch through narrowed eyes as he runs a hand through his hair. A guilty action of a guilty man. "I didn't hurt her."

I scoff. "Would she say the same thing?"

The muscle in his jaw twitches. It's clear by his expression that he regrets whatever he did to her, but I'm not going to let him off easy. She's fragile, and he can't just sweep his actions under the rug.

"I told her she needs to fuck Gray or I'm going to send her to an incubi den," he admits. "I'm not going to do it, obviously. It was just a way to inspire her to take action."

I close my eyes and shake my head as I try and fail to rein in my anger. Being around these two makes me feel more like a parent than a friend. I don't know what's going on between Aziel and Gray lately, but whatever it is, they need to sort their shit out.

We tend to go through phases where things are tense and uncomfortable, but this is getting out of hand.

"Gray's going to be upset when he figures out what you've done," I warn him.

Aziel shrugs, his mask of indifference returning. "I don't care."

I want to strangle him. It's his stupidity that's landed him in this position. He's the one who bought the female, and he doesn't get to go around acting like an asshole now that she's here.

"Threatening Charlie will only make Gray retaliate," I say.

"Maybe, but it will sure keep her the fuck away from me."

Keep her away? I thought he wanted to keep *Gray* away. Does Aziel have a little crush? The thought alone has me holding back laughter. I knew Gray purposefully chose a female Aziel was attracted to, but I didn't anticipate she'd have him frazzled so quickly. She's only been here for a day.

It's comical.

Aziel's frown deepens as he watches my attempts to hide my laughter.

"Contrary to popular belief, being mean to a woman isn't a good way to express your soft emotions toward her," I tease. "I'd recommend apologizing if you want to feel her body on yours."

My laughter continues as Aziel turns and storms out of the room, and I watch him leave before shifting my attention to the book he attacked earlier. He's an idiot, but I'm sure he'll figure it out eventually. As long as he's not physically harming her, I don't want to get involved.

I crouch and slide my finger over my book's rough edge, grimacing at the sight of the ripped corner. Aziel's anger is always getting the best of him, and it appears today it got the best of my book.

My old, incredibly expensive book.

It's not every day one has the opportunity to acquire a spell book from one of the oldest witch covens, and I wonder how long it'll take before I have the chance again. They may have ripped out most of the meaningful spells, but it's still fascinating to read through.

Or at least it was.

I straighten out the pages and stick them neatly between the book cover. I'll have to glue them back together later. Sighing, I push myself off the ground as Gray's shouting reaches my ears.

I knew it was only a matter of time before he made his way to Aziel's office, but I figured it would take a bit longer than this.

Wanting to make sure neither takes things too far, I stroll out of the library and down the hallway that leads to our offices. Aziel has the first one on the left, and their shouting grows louder with each step I take.

Neither man pays me attention as I enter and make myself

comfortable in the chair along the far wall.

Aziel sits behind his desk, his attempt at appearing relaxed painfully subpar. Gray doesn't look much better, his chest heaving as he stands before the large wooden desk.

"What the fuck did you say to her?" Gray shouts, shoving a finger against Aziel's chest.

Aziel dips his chin and looks at the finger with disinterest. He makes no moves to answer, and wanting to hurry up and get this argument over with, I lean forward and answer for him. "He told Charlie he'd send her to an incubi den if she didn't feed you."

The heated glare Aziel shoots my way doesn't bother me much. I ignore it in lieu of watching Gray's face redden.

"And how do you know that?" Gray asks. "Did you sit back and watch him threaten my female?"

I blink, unhappy with the accusation. I've never been that type of man, but Gray is blinded by his anger. He's ready to accuse anybody of anything, including me.

"Of course not," I say. "Aziel came storming into the library afterward and told me."

Aziel scoffs. I don't know what else he's expecting from me. I've made my desire to live in peace with the female quite clear, and it was foolish for him to think I'd back him up on this.

What he said was cruel, and I won't defend it.

As much as he wants to push Charlie away, I know he's unwilling to risk losing Gray over it. Besides me, the incubus is the only person who can stand to be around him. Everybody is too terrified of Aziel or too desperate to please him to be genuine in their words and actions.

He needs us, which means he needs to stay on Charlie's good side.

"Leave Charlie alone," Gray threatens, returning his attention to Aziel.

Aziel shrugs, unfazed. "She isn't doing her job. If she's unable to fulfill your needs, I'll take her back and purchase you a new one."

My back stiffens as Gray lunges. I grab my thighs to keep myself from intervening, my muscles taut. What the fuck is Gray doing? He's never been one for fighting, but to attack Aziel is pure stupidity. Aziel can't stop himself once he gets going, his wrath taking over until he's torn apart every person who stands in his way.

I'm sure the bond protects Gray from death, but that doesn't mean Aziel will be able to stop himself from causing harm.

I scan Aziel as he pins Gray to the desk, checking for any signs of his wrath emerging. Gray flails, his sad attempts at hurting Aziel unsuccessful. Gray tends to stray from the incubi ideals on several fronts, but the need to please and keep the peace are ones he still thrives on.

It's hard to feed when the people you're trying to seduce are filled with anger and hatred.

Aziel wraps his hand around Gray's throat, his arm stiff and unmoving despite Gray's powerful punches to his face and chest.

I continue to monitor as Gray spits insults at Aziel, but I jump to my feet when Aziel looks to me for help. Rushing forward, I shove him away and take over holding Gray down.

Gray's fist makes painful contact with my chin as he blindly continues to attack, his knuckles smashing into the bone and breaking it. I grunt, my fingers digging into his throat until he's struggling to breathe. That hurt.

Aziel moves to the far wall and works to calm himself down, his shoulders shaking at the effort.

Maybe it *would* be best if we got Gray a new female. Charlie's creating quite a rift between these two men, and it'd be best to get somebody only Gray likes. Aziel's attraction is making things too complicated.

The fates say she's to stay with us, but maybe they're wrong.

"Let go of me, Silas." Gray chokes, clawing at my hand.

I take a moment to evaluate him, checking to make sure he's not going to attack the second I release him, before letting go. My hand lingers in the air as I step back, and I'm careful to remain close in case he decides to launch himself at Aziel again.

"Are you two done?" I ask.

Both men hesitate before nodding.

I rub my jaw, prodding at the fractured bone. The bastard got me good. This one's going to take a while to heal.

Aziel gives Gray a wide berth as he walks around us and sits behind his desk. He avoids looking in Gray's direction, but the incubus glares daggers at him each step of the way.

"You," I say, pointing to Aziel, "are going to leave Charlie alone."

Aziel's jaw clenches before he gives a jerky nod. Gray smirks, but his haughty expression falls as I turn toward him.

"*You* need to stop instigating and messing with Aziel. If you get hungry, spend the night with Shay. I'm sure she'll be happy to feed you."

Gray looks like he wants to argue, but he's smart enough to shut his mouth and nod. Shay's one of his favorite females to feed from, and I'm sure Charlie won't be too upset if he visits her. Besides, if she doesn't want Gray seeking nourishment elsewhere, she can give herself to him.

"If you two start this shit up again," I add, "I'll be returning the female and buying a new one of my choosing."

Gray immediately begins to argue, not realizing I'm saying this only to keep Aziel in line. As much as the Wrath tries to hide it, it's clear he's harboring some emotion toward Charlie. Aziel feels comfortable threatening to get rid of her because he knows he won't follow through, but that assurance is not a guarantee with me.

He'll leave Gray and Charlie alone because deep down, for some reason I don't understand, he likes her. He doesn't even know her, but it seems that doesn't matter. She has a cunt and lives in our home, which must be enough for the thousand-year-old virgin.

I lean against Aziel's desk as Gray storms out of the room. I've been friends with Aziel long enough to know his tells, and the way he furrows his brow and purses his lips are two clear indicators he's still struggling to calm himself.

Gray was stupid to provoke him, especially knowing how worked up Aziel already is today.

"Are you okay?" I ask, the worry I feel seeping into my tone.

Aziel hesitates, his back straightening before he rolls his shoulders and stretches.

"I need to go to the pits," he admits.

Shit. I pinch the bridge of my nose, more than a little annoyed. Aziel can't casually go to the pits and be back for dinner. If we're lucky, he'll only be gone a few days, and if not, it may be months before we see him again.

The moment the scent of death hits his nose, he's lost in the fighting, his wrath coming out full force.

"Should I get Gray?" I ask.

I know he will reject the offer, but I ask anyway. He hates when I suggest he let the incubus use lust to calm him, but it would make things so much easier if he just gave in to their bond. That's the whole point of having a bonded mate. Somebody to bring you calm when you get worked up.

I know he's mad Gray forced the bond on him, but it wasn't Gray's fault. The incubus was starving when we found him, probably only hours from death, and he wasn't in control of himself. He tore through the head of the first body he could, his actions inadvertently triggering Aziel's bond.

Aziel blamed me for a while, thinking it was my fault since it was the fates who put the sex curse on his bloodline, but I had nothing to do with it.

"I'd rather go to the pits," Aziel decides.

That's not what I want to hear, but I don't push. I'm just glad he's self-aware enough to know he needs to go to the pits and isn't trying to wait out his urges. There's a human female in our home now, and I don't want to risk him accidentally killing her in a fit of rage.

Gray would never let us hear the end of it.

"You need to be back before the annual gathering," I remind him, glancing at the calendar on the wall. "Asmod is hosting this year, and you must present Charlie as yours."

It's next week, but that should be enough time for Aziel to get the fighting out of his system and crawl his ass back home.

Aziel nods, silently agreeing. *Good.* I'll have to take Charlie if he's not here, which doesn't sound particularly enjoyable. I like her, but my interest in pretending to care for a female is nonexistent. Besides, Aziel agreed to this when he bought her for Gray.

"Promise me you'll be back in time for the gathering next week," I order. "Say it out loud so I know you understand."

Aziel sucks his cheeks into his mouth, then points to the door. "Get out."

He doesn't wait for me to leave before beginning to tidy his desk, which Gray messed up when he lunged over it in attack. I still can't believe the incubus would do something so foolish.

I walk to Gray's office. He's lying on his back in the middle of the room, and his head lolls to the side as I enter. He spreads his arms and legs out, turning himself into a star, before shifting his gaze back to the ceiling.

"What was that all about?" I ask.

Gray continues staring at the ceiling, and the dried blood smattered on his lip and cheek cracks. Aziel refrained from hitting him, so the blood that covers his face is either from Aziel or me. Probably me.

I unhinge my jaw and move it left and right, pleased it's already almost healed. Gray's got a mean right hook.

"He won't kill me," Gray says. "Little Wrath Baby could never hurt me."

He doesn't get it. "No, but if not you, then probably Charlie," I say. "He's going to the pits."

Gray's eyes soften, his pissy attitude deflating at the knowledge of what he's making Aziel do. The pits always mess with Aziel, and the things he sees in them haunt him for months after he returns. He hides it well, but we all see it.

I hope Gray regrets his rash actions.

"I'll settle him," he says, standing.

I lift my hand, stopping him. He needs to give Aziel space.

"Charlie wants a tutor," I say. "And you should prepare her for the annual gathering next week."

Gray lies back on the ground. He seems surprised by my statement, but that quickly turns into an excited expression I don't want to know the meaning of.

"Noted," he says. "What do you think of her?"

I shrug, not having any strong opinions. She could be a fun addition to our home if she learns to accept Gray. She seems to have the potential to be intelligent, which is always a positive.

A small part of me thinks she's fun to look at as well. I have no interest in intimacy with an owned female, but I can't deny that I find her attractive.

I'll enjoy listening to her feed Gray.

It might be the first time I overhear him and don't want to scrub my ears out afterward.

"I like her," I eventually say. "She'll make a good addition to our home."

Gray laughs, agreeing. "You want to fuck her."

I pretend his statement was a question and hum as I think it over. What he says may be accurate, but that's none of his business.

"Not really," I say, knowing he's already well-acquainted with my preferences. "I prefer my females with black eyes."

I've never strayed far from my species, and I don't have much interest in doing so. Demon women are strong and able to give me what I want. Charlie could never take me the way I need.

Chapter Eleven

CHARLOTTE

SWEAT BEADS ALONG my upper lip as I wedge my spade into the ground and pull up a chunk of hard dirt. I dump it onto the grass next to my left thigh as I admire my newly created hole.

I've only been here for three days, but mind-numbing boredom has already begun to sink its claws into me. In a last-ditch attempt to fill my days, I asked Gray to let me plant some seeds in the backyard below the library window.

He was more than happy with my request, claiming I can do whatever I want, before waggling his eyebrows and asking if there was anything else I'd like to do.

That question was met with a firm no.

I wipe the sweat off my forehead with a huff before grabbing a few seeds from the packet I found in my room. Gray brought it over with my stuff, mistaking my dad's seeds as my own. Sprinkling a few into my hole, I ensure they're spread evenly before covering them.

My parents made gardening look so easy, but now that I'm the one doing it, I realize just how tedious it is.

Especially within the sweltering heat of the Wrath kingdom.

Silas is in the library, and I peek at him through the windows. He looks over as if sensing my gaze, and he raises an eyebrow when he notices I'm spying on him. I'm almost always spying on him, and I'm not proud of it.

I perk up, offering him a wide grin and a small wave. The corner of his lip twitches before he dips his head in greeting. He and Gray have taken it upon themselves to be extra kind to me after my run-in with Aziel, offering small assurances that their counterpart will not mess with me anymore.

I'm not sure whether or not I believe them, but I figure I won't know for sure until Aziel returns from the pits. They briefly explained that the pits are some sort of fighting ring, and they promised he'll be much calmer after returning.

I hope they're right.

The fact he had to go to a fighting pit to release his anger is reason enough for me to be scared of him.

I honestly wish he'd stay away forever. The house is much livelier with him gone, and I'm growing to love my exploration of the place now that I don't have to worry about Aziel popping around every corner and hurting me.

"Spying on Silas?" Gray asks, startling me.

I turn toward him with a gasp and place a hand over my chest as he approaches. He's quite quiet when he wants to be, and he chuckles as he crouches to my right. I know what he's seeing, and my cheeks turn red as he makes eye contact with Silas through the window.

I will the flushing of my cheeks to go away as I return to my seeds. Gray's been so busy these past few days that I've hardly had a chance to speak to him. Even when he's in the same room as me, he's too busy to pay me any mind. I want to ask what he's doing, but I haven't found the courage.

I thought I'd like the alone time, but I'm beginning to get

lonely.

My desperation for intimacy has led to me almost offering him to enter my dreams again. I can see the effects of hunger on him, his cheeks sinking inward and undereye bags growing with each day.

Despite it, though, I can't bring myself to offer to feed him.

"What're you planting?" Gray asks, dropping the topic of me watching Silas.

I point to the packet. He looks at the photo of lettuce printed on the top, and my heart lurches when his lips spread into a wide, genuine smile. I want him to smile at me like that every moment of every day. I need him to. He's so beautiful.

"I don't think you'll have a lot of luck growing human food in demon soil," he admits. "But I'm excited to see how it turns out."

I shrug. "Me too."

The sun feels good on my cheeks, and I shut my eyes and look upward.

I have a feeling the seeds won't work, but I want to try it anyway. Wrath is hot, but parts of the human world are just as warm. What more do vegetables need than oxygen, sunshine, and some water? Nothing that I know of.

I hold back the urge to flinch when soft fingertips graze the exposed skin on my chest. It's not the first time Gray's taken it upon himself to touch me, and I've grown used to it over the past few days.

Gray must take my lack of resistance as a good sign, as seconds later, his fingertips are replaced with his mouth. This touch is new, and I tense as he slides his lips from the center of my chest toward my collarbone.

They're soft and warm, and Gray takes the opportunity to lick my salty skin.

My jaw clenches as he releases some of his lust. This must be another one of his attempts to desensitize me to it. The first couple of times he did this, I almost immediately turned into putty, and I pride myself on remaining still as his intoxicating scent hits my nose.

I hold back a moan as his teeth scrape along my neck. It feels so good.

Pushing further, Gray grabs my hands and shoves them underneath his shirt, encouraging me to touch his bare skin. My breath hitches as my fingers meet stiff muscles, and I can't help but visualize how they look as I run my fingers over his torso. I'm scared that opening my eyes will break the illusion, so I keep them shut as I explore the hard planes of his abdomen.

His muscles flex underneath my hands and his breath grows ragged as I wrap my arms around his waist and feel his back. His skin is so soft.

Gray rises to his knees and fiddles with the hem of my skirt, his teeth nipping at my skin before he pulls back and sucks the spot instead. I pant, my movements growing more confident as I dig my fingers into the taut muscles of his lower back.

"Do you want to feed me?" he asks, finding and pinching my nipple through the fabric of my shirt.

I'm supposed to say *no*. I know he wants me to say *no*. Instead, I gasp and nod my head *yes*, desperate for him to continue. He feels so fucking good. I don't ever want this to stop.

"Use your words."

I moan. "Yes. Please touch me." I don't care how desperate I sound at this moment.

Gray pulls away, his retreat leisurely as he soaks up the last moments of contact between us. A loud, embarrassing whine slips from my throat as he grabs my arms and pulls my hands out from under his shirt.

"That was good," he purrs. "When you first arrived, you'd have been begging for me before I even touched you."

I gulp. I like his approval, more than I should. Gray is being kind to me because he wants something from me, something he morally feels he can't take without my permission. Once I've given it to him, though, he'll no longer be burdened by his moral dilemma. I don't want to find out what that's like. I can't take the risk, especially when I'm still so susceptible to his lust.

This practice is going to make me strong, though.

At the end of the day, I'm grateful Gray is taking the time to help me acclimate to his scent. I was under the impression nothing could be done about my response to his lust, and I would wither away until all I could think about was his pleasure, but he's explained it doesn't have to be like that.

Most weaker species aren't given the opportunity to build immunity to the power stronger demons emit, and by the time their bodies start to adapt, it's already too late. Gray's promised he and Silas would keep it at bay until it no longer has such an intense effect on me.

I didn't initially believe him, but I'm seeing a real improvement after only three days. Hopefully, after a few more weeks, Gray's won't bother me at all. Not unless I purposefully give in to it.

My lips purse as I think about what comes next, though. Gray's strong, but there are two other demons I'll have to go through the same process with. I'm not so worried about Silas, but the thought of Aziel trying to train me not to submit fills me with dread.

I hope Gray won't leave me alone with him when the time comes. I can't be left alone with Aziel. I won't make it out alive.

"I have a surprise for you," Gray says, pulling me from my thoughts.

Another surprise?

He grins before bouncing to his feet and holding his hand out for me to take. I stare at it before taking the bait and letting him pull me to my feet. I love surprises.

"What is it?" I give in and ask.

Gray's smile grows. "I've hired you a tutor."

Without meaning to, I turn toward the library windows and peer through them in search of Silas. I never mentioned wanting a tutor to Gray, meaning Silas must have told him on my behalf.

I spot Silas almost immediately, and my eyes widen as I take in his current state. The book he was once reading is long forgotten, haphazardly thrown onto the table next to his chair. His legs are spread as he stares at Gray and me, his hands clenched into tight fists on the top of his thighs.

I refuse to look at or acknowledge the noticeable bulge in the front of his pants.

He seems relaxed, but I know without a doubt he watched the entire scene unfold between Gray and me. I can't believe I forgot so quickly that he could see us. We're sitting directly in front of the window, for fuck's sake.

I hope he knows my begging is just a product of the lust Gray seeps.

Despite it being what I was purchased for, it's one thing for others to know it happens and another for them to see it themselves. My parents raised me to believe intimacy should be kept private, and I need to do a better job of being discreet.

"Oh, don't be shy," Gray says. "He likes to watch."

I frown. "I've gathered that."

Silas has made that quite obvious, but Gray fails to realize that just because somebody likes to watch doesn't mean the other person wants to *be* watched. Despite my inappropriate and secret attraction toward Silas, I know better than to try anything with him.

He's kind and friendly toward me, but he clearly has no interest in a romantic relationship. In some twisted way, his viewing me only as an acquaintance makes me even more desperate.

Gray heads toward the back doors of the estate. I trail silently behind him, intrigued as he leads me past the library and down the hallway where all their offices are.

I tense as we pass the library, but Silas remains inside.

My muscles relax as we halt in front of Gray's office doors, and I turn toward them before realizing Gray is looking at the room opposite it.

"We don't have a formal fourth office, but we have a pretty large supply closet I set up for you." Gray pushes open the door, revealing the converted room.

My own office? I step inside, pleasantly surprised with what he's done. Whatever was once stored in here is long gone, and you'd never be able to tell this was a supply closet. A desk sits directly opposite the door, and a small seating area is in the corner to my left.

The shadow sitting in the chair opposite my desk captures my attention, and I instinctively lean into Gray's side as he turns and stands.

"This is…" Gray pauses, hesitating. "Uh, he has a fairly traditional demon name. You can call him *Rock*. It's the closest translation. He's in charge of the grounds and has volunteered to be your tutor."

Gray places a hand on my back and gently nudges me forward. My heart thunders in my chest as I offer Rock a small smile. I can't make out any part of him beyond the vague shape of his body and the blurry outline of a face.

"It's nice to meet you, Charlie." His voice is quiet.

The lips that meet my forehead tickle, and I turn toward Gray just as he pulls away and announces he'll be in his office. He shoots both Rock and me a wide smile before leaving, and I'm happy to see he keeps his door open.

I don't like being left alone with males I don't know.

Turning back around, I face Rock and try not to let my discomfort show as I walk around him and sit behind my new desk. It's smaller than Gray's, but I'm not offended by that.

This fits me perfectly.

A large stack of papers sits on top, and I look them over with a low hum. Rock gives me a minute to adjust and peek through the desk drawers. Gray has filled the top two with brightly colored office supplies, and I happily sift through them before moving to the very bottom drawer. My jaw drops as I take in its contents, shock turning into excitement as I note the pile of human junk food inside.

Not wanting the shadow to see and ask for any treats, I force myself to remain calm and carefully shut the drawer. I will be munching on these later.

Grabbing a pencil from the holder in the top corner of my desk, I politely make eye contact with Rock. It almost appears as if he's smiling at me, but it's hard to tell through the dark haze that blurs his form.

I'm not sure if I'll ever grow used to that.

"I figured we'd do most of your learnings in the language you know best and slowly shift to universal as you grow more comfortable with it," Rock says, grabbing the stack of papers off my desk. "Gray has requested you also learn to read, write, and speak demon, but there's no rush on that."

He finds what he's looking for with a happy grunt, his blurry fingers pulling a sheet from the stack before returning the rest to my desk. He holds the paper out for me. "This is a quick assessment I made to see where you are in all the base subjects. I figured that'd be a good place to start, and once I see where you're at, we'll decide what subjects interest you most and how you want to move forward with tutoring."

I nod, feeling overwhelmed but still glad I'm getting the opportunity to learn. This is more than most females are given, and I didn't even have to welcome a man into my body for the privilege.

—————

Silas peers at me from over the top of his phone as I rush into the dining room, and he looks mildly intrigued as I frantically scramble into my seat beside Gray. I'm usually on time for dinner, my favorite meal of the day, but I lost track of time while in the shower.

"Sorry I'm late!" I pant.

Gray purchased dozens of soaps and lotions for me, and they make it next to impossible to leave the bathroom. I want to live in there, and I don't think my skin has ever been so soft.

"There's no need to apologize," Gray assures me, reaching for my plate.

I flush, noticing neither of them has begun to eat. "Did you wait for me?"

Silas laughs. "I didn't have much of a choice."

He shoves his phone in his pocket before throwing a pointed look in Gray's direction. His expression is playful, and I can't help but frown as I turn toward the smirking incubus. Gray ignores us as he fills my plate, but the wink he shoots in my direction as he sets it in front of me tells me he was listening.

Gray serves Silas next.

He insists on doing it, and I'm starting to think it's an incubus trait. Silas told me they're desperate to please, and filling our plates makes Gray happy. Either way, I appreciate it.

Gray isn't nearly as bad as I thought he would be, and while Silas is still a bit harder to read, he's been nothing but kind to me, too.

"Thanks," Silas mutters as Gray hands him his plate.

Gray dips his chin and finally serves himself, and Silas and I patiently wait until he's settled before grabbing our utensils and beginning to eat. I don't recognize this dish, the meat and grain foreign, but it tastes similar to a curry my dad used to make.

"How do you like your tutor?" Silas asks.

I clear my throat and shoot Silas a pointed look. I had no interest in asking Gray to hire me a tutor, and I know Silas was the one who gave him the idea. I hate asking people to do things for me, and I don't want Gray to think I'm greedy.

Silas meets my glare head on, the fate clearly not the least bit scared of me. Gray watches us with poorly concealed interest, but he doesn't interrupt. He never does, and if anything, he seems to actively encourage me to develop a friendship with the fate.

"Rock is nice, and I love my office," I admit, shifting my attention to Gray. "Thank you."

He beams, and I can't help but mirror the action before I take a bite of food and reach for my water. Gray must've done some research recently on humans, and he's been forcing water down my throat every chance he gets.

It's ice cold and feels refreshing after the long day I've had. Rock and I only spent a few hours together before he had to leave, and most of that time was spent with me taking random little assessments. He had one for just about every subject in existence, and I have a feeling I did poorly on most of them.

Gray places a hand on my thigh, his touch distracting. It takes everything in me not to react to it as I eat, and that task becomes even more challenging when his lust hits me a second later. It fills my lungs, and I shut my eyes and take a moment to calm myself before shaking my head and resuming eating.

I can practically feel Gray's pride as I ignore his lust.

Silas keeps his power tucked tightly inside him, which I appreciate. He isn't a sex demon like Gray, and his power doesn't evoke the same reactions from me. His makes me tense and uncomfortable, like Aziel's.

My lips purse at the memory of the Wrath pinning me against the wall the last time I saw him. He looked crazed, and I'm not excited for the day he decides to return. Maybe if I'm lucky, he'll remain in the pits indefinitely. I've grown comfortable with Gray and Silas, and I just know everything will go back to being tense and awkward when Aziel is back.

"Were you able to fix your book?" I ask, turning to Silas.

He's spent the past few days organizing the pages of an old book he broke, and today was supposed to be the day he finally glued them back together. I'm doubtful it will work. The pages are cracked and look so old that I'm surprised they haven't turned into dust.

Silas leans back in his chair and shakes his head, the action causing a strand of hair to fall in front of his eye. He pushes it to the side with a huff. "I'm going to try again tomorrow."

I grimace. He said that yesterday and the day before that, too.

"It might be time to call it," Gray says.

He reaches out to place a hand on Silas's shoulder, but the fate brushes him away. He doesn't look happy, but he doesn't argue Gray's statement like he did the first time the incubus suggested it.

"Maybe this is a sign you should be more careful with your things," I tease.

My parents used to say that to me every time I broke

something, and it pissed me off beyond belief. It seems to have the same effect on Silas as he works his jaw side to side.

Then he does something I'm genuinely not expecting, and all I can do is gape as he reaches across the table and flicks my forehead.

It doesn't hurt, but I still jolt in surprise.

"Are you flirting with my female?" Gray laughs.

That sours the mood, and Silas clears his throat before shaking his head and fishing his phone from his pocket. I know Silas doesn't have any interest in me, but Gray hasn't gotten the memo.

He's always trying to read into our every reaction, which I'm starting to think is another incubus trait. The meal passes in comfortable silence, and I eat until my stomach feels like it's moments away from bursting.

My mind flickers from topic to topic, but almost always comes back to the females. It's impossible not to think about the women I met in the facility—not to wonder what happened to them and where they are now while I'm eating dinner.

Gray may not be like my father, but he hasn't harmed me.

I should consider myself lucky. *I do consider myself lucky.*

"Have you ever thought about how weird it is that all the species began experiencing low female birth rates at the same time?" I ask. "I've always wondered if it was some sort of virus."

Gray taps his fork against his plate and glances at Silas. The fate clears his throat before awkwardly reaching over the table to grab a dinner roll.

Odd reaction.

"What?" I ask.

"I think it was fate," Gray blurts.

My head snaps toward Silas so quickly I'm surprised I don't give myself whiplash. "You did this?"

Silas's chest expands as he sets his roll down and meets my

gaze. His eyes are pleading, but I don't care. He did this? I struggle to believe it, but his weird reaction is hard to ignore.

"I don't control fate," he eventually says. "I'm just the vessel that connects fate to the physical world. It speaks to me, and I assist when the balance is off."

I sink my teeth into my bottom lip, not understanding what any of that means.

"What's the balance?" I ask. "And what do you assist with?"

Gray leans forward, seemingly interested in hearing the answer as well. Silas is, and I assume fates in general, secretive about what goes on in his mind, but I need to know. Silas is kind, and I can't imagine him hurting anybody.

"Everything that exists is interconnected," he starts, "like a big circle. There's no start and no end. It's been that way since the beginning. When things threaten to uneven the balance, either by breaking the circle or severing a connection, a fate's purpose is to right it."

I lick my lips. "And how exactly were females unevening the balance?"

Silas shrugs and taps his temple. "That question is above my pay grade. I don't think…" He trails off with a frown.

"Go on!" Gray urges. He does a poor job hiding his excitement, and he practically bounces in his seat as he waits to hear more.

Silas shrugs. "If it *was* an act of fate, which I have no insight into, it could have been a solution to a completely unrelated problem."

Gray scoffs, and for once, I agree with him.

"I struggle to believe that the fates could be so cruel as to condemn an entire gender for no good reason," I say. "That's bullshit."

Silas cracks a smile, but it doesn't meet his eye. I'm sure he knows more than he's letting on. He may call himself a vessel all he wants, but he's a vessel with a direct line to the fated world. I have no idea what that is, and I doubt he'd answer me if I asked, but I'm sure it grants him more information than he's openly sharing.

"I never said it wasn't," Silas admits. "It's just a thought, and if it was an act of fate, I doubt we'll ever find an answer."

I hum, choosing not to push the subject. I enjoy my dinners with Gray and Silas, and I don't want to ruin them by prying for information Silas is unwilling to give. What's done is done, and knowing what caused the female decline isn't going to fix the problem.

"Did you see the new soaps I put in the shower?" Gray asks, changing the subject.

His eyes dart toward my still-wet hair, and I fiddle with the strands before meeting his eye and dipping my chin. It was hard *not* to notice them. Gray installed a whole new shelf and filled it with more products than I think I'll ever need.

That's part of the reason I was late for this meal in the first place. I couldn't stop myself from smelling and testing everything. The minty shampoo is my favorite, and even now I can still smell subtle hints of it.

I'm sure Gray and Silas can, too.

Their senses are a thousand times better than mine, and I assume if I can smell, see, or hear something, so can they. That's why I've taken to using the toilet in the bathroom hidden in the farthest corner of the house, and I run the sink the entire time. I'm sure they know exactly what I'm doing, but I'd rather make it obvious by running the water than have them overhear anything private.

"I also saw all the lotions you left on the sink," I say.

Gray straightens his spine, the man looking awfully pleased

with himself. I can't help but laugh, and he squeezes my thigh before leaning forward and pressing a quick kiss to my cheek.

I wait for his lust to come, for this kiss to be another one of his tests, but then he pulls away and resumes eating.

Chapter Twelve

CHARLOTTE

"CHARLIE!" GRAY SHOUTS, barreling into my room.

I shriek, jumping a good foot in the air and dropping the candy I snuck out of my office earlier. The hard, fruity balls fall to the floor and scatter, and I drop to my knees and begin frantically grabbing at them.

Gray's by my side in seconds, his position matching mine as he helps to pick them up.

The fact that he pops a few into his mouth doesn't go unnoticed by me, but I pretend I don't see. He's the one who bought the candy, so it's not as if I can get angry with him for eating some of it—even if I want to.

"Sorry, my female," he says between chews. "I didn't mean to startle you."

I shoot him a playful glare. Knocking would probably be an excellent way to prevent that.

My lips purse as I stand and shove as much candy as possible into the small package they fell from. Gray's been extra happy today, seeking me out every hour or so to check how my day is going.

He did it even when I was studying with Rock, much to the shadow's amusement. I found it annoying, but Rock was choking back laughter every time Gray interrupted his teaching.

Today was supposed to be my first official day of tutoring, but instead of learning anything, I spent the entire time flushed and on edge. Rock has spent the past three days testing me on all the core subjects, and after much deliberation, we've decided to start from the beginning.

My reading comprehension is fine, but I'm lacking in pretty much everything else. Math feels entirely foreign, and science and history are no better.

Rock hasn't once made me feel bad for my lack of knowledge, and he even went out of his way to scratch out the age ranges on the workbooks he purchased and gave me this morning. I appreciate it and was more than a little excited to jump in head-first.

Until Gray ruined it.

I should've known better than to think I'd find sanctuary in my bedroom.

Gray ignores my annoyance as he drops my candy into its packaging and steps back. He looks me up and down with glee, his face twitching as he takes in my current outfit. I debated whether or not showing so much skin was a good idea, but the sweltering heat made that decision for me.

I made sure to throw on one of my more modest sports bras, the fabric tight around my chest and flattening my breasts in an unattractive fashion. The spandex shorts don't leave much to the imagination, but considering Gray's an incubus, I doubt the shape of a woman's butt is hardly a new sight for him.

"It took you long enough to finish with Rock," he says. "I was going to take you earlier, but Silas told me it would be better to wait until after your tutoring,"

He doesn't seem to realize I have no idea what he's talking about, but I draw conclusions. Take me? I gulp, reassuring myself that he doesn't mean what I think he means. He promised he wouldn't take me until I wanted it.

Shoving away my fear, I lift my chin and meet his eye. "Take me?"

Gray blinks before shaking his head.

"No, not like that. Take you out," he explains with a smile.

Grimacing, I turn and look out of my bedroom window. It's hotter than usual today, and I've already decided I'm not going outside. I fear I might melt if I do.

Gray snorts, his smile wide as he darts forward and steals a piece of my candy. He's too quick, and I scoff as I yank the box out of his reach.

He's already eaten enough, and these are my favorites. Wanting to keep them and myself away from Gray is the entire reason I ran and hid up here in the first place.

Gray crosses his arms over his chest. "You've grown quite an attitude these past few days."

He says it with a joking tone, but my annoyance still shifts into worry. What if he's not joking?

My confidence around him has grown drastically since arriving, and I haven't been holding back from snapping and arguing with Gray when he bothers me. Have I pushed too far? I should've known better than to get so comfortable. I've been warned of the dangers of males, yet here I am acting as if I'm equal to one after only a few days of knowing him.

Gray sighs, his smile falling as he wraps his arms around my waist and pulls me into his chest. Despite my worry, I find myself relaxing into his touch, comforted as he rubs his hand down the center of my spine.

I allow him to hold me for a moment longer before pulling

back, and my lips flatten into a thin line as I realize how eagerly I accept his touch. I've been purchased to be a sex doll for him, yet I continue to let my longing for intimacy cloud my vision.

Even without Gray's lust, I find myself wanting him. A small part of me wishes he'd use it more. At least then I could have something to blame my feelings on.

Mom and Dad ingrained in me not to give in to a man before he's proved he genuinely cares, but they never told me what it looks like when a man does. Gray seems like he cares. He's kind and makes efforts to comfort me, but I can't tell how honest that is.

Is he only doing this so I give in and agree to be a lust source for him? It would make sense, but sometimes it doesn't seem that way. Why train me to resist his lure if that's all he wants?

"Get out of your head, Charlie."

Gray locks his arms around my back and lifts me a few inches. My toes graze the ground as he waddles us to my closet. I'm sure he can hear my heart pounding as he pulls open the door and steps inside.

"I like your attitude, and there's no need to be ashamed for being happy to be around me," he assures me. "I'm sexy and kind. There's no better combination." Gray laughs at his self-preening.

He sure thinks highly of himself.

I can't hold back a slight scoff, but I try to turn it into a cough last minute. There's a lot to be ashamed of, but that's not an argument I want to have with him right now.

Gray politely ignores my slipup, his nose wrinkling as he looks over my clothing rack. Despite the large closet size, all my items fit comfortably on a tiny rod in the back.

It makes the closet look sad and empty, but I don't mind. I'm just happy to have my things, especially the ones Gray brought from my home.

"What're you doing?" I ask as he begins to finger through the clothing.

Gray takes a moment to answer, a quiet hum emerging from his throat as he searches through my items. He pauses and grabs the fabric of one of my dresses, his eyebrows rising as he pulls it out and looks it over.

It's not one of my favorite items, the brown material long and poorly fitting, but Gray seems to like it as he pulls it from the hanger.

"We're going on a date. I want to hear all about your day," he explains, looking between me and the dress.

I flush. A date? What does a date even consist of?

They frequently occurred in my romance books, but they were all written before the female decline when it was normal for women to be out and about in society. I imagine they've evolved since then.

Is it common for demon males to take their females on dates? Thoughts continue to swirl inside my mind as Gray sticks my head through the neck hole of the dress.

I hold back a laugh as he grabs my arms and shoves them inside, finding an odd sense of humor in the sight of him trying to dress me. Luckily, the dress is high-necked and long-sleeved, easily covering the clothing I already have on.

Would he have tried to undress me if I weren't lounging around in a sports bra and short spandex shorts? I shiver at the thought.

I fail to hide my laughter as Gray pulls the loose dress over my body. He then reaches under the hem and yanks down my shorts, leaving me in only my underwear. My knees buckle at the force he uses, and I grab his shoulders to steady myself.

"Aren't you supposed to be good at undressing women?" I joke.

Gray's attention snaps to my face, his eyes narrowing.

"I am, but if I don't distract you by doing a thousand different things at once, you get lost in your head and pull away from me. I don't want you all moody for our date." He plants a swift kiss on my cheek before forcing my feet into a pair of black sandals.

This is all happening so quickly.

I don't have time to process his words as he grabs my hand and pulls me into his chest.

"I'm going to teleport you, but we're staying in Wrath, so it shouldn't be too bad," he says just seconds before the world fades.

I'm blinded and disorientated as the environment disappears and re-materializes around me. I hold Gray in a panic as loud noise and chatter make their way to my ears, my head ringing as I adjust to my new surroundings.

If there's anything I've learned since being bought, it's that I don't like the demon's preferred form of travel.

"You okay?" Gray rubs my back.

Turning in his arms, I try not to let my surprise show as I look around the room. Demons mill about in front of large, waist-height tables. Almost all of them hold what appear to be long wooden sticks, and I watch with interest as one of them bends and uses the stick to hit a ball on the table.

There are at least fifty demons in here, and as I look around, I note that not one is a female. Am I supposed to be here? Gray is strong, but I'm not too fond of being surrounded by so many males.

"This is a pool hall," Gray says, running a hand down my spine. "It's a game that originated with humans, but over time, its popularity grew. Demons are big fans of it."

A few demons turn and watch as I grab Gray's arm and let him lead me across the room, their expressions blank and uninterested as they look me over. Their gazes almost immediately lift to Gray before returning to their conversations.

That's not what I expected.

Maybe it's because Gray put me in a dress suited for a grandma. They probably can't tell I'm a female underneath the oversized, unflattering clothing.

Gray leads us to an empty table in the corner of the room, his unhurried and confident movements bringing me some comfort. Most of the power that overwhelms the room dissipates as we step away from everybody, and I breathe easily as we come to a halt.

How lucky for us that there was an unoccupied table in the far corner of the room.

I take a moment to evaluate the building in more detail. It's full, and I'm utterly shocked nobody seems to care there's a female here. Either Gray is more dangerous than I thought, or something weird I'm unaware of is happening.

"Do you come here often?" I eventually ask, turning to Gray.

He's already looking at me, and I flush as I realize he was doing so the entire time. Pretending it doesn't affect me, I raise my chin and hold his gaze.

"I used to," he says.

I lean forward and watch as he places a bunch of numbered balls into a wooden triangle. He shakes them back and forth before removing the triangle and handing me one of the long sticks.

"Come here." Gray leads me to the end of the table opposite the balls. "I bought this place a few years back and spent a lot of time training the staff." He bends me slightly over the table's edge and walks behind me, out of sight. "It runs itself now, but I enjoy a game now and again."

He owns this place? I suppose that explains why nobody is leering at me. They probably know he's the owner.

My pulse quickens as Gray's chest and hips press against my back, but he doesn't make any dirty remarks as he shows me how to hold the stick and explains the game's rules. They're easy enough to remember, and I find myself having fun as I fumble through the first round.

I can tell Gray is purposefully missing shots so it doesn't end too quickly, but I don't mind. I'm a sore loser, and I'm not above counting a pity win.

"Let's make a game out of this," Gray says as he pockets the last striped ball. He points his stick toward a corner before going for the black eight. "For each ball I sink, I get to ask you a question. You get to do the same for the ones you get."

I pause, caution making me slow to answer. I don't have much to hide, but I don't doubt Gray will ask questions I'm uncomfortable answering.

My chest expands as I suck in a deep breath. "What if I don't like what you ask?"

Gray cocks his head to the side as he thinks, his back straightening as he sinks the last ball and wins the game.

"You can avoid a question by giving me a kiss."

I laugh, having expected nothing less. "Okay."

There are a thousand things I'd love to know about Gray and the demons, and I'm not going to pass on such a perfect opportunity to ask them—especially when the only punishment is a kiss.

"And if *you* don't want to answer one of *my* questions...." I say, thinking over a proper punishment for his avoidance. "I get two more in its place."

"Fair deal!"

My excitement grows as Gray pulls the balls from the pockets on the green velvet-covered table and starts a new game. He organizes them in the wooden triangle and sets the leftover white ball on the opposite end of the table.

I hold my stick as he takes the first hit and sinks a solid. It flies into a pocket, and I realize immediately I've potentially made a big mistake. Gray wasn't putting in his full effort the first time.

He smirks as he walks around the table and sets up another shot. "Let's start with something easy. What's your favorite thing to eat?"

I hum, thinking it over as he misses his next ball. He hardly seems surprised as it bounces off the wall and rolls to the opposite side of the table.

"Spaghetti," I say, my mouth watering at the thought. "With meatballs."

Gray laughs as I walk around the table, searching for the best shot. I'll be damned if I don't get any questions in. I have a feeling he won't be taking this game as easy as the last. I find a shot I like and cheer as I knock one striped ball in.

I turn to Gray with a smirk, proud of my achievement. "How did you meet Silas and Aziel?"

The corner of Gray's lip twitches downward, but he quickly hides the reaction behind a laugh. That's odd.

"If you get your next ball, I'll give you the full story," he says, gesturing to the table.

Bouncing on my heels, I turn and look at the damage. One of my balls rests directly in front of a pocket, and I grin as I realize I have a clear shot at it. Lucky me.

I can practically feel Gray's eyes on my butt as I bend and sink the ball. I've never felt so accomplished, and I spin and shoot him a cocky smile.

It falls when he makes a slow step toward me, his expression unreadable. He takes hold of my waist, his touch soft before he tightens his grip and lifts me until I'm sitting on the table.

Slotting his hips between my thighs, he grabs the hem of my dress and tugs it higher so I can spread my knees for him. I scowl but don't fight him on it.

"Even Aziel and Silas don't know the full story, so you should feel very special," he says, kissing the corner of my lips. "I'm sure you've noticed I'm a bit odd for an incubus, and my differences ostracized me from my den at a young age. The biggest issue has always been my possessiveness."

I find myself on the edge of my seat as he shares his story.

"There was a woman I fell in love with many years ago. I was eager to introduce her to my family as my female." Gray's voice lowers as he speaks, his fingers sliding up my arms and causing goosebumps to pebble along my skin.

"They laughed as I claimed her as my own, arguing that incubi always share. We never bonded, so she was susceptible to their lust. They made me watch as she begged them to take and pass her around the den." Gray pauses and clears his throat before continuing. "I thought the lust made her act that way. I wasn't mad at her. I knew it wasn't her fault. She, well… it turns out she truly did want it. She wanted to stay in the den."

Gray lets out a dry laugh and shakes his head. Unsure what to do, I grab his hands.

"You don't have to tell me this," I say, regretting asking such a personal question.

I thought he would tell me some goofy story about him stumbling upon them and latching on. Never in a million years did I think he'd share something so painful.

Gray hums before pressing a kiss to my temple.

"It's okay," he says. "I stuck around because I loved her and all that, but it was hard to watch her with others. After a few months, I tried to take her away, but she screamed and alerted the den. She told them I was trying to steal her. They kicked me out of Lust, and I was too young to know how to feed properly, so I wandered around Wrath until Silas and Aziel stumbled upon me."

Gray's excitement visibly grows as he gets to this part of the story, and I force my tense muscles to relax.

"I'm not sure how I did it, but I accidentally broke through Aziel's mind and fed." Gray pauses and laughs, the noise hearty as it bubbles up out of his throat. "He dropped to his knees and cried out like a canary. Sex is what triggers his bond, but somehow, I was able to bond him to me without it. Aziel and Silas brought me home, and I've been with them ever since."

I blink, my mind blank as I think of an appropriate response. How does one react to being told something like that? I'm sure Gray doesn't want my pity, but laughing at the story as he did doesn't feel right, either.

Instead, I lean forward and kiss his cheek, hoping it expresses the emotions I'm unable to vocalize. I'm grateful he shared this with me, and I feel closer to him.

If I didn't know any better, I'd say Gray's cheeks redden as he pulls me off the table and gestures for me to take my next turn. I move to do so, but then I pause as the second part of his story registers.

"Wait!" I spin toward him. "You and Aziel are bonded?"

Gray looks confused before he leans back and nods.

"Did you not know that? I thought it was common knowledge. The fates made it so anybody descended from the royal Wrath bloodline bonds when they have sex. Bonding with another person can be seen as a weakness, and it prevents Aziel from taking hundreds of women and making an army of super-strong Wrath children. I fed from him, made him orgasm, and that was enough to bond him to me."

What the fuck? I had absolutely no idea.

"But since you two are already bonded, does that mean Aziel can never have a female?" I ask.

Gray shakes his head. "No. Aziel could bond with multiple people if he wanted. Having a bond is a weakness, though, so he obviously wants to keep the number as low as possible."

I suppose that makes sense.

"So, you two are…" I trail off, looking for the right words. "Together? Why did he purchase me, then?"

Gray chews at his bottom lip. "We aren't together, not like that. He doesn't recognize our bond, so we live together as friends."

"And you're happy with that?"

"The bond makes things complicated. Our souls are entwined, which makes us want to be together, but Aziel's mad about the forced bond, so he ignores it. It's all very angsty, but I'm content with our life—especially now that I have a beautiful female to whom I can give my affection. She's quite feisty, and I like it." Gray steps forward, always flirting, and I wave him away and return to the game.

That's a lot to digest, but it explains so much about their relationship.

I take my next shot, pouting when I miss it. Wanting to lighten the mood after such a painful story, I turn my back to the room and sit in the nearest chair.

Gray's gone out of his way to be kind to me, and I want to trust him. I should give him the opportunity to gain my trust.

Sucking in a deep breath, I tell myself this is okay as I lift my feet to the seat of the chair and let my dress slide to the tops of my thighs. I pretend I don't notice he has a complete view of my underwear as I rest my chin on my knees and watch him step forward to take his turn.

It takes Gray a moment to notice, his attention on the table, but the moment he looks at me and his body stiffens, I know he's seen. My lips split into a wide grin as I gesture for him to shoot.

He makes no effort to hide his line of sight, his eyes locked between my thighs as he halfheartedly aims and misses. He doesn't wait for the balls to stop moving before stalking toward me.

I drop my legs before rising, and a quiet groan tumbles from Gray's throat as I walk past him, bumping my shoulder against his.

"You cheated," he complains.

I shrug, my face warming at my brazen actions. I can't believe I just did that.

Trying not to appear as flustered as I feel, I rush to take my turn. I manage to pocket a ball and breathe out a sigh of relief.

"What's your favorite thing to eat?" I ask, copying Gray's initial question.

He enters my personal space instead of answering, a dangerous glint in his eye. It has my heart pounding.

"It's not something I've had the pleasure of trying before," he says, pinning me against the table and sliding a hand up the front of my dress. "But I can only imagine it's delicious."

I worry the other demons in the room will be able to tell what's happening in our corner, but thankfully, Gray's body blocks any view they may have. My jaw clenches, and I grab Gray's hand as he traces the seam of my underwear.

Teasing him like this was stupid. He's going to take it as an invitation.

"Hey, hey, Charlie," Gray says, his wandering fingers coming to a halt as he uses his other hand to tilt my chin up. "We're just teasing. This doesn't mean I expect anything from you when we go home."

I gulp, still wary. As much as I don't want to send him the wrong message, I can't deny our teasing turns me on. I like it. I like it, and I can't even blame his lust. He's keeping it tucked securely away.

Gray refuses to let me look away as his fingers move slightly, gently grazing against my clit. He leans in and presses his lips to my ear before hooking his finger into my underwear and pulling it to the side.

"I'm going to ease my finger in and take a few selfish seconds to enjoy the feel of you. Then I'm going to take it out and taste," he whispers into my ear. "After, we'll return to our game and move on from this."

He pulls back and stares at me, and I let my eyes slip shut before giving him a tentative nod. I want that. Gray moans, sliding his hand upward and sinking a finger into me. He moves slowly, giving me time to adjust until it's buried entirely inside.

I'm sure my face is a thousand shades of red as I clench around him, silently begging him to continue.

Gray nips at my ear as he eases his finger in and out, the feeling foreign but good. My fingers are the only thing that has ever been inside me, and Gray's are much thicker.

I let out a quiet gasp, enjoying what he's doing. I was under the impression female pleasure only came from the clit, but as he curls his finger, I realize just how wrong I was.

Gray's pulling out of me before this goes any further, and I'm frozen as he brings his hand between our bodies and slide his middle finger into his mouth. His eyes flutter shut as he tastes me, a quiet moan rumbling from his chest and making me clench my thighs around his hips.

"Delicious."

Stepping away, he chuckles as he looks over the table. I scan the room for any sign we were spotted, but nobody pays us any attention. I'm still shocked over the lack of interest everybody seems to have with a female being here, especially after spending most of my life hearing about how males love to leer.

Gray waits as I struggle to get my bearings, his smirk growing when I miss my next ball.

As promised, he makes no comments about what just happened and doesn't try to touch me again for the remainder of the game. I'm visibly on edge at first, missing almost all my shots, but over time, I relax.

We play until late into the night, our laughter growing with each shared snippet of information and lighthearted joke. I'm hardly ready to stop when he pulls me flush against his chest and says it's time to go. Maybe it's not so shameful to find enjoyment with him. I grab his shoulders and bury my face into his torso, preparing for the travel.

Despite being unable to see the world swirl around me, I still feel it in my stomach. Gray's hold tightens as the ground beneath my feet hardens, his breath coming out in a loud pant as I stumble out of his arms.

Shaking away the dizziness, I look up at him in worry. Sweat beads along his forehead, and it's clear he's fighting off the urge to hunch over. Is he okay? I know he's hungry, but I didn't realize how bad his hunger was.

I grab his forearms. "Are you okay?"

Gray plasters a smile on his face. "Of course I am." He pulls me into a bone-crushing hug before I can pry any further. I laugh, a slight flush warming my cheeks.

"Did you have a good time tonight?" he asks.

I hold back a smile as I nod. Gray looks relieved as he bends and presses his lips to mine. For once, I try not to let myself overthink it as I inch up on my toes and return the kiss. His lips are warm and soft, and I feel my excitement grow as he opens his mouth and slips his tongue between my lips.

I almost want to pout when he pulls away, but I push that thought aside as I take in his nervous expression. What's wrong with him?

Gray frowns before releasing me altogether. "You should go

to bed now. I will be out of the house tonight, but Silas will be here if you need anything.”

I cock my head to the side. “Where are you going?”

Gray shifts uncomfortably, and he looks at the ceiling before finally meeting my gaze.

“I’m starving, Charlie,” he deadpans. “And if I’m not going to feed off of you or Aziel, I need to get nourishment elsewhere.”

The intensity of my jealousy practically knocks me off my feet. Is he going to spend the night with another female? Why would he do that when I’m here? I answer my question with the angered realization it’s because he’s trying to be respectful of my wishes.

I could give him permission to feed from me. He could enter my dreams as he did before. The thought makes me nervous, but the idea of him going out and touching another makes me feel worse.

“If you were to enter my dream, what would that consist of?” I ask.

Gray licks his lips. “I’m assuming you’re not looking for me to dirty talk you right now?” He chuckles as I narrow my eyes and shake my head. “It would be just me, and I wouldn’t touch you with anything other than my hands and mouth.”

I nod, happy with that response but needing more.

“If you did, I wouldn’t want you making me do all the things you did last time,” I say, still embarrassed by the memory of his last feed.

Gray appears solemn as he nods. “I’m sorry about that. I know better than to come on so strongly. It won’t happen again.”

I pull my lip between my teeth as I look over his body, saddened by his current state. It wasn’t nearly this bad on our date, and if I had to guess, I’d say the teleporting takes a lot out of him.

Gray makes no movements as I scan him, but he does suck his

cheeks into his mouth in a visible attempt to keep any hope or excitement off his face. I hope I don't come to regret my decision as I cup his cheeks and press a kiss to his chin.

"Then, well," I start, blushing, "I'd rather you feed off me tonight than another."

Chapter Thirteen

CHARLOTTE

MY HEART IS practically beating out of my chest as I lie in the center of Gray's bed. It's surprisingly comfortable, and I pull myself into a sitting position before leaning against the headboard.

The dress I wore on our date tangles around my thighs and bunches at my waist, and I take a moment to straighten it out before continuing my search around his room. I thought I'd taken it off before bed, but as I rub my eyes, I figure I must have forgotten.

Did Gray carry me in here after I fell asleep? It's the only explanation that makes sense. If he did, where is he?

The room is dark, the moonlight streaming through the window providing just enough light to make out his furniture's vague shapes. I don't remember him feeding on me tonight, and I wonder if he somehow took my memory of it.

I'm going to be pissed if he can do that yet chose not to the first time he slipped inside my dreams.

My eyes narrow as I search around the large bed for any signs of Gray's form, feeling both relieved and disheartened as I note I'm here by myself. There's a tightening in my chest as I look around the room again, almost frantic.

What if he left to feed on somebody else?

Did he not think my offer was genuine? Has he carried me to his bed to soften the blow? My jealousy spikes. Why has he chosen another woman over me? I've never asked if being a human means I can't feed him as well as a stronger species female could, and I'm now regretting that.

"Why are you so angry?" Gray asks from somewhere in the darkness. "I thought the mystery of waking in my bed would turn you on."

My head snaps toward his voice, my stiff posture relaxing as I realize he's here with me. He stands in the corner of the room, hidden almost entirely by shadows.

If it weren't for him speaking, I don't think I would've ever spotted him.

I watch through wide eyes as he approaches, his features materializing as the moonlight touches his body. He still looks gaunt, his cheeks sunken and eyes darty. Despite it, his movements are almost predatory as he kneels on the bed.

"Why am I in your bed?" I ask. "I thought you were going to feed through my dream."

Despite my attempts to sound confident, my voice comes out in a whisper. I don't know how comfortable I am feeding him outside of sleep. It feels different when it's just a dream, and knowing it's not real brings me comfort.

"You *are* dreaming, Charlie," Gray says. "I thought you'd appreciate the sense of normalcy over the confusion of our last feed."

I stare at him, unsure how much I believe that. This feels so real, a far cry from how it was the last time. Gray chuckles and gestures to my body as if he can feel my hesitation. Following his line of sight, I glance down at myself and gasp.

I'm naked.

I scramble to grab the forgotten covers off the bed, my cheeks flaming as I rush to cover myself. I could've sworn I was just wearing the ugly dress Gray put me in for our date. He sits by my feet as I pull the sheet away and glance at my naked body.

This is not what I look like.

My eyebrows furrow as I glance over the changed slope of my breasts and my unmarred skin. It's hard to tell in the dark, but it even looks like the stretch marks along my thighs and hips have been removed. Why did he change my body?

"Do you not like the way I look?" I ask, trying and failing to keep the hurt out of my voice.

Gray detects it anyway and frowns as he crawls over me and tugs at the sheet. My grip tightens on it before I sigh and let it go. He's already seen everything.

"I've only seen you naked at the auction, and I admittedly wasn't paying much attention. I had to make some guesses to fill in the gaps of what I don't know," he explains, trailing his finger down the side of my breast. "Tell me what I've gotten wrong."

I blink, unsure how to describe what my body truly looks like. The differences he's made are slight, and it would be hard to fix every one of them.

"I don't understand why my mind doesn't fill in those gaps for you," I say. "It's *my* dream."

Gray smiles, his hand trailing up my leg. "My presence in your mind takes that ability from you. I'm controlling every aspect here, including how you look."

My lips twitch. I'm relieved he hasn't *chosen* to remove the features he doesn't like.

"Would you like me to look at your body and fix it? It'll be quick," he asks, squeezing my thigh. "I want you to be comfortable."

Does he mean leaving my dream to look at my sleeping body? The excited gleam in his eye answers that question for me, yet despite how weird it is, I find myself saying *yes*.

If I'm going to be feeding him, I'd like to do it in my own body.

Gray's smile softens, his eyes slipping shut as he bends and kisses the skin directly below my belly button. I gulp, nervous about how close his face is to my sex, but he's gone before I work up the strength to move away.

Alone once more, I bring my knees to my chest and wrap my legs around them. Gray didn't give me my clothing back—probably on purpose.

The real-life him is probably entering my bedroom right now, his footsteps light as he creeps toward my bed. I'm not sure how he plans to do this without waking me, but I figure he has ways to keep me asleep.

It's what incubi are known for. Sneaky dream fuckers.

I shiver and squeeze my legs as a cold breeze suddenly covers my skin. It's weird, and I let out an audible gasp as warm pressure presses against me. Is that Gray? Is he touching me?

I release and stretch out my legs in shock, speechless as my skin changes before my very eyes. The adjustments are minor, and a slight tingling sensation spreads through me as my body hair changes and my blemishes appear.

The warmth from his hands traces a large scar on my thigh, the touch feather-light. It's gone seconds later, replaced by a tight hold on my hips. Despite the intimacy of the action, I don't feel uncomfortable as the soft tingles begin to spread across my back.

The sensation fades just before the hands are removed, and the cool chill over my body disappears. I assume it's due to him covering the real me with my sheets, and I take it as a sign to slip under his and wait for his return.

Gray doesn't disappoint, reappearing on the bed mere seconds later.

He's beaming as he crawls over me, his clothing disappearing as he pulls back the sheet I've hidden under and slides beneath it. I've never seen a naked man before, and I can't help but *stare*. Gray is exceptional, with long muscular limbs and smooth skin.

I don't get a good look at the more intimate parts of him before he's under the sheets, but I hide my disappointment well. I shouldn't get carried away.

"We can stay covered if you prefer," he says, pressing a small kiss to my cheek. My face flushes as he follows it up by pushing a strand of my hair behind my ear. It's a gesture I'm learning to associate with him.

"Do you feel better?" he asks. "I hope you don't mind, but I adjusted your position in bed. You were all twisted about, and it looked uncomfortable."

I've always been bad about my sleeping positions, and I frequently wake up with back and hip pain. It's not fun, and I'm glad Gray took it upon himself to adjust me.

I shift under the sheets, painfully aware of how close his naked body is to mine. He promised he wouldn't do anything beyond touching me with his mouth and hands, and as much as I want to trust him, a small part of me is still scared.

Gray moves slowly, his eyes never leaving mine as he finds my waist under the sheets, his fingers wrapping around my hip bone and pressing into my back. He wastes no time trailing his hands lower, grazing the outside of my thighs before reaching my knees and pausing.

I'm rigid with anxiety. Am I supposed to touch him back? I don't even know how.

Gray's eyes soften as he senses my nerves, his face nearing mine before he kisses me. I relax, happy to have something to focus on that isn't his wandering hands. He waits until I'm kissing him back before deepening it, and a quiet moan rumbles from his chest as our tongues finally meet.

"Fuck," he gasps. His hands return to my legs. "I'm so hungry for you."

His actions are teasing. His fingertips run up and down the inside of my thigh, trailing a little higher each time before infuriatingly dropping back to my knee.

I thought the point of this was to get me off. Isn't he supposed to touch me for that to happen? The suspense is killing me.

I spread my legs to give him more room, and his lips twitch against mine before he drags his hand to the apex of my thighs. It feels good, and my hips jerk toward him on their own accord.

Gray seems to enjoy it as he groans and buries his face in my neck.

Some of his lust slips out as he runs his pointer finger along my slit, so close to where I want him, but he pulls back on it almost immediately.

"Sorry," he says, clearing his throat. "I didn't mean to do that."

I pull my neck out of his mouth's reach. "Is it hard to hold it back?"

Gray shrugs, his gaze meeting mine before he sheepishly nods. He looks embarrassed.

My mind races as I think over my following words. I already agreed to this and want him to get his fill tonight. I don't want him to seek nourishment elsewhere.

"You're only going to use your hands and mouth?" I ask, wanting confirmation.

If I tell him it's okay to release his lust, I don't doubt I'll end up begging for more. It makes me crazed, and I don't want him going beyond our agreed plan just because I ask for it in a lust-induced haze.

"Of course," he says. "I'll only do what you agree to in your waking state."

My lips purse. That's good to hear.

"Then, well…" I start, bravely reaching up to grab his cheeks. "You don't have to hold it back. I'm okay with what we agreed to, and as long as you don't let me embarrass myself, I'm not going to be upset."

Gray stares at me for a long minute before relaxing. I wasn't even aware of how tense his body was, but as he melts into the mattress, I realize how much he was struggling. His intoxicating scent hits me with my next breath, and my body sags as my eyes roll back.

It's so good.

My hips twitch toward his hand, desperate for him to soothe the deep ache settling within me. I need Gray, and every inch of my body is desperate for the pleasure I know only he can bring. I'm about to give in and beg when he finally climbs over me.

He straddles my legs, the insides of his thighs pressing against the outsides of mine, and his hard length grazes my stomach. I look down, horrified by the sight of *him*.

He's too big, too thick and too long, and I feel bad for every woman he's ever been with. I don't want that inside me, and his suffocatingly sweet scent isn't enough to change my mind.

Gray politely ignores my terror as he crawls down my torso, spreading my thighs in the process. He's not wasting time, and I gasp as his mouth abruptly connects with my sex seconds later.

The explosion of euphoria is too much as he licks my clit, and I squeeze my legs around his head as I rock against him.

"Fuck," I choke out, grabbing and holding his hair for dear life. "That's—*oh!*"

My words are cut short as Gray closes his lips around my

sensitive skin and sucks, his tongue flicking as he wiggles his hand between my legs and works two fingers into me. His scent amplifies everything, but I know this would feel amazing even without it.

Gray eagerly licks me, his face practically buried between my thighs, before he pulls back and runs the flat of his tongue from my entrance to my clit.

"Want you to cum on my tongue," he says, peering up at me through his lashes. "Feed me, Charlie."

I cry, bucking against his mouth until he brings his focus back to the spot that makes my toes curl.

Gray tightens his grip on my hip as he pins me down, putting a forceful stop to my writhing. The sheets around his hips move as he rubs himself against the mattress, and knowing he's finding pleasure in this is enough to push me over the edge.

Gray continues to lick me as I cum, his moans loud as I squeeze his head and fall apart. When he finally pulls away, he pauses to bite my thigh, the sharp pain shocking.

"You're so fucking amazing," he says, climbing back up my body. "And you feed me so well."

I flush, my confidence soaring.

His lust remains thick in the air and urges me for more, and I hardly think through what I'm doing as I spin and push Gray onto his back. He laughs as he falls onto the mattress, the incubus more than happy to let me take the lead.

I don't notice him tense, but it becomes incredibly apparent as I grab his cock and begin to stroke it. His eyes narrow, but he doesn't stop me.

I've never touched a man like this before, and I enjoy the feel of his hard, silky length in my hand. It's heavier than I imagined, and the skin is softer. Do men need to moisturize themselves?

My nerves are on fire, and my swollen clit throbs as I throw my leg over his waist and straddle him. With another deep inhale, I'm losing all sense of modesty and taking charge to get what I want.

Ignoring the hard look in his eyes, I try to emulate what I've read about in my books and bring the tip of him to my entrance. I didn't want this a minute ago, but that was before his lust robbed me of all coherent thought. I just might die if I don't get him inside.

Gray grabs my hips, stopping me, and I immediately begin to tear up as I see his unhappy expression. Is he not going to let me have him?

His lips soften at my impending tears, and he slides one hand over mine. I glance at it, excited as he slots his fingers between mine. I like the sight of us both holding his dick.

With gentle movements, he lays it flat against his belly.

"Sit on it this way," he says, prying his fingers beneath my palm and forcibly pulling my hand away.

I frown, but I do as he says and sit on the side of his shaft. He reaches between my thighs and spreads me so his cock sits nestled against my clit.

"I'm only letting you do this so you don't cry," he says. "Don't be getting all pissy with me tomorrow. Lean forward."

His hands return to my hips and help guide my movements, flexing and pulling me forward before relaxing and pushing me back. The angle has my clit rubbing directly on his shaft, and my arousal keeps the motions slick and smooth.

I moan as my clit gets caught on his tip. It feels so good, and I begin to rock faster. Gray twitches below me, his lust once more pouring out as he struggles to hold it back. I greedily breathe it in, panting as he pushes onto his elbows and connects his mouth with mine. The kiss is sloppy, all tongue and teeth, before he moves to my neck.

He sucks on the skin and licks over the sore spot.

"I can feel your pussy twitching against me. It so badly wants me inside," Gray breathes, his hips bucking beneath mine. "But I'm not going to give it to you. You're going to cum without even feeling an inch of me inside you."

I gasp, my trembling growing. It feels so good, and his dirty words are going to push me over the edge.

"You're mine." Gray groans, throwing his head back as he continues guiding my rocking.

The pressure builds as I drop my chest against his and let him do all the work. Gray does so happily, wrapping his arms around my back and holding me still so he can thrust against me.

I let out a silent moan as I'm pushed over the edge, my thighs clenching around his waist. Unlike before, Gray doesn't slow. I'm flipped onto my belly before I've come down, my face smashed into the pillows as Gray pushes my thighs together and shoves himself between them.

He rubs against my sensitive clit, but I make no complaints as he begins to desperately fuck my thighs.

He grunts as he grabs a fistful of my hair and pulls my head to the side. The roughness feels good, and I can't stop a throaty moan from slipping out as he buries his face in my neck.

"Fuck." Gray drops his forehead against my shoulder. "I told myself I wasn't going to cum tonight. I was going to make this all about you." He picks up speed, practically slamming into my thighs. "But you, my naughty fucking female, just had to rub your soft pussy against me until I cracked."

His hips stutter, but he doesn't let it deter him as he finds his pace once more.

"Do you want to know why I was holding back? Do you want to know what happens when you make an incubus cum?"

His cock smacks my clit with each thrust. The pleasure builds until I'm clenching around him again, my body greedily accepting the thumb he abruptly sticks in my ass.

I pause momentarily, distracted by the foreign entrance, but quickly rock back as Gray stills and finds his release. My vision is lost as complete euphoria overtakes my body, rocking me to the core as it spreads to every cell. It's overwhelming, and I can't tell what's up and what's down as I scream into the sheets. I'm hardly aware of Gray spilling between my thighs and collapsing on top of me as I come down from the high.

If that's the orgasm I get when I make Gray cum, I just might have to make a habit out of it.

Exhaustion overtakes me as I sink into the mattress.

Fuck.

"Are you okay?" Gray asks, pulling his thumb out of my ass. "I know that was more than we discussed."

He pulls back on his lust, tucking it inside himself until only what's stuck to the mattress and my skin remains. I blink before rolling onto my back.

I'm sure I'm a sight to see, my hair a wild mess and face beet red, but Gray still looks at me like I'm the most beautiful thing he's ever laid eyes on. It makes me feel better than I'd care to admit.

"Are you full?" I ask, eager to know how well I've fed him.

Gray smiles, a softness I rarely see taking over his features.

"You've done an amazing job feeding me tonight, Charlie," he answers, cleverly avoiding my question.

I prop myself up on shaky elbows. "But are you full?"

He purses his lips. The reaction is enough for me to know the truth, and my heart drops at the realization that this isn't enough for him. Gray's quick to comfort me, grabbing my cheeks and forcing me to look him in the eyes. I fight it for a moment before giving in and meeting his intense gaze.

"I'm practically full, I promise," he says. "I don't even think I could take everything you release from another orgasm."

Finding his words encouraging, I take a deep breath and nod. I'll be damned if we stop now when all he needs is one more. It's not like the orgasms are unenjoyable, and my newfound jealousy urges me to prove I can feed him better than some random female.

"If we're going to do this, we're going to see it through," I say, guiding his hand between my thighs.

Gray hums, hesitating, before bringing his fingers to my sex. I jolt at the contact, grabbing his wrist before adjusting my hips into a more comfortable position.

"I know you're sensitive, my female, but we'll go slow. You're doing so good." His thumb strokes my clit before he sinks two fingers inside. "Just one more and I'll be so full."

Gray's actions are gentle as he brings me to another orgasm, his eyes fluttering shut as I cum around his fingers after only a few minutes of touch.

His chest expands as he breathes it in, taking his fill, and he finally looks at ease as he pulls his hand away. His lust has completely dissipated at this point, but I still whine as he removes himself from me.

My eyes slip shut as exhaustion takes over, my body fighting sleep even in my sleep. I can tell Gray's looking at me, his body still hovering over mine.

"Can I sleep with you tonight?" he asks, drawing me from my rest.

I blink up at him, confused. "I'm in *your* bed. It should be *me* asking *you* that."

"No." Gray cups my cheek and strokes his thumb over my eyebrow. "I want to sleep with the real you."

I'm not sure how to feel about the request. It sounds enjoyable right now, but I don't know if I'll feel the same way when I wake up tomorrow.

"Will you wake me up and ask again?" I'm unsure how much being in a dream alters my state of mind.

Gray beams as he dissipates into the air. I remain still, unsure of what to expect, when my pulse suddenly quickens and I jerk up in bed. My eyes widen as I look around, confused and disorientated as I realize I'm in my bed and Gray is hovering above me like a horror movie serial killer.

To my utter relief, though, I feel no change in my mind and thoughts. The only difference is that sticky cum no longer covers my skin and our accumulated sweat is gone.

"Can I sleep with you?" Gray asks, his face nearing mine.

I glare at him, groggy and grumpy as I scooch over and make room.

I shouldn't have asked him to wake me up.

He crawls in without hesitation, quickly slipping underneath the covers before pulling me flush against him. I grab his nipple before I can think better of it, pinching and twisting it between my fingers.

Gray chokes as he rips my hand away from his flesh. "What the fuck?"

"Stay away from my butt."

Chapter Fourteen

SILAS

MY SHOES ECHO through the hallway as I head toward Aziel's bedroom. His corridor is dark and depressing, and I make a mental note to buy him some paint for the human gifting holiday Charlie's always talking about. She was obsessing over it yesterday during dinner, her voice loud as she told story after story of a man who sneaks into homes and leaves presents for children.

I forgot how peculiar humans are, but she's sure reminded me.

Aziel's bedroom is just up ahead, and I glare at the wooden door as I approach. *Please be in there.* The party is tomorrow afternoon, and if he's not here, I'll have no choice but to go to the pits and get him myself.

I hate going there. There are no laws, and that leaves me vulnerable. Fates are a hunted species, and the second word gets out that I'm there, they'll swarm. I'll be lucky to make it back with anything less than a few broken ribs.

My irritation grows as Charlie lets out another particularly throaty moan, her noises growing louder with each passing minute. I'm willing to bet Gray didn't tell her sleep-talking is a common side effect of dreaming with an incubus.

I shove Aziel's bedroom door open and step inside just as she begs Gray to keep going. Her words threaten to distract me, but my attention is quickly captured by the giant demon standing in front of his closet. Aziel doesn't acknowledge my presence as I make myself comfortable in the chair opposite his bed.

The thick walls do nothing to dull Charlie's moans, and I readjust myself as she's brought to another orgasm. What I wouldn't kill to be Gray right about now. While I'm running around in a tizzy, he gets to enjoy the pleasures of the spitfire female who's infiltrated our home.

"She's a bit dramatic, don't you think?" Aziel says.

I shrug. I like my women loud.

"I was worried I'd have to go the pits and get you," I respond, watching through narrowed eyes as he pulls out an assortment of ties.

He spins and holds them up for me to see. "What color is she wearing?" he asks. "And I told you I'd be back in time for the party, didn't I?"

He frowns at the humorless laugh I let out. I hold very little faith in the promises made by a man overcome with wrath. Wraths aren't exactly known to be the most reliable, and it wouldn't be the first time Aziel missed an important engagement because he was too busy lurking around the dark corners of the pits.

Ignoring me, Aziel turns and holds the ties under the light.

He's got quite an assortment, each one probably collected during the years he decided to hunt for a bonded female. It was so long ago that I hardly remember what came of his search, but knowing Aziel, I wouldn't be surprised to hear he grew bored and abandoned the idea after a particularly bad date.

I shrug. "I'm not sure. Gray hasn't even told her about the party yet, let alone helped her pick a dress."

Tradition states males match their ties to the color their

females wear, a subtle claim. The three of us have always chosen to go without, opting to wear our shirt collars loose and open, but to keep up appearances, Aziel is expected to match Charlie's dress.

I'll do the same to show my support, but I'm not nearly as worried about it as Aziel is. My lips twitch, and I place a hand over my face to hide it. Aziel hates being laughed at, but seeing him so worked up is amusing.

Charlie's got him picking out his outfit the night before like an overeager teenage boy.

Aziel shuts his eyes and sucks in a sharp breath as Charlie moans again for Gray. I briefly let myself wonder what he's doing that's making her cry for him to continue, but I shake that thought away before it derails me.

It's none of my business.

Aziel doesn't seem to share the same thought process as he palms himself, his hand curling around his length before giving a hard tug.

"I'm right here," I remind him, gesturing to his hand.

Aziel releases himself with a shrug. "Don't act all high and mighty," he snaps. "No amount of clever hand placement is going to hide *your situation*."

Instead of arguing, I glance down at myself and frown. Charlie's sounds might entice me, but that doesn't mean I plan to act on it. Gray will know immediately if Aziel or I touch ourselves, the damned incubus able to sniff out any arousal within the estate.

I need to hide in corners or wait until he's out of the house to masturbate, neither of which will be happening tonight.

"You need to be kind to her tomorrow," I say, dropping the subject of our mutual arousal. "The incubi are going to be keeping a close eye on your relationship."

Aziel scoffs and waves my worries away, but the slight tightening of his jaw tells me he's aware of the dangers tomorrow holds. Gray will be furious if Aziel fucks up and allows his female to be taken, and the last thing I want to deal with is another ten-year-long fight between the two.

The last one ended only three years ago, and it made living here insufferable.

"Gray has requested you apologize to Charlie," I continue.

If you told me a month ago Gray would be demanding Aziel apologize to a small, human female, I'd have doubled over in laughter. Gray probably would have, as well.

Charlie's had a more significant impact on the incubus than anticipated, and I can't say I'm upset about it. He makes her happy, and I enjoy having her around. She's fun to talk to, and her human ideals and expressions are entertaining.

She lets out another strain of cries, her noises ending in a whimper as Gray soothes whatever she's found herself upset about. I resist the urge to turn in the direction of the noises. I want to know what they're doing.

Aziel seems to be in the same boat as me as he goes quiet and steps in her direction.

We both sit in silence and listen to her heavy breathing. It turns into pants as Gray pushes her toward another orgasm, and if I focus hard enough, I can even hear her shifting unconsciously in her bed.

Aziel visibly shivers as she chokes out a particularly guttural moan, her breathing halting for a few seconds before coming out in a deep exhale. It looks like orgasm number three has been completed.

"I'd sooner cut off my balls than apologize to the female," he eventually spits out.

He turns and storms into his closet, but not before pausing to readjust himself. I have a feeling he'll come to regret those words.

"Did you get your fill in the pits?" I ask, changing the subject.

I'm already going to be taking a cold shower tonight, and speaking about Charlie is doing nothing to curb my arousal. I blame my reaction to her on the fact it's been years since I was last with a woman. Maybe I should indulge while we're at the party tomorrow.

It's being held in Lust, and that kingdom is notorious for providing its guests with pleasure. I've found some of my best times to have been at the hands of the succubi. They're eager and experienced, and I know they like when I give in to them. It's not often they come across a man of my status and interests.

Aziel doesn't like it when I ask about the pits, and his face hardens as my question filters through his mind. We have an unspoken agreement that I don't ask and he doesn't share, but I need to know tomorrow's going to go smoothly.

"I'm not going to mess with her again, all right?" he snaps.

The power that pours from him is enough to have me dipping my chin in forced submission. I hate when he does this, and I clear my throat before leaving the room.

Asshole.

Chapter Fifteen

CHARLOTTE

I FLING MY arm out and smack Gray's neck as I wake up, momentarily terrified by the sight of his black eyes staring down at me. Who the fuck does that? I don't think he understands how many of his demonic traits are used in human horror films.

Gray hardly flinches as my hand makes contact with his throat, the only change in his expression being the slight widening of his eyes.

"How long have you been staring at me?" I ask.

I refuse to feel regret for last night as Gray smiles and hooks his leg over my waist. I had fun, and there's nothing wrong with enjoying his presence. He's kind and treats me well.

His eyes don't hold the sexual malice they did after the first time he fed on me, and my heart blooms at the knowledge that he isn't going to humiliate me as he did before.

"Why did you hit me in the throat? You said I could sleep in here," he says, ignoring my question. "Do you remember that? It was seconds before you ripped my fucking nipple off."

His voice lowers as he brings up my attack on his chest, his eyes narrowing before sliding to the sheet that covers mine. I fling my arm over my breasts in a panic, scared he's going to take revenge for my attack. Instead, he laughs, his eyes lighting up at my reaction to him.

"I was only looking at you for a few minutes." He finally answers my earlier question. "Stop being so weird."

My jaw drops. Does he really think it's *me* who's being weird? He must be joking. Gray smirks, confirming my thoughts, and I take a moment to look him over, scanning every bit of him in search of any telltale signs of hunger.

My face warms as I find none, a feeling of pride seeping into me as I see only filled-out cheeks and bright eyes. He looks good.

Gray's smile wavers, and the sheet covering us moves seconds before I feel his fingers touching my palm. I'm sure my cheeks are red as he entwines his fingers with mine, our palms pressing together. The handholding feels more intimate than anything we did last night, and it makes my heart flutter at an embarrassingly fast pace.

"Is there anything about last night you want to talk about?" he asks.

I shake my head, declining the offer. I appreciate that he's opening the conversation, but I'd rather the world swallow me whole than speak about what we did in my dream.

"Is there anything you're upset about?" He continues. He's apparently not accepting my *no* as an appropriate answer. "We don't have to go into detail, but I'd like to know if I went too far at any point. We need communication if this relationship is going to work."

Our relationship? I want to ask about that, but fear of the answer keeps me silent. Am I his girlfriend? The thought frightens and excites me at the same time. Gray's been so kind and patient with me, and I wouldn't be upset to have a label—especially the one of girlfriend.

Do incubi even have relationships like humans? I know there was a female he loved once, but that was a long time ago. My heart aches as I consider the possibility he doesn't feel any emotions for me beyond lust.

I work up the courage to ask, but as he tightens his grip on my hand, I chicken out and push the words back down my throat. I don't think I can handle the disappointment of being told he doesn't share the same feelings I do.

"I'm not upset about anything. I liked what you did," I say instead.

"Even the butt thing?"

My eyes narrow, and after a moment, I shrug. "It was unexpected, and I don't think I'd like it to happen again without warning, but I'm not mad," I admit. "It felt good."

Gray's lips curl into a sly smirk before he forces it back down. The mattress shifts as he rolls onto his side and cups my cheek. I expect him to kiss me, but instead, he buries his head in my neck and latches on to the skin. His lips are soft as he bites and sucks, and I do everything in my power not to let my shaky breaths be heard.

I can't do anything about the arousal that's no doubt pouring out of me, but I clench my thighs together anyway, desperate to keep it hidden.

Gray politely ignores it as he moves his mouth to a new spot, quiet grunts slipping from his throat as he marks up my skin. He takes his time to cover me in what I'm sure are embarrassingly large and dark hickies.

When he finally releases me, he does so with a grin. He seems awfully proud of himself as he evaluates his work, and his smile grows before it abruptly falls.

"There's something I've been meaning to talk to you about." His hushed words make my heart race.

I gulp, nodding for him to continue.

"Before I tell you, I want to promise that Silas will be with you the whole time, and he won't let anything bad happen," he starts, his words only worsening my anxiety. "There's an annual gathering tonight. It's essentially a dick-measuring contest among the demon leaders. Word's gotten out that Aziel bought you, and it's expected you make an appearance."

Gray grabs my hand, his grip tight as he pulls it to his mouth and presses a soft kiss to my knuckles. I try not to let my nerves show as I sit up.

"A gathering?" I ask. "Where is it?"

I hope not here. I don't want people touching my things.

This isn't ideal, but it's far from the worst thing I've ever had to do. I trust Gray and Silas to keep me safe, and I knew I'd be expected to interact with others at some point.

Gray grimaces. Why does he look so nervous? I frown, already knowing I won't like what he's about to say. When he wears that expression, I almost never do.

"It's held in Lust this year, which I'm sure you've gathered is where I'm from. I, well… There's something I haven't told you." Gray frowns and shoves a piece of hair out of his face. "Asmod, the king of Lust, is my dad. He's got like a thousand children, and I'm far from being one of the oldest, so it's not a big deal, but being a direct descendant means they'll be keeping a close eye on me. I need to keep my distance from you tonight."

My blood runs cold. If he's not going to be accompanying me, then who? He mentioned Silas would be with me the whole time, but his wide, panicked eyes and nervous explanation tell a different story.

I gnaw at my bottom lip. The story is that Aziel purchased me. I shake my head, refusing to believe it. There's no way Gray would ask me to go with Aziel. The Wrath threatened to send me to an incubi den the last time he saw me.

"Who am I going with?" I ask, wanting verbal confirmation of my assumption.

Gray squeezes my fingers. "Aziel. But Silas has promised to remain by your side the entire night, and you only need to stay for an hour or so. Silas will stay with you until I come back later. He's promised."

My anger flares, and I scramble back in bed to put some distance between us. Aziel has already threatened to hurt me, and I highly doubt he's one to make empty promises. I'm not dumb enough to believe Gray or Silas could hold back the Wrath should he decide to attack me.

"Why can't you take me?" I ask. "You don't live in Lust anymore, and you don't have to listen to everything they tell you to do."

Gray reaches for me but freezes when I jerk away from his touch. He sighs as I wiggle out of bed and put more space between us, and he politely averts his gaze as I realize I'm naked. I rip the sheet from the bed and wrap it around myself.

"Because they won't ask, Charlie," Gray says. "They'll grab and teleport you to some hidden location before taking turns raping you until you're a shell of a fucking person. The issue isn't me not listening to them. The issue is they don't respect me."

My jaw clenches, and I push down my fear so I can continue being angry. "And what's the difference if Aziel takes me?" I ask, knowing there isn't one.

Gray scoffs before sitting up and throwing a pillow at the wall. "Because people don't fuck with Aziel. What do you want me to say, Charlie? I'm a weaker demon and don't command the same respect as him. Do I need to spell it out for you? Aziel is strong. People don't touch what's his. I am not. I can barely teleport you places, and my family won't think twice about stealing you away if they know you're mine."

Gray's cheeks turn red as he voices his insecurity.

I lick my lips, remembering the story he shared with me yesterday. His family already took away one woman he cared for.

Gray grabs the comforter at the end of the bed and yanks it over his lap. The visible vulnerability cracks my anger, and I find myself suddenly desperate to console him. He refuses to meet my eye as I climb on his lap, but he still opens his arms and welcomes me into them.

His shoulders slump as he pulls me into a hug.

"I know it's a lot to ask, but I promise Aziel isn't going to hurt you," Gray murmurs, kissing my temple. "He has to go because he's the king of Wrath, and I have to go because Asmod is my dad. If we don't make an appearance, the other leaders will find some reason to come here and inspect our relationship themselves."

I sigh. I still don't like this. "Can't you just turn them away?"

Gray shakes his head before tightening his arms and pulling me further into his lap. "Not if we want to keep the peace. You must understand the influence Aziel holds. He's a king, and he must maintain good relationships with the other royals. He'd be doing bad by his people if he didn't."

As much as I'd love to pretend I don't understand and continue arguing, I know what Gray says is the truth. Aziel has responsibilities, and by extension, so do Gray and Silas. I suppose that means I do, too.

"Silas and I tried to get them to postpone, but too much was already in motion," he says. "I was avoiding telling you until I got a final confirmation, which happened yesterday afternoon. And with our date, I was scared to ruin the mood by telling you beforehand."

I nod, having no response. I don't have a say in this, and if I continue arguing, it will do nothing but stress Gray and me out. It's only one hour. I can suck it up for one hour.

"Do you want to see the dress I picked out while you were sleeping away the morning? It's very expensive and very comfortable," Gray whispers into my ear, his attempt to lighten the mood incredibly apparent. "And if you let me, I'd love to do your hair. I'll deny this if you ever bring it up in public, but I went through a cosmetology phase about seventy years ago and am pretty good at an updo."

I choke back a laugh, my interest piqued as I pull back and look into Gray's eyes for the truth. He seems nothing short of earnest, his eyebrows raised as he waits for my response.

This man is such an enigma. Not having the heart to tell him what was fashionable seventy years ago is no longer going to be popular today, I agree to his request. He's excited, and it's not like I'd be able to do any better. The most I've ever done to my rat's nest is throw it up in a loose, scraggly braid.

Fashion isn't exactly at the top of the mind when your parents are the only people you ever interact with.

Gray's grin is nothing short of infectious as he carries me out of bed and into his bedroom.

Gray squeezes my hand as we walk downstairs to meet Aziel and Silas. No words are exchanged, but as he pulls me into his side, I know he's more nervous than he lets on. I wish I knew if those nerves were caused by seeing his family or by seeing Aziel.

I bundle up and lift the fabric of my dress as we make our descent.

Sucking in my stomach, I allow Gray to lead the way. The emerald-green silk is admittedly incredibly comfortable, but it's more form-fitting than anything I'd have ever chosen for myself.

Gray's lusty gaze as he helped me into it made me feel slightly better about my figure. Still, no amount of admiration will make me feel completely confident about the soft lower belly that protrudes from the fabric.

"You look beautiful," Gray says as we reach the bottom landing, his eyes trailing down my frame before settling on the high slit that runs up my leg. I wasn't aware they could go as high as this one, and I'm anxiously mindful that one wrong move will expose my underwear.

Hiding behind the face-framing pieces of hair Gray left around my hairline, I will my cheeks to return to their natural color. Gray pulls me into the sitting room. Aziel and Silas are already waiting for us, and I avoid making eye contact with the Wrath.

They're dressed in stuffy-looking suits, their ties matching the green of my dress. I'm surprised both decided to wear the formal, slim, matching tie. Gray said matching is a way to publicly claim a female, and I only expected Aziel to do so.

Turning to Gray, I frown as I take in his half-unbuttoned shirt. He could read my emotions the moment he slipped on his jacket, and he promised he'd have coordinated with my outfit in a heartbeat if he could, but it didn't make me feel better.

At least I'll get a good view of his chest all night.

I refuse to let my fear show as Aziel and Silas step forward.

"It seems I've missed a lot this past week," Aziel says, holding his arm out for me to take.

Gray clears his throat and pulls me back before I accept it.

I stumble into his chest, more than a little surprised. Aziel rolls his eyes as Silas coughs to cover his laugh. What's Gray doing?

Aziel glares at the incubus over my head, and a second later, his chest expands as he sucks in a deep breath.

"I promise to be on my best behavior tonight," Aziel says, his tone full of thick sarcasm. Nobody moves, and Aziel looks like he's about to murder somebody as he clears his throat and tilts his head back, staring at the ceiling. "I'm sorry, Charlotte. I have no intention of sending you to an incubi den."

I blink, shocked. He apologized and his throat didn't catch on fire? Consider me surprised.

Gray nods and nudges me in Aziel's direction. I gulp, my pulse racing as I accept the Wrath's outstretched hand and let him pull me against his side.

I'm standing in the middle of a bustling room before I can register what's happening, the blaring music almost as overwhelming as the hundreds of people milling about. I'm blown away by the lack of pain or discomfort that accompanied the teleportation, and I look around until I spot Gray and Silas appearing on the other side of the room.

Silas holds Gray's arm but lets go almost immediately after they solidify. I wonder what that's all about, but I won't shame Gray by asking.

I bet Silas teleported them here, taking the pressure off the incubus. Gray doesn't even look for me as he turns and walks away, and I try not to let my disappointment show as Silas locks eyes with Aziel and gestures to the bar.

Gray said that the fate would be by my side all night, but I guess not.

Aziel slides his arm around my waist, his touch making me nauseous. He's no longer holding back his power, and it makes concentrating nearly impossible.

Several demons turn in our direction.

This is more than I anticipated. The room is cast in a dark, red glow, making it hard to see. Loud music beats all around me, seemingly having no source as it hits me from every angle. I'm overwhelmed, and my knees grow weak as I breathe in and the suffocating amount of power within the room fills my lungs. I practically slump into Aziel's side as it consumes me, tears prickling in my eyes as my body is rendered immobile.

Aziel smoothly supports most of my weight.

"Where are our seats?" I whisper, desperate to move out of the center of the room. There are round dining tables placed evenly throughout the room, and I'd like to sit.

Aziel shrugs, leading me forward. "We're probably at the head table."

I'm surprised by his straightforward answer, and I'm slightly relieved as he continues to support most of my weight. I doubt my knees have the strength to move on their own right now.

Aziel pauses as I stumble over my feet, his breath hitting my cheek as he bends and places his lips near my ear.

"Breathe through your nose," he whispers. "It won't fix the problem, but it will help." He presses a quick kiss to my cheek as his words cause two nearby men to look over.

I flinch before snapping my jaw shut. It's harder to breathe through your nose when your body is desperately saying it needs more oxygen, but after a minute, I do start to feel a bit better.

Aziel remains still as I calm myself down, and only once my breathing has returned to normal does he continue to guide us forward. He leads me to the largest table in the front of the room, and I scan the small name cards on each plate before finding my own.

I practically throw myself down the second I see it.

Aziel lowers himself into the seat next to mine before switching Gray's and Silas's spots so Silas will be on my other side. I don't love the idea of Gray being a person away, but I understand why Aziel did it.

Sucking in a slow breath, I lift my head and look around.

"There are..." I start, pausing as I take in the faces of the demons surrounding me. "There are so many women."

It seems like a female accompanies every man. I've never seen so many in one place, not even at the facility.

My mouth runs dry as the absurdly beautiful women stroll around the room, their posture showing no signs of the hesitation or fear I'm used to seeing in females.

Almost all their eyes are black, signaling them to be demons.

Aziel's laugh draws my attention. Where did all these females come from? It's unrealistic that all these men would've been able to find and acquire one of their own species.

"Your shock is amusing," Aziel says, not answering my unspoken question.

I fight the urge to glare and remind myself that while Gray and Silas seem to enjoy my attitude, Aziel will not. The last thing I want is to make him angry.

We sit in tense silence as I continue to scan the large room.

Silas finally approaches a few minutes later with three drinks. His presence is an immediate comfort, and I shoot him a weak smile before looking for Gray. He's nowhere to be seen, but an approaching couple puts a stop to my hunt.

The lust the newcomers emit has me clenching my thighs, and I nervously remain still in the hopes they won't smell my arousal. I know it's not my fault, but I can't help but worry Gray will be upset about my reaction toward the other incubi.

Aziel slips his hand under the slit of my dress and grabs my thigh, his grip painful. I hate it, but the pain *does* help to distract me from the lust.

My throat is dry as I meet the gaze of the couple.

The pair are gorgeous, clearly lust demons, and they wear matching maroon attire. They're both tall, unsurprisingly, with long, dark hair and full lips. I gulp, shifting in my seat as I make the mistake of locking eyes with the man.

He's beautiful.

"We wanted to stop by and say *hello*," the man says. "We've heard so much about you, and we're excited to finally put a face to the name. I'm Asmod, and this is my wife, Nicolette."

Oh. I will my thundering heart to settle as I nervously laugh and sink into Aziel's side. The Wrath slides his hand farther up my thigh, his movements dramatic to draw attention. He wants Gray's dad to see it.

The pair lower their gazes to our connection, and Asmod's lips twitch downward before he clears his throat and turns to Nicolette.

They don't look a day over forty, making me wonder how old Gray is.

With a frown, I note I've never taken the time to ask. As much information as he knows about me, I don't know much about him.

"We appreciate you coming over," Silas says, taking the attention off Aziel and me. "I'm sure you're incredibly busy tonight, but we do love it when you host the annual gatherings."

Asmod grins, his gaze predatory as he watches the debauchery happening in the dark corners of the room. I've made a pointed effort not to look over there, my interest in watching people get fucked nonexistent.

"Ah, there he is." Asmod laughs and grabs his wife's arm before gesturing toward one of the sinful corners. His gaze slides back to us three, but it lingers on me. "Excuse us. Nicolette is quite excited to see her old friend."

Aziel nods as I give the couple a weak smile, my clenched hands finally softening as the pair leave. I turn to see where they're heading, my attention captured as I realize their target is Gray.

Red-hot anger flares inside me as I notice he's standing eerily close to the sex. He wears a wide grin as he speaks to an admittedly quite beautiful woman. I can only see the side of her face from this angle, but it's enough to ignite my insecurities.

She's tall with black hair, two telltale signs she's a demon, but she doesn't hold the same unique glow the sex ones have. She must be from another kingdom. Maybe Wrath. Her red dress is form-fitting, and I scan her figure with a frown.

I sit up straighter and fix my posture, my eyes narrowing as Gray tucks a strand of hair behind her ear. I thought that was a special thing he did with me.

I guess not.

Gray guides her farther into the darkened portion of the room, weaving through the sex. Is he going to have sex with her?

I understood he wasn't going to spend any time with me tonight, but I didn't realize he would be whoring himself out as well.

Aziel groans and pulls me onto his lap, his hands pinning my arms to my sides. I try to fight, my body jerking to the side as I attempt to wiggle off his lap, but it's no use.

"Charlie, you need to calm the fuck down," he says, his arms tightening painfully around me.

I wince as he grabs my chin, forcing me to look away from Gray. He continues to push out his power until I have no choice but to submit, my body slumping on top of his. Tears prick my eyes, the only reaction I can muster.

His voice is much quieter as he continues his scolding. "To stare so publicly is a claim. Now, sit on my lap and stop fighting. Silas will take you home after dinner."

I turn to Silas for help, but he offers none. His gaze flickers uselessly around the room, and I pry my arm free from Aziel's grip so I can grab my drink.

It seems the fate isn't going to be any help.

My hand is visibly shaky as I grab my glass, my nerves at an all-time high as I take a sip. The alcohol is bitter, and I wince as it slides down my throat.

Both Silas and Aziel chuckle at my reaction, Aziel's heartier as he pries the drink from my hand and moves it out of my reach.

"We don't need you getting drunk tonight, my love," he teases, drawing the attention of the nearby demons.

I shrivel into his chest and search for Gray. He's nowhere to be seen, but I know he's still with that woman. What are they doing right now? I understand he can't give me attention tonight, but I don't get why he can't hang around Aziel and Silas.

My head continues to swim, the power in here suffocating and overwhelming. Being so close to Aziel and Silas doesn't help.

"Let's take a lap of the room," Aziel suggests. He taps my thigh, and I more than happily slide off his lap. "Try to keep your staring to a minimum."

Silas rises and hands me my drink.

"Take small sips," he says.

He doesn't have to tell me twice. The last thing I want tonight is to lose control.

I finally catch sight of Gray, and despite Aziel's warning, I can't stop sneaking peeks at him and the woman as I'm led around the room.

Not once does Gray look in my direction, his posture relaxed as he chats with the demon. There's an excited glint in his eye that I foolishly convinced myself was only ever directed at me, and it hurts to see. I severely misjudged our relationship.

That's a mistake I won't make again.

Gray finds a seat beside a couple very openly having sex, and he eyes them for a moment before gesturing for the woman he's been speaking to to slide on his lap.

His smile grows as she places a hand on his thigh and whispers something in his ear, her lips grazing his skin, and I wince he grabs her hips and pulls her onto his lap. She straddles him with ease, her pelvis rolling against his as she brings her lips to his neck.

All he's ever cared about is getting fed.

Gray finally looks at me as he wraps his arms around the woman, his expression conveying an emotion I don't understand. A second later, he's standing, his abrupt action causing the woman on his lap to flail and grab his bicep for balance.

Aziel sighs, noticing what's happening, and pulls me to the side until Gray's no longer in my line of sight. I wince at the sudden tug on my shoulder and stumble into his chest.

A few nearby demons move out of the way, their expressions guarded as Aziel wraps his arm around my waist and brings his mouth to my neck.

I wince, trying to shove him away as he licks the hickies Gray put on me.

It only encourages him to tighten his grip, trapping me against him. His power pours out in waves, overwhelming my senses until I'm again sagging.

Tears fill my eyes as Aziel sucks my skin, the sensation making me shiver despite my hatred. Is this why Gray gave me the hickies? So people would think they were from Aziel and believe we're closer than we are?

I shut my eyes as Aziel slides his mouth to the shell of my ear, his stubble rubbing against my cheek.

"Stop fucking staring and I won't be forced to do this," he says, his voice hoarse. "Every time you look at him, I'll put my mouth on you. It's one fucking hour. You can't get your head out of your ass and behave for even one hour?"

I stumble back into another body when he releases me, and my heart plummets as another unfamiliar set of arms wraps around my waist.

"It's just me," Silas says.

He's the only one I can trust.

I thought I'd be expected to sit silently at a table for an hour until I was taken home. Instead, I've been forced to watch Gray parade around with another woman while Aziel makes me constantly endure his touch. Silas is the only person who hasn't lied to or tricked me—the only one who's been genuine.

He tucks me under his arm and leads me away from the watchful crowd.

Laughs and sneers make their way to my ears as we return to our seats, making me wonder if it's embarrassing for them to have me as their female. It doesn't seem like demons have the same limited number of women as the other realms.

These men could have had their picks of the demon litter.

Why did they choose to purchase a female, then? Why me? There must be something I'm not understanding.

I hold back my burning desire to ask these questions as Silas pulls out my chair, and I refuse to look in Gray's direction as I take a sip of my drink. Despite my sheltered upbringing, I'm not going to get drunk from one drink. Two's a different story, but I won't let myself get anything remotely close to tipsy here. I won't let my guard down around these demons.

Especially while in Lust.

"He may not have a good way of showing it, but Aziel is trying to keep you safe," Silas says after a few minutes of silence.

I scoff and shake my head. "Aziel is a dick."

I don't care if my rude remark makes its way to the Wrath's ears. Let him hear it.

Silas's laugh startles me, the abrupt noise unlike him. His words and reactions always seem so calculated and thought out.

Wanting to know where Aziel is and if he heard, I scan the room until I spot him standing along the wall only a few feet away. He quirks a brow as we lock gazes, a lazy grin spreading across his lips as he tilts his drink in my direction and takes a sip.

I relax as I take in his reaction. I was worried he'd be angry and try to punish me, but it looks like he finds my insult amusing more than anything else.

"Aziel *is* a bit of a dick, isn't he?" Silas snorts.

I don't think what I said was funny, but I'm glad Silas finds humor in it. I'm sure people don't insult the Wrath often, and I make a mental reminder to hold my tongue next time.

Aziel's threat to send me to the incubi den still lingers in my mind. I bet it wouldn't be hard for him to sneak into my room while I'm sleeping and pull me away before Gray or Silas even notice.

Gulping, I look at the hundreds of demons standing around. I'm surprised Aziel isn't making any effort to converse with them. He probably plans to do so after Silas takes me home.

There are a few non-demons here, but all the other species are also from powerful lines.

What looks to be a group of elves is near the bar, their dark, spiraled hair and deep-purple markings a clear indicator of their identity. I even see what looks like a vampire or two meandering about, their dark red eyes standing out against their pale, nearly translucent skin.

I don't belong amongst the elite.

Their prejudices against humans are the reason we were one of the last to join their worlds. If we hadn't accidentally stumbled upon a portal, we wouldn't have ever known they existed.

I watch the bartender as I get lost in thought, amazed at how quickly he serves his intricate concoctions. He hardly seems affected as over a dozen demons stand around placing orders, his focus never wavering from the task at hand.

And to think I felt so fancy when making my parents a simple mojito.

The bartender smiles as he slides two glasses across the counter. I follow them, my throat drying as I realize he's serving Gray and his new female. I lock eyes with the woman before dropping my head toward the table. I didn't even realize I was unintentionally watching them, my focus on the bartender.

Silas pulls me out of my chair before I have the chance to react. I gasp, struggling to get my bearings as I'm pressed against his chest. What's going on?

"Fuck off, Shay," Silas spits, his tone taking on a venomous edge I've never heard him use.

I blink and curl into him as I realize the woman Gray's been with all night is barreling her way toward us. I open my mouth to explain I didn't mean to stare, but the murderous expression on her face renders me silent.

It'd probably be best to let Silas do the talking.

"I want to know why this fucking" —Shay's gaze narrows on me— "*human* keeps looking at Gray." Her sneer turns into a sickly-sweet smile, but I can tell it's not genuine. "If you want him, baby, all you need to do is ask."

"She's looking at Gray because she's nosy and we all live together," Silas says. "You know she belongs to Aziel."

Gray approaches, his face blank as he wraps his arm around Shay. The bulging of his biceps tells me he's using considerable force to keep her held back, though.

"Stop being so jealous, babe." Gray laughs, smiling as her cheeks redden in anger. "I don't want her."

I try not to wince as his words cut through me, but I'm sure my pained expression gives away the emotions I wish to remain hidden.

I've never had to hide my emotions before. My parents were always eager to know how I felt and wanted to hear my frustrations whenever they arose. I don't know how to hold back tears or keep my face expressionless as the demons before me do.

Asmod and Nicolette approach on my left, pushing through the ever-growing crowd until they're directly in front of Silas and me.

"Where's Aziel?" Asmod asks. "You think he'd be eager to come to the defense of his female."

Aziel was standing against the wall the last time I saw him, but now that space is empty. I'm willing to bet this was his plan all along. He's probably hiding in a corner watching this all go down, the man happy to finally be rid of me without taking the blame.

It's not his fault I looked at Gray and attracted attention to myself.

Silas pulls me to the side, his actions too quick for me to follow as I'm abruptly yanked away from a lunging incubus. The man's fingertips graze my arm before my face is smashed into Silas's chest. I turn just in time to see the incubus who attacked fall into the forming crowd of demons, his body making painful contact with the ground before he's back on his feet.

He turns and looks between Silas and me, sizing us up.

Silas wraps his arms around my torso, holding me tightly and preventing me from moving—not that I'd want to. I'm not dumb. I'm no match for these demons, and I'll do well to stick close to and follow the instructions of the only one who seems willing to protect me.

Silas tuts. "I'd refrain from trying that again. You don't want to bring out Aziel's wrath, do you?"

The intoxicating scent of the nearby incubi reaches my nose with my next inhale. It's stronger than Gray's, and I feel my muscles stiffen before melting, my body paralyzed by their lust.

It's so good.

I hardly care if they can smell my arousal, and I try to wrestle out of Silas's arms in a fit of desperation.

I want them.

"This is always my favorite part," Nicolette laughs.

I don't listen as I continue struggling against Silas, my arms pushing against his as I try to break free and seek out the incubi. Silas shoves me to the side before twisting and landing a punch on another lunging incubus. Blood spews out of the man's nose and lands on my hands, but I ignore it.

I need them.

Chapter Sixteen

GRAY

WHERE THE FUCK is Aziel?

The incubi surrounding Silas and Charlie are growing more daring, and I'm starting to get concerned. My arms tighten around Shay as she not so subtly tries to break free from my hold.

She wants to fight my Charlie, but I'm not going to let that happen.

I had no idea she would be here, and I hate myself for not warning Charlie of the possibility. The demon female sends me pictures of herself every day for weeks leading up to the event, each image dirtier than the last so I'm desperate for it by the time the party comes around.

There were no images this year, and I took that to mean she wasn't coming.

I never wanted to hurt Charlie, and I had no desire to be with Shay, but I knew I had to stick with her once I realized she was here. It would've been too suspicious if I didn't, but I desperately hoped Aziel or Silas would explain to Charlie that it was only an act.

The pain in her eyes tells me they did not.

The sight of Charlie's tears will haunt me for a long time, and the betrayal that shone in her eyes cuts me to the core.

When all has calmed with Aziel, I'll assure her she's the only female for me. I'll let her know I have no desire to touch any other, and I only allowed Shay to sit in my lap. She kissed my neck, but I hated every second of it and tore her mouth away as soon as I could.

Silas twists Charlie out of the way so he can snap the neck of a darting incubus. He looks confident and in charge as he protects Charlie, but I know him well enough to see the underlying signs of stress in the curl of his lip.

I want to help, but my involvement will only draw unwanted attention. The incubi are testing us, making half-assed attempts at grabbing Charlie to see my reaction. And Aziel's. Wherever the fuck he is.

Shay tries to wiggle out of my arms as I turn in search of the Wrath. I'm going to snap his neck. He had one fucking job.

Charlie moans, her arousal less than ideal.

The incubi purposefully push out their lust, the scent thick in the air. They have a lawful claim on her the moment she asks for them, and I desperately hope she keeps her mouth shut until Aziel returns from wherever the fuck it is he's disappeared to.

All this lust will throw her into a frenzy, and I can tell by how she fights Silas that it's going to happen sooner rather than later. Incubi lust is potent, often acting like a drug for many weaker species. The comedown will be agonizing, and the more she breathes in, the worse it will be.

Shay tries to spin in my arms just as the scent of her arousal reaches my nose, but I refuse to touch her. My focus is on Charlie only.

I want to take her from Silas and bring her home, but that'll only exacerbate the situation. It was naive to think the incubi wouldn't try something tonight. They love chaos way too much.

The room is tense as everybody waits to see what's going to happen, and I resist the urge to groan when the music cuts off and we're thrown into an uneasy silence. The non-lust demons gather around and watch in mild interest, always finding the drama that follows me to be a fun source of entertainment.

My anger spikes as one of my brothers lunges for Charlie, his actions quick. They'll teleport her away the moment they get their hands on her, but Silas is good about keeping her out of their grasp.

I rock back on my heels, my desperation growing.

Humans are fragile, and I don't like the danger I've foolishly put mine in.

"Calm, calm," Asmod says, his words vibrating through the air as lust pours from him.

Fuck.

Charlie's body is a thousand times more susceptible than most, and I can't imagine how much this must be affecting her. Her shivering form is answer enough, though, and Silas shoves his thigh between hers in a sad attempt to keep her sated.

She almost immediately begins to rub against it.

I know she'll feel shame for this later, but I'd rather have her embarrassed and safe than be passed around as my last female, Nicolette, was. I'd be wrecked if I had to watch another one of my loves be paraded around the den, her soft skin slowly turning purple as they cover her with love bites and fingertip-shaped bruises.

"Just because Gray's gotten himself another female doesn't mean we need to act like animals." Asmod laughs, his eyes darkening as he watches Charlie writhe against Silas.

My pulse races, and it takes everything in me not to respond to his words. He's trying to make me react. He doesn't know

Charlie is mine, and I intend to keep it that way.

Charlie pants and cries into Silas's bicep, her noises growing louder as he grabs her hips and pulls her harder against him. It's good he's keeping her distracted.

"Aziel will be furious you're forcing his female into a frenzy," Silas says.

Asmod laughs, his eyes shining with amusement as he takes a threatening step forward. I struggle to maintain my unaffected, uncaring expression.

"Is that so?" Asmod asks.

He lifts his arms and gestures around, alluding to the fact that Aziel is nowhere to be found. Leave it to the Wrath to disappear the second he's needed.

The air around us ripples, and Aziel materializes behind Nicolette a second later. He takes only a moment to look around, his eyes narrowing before his lips curl into a snarl and he shoves an arm through her back.

I shut my eyes to hide my pain. This is my fault.

Nicolette has only enough time to let out a gust of air before she crumples to the ground, the sound drawing Asmod's attention. He and Aziel make eye contact, and Aziel makes a show of dropping the heart he pulled from her chest onto her body.

Asmod hardly reacts. He never cared for her, and I know he only took her as a wife to hurt me.

Her heart lands on the back of her head before rolling away, the squelching sound it makes uncomfortably loud within the newly silent room.

I flinch, but that's the only reaction I allow myself to have. Now isn't the time to mourn.

Nicolette's blood drips from Aziel's fingertips as Asmod's lust dissipates, vanishing deep inside him.

Charlie cries in response to its abrupt removal, the noise

drawing Aziel's attention.

I anticipate she'll come to awareness shortly, but it will be painful for her not to cum after ingesting so much. I've never experienced a comedown, but from the descriptions people have given me, it's similar to the withdrawal weaker species are subjected to after ingesting heavy drugs.

Aziel steps toward Charlie, but he freezes as he passes the incubus who lunged for her earlier. The incubus grazed her arm with his fingers, and I'm sure he carries her scent. Aziel cocks his head to the side, scanning the man before he rips out his heart as he did to Nicolette.

It happens so quickly I don't have time to process it. Neither does the incubus.

Aziel smiles as the body drops to the floor, his pupils dilated. I exchange a panicked look with Silas. This is less than ideal.

Shay wiggles once more, but this time, I release her. I hate the feeling of her in my arms, and I know she won't try to harm Charlie when Aziel is here.

"Is there anybody else who'd like to stake a claim on my female?" Aziel asks.

Asmod smartly steps back, knowing better than to get in a fight with Aziel. It's not one he'd win, especially while the demon is very quickly losing himself to his wrath.

A tense silence stretches as the incubi begin to vanish, their bodies disappearing as they take this as their cue to leave.

I sigh and run a hand through my hair. Aziel shivers as he fights to contain his rage, but the moment Charlie's loud cry echoes through the room, I watch his last sliver of control snap.

Aziel's muscles loosen as he succumbs to it, his body preparing to fight as the full extent of his power emerges from him. Silas buries Charlie's face into his chest to keep her from breathing it in, which I'm grateful for.

"Aziel," I say, drawing his attention. "That's enough. Charlie's fine."

I step forward and try to reach him through the bond. He rarely lets me in, but it's worth a try. I know he's got some hidden feelings toward Charlie, but he doesn't need to be going full Wrath in the middle of this party.

Asmod has backed off, and the others will follow.

Aziel turns toward me, blinks, and disappears.

Fuck.

I watch in horror as he materializes behind an incubus who's yet to leave. The poor man doesn't even have the chance to react before dropping to the floor, his blood pooling from the open wound in his chest.

The demons too weak to teleport begin to run, their frightened motions only acting as fuel. Aziel loves the chaos, but I don't have time to calm him as Silas captures my attention and gestures to Charlie.

She's twitching, her body begging for the release Asmod's lust promised her.

"Take her home," Silas orders, removing his thigh from between hers. "I'll get Aziel to the pits."

She cries as the pressure vanishes, and I hurry my footsteps, only to break out into a full sprint when Aziel abruptly stills. I attempt to teleport to her, but I'm too slow and by the time I make it to Silas, she and Aziel are gone.

Double Fuck.

"I'll check home," I shout, traveling home a second later.

I don't wait for Silas's response, but I know he'll be searching the pits for the pair. Those are the only two places Aziel would go.

A demon overcome with wrath is typically unpredictable, but Aziel is a creature of habit.

The two consecutive teleports take a lot out of me, but I refuse to rest as the sitting room of our home materializes around me. I hold my breath and listen, relieved when I hear two heartbeats upstairs.

Aziel has taken Charlie to his bedroom.

My legs feel like gelatin as I force myself upstairs and into his room. The door smacks against the wall, and Aziel is on me in a heartbeat.

"Go away," he spits, his fist making painful contact with my cheek. "You're not welcome here."

I stumble backward and swallow a mouthful of blood. Where's Charlie? I can hear and smell her, but Aziel is blocking my view.

Aziel's lips curl as he pins me against the wall and brings his lips to my ear. "Hurt my female again, and I'll kill you."

I freeze, and every muscle in my body becomes rigid. *His* female? What?

I know he has feelings for her, a childish crush stemming from her dislike for him, but I didn't realize he had begun to think of her as *his*. Charlie lets out a pained groan, and in a panic, I lift my knee and slam it into Aziel's balls.

He can't be near her when he's this out of control. He'll hurt her.

Aziel hisses, his grip tightening on my shoulders before his head smashes into my nose. The bone cracks, and an immediate headache forms.

Shit. That hurts.

"Fuck you," I grunt, desperately trying to keep his attention on me.

Charlie will be in pain for hours until the effects of the incubi lust wear off, and the only way to end it now is through touch. It'll be a cold day in hell before I let Aziel touch her.

He's going to hurt her. The oversized, inexperienced fucking brute is going to break my female, and I'll be damned if I sit idly by and watch it happen.

In a fit of desperation, I muster up every bit of lust I have and push it out. Charlie's cries amplify as it hits her, but I don't have the capacity to worry about that as I grab Aziel between the thighs.

He never lets me touch him outside his dreams, but it's worth a shot. He's already hard, and the knowledge that he was ready before I tried to lure him has red-hot anger pulsing through my veins.

Was he planning on taking Charlie after he had beaten me? Is he that fucking blinded by his wrath that he was willing to rape my female?

Fear for Charlie has me dropping to my knees, my hands shaky as I grab at and try to remove Aziel's pants.

He shoves me away with a scoff, his rage stronger than my lust. I try again to distract him, my bloody body trembling as I practically crawl after him. He turns away without a second glance, his attention shifting to Charlie.

She's lying on his bed, her body curled in on itself as she buries her face in her knees and sobs. I scream every insult I can think of as he approaches her, hoping it lures him back to me. It doesn't, and my knees wobble underneath me as I struggle to get my footing.

Aziel rolls her onto her back. She reaches for his arms and curls her fingers around his biceps, my female desperate for touch and not caring who it comes from.

The Wrath continues to try to determine her source of pain as I approach. He hovers over her in a way that has me nervous, his body caging hers against the mattress. My panic continues to build as he strokes her cheek.

He's either unaware of or doesn't care about my presence as I crawl on the bed and shove at his side. He doesn't move.

"Get the fuck off her." I groan.

Aziel ignores me as he grabs Charlie's chin and pushes her head to the side. His body lowers over hers, the action making her moan.

"What's wrong with her?" Aziel asks, turning to me.

I shake my head, refusing to give him an answer. She's feeling this way because she hasn't cum, but the less he knows, the better. Charlie doesn't like him, and she wouldn't want any part of him touching her if she were in her right state of mind.

I lean forward and physically ram my body against his. I want him off Charlie.

Aziel laughs, his lip curling before he shoves me off the bed. I land in a painful heap on the floor, my skull bouncing off the hard ground and intensifying the headache that's already cemented inside my head.

I can barely hear footsteps over the ringing in my ears, but the sight of Silas's legs rushing past me brings immediate relief.

Pushing myself back to my feet, I lean heavily against the bed as Silas rips Aziel off Charlie. The Wrath's ebbing anger is renewed as he spins and tries to hit Silas, but the fate easily avoids it.

Charlie rolls onto her side as I shuffle past her, her sweaty forehead and begging eyes hard to ignore. He's the bigger issue right now. Once I'm done with him, I'll take care of her.

Silas and I get Aziel onto his back, narrowly avoiding his swinging arms. Silas is strong, but he can only pin Aziel for a few seconds. I never anticipated him getting this worked up over the incubi testing his claim, and I hope it's more of a pride thing than a Charlie thing.

I want him to want her, but not if he's going to be this intense about it.

Charlie isn't like the demon females he's been around. She

doesn't find his shows of strength attractive, and all he's going to do is frighten her.

"You're scaring Charlie," I whisper.

Aziel slows and turns in her direction. She's rolled over, facing us, but I know she's unaware of what's happening. I'm willing to bet all she can think about right now is the lustful burn coursing through her, but I'll soothe it the second I'm done with Aziel.

The Wrath continues to fight as I shove his pants and underwear down his thighs. His muscles twitch as he tries to calm himself, the Aziel I know desperately trying to break through the shroud of anger that's taken away all sense and reason.

"Are you sure this is the best option?" Silas asks, his muscles straining as he continues to pin Aziel's shoulders

"What else do you suggest?" I snap. "I'm an incubus. This is the only way I know to calm him."

Silas winces as Aziel frees his arm and tries to land another hit. *Fuck.* I sit on his knees so he can't kick up at us. The action makes me dizzy, my body still struggling to heal from the punches I took to my temple earlier.

Aziel and I have gotten into our fair share of fights, but he's never genuinely hurt me before. The bond usually doesn't let him.

Charlie lets out another loud cry, and I put a hand on her thigh to quiet her. The touch of an incubus should calm her enough for Aziel to relax. Her eyes snap open as I make contact, the unspoken promise of relief making her alert.

I offer her an encouraging smile as Aziel curls his fist into my hair and yanks my head to the side. I instinctively try to dislodge him, but Charlie groans the second I release her.

"Shit, Gray. Hurry up." Silas places a knee on the bed for more leverage.

Ignoring the pain from having my hair ripped out of my scalp,

I grab Charlie's leg again.

"Do you trust me?" I ask her.

She won't like this, but it's all I can think to do. Her pain is only riling him, and I'm not going to be able to calm him if she's too worked up. I wish Aziel would go to the pits and sort out his shit, but I can tell he's not going to be leaving Charlie without a fight.

Even if we managed to get him to the pits, he'd be right back here trying to take her with him.

I refuse to let him bring her there. They would destroy her.

"Come here," I whisper, urging her to crawl over. "Let me help you."

She moves surprisingly fast. Aziel settles slightly as she nears, his grip on my hair loosening as I help her swing her leg over his hip and sit on his stomach.

Her back is to me, and I look down to ensure she's a safe distance away from his exposed manhood.

"If you move, you're going to hurt her," I say, peering at Aziel over her shoulder.

He frowns but ceases his fighting and finally fucking releases my hair. My scalp burns, but I ignore it and snatch up his hand before he touches Charlie.

"What'd you do to her?" Aziel groans, his knee suddenly rising and burying into my balls.

My eyes roll back as the urge to vomit overtakes me, my throat moistening and my breath hitching. "Fuck," I groan, heaving. "I can't help her if you're hurting me."

Aziel frowns, his eyes narrowing as I slide my hand up the slit of Charlie's dress. The long fabric has ridden to her hips, and it's easy for me to place my palm on her bare belly.

She moans, her body reacting positively to the promise of touch. I have no intention of pleasuring her when she's on Aziel, but it's enough to calm her down and let me focus on the Wrath.

"Gray." She moans my name, her hips rocking forward.

I'll never make the mistake of trusting Aziel again. All he had to do was defend his stance that Charlie is his female. One simple, straightforward fucking task, and screwed it up.

Chapter Seventeen

CHARLOTTE

GRAY'S TOUCH HELPS to soothe my burning skin, the heat simmering into a dull, manageable ache as he holds my stomach.

"Look at her, Aziel. She's okay," Silas says, drawing my attention.

I turn in his direction. He's pinning Aziel's shoulders to the bed. I faintly remember them fighting, but most of it was a blur.

The men moved too quickly for my eyes to follow, and the pain was too distracting for me to pay attention. Even now, it feels like my entire body is burning from the inside out. It's better with Gray's touch, but the need hasn't lessened.

Sex is the only thing I can think about, and I plant my palms on Aziel's chest before rocking myself against his abdomen. It feels good, but I need more. I need to feel his bare skin against mine.

I reach for Aziel's shirt buttons, my fingers barely grazing them before Gray pulls me away.

Aziel twitches before he breaks his arms free from Silas and rips his shirt open.

"Mine," he hisses, slipping his hand under my dress.

Gray snatches Aziel's arms and pins them to the bed, and the Wrath's black eyes bore holes into my face as I writhe above him. I enjoy the feeling of his hard body below me.

He breaks free of Gray, grabs my waist with his left hand, and slides his right up the column of my throat. His fingers curl around my neck before pulling me down, his face showing no emotion as he buries his face in my hair.

I can't stop moaning as he licks and sucks at the skin of my neck, his tongue wet and sloppy as he trails it from my collarbone to my ear. I can vaguely hear Gray saying something before I'm pulled back up.

"Don't touch her," Gray snaps.

Aziel grunts, but he doesn't put up a fight.

There's movement behind me, but when I try to turn and see, Silas plants a hand on my shoulder and stops me. He's no longer holding Aziel.

The Wrath's hand finds its way back to my thighs, but this time, he moves slowly not to draw attention. I lean back, accidentally letting out a gasp as he pulls my underwear to the side and slips two fingers through my folds.

The touch feels amazing, but my patience runs thin when he doesn't put them inside me. He prods and explores instead, two things I do not want.

"I, ah—*fuck*." I snatch Aziel's wrist and guide his fingers to my clit. "*There*."

Aziel groans, his abs flexing as the noises behind me grow louder. Whatever's happening is wet, and I can only imagine what trouble Gray's gotten himself into. The incubi's mouth connects with the back of my neck a second later, and Gray kisses my sweaty skin before peering over my shoulder to see what's happening between Aziel and me.

"Is she still high?" he asks Silas.

Silas grabs my chin and forces me to look into his eyes, and he scans my face before shaking his head.

"She's alert," he says.

Gray doesn't pull Aziel away again, and he instead adjusts the Wrath's fingers currently pressing against my clit. I sigh as he moves them into a better position.

"Circles," Gray instructs. "Don't get excited and press too hard. Keep it just like this."

My head rolls to the side. It feels so good.

Silas sinks his teeth into his bottom lip as he watches, his gaze heavy with interest, and Gray's claims that he likes to watch flicker through my mind.

"I'm going to make you cum," Gray says. "We've got to calm you down."

I let out a happy sigh. That's exactly what I need.

Gray chuckles. "Not you, princess." He trails his lips down my neck toward the exposed skin of my back. Never in my life have I been so happy to be wearing a backless dress.

I cry out as he reaches the center of my spine, his tongue darting out to lick along the protruding bone just as Aziel lets out a loud grunt.

I peer back at Gray, and the incubus meets my eye with a sly smirk as he strokes Aziel. He's gripping the Wrath tightly, his fingers curled around the hard length as he slides his hand from base to tip and back down again.

Fuck.

I thrust faster against Aziel's fingers, the heat pooling in my lower belly soothing the ache I feel everywhere in my body. I'm close.

"Please," I beg.

"I know, baby, I know," Gray whispers, his skin practically glowing as he feeds from Aziel and me. "I'm going to make you both feel so good."

Overcome with the urge to be filled, I plant my hands on Aziel's chest and lift my hips. Aziel quickly adjusts, following my lead so he can continue rubbing me. Gray presses a hand to my lower back to stop my movements.

"Let her," Aziel groans.

Gray tuts, shaking his head. "Can't do that," he says, his face grave as Aziel lifts his knee and tries to push him off. "Aziel, stop. That's not what she needs right now. Trust me, please."

Aziel stops fighting, his body slumping against the mattress before he wraps his arm around my waist and pulls the front of my body against his.

"The next time you ask for my cock, you're getting it. I don't care if the incubus approves," he whispers. "You're mine. This soft little pussy is mine."

His grip on me tightens as I cry out and shake, my eyes rolling back. I'm so close.

"Say it. Tell me you're mine."

His fingers slow when he realizes I'm too close to orgasm to speak, my nerves on fire as I convulse above him. I whine at the teasing, desperate to cum.

"Please," I beg. "I'm yours. I promise I'm yours."

Aziel resumes, his fingers circling my clit just as Gray taught him. He doesn't stop until I'm collapsing on top of him, my flushed skin breaking into a cold sweat as the desperation and burning leaves with my orgasm.

I tell myself not to freak out as Aziel holds me against his chest, his grip borderline painful as he buries his face in my neck and uses my skin to muffle his moans.

I can hear the slapping of skin as Gray continues to touch the Wrath. Is this going to trigger Aziel's bond? I don't want Aziel to be bonded to me.

Aziel's quiet moan interrupts my thoughts. He licks me a second later, his tongue running up the column of my throat.

I feel ashamed of the warmth his touch brings, my body responding to his pleasure in a way I'm not proud of. I only hope Gray can't sense it as he palms my ass and brushes his head against the back of my thigh.

Despite my desire to turn and see what he's doing, I remain still. I'm wary of what Aziel will do if I try to get up, and I figure I should stay here until given directions to do otherwise.

Gray's hoarse cries make their way to my ears as he feeds, the noise identical to the ones he makes in my dreams. My eyelids feel heavy as I turn and look at Silas, and I feel my pulse race as he licks his lips and stares at the skin exposed by my ridden-up dress.

Aziel releases another loud, choked moan as he's pushed over the edge.

I remain frozen as he comes undone, unsure of what to do. Gray's quick to jump into action and make that decision for me, his arm forcing its way between Aziel's and my sweaty bodies and carefully prying me off his friend.

Aziel shuts his eyes and licks his lips, his arms falling away as I'm picked up. I only have a brief moment to look at his body as I'm pulled off the bed, and my eyes linger on his still-hard cock and the cum that coats his shaft and lower abdomen.

There's less than I expected there to be, and as I turn my head to look at Gray's puffy, wet lips, I realize why.

Silas leaves with us, but he breaks away and heads downstairs as Gray carries me into his bedroom. I hold my tongue until the door is closed behind him and we're alone.

"What the fuck was that?"

Gray runs a hand through his hair, looking about as stressed as I feel. My knees are shaky, and I struggle to hold myself upright as the burn spreads through my veins once more. It's not nearly as intense as before, but it's bad enough that I don't argue as Gray leads me into our bathroom and runs a bath.

He messes with the knob before finding a temperature he likes and grabbing me a towel.

"It will help," he promises.

I grind my teeth, debating arguing as the tub fills. The burn continues to grow, and with a huff, I rip off my dress and lower myself into the water. It's lukewarm but brings immediate relief.

Gray sits on the tub's edge, but his expression holds no arousal as he scans my bare form. He's already seen everything, so I don't bother covering myself as I grab some soap and mindlessly clean my torso.

"That woman you saw me with, Shay, it's not what it looked like," he explains. "She and I have a history, and I had to be near her or people would've suspected. I didn't think she'd be there tonight, which is why I didn't say anything to you."

I avoid eye contact.

"You're the only female I want to be with," he continues.

I want to believe Gray, but my blood still boils when I think about him and that female. He looked so happy as he held her in his arms, and a look like that is hard to fake.

"Lean forward," Gray says, scooping up a handful of water.

I hug my legs to my chest and drop my chin onto my knees. Gray pushes my hair off the back of my neck before pouring the water on it, the coolness refreshing. He wasn't lying when he said the bath would help. The burning has already simmered to a dull ache.

"Has tonight ruined how you feel for me?" Gray asks.

"I don't know."

It's not what Gray wants to hear, but it's the truth.

"What can I do to fix it?"

Gray sounds so earnest, and I turn my head so my cheek is

resting on my knees and I can see his expression. His eyebrows are pulled together, and he stares at me with so much intensity that it steals my breath. His sleeves are wet, and the ends dip into the water each time he scoops up more. I stare at where the fabric sticks to his forearms before working up the courage to look him in the eye.

"What are we?" I ask.

Gray's lips twitch as he fights back a smile. "I'm your boyfriend." He grimaces before continuing. "That is the correct term, right? Demons don't use it."

I clear my throat. "That's the correct term. Are we exclusive?"

"Does that mean I can't feed from Silas and Aziel?"

I shrug. My jealousy doesn't expand to them, and they've made it clear they don't like when Gray tries to seduce them. It's the entire reason they bought me.

"If you find yourself lucky enough to have the opportunity with them, I won't stop you." I crack a smile but quickly remember I'm angry and force it away. "I don't want you with anybody else, though."

Gray nods, agreeing to my demand with no hesitation.

"Are there any other females I should be made aware of?" I ask.

Another scoop of water is placed on the back of my neck, and I sigh as it trickles down my spine. Gray leans forward to blow on it but stops when he realizes his action will have the opposite effect of what he wants.

"There are not many demon women I haven't fed on at some point," he admits, shrinking at the glare I shoot in his direction. "But the only other noteworthy relationship I've had in my lifetime has been with Nicolette."

The woman who was with Asmod?

"Your dad's wife?"

Gray sucks on his teeth and gestures for me to stand. He grabs a towel while I do, and I shiver while I wait for him to wrap it around my body and help me step out of the tub. I feel better, albeit like I'm recovering from a fever, but it's manageable.

Gray leads me into his bedroom.

"She was the woman I told you about on our date, the one who left me for my den. She ended up marrying my father, but you don't have to worry about her. Aziel killed her tonight."

My heart aches for him, and when he pulls back his sheets and gestures for me to climb into his bed, I do. He doesn't hesitate to join and curl his body around mine.

Jealousy continues to flare inside me, especially now that I know there aren't many demon women who haven't been with him, but I understand that incubi have different customs than me. They need sex to survive, so I can't be angry with Gray for having a long history of it.

"I'm still mad at you," I whisper, shutting my eyes.

Gray hums. "You should be."

Chapter Eighteen

AZIEL

I STARE AT the ceiling as Silas, Gray, and the human rush out of my room, their presence unwelcome and unappreciated. Who do they think they are?

This fucking human is ruining my life.

A frustrated groan slips from my lips as I slam my fist into the mattress. Her scent is everywhere, mixing with Gray's and preventing my cock from softening. It's been fifteen years since I last allowed Gray to touch me, and our bond is begging for more.

It's not usually this bad, but Charlie's sweet scent only makes it worse. My body wants her, the thought frightening.

Despite my anger, I don't feel the familiar urge from my wrath to strike out. Gray managed to calm me with his touch, not that I'll ever let it happen again. The little fucker's always looking for an opportunity to get his grubby hands around my dick, and I'm pissed I gave it to him.

Not that it didn't feel fucking fantastic, though. I wonder if he's that good or if I only think that because he's the only person who's ever touched me. Probably the latter.

I squeeze my eyes shut as I listen to them scamper around the house. This is simply a momentary slip that will never happen again. I'd rather spend a year in the pits than let that weak female get me in such a state again, her infuriating voice and temperamental personality proving dangerous for my temper.

She's nothing more than a nuisance I'll need to endure for the next sixty years. She'll grow old and lose her use, and I'll buy Gray a newer, better female who doesn't frustrate me so much.

At least, that's what I tell myself as I slip my fingers that were just on her into my mouth. She tastes sweet, and I can't stop imagining her low moans and desperate cries as I curl my fist around my length.

Licking her residual wetness off my fingers, I moan and thrust my hips, fucking my hand. The skin's a bit sensitive, thanks to Gray. My cock doesn't heal as quickly as the rest of my body, the skin more susceptible to injury, and Gray touched me dry.

Probably to punish me.

He even went as far as to take me in his mouth as I came. I'll never admit that I enjoyed the feeling of his lips around me, his tongue flicking over my slit as he swallowed.

I groan as I remember ordering him to let Charlie sit on me. Gray was smart enough to keep her away and prevent my bond from being triggered.

I would've cum the second my dick touched her wet folds, and I fear the contact would have bonded us. What happened today was already too close. One wrong move and I'd be tied to the filthy human.

My cock aches due to Gray's rough touch, but I ignore the slight pain as I massage my shaft and desperately chase another high. The fucker probably did this to ensure I wouldn't touch myself after, the greedy incubus angry whenever I get off and he isn't around to feed on it.

I don't bother muffling my moans as I suck on my fingers, my imagination running wild with images of my tongue on Charlie. *Fuck.* I bet she'd love that.

My motions grow frantic as I find my release, and I spill over my stomach and chest with a deep grunt. I sigh as my arousal dissipates, shamed slightly by the thoughts that pushed me over the edge.

I'm sure Silas and Gray heard, but I can't bring myself to care as I head to my bathroom. Both are probably furious with me right now—Gray because I left his female alone at the party and Silas because I hit Gray.

The familiar tingle of guilt lingers in the back of my mind as I recall my attack on the incubus. I never hit him, at least not with the intent to harm, but I took it too far today.

My guilt continues to grow as I remember the sheer desperation in his voice as I lay with Charlie on my bed. Despite my clouded judgment, I had no interest in raping his female. I just wanted to soothe her pain, but there was no way for him to know that.

He probably still thinks I had intentions to take her against her will.

I hate how she makes me feel, and the way she's constantly begging for Gray's affection infuriates me. Watching her cry over him at the party made me ready to snap both of their necks.

I've never particularly enjoyed Gray being with others, our bond aching whenever he touches them, but I've never felt such a strong need to claim him. Seeing Charlie cry provoked my wrath, and I had to leave the party for a few minutes when the need to storm over and claim her and Gray as my own in front of the entire fucking Lust horde grew too strong.

I thought she'd be okay with Silas for a few minutes. He's perfectly capable of keeping a tiny human woman seated in a chair by herself.

Or so I thought.

I didn't realize there was an issue until I felt Gray tugging at our bond, his mind slamming into mine with panic. By the time I'd noticed and returned, too much had already gone down. The sight of Charlie sobbing into Silas's chest instantly had me in fighting mode.

My frustration with myself grows as I step into the shower. Charlie fucking leaked all over my chest, and I tell myself I hate it as I scrub it away.

I want to seek out her and Gray, and I slam my hand against the shower wall before shutting off the spray. I need to get out of here before I do something I regret.

Again.

There's a fresh towel hanging on the rack next to the shower, and I roughly dry myself before heading into my bedroom and throwing on a pair of loose shorts and a ratty T-shirt—the perfect attire for the pits.

Gray apologizes to Charlie, his voice soft and pleading as he explains what happened tonight. I scoff as he says Shay means nothing and he only wants Charlie. He should have warned Charlie about her.

He put his human at a disadvantage tonight, and while Charlie should've been better about keeping her emotions contained, he should've been better about setting expectations. All of this could have been avoided if she had stopped fucking staring.

I'm willing to bet Charlie's glaring at Gray with her arms crossed over her chest right now, her lips pursed as she politely listens to his excuses. The sudden urge to teleport to them and pull her onto my lap as Gray pleads has me running my fingers through my hair.

I shouldn't want to soothe her. My heart shouldn't thump painfully when I hear her quiet sniffle and shaky breath. She's not my problem to worry about. Gray's the one who fucked up by not setting proper expectations, and it's his job to comfort her.

Not that my presence would help, anyway. The female clearly dislikes me. The only interest she's ever shown in me has been today, but I'm not sure if that counts. I know she's attracted to me, the arousal that slips from her whenever I'm near proof enough of that. It's almost always suffocated by fear and anxiety, but it's still there.

My lips curl as I recall her moans. Gray was practically humping my leg as he placed my hand on her swollen, sensitive clit and taught me how to pleasure her.

Charlie sniffles as she admits to Gray she didn't like watching him with Shay, and I can practically visualize Gray's pained expression as he pulls her into his arms and promises she's the only female he wants. I wait to see if they discuss their interaction with me, but Charlie doesn't bring it up and neither does Gray.

I'm sure she feels embarrassed and guilty about her want for me. Gray's probably telling himself her desire was caused by lust and she wasn't in control of it, but he couldn't see her face.

He didn't see how her pupils returned to their standard size well before she came or how she bit her lip as I called her mine. She loved having two men fawning over her.

I suppose I shouldn't be surprised, though. She's never had a man show her any interest. I'm willing to bet my dick is the first she's seen.

What a lucky day for her.

My muscles tense as I realize she's the first female to see mine, but those situations are different. She's the only female I've *allowed* to see me, but I'm probably the first man who's ever given her the opportunity.

Traveling into the pits, I inhale the scent of death and will my wrath to return. It doesn't fill my bones as it usually does, the damn incubus having settled me too much. Shaking out my limbs, I curse the bond for tying me to the annoying, pesky demon and head in further.

The pits were designed by my father when I was a small child. He wanted a place for evil, and what's better than a pitch-black void of nothingness full of demons set out to kill one another?

My wrath stirs as a spear strikes me from behind and slices through my skin. Smiling, I crane my neck to the right to look at it. The tip protrudes from the front of my shoulder, and I laugh as I rip it the rest of the way through my body.

A good shot.

Now armed with a weapon, I turn and throw it at the demon who attacked me. It sails evenly through the air before lodging into his neck.

A better shot.

My mood perks as I approach the demon. He tries to cry out, but all that emerges is a pained gurgle. He's a weak nightmare, his face contorted and stretched in agony.

His eyes beg for mercy as I grab the end of the spear and drive it further into his neck. Stupid demon. They always forget that they can and likely will die in here. Some come to have fun and burn anger, but that's not the game I play.

I'll be merciful and leave his body here for the others. They'll be able to smell me on his clothing. Most will choose to leave and come back after I've returned to Wrath, but the few who stay will make for a fun challenge.

I forget all about Charlie as I succumb to my inner desires and drive the spear the remainder of the way through the nightmare's neck.

Chapter Nineteen

CHARLOTTE

I ADMIRE GRAY as he sleeps, intrigued by the tiny freckles that line his cheeks and the stubble growing along his chin. The stronger species are always near-perfect, their skin flawless and free of markings.

Gray fits that bill, only occasionally marred by a scar or spot. I like them, and I shift my gaze to the hole in his ear where he once wore an earring. It's hard to imagine him with one, and I wonder if I can convince him to put one of mine in when he wakes up.

His chest expands as he breathes, and I trace my finger down the bridge of his nose before kissing his cheek. His skin feels like it's growing colder, making me worry about his current state of hunger. He was full after feeding on Aziel and me, but that was almost a week ago.

He hasn't asked to touch me since the incident, but I can tell he's starting to feel the effects of hunger. My lips purse as I debate offering, but the memory of that female on him prevents me from doing so.

My bottom lip trembles, my feelings getting the best of me as

I recall how it felt to see him with Shay. He's been genuine in his attempts to earn my forgiveness, apologizing thousands of times. He also hasn't let me out of his sight.

I must admit I appreciate it, my jealousy urging me to keep him close so he can't meander off to wherever it is he goes to during the day. It's unhealthy, and Gray's been more than happy to whisper that gentle reminder when I get too clingy, but he still hardly seems upset by it.

Gray's arm snakes up the blanket and his fingers curl around my wrist, his touch gentle as he pulls my hand to his lips and kisses my knuckles.

"Do you want to talk about last night?" he asks.

I shake my head, not wanting to think about it.

It's too embarrassing. I was so angry when I woke up, and I immediately turned and punched Gray's shoulder until he woke up, too. My voice was loud and shrill as I accused him of entering my dreams without permission, and Gray was so confused as he explained he wasn't anywhere near them.

"No," I say, rejecting his offer to speak about it.

I'd rather die than discuss my dream. I'm still in shock that my twisted, sick mind conjured up those intimate images of him and Aziel.

Gray sighs and props himself up on his elbows.

"You know there's nothing wrong with being attracted to us, right?" he asks. "It's okay to fantasize about what happened last week."

I clench my jaw, not wanting to talk about this. Gray's being kind, but I'm still so mad and it's confusing. I want things to go back to the way they used to be. I wish the party had never happened so I could continue pretending I'm Gray's only female and Aziel doesn't have some weird crush on me.

Gray runs a soothing hand down my cheek before tucking my

hair behind my ear. I lean into his touch, comforted.

"It's not okay." I choke back a cry. "We raped him."

I've been avoiding talking about what happened between the three of us, but the guilt is eating away at me. Aziel didn't want us to touch him, and he went as far as to hit Gray the first few times he tried.

Just because he gave in at the end doesn't mean it's okay, and I feel nothing less than complete shame over the part I played in it. I didn't think anything of it at first, but the more time that passes, the more I realize how terribly we acted.

Gray visibly hesitates as he watches me come apart, his mouth opening and closing as he searches for his following words.

"Charlie," he eventually says, his voice hard. "We did not rape him. Aziel is a strong demon. If he didn't want what was happening, he could have fought us all off or teleported away. This isn't the first time we've attempted to calm his wrath using my lust, and I can assure you from experience he has no issues disappearing if he gets bored with our antics."

I suck in a shaky breath.

I know he can teleport and could have easily gotten himself out of that situation if he'd wanted, but I still feel guilty. He's in the pits right now, but the second he returns, I'll apologize and hear the truth from his mouth.

Aziel may not like me, and I may be scared shitless of him, but if we're going to live together, one of us needs to put in the effort to be cordial. I thought it would be the older-than-dirt demon, but leave it to the twenty-five-year-old human to be the bigger person.

"Are you hungry?" Gray asks, stroking my cheek.

I'm not a big breakfast person, but after seeing how much food Gray has scarfed down these past few days, I know he's asking more for himself.

"You eat more when you're hungry," I note.

Gray looks at me like I've grown three heads. "Yeah, that's kind of how appetites work."

I snort and shove at his chest before rolling out of bed. Gray begged me not to make him sleep alone after our big fight, and I must admit I like cuddling with him.

"I mean when you're hungry-hungry," I clarify, pointing to his hardened length.

Gray frowns and drops his chin to look at it. I try not to appear too shocked as he curls his fingers around the base of himself and squeezes. He does this every morning, pawing at his dick like a horny, temperamental young boy before remembering it's not normal for me and dropping it like it's on fire.

It makes me wonder what his life was like before I arrived. Would he openly touch himself whenever the mood struck? Probably.

"Yeah, it's a side effect. Don't worry about it, though. I'm fine," he says, releasing himself before sliding on a pair of underwear.

I frown, wanting to push the subject. "How long can you go without feeding?"

Gray shrugs, his eyes narrowing as he snaps the elastic band around his waist and heads to his closet. I follow.

"I told you I'm fine," he repeats, his tone sharp.

"Gray."

"Charlotte."

I stomp into his closet and insert myself between him and his clothing. I don't think it's too much to want to understand his needs better—especially if he's to be my boyfriend.

Running his hand through his hair, Gray lets out a shaky breath and lowers his face into my neck. He has to bend his knees to reach, and I push up on my tippy-toes to help.

"I can go about a week before getting hungry and irritable. After two or three, I'll grow desperate and won't be able to stop myself from, at a minimum, sneaking into your dreams," he admits. "But please don't be scared of me. I swear I'll go to a brothel if I get too hungry."

My heart thumps as I rip myself out of his arms. Does he still intend to feed off others? I step back into his clothing rack, my arms moving instinctively to cover my chest. I thought we discussed this and agreed to be exclusive. Other than Aziel and Silas.

Gray's quick to backtrack as he realizes his mistake, his hands grabbing at my cheeks and forcing me to look up at him.

"It's not like that, Charlie. I'm trying to be compassionate. I won't have sex with anybody; I'll just feed off what's already happening there. This isn't me being an asshole and feeding for pleasure. I need to do it to survive."

I push his hand away. "If you get so hungry, why wouldn't you just feed off me?"

Gray screeches, the noise high-pitched and full of frustration. "If I'm to that point of hunger, it's safe to assume it's because you aren't letting me." His voice deepens as he levels his face with mine.

"I'm more than happy with you being my only source, but if that's something you want, you need to learn to disconnect our romantic relationship from intimacy. Imagine if I got angry and starved you as punishment. Made you go days without food. That would be cruel, wouldn't it?" Gray asks, his thumbs softly stroking my cheeks. "That's what you're doing to me by demanding you be the only person I feed on but also holding out when you're unhappy."

My palms grow clammy as he explains this. It makes complete sense, and realizing what I'm doing to him makes me feel awful.

"I want you to feed off of me when you're hungry," I decide.

Gray smiles, but it doesn't meet his eyes.

"Why don't you think some more about it before deciding? If this is truly what you want, I need you to understand I'll be in your dreams even when you don't expect it. I don't want you attacking me in the night because I fed. I'll stick to your limits, but I won't ask permission whenever I want to eat for the rest of our lives."

I nod, absorbing his words.

I can't say I'm entirely comfortable with him entering my dreams whenever he wants, but I understand these needs are part of him. It'd be like him demanding I stop needing food. I don't have control over that part of my body, and he doesn't have control over his.

My mouth goes dry as Gray releases my cheeks and grabs my hands. He maintains eye contact as he brings them to his mouth and kisses my knuckles.

"Think about it," he urges.

The air between us feels tense as I leave his closet, heading into my room to get dressed. My mind reels as I tear off my pajamas and slip on some athletic clothing.

Gray's taken it upon himself to buy me a handful of sets after seeing how much I love them, the action warming my heart. My parents always complained about how expensive women's clothing has gotten since it's no longer made in bulk, and I don't even want to think about how much these new sets cost.

I peek into Gray's room once I'm finished, but it seems he's already left for breakfast. He must really be hungry.

I continue thinking about our conversation as I head downstairs. I understand I can't have all of him while also keeping him from my body, but I don't know how to disconnect sex from our relationship.

My parents raised me to believe the two go together, and I worry I won't be able to separate them the way he needs me to. It feels like giving up a piece of myself.

Gray smiles as I walk into the dining room, his plate piled high with food. My guilt grows as I realize just how much he's served himself.

"Stop," he orders when I try to sneak through the room.

I turn, my lips twitching as I see him holding a fork full of scrambled eggs in my direction. He's made his dislike for my disinterest in eating breakfast known these past few days, and I hurry over and accept the food with a quiet laugh.

My teeth clink against the fork as he shoves the entire thing in my mouth, his eyes narrowing as he makes sure I eat it all.

"Happy?" I joke as he scoops up some more.

Unsurprisingly, the food is delicious, and I happily accept what he's giving. The shadows are excellent cooks and have excelled at the human foods Gray's been asking them to make lately.

Gray nods and lets me leave after three more bites.

With a mock bow, I turn and begin my search for Silas. He spends most of his mornings in the library, and I need his help finding some books.

Both Gray and Silas have brushed off my questions about why there were so many demon women at that party, and I want answers. There were at least a hundred there, and judging by the way none of the men were fawning over them, I'm willing to bet that seeing so many women is not uncommon.

Demons aren't struggling with female births as much as they let on, and I want to know why.

I burst through the library doors, immediately locking eyes with Silas. He's sitting in his reading chair, and he looks up with a raised brow as I hurry toward him. Things are still a bit awkward after he watched me throw myself at Aziel, but he isn't making a big deal about it.

He's as indifferent as ever.

"I need your help finding books," I say, rocking back on my heels.

Silas stands, his expression shifting into surprise before he recovers and slips his mask of calmness back on.

"And what books would those be?" he asks.

"Whatever you have on demon females."

The sudden stiffening of Silas's body and the flexing of his hands tells me I was correct in my assumption. There's something they aren't telling me. Hopefully, I'll find the answers I need in a book.

I still can't read the demon language, but my tutor, Rock, gave me a tablet that helps translate. I should be able to make do with that.

Silas steps around me and walks down the first aisle, his back stiff as he scans the titles.

"What are you looking to find in there?" His voice is deceptively calm as he pulls one off the shelves. "They aren't going to be very interesting."

"I want to learn about female births," I admit. "There were a lot of women at the party."

Silas pauses, hesitating, before laughing. I can't tell if it's genuine as he spins and places a book in my arms. I stare him in the eye as I accept it, silently challenging him to tell me the truth.

He doesn't.

Chapter Twenty

CHARLOTTE

ROCK SITS IN the corner of my office reading a thick paperback, and I watch as a shadowy hand pops out of his robe and flips the page. Being a shadow must be hard.

He's told me his body will gradually materialize as he grows older. Most demons are born into solid bodies, but occasionally one will come out too weak to hold a physical form.

Rock doesn't talk much about his family, but from the information I've gathered, it seems his parents weren't happy to give birth to a shadow. He mentioned that they're Wrath nobility, which isn't surprising.

The Wraths seem to value strength above all else.

Rock flips to the next page in his book.

I wonder if he has a hard frame or if his physical body is hazy to the touch, too. I tried asking Gray, but his only response was to suggest I touch Rock and find out. The glint in his eye as he said it, though, tells me doing that would be nothing short of a bad idea.

I'm not going to ask Rock, not wanting to offend him, but I can't stop thinking about it as his blurry fingers reach out to turn another page.

He's got to be at least partly solid if he can pick up and move things around.

Rock politely ignores my staring as I trail my gaze down his cloaked figure. He wears shoes, a shiny, black pair that look expensive. He wore simple, faded brown ones before, but I'm sure Gray's paying him well and is the reason for the upgrade.

He sighs. "Can I help you, Charlie?"

I shake my head and get back to work.

The book Silas gave me this morning was useless, and I've taken it upon myself to go to the library and grab three more. The fate watched me the entire time, cracking jokes about my obsession, but I know I'm not crazy.

These books are surprisingly dense, though, and they're taking me forever to get through. They aren't even engaging, making the task drag. I've learned an incredible amount about demon skincare and the process of childbirth, but nothing at all relating to gender rates.

"What do you know about female births in the demon realm?" I ask.

Rock grows still.

He knows something.

Does everybody but me know what's going on? I clench my jaw and take several slow, deep breaths to calm down. Getting worked up and angry isn't going to help me any.

"I don't know anything," Rock eventually says. "It would be best to go to Gray or Silas with those questions."

His voice shakes, so I drop the subject. The last thing I want is to get him in trouble. I'll ask Gray about it again tonight.

I'm hoping he'll be in a good mood when I tell him I've definitively decided I want to be his only source of lust, even if that means he feeds from me without asking. Hopefully, that good mood will also translate to him giving me the information I want.

I hope it's his hunger making him grumpy and uncooperative.

I work through three more pages of my anatomy book before giving up and tossing the translator aside. This would be so much easier if I didn't have to translate every word individually, and I make a mental note to return to this when my reading comprehension is better.

Rock looks up as I stand and stretch, his body wincing at the loud cracks that emerge from my spine. Shadows probably can't crack their bones.

"Are you done for today?" he asks.

I nod. "I think my brain will explode if I read one more word."

Rock's chuckle sounds nervous, his anxiety making me concerned until I realize he probably can't tell if I'm being serious or not. I'm sure he was raised believing humans are incredibly frail and helpless creatures, their bodies failing at the slightest hint of stress.

"I'm joking," I say.

He sighs, and I shake my head as his body relaxes into the chair he's lounging in. Humans may be small and weak compared to demons, but we don't spontaneously combust. Should I tell him about brain aneurysms and cardiac arrest?

It would be funny, but it's probably best to keep that information to myself. Poor Rock would likely refuse to tutor me out of fear I'll suddenly die.

He hums a tune I've never heard before as he stands and follows me into the hallway, his shadowy hand reaching out to tousle the hair on top of my head. I frown and fix the ruined strands as he leaves.

Gray's office door is closed, and I bounce on my toes as I push it open and peek inside. He's on the phone but waves me in with a smile. He also gestures for me to sit on his lap, which I happily do.

We haven't spoken since our conversation this morning, and if I didn't know any better, I'd say he's been avoiding me. As annoying as I find it, I'm grateful he gave me uninterrupted time to think.

Despite knowing I was purchased for the sole purpose of feeding Gray, somewhere along the line, I grew comfortable and started to take back ownership of my body. It felt good having the power to deny him, and it felt even better knowing he would respect it.

With a slow inhale, I remind myself it's still my body and I'm deciding to let him do this. He'll back off and respect my wishes if I change my mind and say this isn't what I want. I know he will.

I try to eavesdrop on Gray's conversation as I settle on his lap, but the person on the other end of the line is too quiet to hear. Instead, I lean into his chest and listen to his heartbeat. It thumps rhythmically and increases as I slide my fingertips up the hem of his shirt and press against the bare skin of his belly.

We've come so far since I was purchased. A part of me is still scared I'm being silly with my emotions toward Gray, but that fear grows smaller each day. I've never been in a relationship before, let alone had any prolonged interaction with a male who wasn't my father, and I don't know what's normal.

Are the things he's asking of me reasonable, or am I naive and falling for a trick?

My mom would have an answer.

Gray tells me he's looking for her, and I wonder if it's also silly for me to believe he's doing so. He seems earnest, though.

My head spins as I sink further into the dark rabbit hole of my insecurities. Gray rubs gentle circles against my back as he wraps up his call and sets his phone on his desk.

I remain still as he kisses my cheek, his lips lingering before sliding to my mouth to give me a proper one. I'm eager to return it, my lips softening against his as I crane my neck so he has better access.

"Are you and Rock finished?" he asks as he pulls back.

I nod. I enjoy my study sessions with Rock. He's kind and easy to be around, and I'm learning much more than I thought I would.

"Yes. I spent more time reading than working, though," I admit, my face warming.

Gray chuckles and tightens his grip on my waist. I cozy up to him, enjoying the warmth his body emits. I've noticed he's been allowing more and more of his lust out when I'm around, and I'm excited that it's not affecting me nearly as much as it once did.

If I focus on it too much, I'll grow aroused and fidgety, but it fades into the background for the most part. Silas's has been getting better, too, but I still struggle with it. His makes me uncomfortable, my body wanting to submit and be small.

"What's Rock's real name?" I ask. "I feel awful calling him *Rock*."

Gray doesn't immediately answer, and I slide my finger up his chest before pulling away with a gasp.

"Your real name isn't Gray, is it?"

Instead of responding, Gray laughs and digs his fingers into my sides in a sad attempt to tickle me. It hurts, and I grunt and wiggle until he stops. He's been trying to figure out how to do it since learning humans are ticklish, but he hasn't realized that jabbing his fingers between my ribs isn't how it's correctly done.

Not that I'm going to correct him, though. I hate being tickled, and I'm thrilled he doesn't know how to do it.

"It's not, but I've grown to enjoy the name," Gray says, bringing his lips to my ear. "I associate it with your screams of pleasure."

My body warms, but I refuse to give him the upper hand as I

look away and pretend his words aren't affecting me. Cheeky fucker.

"What about Silas and Aziel?" I ask.

Gray's smile grows as a result of my interest in his friends. He practically beams as I scowl at him, loving attention even when it's not good.

"Aziel and Silas are their real names."

"Why have you told me to call you *Gray*?"

Whenever I feel like I've got him figured out, he turns and hits me with another bombshell.

"My name is foreign to your kind. I picked a new one when we decided to go to an auction in the human realm, and I used Aziel's computer to send out a message informing everybody of the change a few weeks before the auction. I thought it would make my female more comfortable," Gray explains, his chipper mood remaining despite my rapidly souring one. "It's not that big of a deal. I'm old, and it's fun to change things up."

I'm going to kill him. "What's your real name?"

Gray rolls his eyes. "That's none of your business. I like Gray. It's both a color and a description."

He beams, his eyes soft as he watches my anger grow. I can tell I'm not getting my answer today, but I store this information in the back of my mind to dig into further at another date.

I don't want to get too distracted. "I came in here for a reason, you know?" I say, changing the subject. "I wanted to ask you about demon female births."

Gray hums, but he doesn't look surprised. "Silas mentioned you were reading up on it."

I force myself to keep my expression neutral. Silas wouldn't have mentioned anything if he weren't hiding something from me. It wouldn't have been a big enough deal for him to bother.

"I know you're keeping something from me," I say.

Gray's eyebrow quirks. "What makes you say that?"

I clench my jaw, unsure how to answer. There isn't anything concrete I can point to that backs up my accusation. It's just an inkling that something isn't right. Maybe Silas is correct in his claim that my obsession is unhealthy and illogical.

"There were so many women at the party," I say. "And the men weren't surprised."

Gray slides his hands from the tops of my thighs to my hip bones. I wiggle as he wraps his fingers around my sides, his large palms encompassing them completely.

"Would you rather we leer at and molest our women just because they're rare?" Gray retorts, his eyes surprisingly hard. "Our customs encourage us to treat our females well, especially in Lust. You continue to compare us to the humans and hunt for signs that we're lying to you, but we're nothing like them."

His grip tightens, and I lick my lips as I absorb his words.

He does make a good point. I've been hammering Gray and Silas with endless questions without ever truly considering that maybe they're just trying to be good people. Guilt worms its way into my chest, but Gray pulls me close and runs his lips across my forehead before it cements.

"Stop fretting, my love," he whispers.

My lungs expand, and I force my body to relax when I exhale. He hasn't given me a reason not to trust him.

"Have you had a chance to think about our conversation earlier?" he asks, changing the subject.

I curl my fingers into his chest, enjoying the feel of his smooth, muscular skin. He's so soft, and I can't hold back my smirk as his body reacts to my touch.

"I did," I say, peering at him through my lashes.

"And?"

"I want to be the only female you feed from, and I'm okay

with what that entails."

Gray's throat bobs as he gulps, and I can't help but squeal as he abruptly stands and carries me out of the room. His hands are under my butt, supporting my weight as I wrap my arms around his neck and hold him close.

"Your dad's coming over for dinner," Silas shouts as Gray carries me past his open office door.

Gray pauses and groans as he steps back and peers through the open doorway.

Silas stares at us with raised eyebrows and an amused grin. He leans back in his chair and continues taking in Gray's current hold on me, his smirk only growing as he pauses at Gray's hips.

I'm sure the incubus's erection is hard not to notice. Not wanting to face the painfully accurate judgment of the fate, I hide my face in Gray's chest.

It wouldn't kill the man to have a little bit of shame.

"Why?" Gray asks, his voice clipped.

A quiet sigh follows a long beat of silence.

"I don't know," Silas says. "It probably has something to do with Aziel. I'll plan to do all the talking, but make sure to be finished humping Charlie and ready to eat by five."

If it was possible to die from embarrassment, I'm sure this moment would be the one that does me in. Sometimes it feels like they're going out of their way to mortify me, making sexual jokes about my relationship with Gray or loudly announcing whenever they smell my arousal.

Gray's the main culprit, but Silas doesn't shy away and loves to chime in with his thoughts. My only saving grace is that he won't do it when Gray's not around, choosing only to partake in my public humiliation when he has an audience.

I don't know what I'd do if he were to act like that in private. I'm already ashamed of my slight intrigue and attraction toward him, and the more he treats me like an annoying younger sibling, the worse it gets.

I squeak as Gray smacks my butt and turns away from Silas.

"Don't tell me how long I can hump my female for," he grumbles, continuing his descent down the hallway.

He doesn't seem concerned about Asmod joining us for dinner, which I'm taking as a good sign. Both Silas and Gray have promised nobody will mess with me after Aziel's dramatic display of possession at the party, and while I'm not sure how much I believe that, it's not like I can do anything about it.

"Stop stressing, Charlie," Gray teases. "This is an exhilarating day for me, and I don't need you ruining it with your anxiety."

His pout has no business being as endearing as it is.

He carries me upstairs, and I chew at my bottom lip as we near his bedroom.

"I'm a bit nervous," I admit.

Gray tightens his grip on my thighs before pushing open his bedroom door and laying me on his bed.

"You have nothing to be nervous about," he says, leaning over me. "You're in control here." He clears his throat. "Are you sure this is what you want? I won't be upset if you decide it's too much."

I lick my lips, my heart slamming into my ribcage. I know this is what I want, but that doesn't stop me from being terrified. Our relationship is more than me just being a female to feed him, and while I love that, I'd be stupid not to realize how vulnerable it leaves me. Gray could decide at any moment that I'm not what he wants. He could choose to sell or give me away, and I'd have no say.

"Why did you buy me when there are a plethora of demon females to choose from?"

Gray grabs my hands. His are warm and soft, and I stare at

them as he slides his thumb across my wrist.

"Most demon women only see me as a way to get to Aziel," Gray admits. "I've tried dating, but women lose interest when they realize being with me doesn't mean they get Aziel and Silas. I thought purchasing a female would be the best way to stay fed without getting hurt."

I open my mouth to respond, but Gray launches into another explanation before I get the chance.

"And I don't want you thinking I only like you because I have no other options or because you feed me. That may have been how it started, but that's not what this is. You're my Charlie."

His sincerity in tone is reassuring, even if his explanation isn't exactly what I wanted to hear.

"How often do you need to feed?" I ask.

His hair falls in my face, the strands tickling my nose and cheek until I swat them away. Gray snorts, his smile returning as he climbs on the bed and sits on my thighs. He's heavy, but I don't complain.

"It depends on the day," he says. "The more I do, the hungrier I am. I'd love to feed four or five times a week, but we can work our way there. I know intimacy is important to you, and I want anything we do in the real world to remain that way. I'll try to feed on your dreams as much as possible."

Intimacy does mean a lot to me, and I don't want the entirety of our sexual relations to be seen as nothing more than a necessary meal.

"I'd like that," I admit.

Gray bounces slightly on my thighs, a giddy smile spreading across his face. I laugh at his reaction, my prior hesitance replaced with excitement. I love it when Gray is like this.

"Can I touch you?" he asks. "I want to show you how much you mean to me."

I want that, too.

I nod, and Gray slides off my legs. He takes my pants with him, maintaining eye contact as he pulls my leggings and underwear off and tosses them onto the floor.

A part of me wants to be embarrassed, but it's hard to feel that way when Gray's staring at me like I'm the most beautiful person he's ever seen. I relax against the mattress as he lifts my legs and folds them against my chest.

"Hold them here," he orders.

My face flushes as I wrap my arms around my thighs. This position has my sex out in the open, but Gray's an incubus and I'm sure what I have isn't anything he hasn't seen a thousand times before. He's not going to think my vagina is weird or different, and even if he does, I doubt it would bother him.

He continues to maintain eye contact as he sinks to his knees, positioning himself between my thighs.

I know what he's planning, but I still let out a shocked gasp when his mouth makes contact with the inside of my thigh. I've only experienced this in my dreams, and the feelings are significantly more intense in real life.

Gray moans, dragging his teeth against my skin.

"I muted your pleasure in your dream," he admits, biting my thigh. "I thought it would be most exciting for you to experience the true feeling of my touch in real life. I was right."

He connects his mouth with me without warning, the sudden contact making me jolt. Gray's tongue is unbearably wet and warm as he slides it up my slit, and his hands soon join the fun as he spreads me with one hand and uses his other to tease my entrance.

I groan, the noise loud and throaty as he sinks one of his fingers inside me. My nerves are on fire as he works it in and out, the pleasure only amplified as he flicks his tongue over my clit. It feels good, so good, and I let out another moan as he adds a second finger.

"I can't tell you how many times I've touched myself to the thought of you this past week," Gray admits between teasing licks.

Fuck.

When he pulls back, I'm graced with the sight of my arousal covering his mouth and chin. His lips are puffy, and his eyes are wild as he leans back in.

He wastes no time teasing, immediately getting to work. I cry and jerk against his mouth, my pants loud and desperate. I would die for this.

Without thinking, I grab a handful of his hair and arch my back off the mattress. I can feel myself clenching around his fingers as my orgasm builds, Gray's determination paying off as I whimper and roll my hips in a desperate plea for more.

Gray's smooth movements drive me to the edge quicker than I'd care to admit, and with a few loud profanities, I'm tightening my grip on his hair and holding his mouth firmly against me.

"Gray, I—you—" I choke out, my head slamming against the mattress as I give up on whatever I was going to say.

He moans as I tense and find my release, my hips stilling before jerking away in sensitivity.

The shit-eating grin on Gray's face when he pulls back makes me scowl, and I wave him away before he can make any teasing remarks. I don't want to hear them, and I happily spread my arms as he climbs up my body and pulls me into his chest.

"And that, my little female," he says, "is why I love my new name so much."

I grunt but don't respond. He'll eventually let his real name slip. I'm sure of that.

I bury my head against his chest before sliding my hand down his waist. I want to touch him, want to know what he feels like in real life.

He grabs my wrist to stop me, his rejection abrupt.

"You aren't ready to make me cum," he says.

I scowl. "What's that supposed to mean?"

"Making an incubus cum is pleasurable and can be overwhelming for humans," he explains. "It might throw you into a frenzy, and we don't have time to work you down from one of those right now."

"Oh," I say, unsure how else to respond. "But you'll let me touch you eventually? You want me to?"

Gray laughs, nodding. "When we have more time and you're less susceptible to my lust, I assure you I'll be honored to feel your touch."

Chapter Twenty-One

CHARLOTTE

MY PALM IS uncomfortably sweaty against Gray's, and my fingers hold his for dear life as he leads me into the dining room. Despite his promise that there's nothing to worry about regarding his father coming for dinner, I'm still nervous.

From what I've gathered during my short time here, Asmod is a sneaky, unfriendly man. I doubt his visit today is friendly, especially considering he's coming when Aziel's gone.

Silas is the first person I see as I enter the room, his expression unnervingly neutral. He sits at the head of the table, taking Aziel's place in his absence, and to his left sits Asmod and a female I don't recognize.

She's unnaturally beautiful, with thick dark hair and full pouty lips. She exudes the same sensuality as Gray, and immediately I recognize her to be a succubus. Asmod probably brought another one of Gray's past lovers in the hopes of upsetting me. Wonderful.

Everybody watches as we enter, and I avoid eye contact as Gray leads me around the table and urges me to sit between him and Silas.

The shadows have prepared a meal I'm unfamiliar with, but

Gray seems more than comfortable with it as he reaches forward and begins filling his and my plates. Silas snorts at the rude entrance but says nothing as he begins to serve himself.

Asmod grunts but also doesn't say anything as Gray begins eating. I'm just glad Asmod is keeping his power tucked away. It's still there, but its intensity is significantly less than the last time I had the misfortune of being around him.

The succubus isn't emitting any, either. Silas must have made them do this. My fists unclench at my sides, and I force myself to look calm as I grab my fork.

Silas clears his throat. "I'm sure there's a reason you invited yourself to our home, Asmod. What do you want?"

His tone is so sharp that even I fear being cut by it.

"Let's enjoy our meal first," Asmod suggests.

Silas purses his lips. "Let's not."

A tense moment of silence passes between the two men, neither wanting to be the first to give in.

Asmod finally gestures to the woman sitting beside him. She straightens her spine, her eyes darting between Gray and Silas.

"I came with a trade," Asmod says. "Aziel has not bonded with the human, and I thought this would be a good opportunity to propose he takes Valentine instead."

Gray shovels another forkful of food into his mouth. I go rigid. A trade? They wouldn't do that, would they?

My heart pounds as I wait to hear the response. It's Gray who provides it.

"Our plans to bond with the same female were made clear over a hundred years ago," he says. "Do you seriously want to suggest that female be my sister? And you can fuck yourself if you think we'd ever give you Charlie."

What? They plan to bond with the same female? Gray's never said anything about that to me.

Asmod ignores Gray and turns to Silas. It's clear the fate's in charge when Aziel's gone, but I'm surprised Asmod expects him to make a decision of this caliber on Aziel's behalf. Is this typical for them?

They've known one another long enough that making decisions involving money or other simple things is expected, but this feels extreme. I couldn't imagine letting Gray barter away my relationships without my input.

"The den won't interfere with Gray and Charlie's relationship if Aziel claims Valentine," Asmod clarifies. "She's set to inherit my throne, as I'm sure you're aware. This is a good trade. We all know Gray was a mistake, and the Wraths will be able to overlook his involuntary bond to Aziel. Most don't even recognize it, considering it's been over a hundred years and the two have not fully mated."

I don't have to look at Gray to know he's hurt by his father's words. The man is cruel and vindictive, openly talking about how easy it would be for Aziel to cast Gray aside. I want to throw my food at him.

Asmod continues. "It looks bad for Aziel to claim the human, and I'm not foolish enough to believe he truly wants her. He's doing this for you, Gray, and I'm giving you both an out."

I sink into my seat and turn toward Silas. He can't seriously be contemplating this, can he? Pretending I'm Aziel's isn't as bad as I initially thought, especially considering the man has been in the pits almost the entire time I've been here. I also don't trust Asmod enough to believe he'd ever truly leave Gray and me alone.

His dislike for his son is concerning.

Silas glances at me and sighs. "No, Asmod, I believe this situation only looks bad for *you*. We've heard the rumors. Your people are angry you're not securing an alliance with your son. Gray is bonded to the king of Wrath, yet he holds no allegiance toward you or your people." Silas picks up his fork, but he doesn't touch his food. "They want their next ruler to be bonded to Aziel, and they don't care which child of yours it happens to be with. You're the one who's desperate for it to be Valentine, but Aziel has already chosen Gray."

Asmod and Valentine frown, both looking equally angry at Silas's rejection. I'm sure they thought they'd march in here with their trade and Silas would jump on the opportunity. I'm happy to watch them be rejected. They deserve it.

"Aziel doesn't even like the human," Asmod points out. "You're not fooling anybody. Valentine will make both of you happy."

Silas blinks. "Aziel is happy with the current arrangement. Gray and Charlie are his, and he has no interest in changing that."

"And what about you?" Asmod asks. "You stand by Aziel's side, yet you're unable to convince him to take a female you find comfort in." His gaze cuts toward me. "We both know Valentine can serve you better than the human."

Silas sucks on his teeth, remaining silent.

I tell myself not to be offended as a hot spike of jealousy flares up my spine. I know Silas isn't interested in me, but I didn't realize he was so opposed to humans that he couldn't even argue the point on my behalf.

I've got the same holes she does.

Gray grabs my hand under the table, his grip tight as he leans in and presses his face into my neck. I remain still as his lips make contact with the sensitive skin there, his actions probably done to settle me.

Valentine shifts her attention to Gray and me, her frown deepening. It's hard to tell if she's genuinely as angry as she appears or if that's her natural expression, but I doubt I'll find out today.

"Don't be stupid, Silas," she says, her voice deceptively soft. "I'm better suited to rule by yours and Aziel's sides than my brother and the human. Gray will get to keep Charlie, and the shame of bonding with them will no longer burden Aziel. This is a good deal."

Silas sucks on his teeth, his hesitance making my palms sweat. Is he considering her offer?

"Plus, we both know how well-acquainted I am with your desires," she continues. "If you'd like a refresher, I'm more than willing."

Gray pulls his face from my neck. "I can give Silas what he needs better than you can."

Silas, for once, shows some emotion. He looks mildly uncomfortable as he leans back in his chair and pinches the bridge of his nose.

"Silas doesn't like men," Valentine retorts.

"Silas doesn't care!" Gray's almost shouting, his voice growing louder with each word. "The gender doesn't matter as long as he's being held down and called a *good boy*."

What? It takes everything in me not to splutter as I turn toward Silas and try to catch his reaction. He hardly has one, and he lets out another sigh as Gray stands from his chair.

"You're a greedy whore!" Gray hisses, pointing at Valentine.

"That's enough," Silas says, putting a halt to the bickering. "Gray and Charlie are staying. We aren't interested in making any changes to our arrangement."

I relax. That's so good to hear.

Asmod scowls as Gray sits back down and resumes eating, visibly pleased with himself. I'm still reeling over the information about Silas, but now's not the time to appear too shocked and confused.

Valentine and Asmod exchange glances. It's tense and

awkward, and I silently shove a forkful of food into my mouth as I wait to see what happens next. My life has become a telenovela.

"I'll be back to speak to Aziel," Asmod says. "I should've known better than to try to do business with a *fate*."

He spits the word *fate*, and I wince at the sheer hatred in his voice. Gray hardly seems to react to the derogatory tone and, if anything, looks to be holding back a laugh. He's always quick to defend Aziel and Silas, so I take it as a good sign that he's not upset.

Silas also appears unoffended.

Asmod and Valentine give me another slow onceover, their heated gazes evaluating and probably dissecting every flaw they see and imprinting it into memory. I refuse to let myself cower under their judgment, and I keep my spine straight until Asmod vanishes.

Valentine's quick to follow, her body there one second and gone the next. I let out an audible sigh when we're left alone, relief flooding my system as my shoulders relax and my toes uncurl.

The two didn't bother serving themselves food, and the shadows slide in and remove their empty plates from the table.

Gray's humming comes to a slow stop as the shadows move around us, and he places a hand on my thigh before rising. I turn to him, shocked to see the glare he's shooting in Silas's direction.

"It wouldn't have killed you to say *we* please you," Gray snaps.

Silas takes a bite of food. He chews it painfully slow, and if I didn't know any better, I'd say he's stalling.

"I'm going to the bathroom," Gray says, storming out of the room.

I watch him leave. Gray's sensitive about his ability to keep everybody in the house happy, and given his constant rejections whenever he tries, I wouldn't be surprised to learn that he harbors genuine insecurities about it.

"Do people think all of us are together?" I ask.

Silas takes a sip of his drink, in no rush to answer. "I'd assume so, yes."

"And they think that because the three of you have…" I pause as I search for the right words, "decided to bond with the same female?"

I bite the inside of my cheek. Gray has made it clear he doesn't care if I'm attracted to Silas or Aziel, but I thought that was just the incubus in him talking. He never said anything about them agreeing to bond with the same female.

Do they intend for me to be that woman?

"We decided long ago that we would share a female when the time comes," Silas says. "It's common knowledge, and most people know we aren't ready for one. Gray was getting impatient, though, so we bought you to keep him occupied."

I clench my jaw and look away, not wanting Silas to see my budding tears. I understand my purpose is to keep Gray occupied for a couple of years, but hearing how little I mean to them in the grand scheme of things still hurts.

"And I'm just the short-term entertainment." I sound pitiful. "Why have none of you taken a female before?"

Silas lets out a dry laugh. "When you live thousands of years, there isn't a huge rush. Aziel went overboard at the annual gathering, and now everybody thinks you're in the running to be our bonded mate. They want to throw their daughters into the ring before we bond with you and it's too late."

Silas rolls his eyes with a laugh, but he stops when he realizes I'm upset. His eyebrows furrow, and a second later he stands and sits in the chair previously occupied by Gray.

"Did Gray not tell you any of this?"

I shake my head, and Silas clenches his jaw before running a hand through his hair. He looks annoyed again.

"Of course he didn't," he mumbles to himself. "Look, it's nothing you need to worry about. Gray loves you, and I assure you that we aren't going to let anybody hurt you."

He's misunderstanding why I'm upset.

"What if I want to bond with Gray?" I ask.

My cheeks warm as I voice the question. It's embarrassing to ask, especially since I don't know Gray's stance on the issue, but things are going well for us and I don't think it's a crazy thing to wonder about.

Bonds are a permanent soul-tying, and they aren't taken lightly. If I bonded with Gray, I'd live as long as he does and maybe even gain some of his demonic abilities. I probably wouldn't be able to teleport or anything, but I might have faster healing and better senses.

It would ruin their plan of finding a female to share when I die in sixty years, though.

Silas takes a moment to think through his response. "I'm not sure if you could ever break Gray and Aziel apart. If you wanted Gray, you'd need to accept Aziel." Silas taps his fingers against the table, almost fidgeting. "Aziel's taken a liking to you, so I'd say it's not out of the realm of possibility."

Is there no way to have Gray without Aziel? The Wrath is cruel, and I don't want to spend the rest of my life with him.

"And where do you fit into that?" I can't stop myself from asking.

Silas looks mildly uncomfortable. "I intend to bond with the same female as them. Since I have desires unique to men of my status, most expect we'll pick a succubus from Lust. Valentine and I had a brief relationship many years ago, and Asmod has been pushing her on us ever since."

Gray appears in the doorway, and I offer him a weak smile

before turning back to Silas.

"Why don't you get your own female?"

Silas shrugs. "I like sharing."

I'm learning more about Silas's kinks this afternoon than I ever imagined. I'm going to continue prying.

"Do you plan to bond with Gray and Aziel, too?" I ask. "Or just the female?"

Silas waves over Gray. "I don't know. It depends on what she wants, but I imagine Gray will push for it to happen."

Gray's footfalls are quiet as he approaches, and I stare at my hands.

"Why haven't you explained this to Charlie?" Silas asks Gray.

"The conversation hasn't come up," Gray argues, his voice quiet. "You'd be open to bonding with me, too?"

Silas ignores the question. "You shouldn't keep Charlie in the dark on the details of our relationship. You're putting her in a position to fail. Imagine if Asmod or Valentine had caught on to her confusion. They'd have preyed on that, and you know it."

Gray scoffs. "There *isn't* a relationship between us, remember? You fucked my sister!" His tone indicates this isn't their first time arguing about this.

The incubus turns toward me, effectively dismissing Silas.

"Come," he orders. "Let's watch a movie."

There's obviously some unspoken, hidden tension between these two men, and I don't want to be here when it finally explodes. I rise, following Gray out of the room.

I hardly ate my dinner, but our guests ruined my appetite.

Gray throws me over his shoulder and carries me upstairs when I get lost in thought and slow my steps. I don't want to think about this any longer, and I refuse to allow myself to ponder the possibility of being with all three of these men.

It will never happen. Aziel doesn't want it, and neither does

Silas. I also could never ask Gray to give them up for me. He'd regret it and would grow to resent me for having made him choose.

I'm going to tuck that information deep down inside and wait until it bubbles up and erupts out of me—like a normal person.

Chapter Twenty-Two

CHARLOTTE

I GLARE AT Gray while waiting for the shadow in his office to finish his business. The incubus visibly flinches beneath my heated gaze, no doubt wondering what he's done to provoke my anger.

The shadow must sense the tension as he snatches the broom sitting in the corner of Gray's office and hurries out. His quick exit blows my hair back slightly, but I ignore it and continue to look at Gray with what I hope is a threatening stare.

If there's anything I've learned these past few weeks, it's that Gray's especially sensitive to negative emotions. Silas wasn't kidding when he said the incubus is desperate to please, and I fully intend to use that to my benefit.

Gray's throat bobs as he gulps. "What have I done?"

I cross my arms over my chest. "Care to tell me why I woke to an empty bed this morning?"

The smile I've been working hard to hide spreads across my lips as Gray realizes I'm teasing and relaxes, and he scowls in my direction before returning to his computer. I knew he had to get up early, so I wasn't surprised when I woke up to a cold, empty bed.

I step through the doorway, entering Gray's office. "Why didn't you tell me you three plan to bond with the same female?"

I've been full of questions since my conversation with Silas yesterday, and I think I might explode if I don't get my answers soon. Gray seemed pretty upset last night, so I decided to wait to ask, but it's been almost fourteen hours now and my patience has thinned.

Gray looks almost hesitant as he gestures for me to step further inside his office and sit on his lap. I reject the offer with a shake of my head, not wanting his lust to distract me.

He's recently decided to turn it up, and it's been getting to me all day.

"There hasn't been a good time to tell you," he explains. "You came here convinced I was going to rape you, and that fear immediately transitioned into believing Aziel was going to murder you or send you away to a den. It's not that I didn't want to tell you. I was waiting until the information would be accepted without fear."

I bite the inside of my cheek as I mull over his answer. I suppose that makes sense.

"What does my future look like here?" I ask.

Gray shoots me what I'm assuming is supposed to be an encouraging smile, but it looks more like a grimace than anything else. I'd be grimacing, too, if I were him. These questions probably aren't ones he's excited to answer.

"Your future's whatever you want it to be," Gray says. "The intention of purchasing a female was to keep me satisfied and fed until Silas and Aziel decided they were ready, but that's no longer what I want. I want *you* to be our bonded, but I'd understand if that's not what you want."

I lean against the doorframe as my eyes narrow into slits. He acts as if I could waltz right up to Aziel and Silas and claim I'm now their female. Aziel would either try to murder or fuck me on the spot, and Silas would probably laugh in my face before walking away.

Besides, I'm not even sure if I want that.

The idea of living forever with Gray, and maybe even Silas, isn't bad, but I'm still undecided on Aziel. He's unpredictable and scary, and even if we *were* to bond with one another, I'd still be a weak human.

My strength doesn't grow the way theirs does, and Aziel doesn't seem like the type of person to be okay with a weak female. I'm sure it'd only be a matter of time before he grows bored and kills me.

What would our relationship even look like? Gray alone is a lot to manage, and I can't fathom having three boyfriends. That sounds like a headache.

A small part of me wants to be petty and ask Gray if he'd ever consider leaving Aziel and Silas to be with me, but I resist the temptation. He's made it clear he wants somebody to love and give his affections to, and even though it would kill him inside, I believe he'd do it for me.

Despite how I may feel toward Silas and Aziel, I could never ask that of Gray.

Those two have been his family for a long time and, as far as I know, are the only ones who have shown him genuine love. It may not be in the sexual manner he'd like, but it's love nonetheless.

It'd be cruel to ask him to give them up.

"If I did want that?" I ask. "Would I be expected to be intimate with all three of you?"

Gray smirks. "We want a healthy, happy bond. I'm the only

one who needs intimacy to survive, but I'm sure the other two will also want it. Especially Aziel. He's desperate."

Gray's eyes are practically shining, and he bounces in excitement with each one of my questions. He probably thinks me asking this means I'm interested and considering the possibility. It's not an incorrect assumption, but I'm not quite ready to admit that to myself—let alone him.

I glance away and clear my throat before asking my next question. "Will you three be intimate with one another?"

Gray sucks in a sharp breath. He shifts uncomfortably in his chair, and I resist the urge to roll my eyes. It doesn't take strong demon senses to know he's turned on.

He's always turned on, though, so I guess I shouldn't be too surprised.

"That depends," Gray says. "Attraction for me is different than it is for you, and if the others let me, I likely will. Silas and Aziel don't prefer men, but they aren't against it, either." Gray wiggles his eyebrows. "Besides, there'll be times when you're unavailable, either because you're pregnant or traveling, and the bond will urge them to keep me fed."

"Traveling?"

Gray nods. "You'll live for thousands of years if we bond with you. I assume you won't want to spend every one of them with us, and I expect there'll be times when you grow angry and leave for a brief period. We do it all the time, especially Aziel."

My pulse races. I never considered the possibility of being free to leave and travel. Gray watches with visible excitement as I try to tamper mine.

"But I'm human," I point out. "Easy to kill."

Gray waves an arm. "Once bonded, we'll be able to reach you wherever you are. We'd feel if you were in danger and could teleport to you in a heartbeat. Plus, you'll be able to tap into our power. You don't need it to survive as we do, but ours will probably give you an extra boost and make you harder to kill."

"I don't exactly understand what your power is," I admit. "Or why you need it."

Gray laughs, his white teeth on full display. "I don't know nearly enough about biology to explain that to you. It's just what keeps us going. Humans get their energy primarily through food, I get mine from sex, Silas from going into the fated world, and Aziel's the lucky bastard whose body regenerates it like a fucking salamander."

He continues. "Our power keeps us alive, just like energy and calories are for you. Food helps, but it doesn't provide enough to sustain us. It makes us strong, and when you hold enough of it, it eventually pours out and permeates the air. That's why your body reacts to ours the way it does."

I nod, my mind reeling. I hate to admit how much the bond is starting to sound appealing, and I'd probably be quick to jump on board if it weren't for the fact that Aziel comes along with it.

The silence between Gray and me is comfortable as I step further into his office and sit on the couch. I have to push away some of the cleaning supplies still stacked on it from when Gray emptied the closet that's now my office, but I welcome the momentary distraction.

I sink into the cushion with a sigh, almost beginning to regret coming in here in the first place. They say ignorance is bliss, and I'm starting to understand what that means. This is a lot to think about.

It hasn't gone unnoticed that Gray's answering all my questions in the future tense instead of hypothetical, but I don't have it in me to correct him.

"I like how interested you are in this," he admits.

The dry laugh that slips from my lips is involuntary, but the shake of my head is not. "It's all hypothetical. Silas and Aziel don't even like me."

Gray stands up and approaches, his movements slow as he crouches by my knees, bringing himself to eye level with me.

"I know this is a lot," he says. "Aziel likes you more than you realize, and I anticipate his feelings will only grow when he returns home. Silas likes you too, but he's not one to give in to his desires." Gray's voice lowers into a low whisper as he leans in and places his mouth by my ear. "You know what he likes. If you want him, you'll need to take him."

My cheeks flush as I turn away, too embarrassed to ask for further clarification. Women dominating men isn't something I read about in my novels, and I don't know what *taking him* would even consist of.

"I could help you," Gray offers, his fingers trailing up the insides of my thighs.

I gulp, my pulse racing. This seems to spur Gray on as he readjusts his position between my knees and presses a wet kiss to the base of my throat.

"When he's eating dinner, I'd tell him to drop to his knees and taste you. He'd be wary at first, thinking we're toying with him. The second he realizes I'm being serious, though, he'd drop to his knees so hard they'd bruise." Gray chuckles.

He knows what he's doing whispering these things to me, and I don't know how to feel about that. Gray returns his lips to my neck as I let out a shaky breath.

"He likes a little pain, and he'd want you to pull his hair and guide his mouth," Gray continues. I gasp as he grabs a handful of my hair and gently pulls my head back, demonstrating. "He'd look up at you with his big doe eyes until you give him permission, his hot breath warming your pussy as he pants like a dog at your feet."

I hate how much I like the sound of that, and I pull my bottom lip between my teeth as Gray presses another kiss to my neck. He then trails them to my shoulder, his lips wet.

"Fuck," he breathes. He slides his hand between my thighs, brushing over my sensitive skin. "Maybe I'll be mean and make him sit and watch as I get you off with my fingers instead."

"I want you to scream his name while I make you cum." Gray moans, his voice hoarse. "I want him to hear us and cry over what he's missing out on."

Those words are enough to snap me out of my daze, and I push Gray away with a grunt. This is too much. I'm already overwhelmed, and his touch is only making it worse.

Gray frowns, but he releases me and steps away as I stand on wobbly legs. He holds out his hand in a silent gesture I don't understand, and I softly place mine on top before turning and rushing out of his office.

––––––––

My reflection is disappointed, but I force myself to look at it anyway. My father would blow a gasket if he saw what my life has become. All he ever wanted was for me to stand tall and play it safe, and it feels like I've done neither of those things.

Here I am, his only daughter, dating an incubus while simultaneously considering the possibility of trying to seduce two other powerful demons—one of whom is arguably one of the most dangerous there is.

Gray may be a beaming light of optimism, but the harsh reality is that Aziel has been gone for more time than he's been here and Silas has made his disinterest quite clear.

I frown, watching as my image in the mirror copies the action. I can't hide in my office forever, and I have to pull up my big girl panties and leave at some point. I'm sure the smell of my arousal has dissipated by now, but I still worry Silas overheard Gray's dirty words. It's not as if the incubus was trying to be quiet.

These men have impeccably good hearing and a startling lack of privacy.

With one final deep breath, I grab the books I borrowed from Silas and begin my journey to the library. I have to face him at some point, and I'd like to get it over with sooner rather than later.

Maybe he'll be feeling generous and let it slide.

Gray stares from behind his desk as I come shuffling out of my office, his dark eyes boring holes into mine as he openly watches my every movement. I bite my bottom lip before nodding in his direction, silently communicating that I'm okay.

The corner of his lip twitches upward, and his tense posture softens as he returns the nod.

One down, one more to go.

I can't decide whether or not I hope Silas is in the library as I head in that direction. I would've been glad to run into him and launch a thousand questions in his direction thirty minutes ago, but after what happened with Gray, I dread the moment we're face to face.

The books I carry are surprisingly heavy as I walk down the hallway, and each step feels like an added weight in my arms. The demons should invest in thinner paper and lighter binding.

I'm on the verge of losing my grip when I finally burst through the library doors. My eyes immediately land on Silas in a silent plea for help, and he's in front of me taking the books from my arms in a flash.

He huffs. "It wouldn't have killed you to take two trips or ask one of us for help."

He holds the books in one arm like they're feathers, which is mildly annoying. He could at least pretend they're heavy. I shake out my limbs, my muscles feeling a bit like gelatin.

"I made it all the way here, didn't I?" I ask.

"Barely." Silas snorts and readjusts his grip. "Did you find what you were looking for?"

I clench my jaw, biting back a snarky remark. We both know the answer to that. I still can't help but feel there's something they're hiding from me, and the more they keep it a secret, the more desperate I am to figure it out.

"I did not," I say, my frustration audible. "Are you sure there isn't anything you want to tell me?" I'm still hoping he'll take pity and share the truth.

Silas turns away instead of responding. I scowl, my irritation growing as he walks down the aisle where I took the books from. I try to be silent as I follow him, but my footsteps are loud despite my best attempts at stealth.

Maybe I should start going barefoot around this place. I feel like I could be really sneaky without the clunkiness of shoes.

Gray's earlier words weasel their way into my head as I walk behind Silas, and for a brief moment, I wonder if I could seduce him into telling me the truth. Gray seems to think so.

Gray thinks that about everybody, though.

"I like your determination," Silas admits as he comes to a halt at the end of the row.

He returns my books to the shelves. His gentleness with them is surprising, and I admire how calm he is compared to the other two demons.

Even when Gray tries to be soft, there's an edge he can never quite seem to erase. It doesn't feel nearly as threatening as it did when I was first bought, and I wonder if I'll ever be able to figure out where it stems from. It would be nice to see Gray in a place where he can truly relax.

I'll see if I can get him in the bath. Those are always calming for me, and I bet they'd help him, too.

"I like your temperament," I tell Silas, returning the compliment. It's true, too. "You're peaceful, and I enjoy being around you."

He looks surprised, his eyes widening for a fraction of a second before returning to his usual unaffected, collected self. My face flushes, unsure if I said something I shouldn't have. I was being honest.

Silas shuts his eyes and tilts his head back, and I lower my gaze to his shins. I should've just accepted his compliment and moved on. He's not going to tell me anything, and I need to stop letting Gray's whispered words get to my head.

Silas cares for me only as a friend or annoying younger sibling, and I need to get that fact through my thick skull.

He groans. "Okay, Charlie. You win."

What? I can barely contain my confusion as he gestures for me to sit in one of the chairs tucked in the corner of the library. Does this mean he's going to tell me about the demon females? I practically sprint to the chairs, almost tripping over my feet in the process.

Is this it? Is he finally going to tell me the truth?

Silas chuckles as I throw myself into the closest oversized chair wait impatiently for him to sit and get comfortable. He takes his sweet time doing so, his movements painfully slow.

"This is private information," he starts, his lips twitching as I lean forward. "But since I don't expect you to be leaving our sights any time soon, I'll tell you."

This is it. This is really it. My feet tap against the ground as I wait for him to continue.

Silas continues. "Demons were initially affected by the female decline just as much as the other species, and we resorted to the same desperate measures most other realms were taking. Nothing worked, and everything we tried only worsened the problem—

until we discovered a couple living in Wrath who had given birth to six females."

I gasp, my eyes growing wide in horror. Six females? There's absolutely no way. I couldn't imagine going through the pain of having six daughters ripped away from me, and I can't believe the couple continued bearing children after the first.

Most human couples decide to stop having children after their first female is born and taken by the Seekers. My mother sterilized herself after I was born, and she taught me at a young age how to do the same to myself should I ever need to.

The procedure is risky when done at home, but she claims it's a necessary precaution.

Silas seems to sense where my dread stems from as he frowns and shakes his head. "We don't take females away from their families here. Even at the worst of times, they remained under their parents' care until they were eighteen. At eighteen, they were given the option to choose a man or undergo insemination."

That's a relief. My shoulders sag, and I nod for him to continue.

"The couple agreed to undergo some testing. We wanted to see what was happening in her body that differed from other females," Silas explains. "Long story short, we discovered the female body has developed to reject all sperm with X chromosomes if there's not enough oxytocin in her system. Oxytocin is produced in response to welcome physical touch, so the more males abused the females, the less they produced."

I'm sure I look like a fool as I stare at him with a gaping mouth, but I don't care. They know the cause of the female decline? This is nothing short of amazing.

"Why didn't you tell me sooner?" I ask. "And why aren't people treating their females better if they know this is the cause? When did you figure this out?"

My mind continues to reel, thousands of questions and ideas flickering through my head. Silas grimaces and glances at the painting on the wall to our right.

"Only the Wraths know," he says.

Before I can think better of it, I jump out of my chair and launch myself into Silas's lap. He grunts as my knee makes contact with his thigh, but he doesn't push me away as I wrap my arms around his neck and pull him into a tight hug.

This is going to change everything. When people find out, men will have no choice but to begin treating females better. We can work to get our rights back and see a world where we pick our males instead of being sold at auction.

In only a few years, we could have a boom in females again. I could find my mother, and we won't have to cower under the painful tempers of men. I won't have to live in fear of delivering a female, and I'll never have to sterilize myself should I find myself unlucky enough to create one.

Silas accepts my hug, but he looks cautious as I pull back and look into his eyes. Our faces are only inches apart, but I'm so excited, I hardly notice.

"This is going to change everything!" I beam, my body practically vibrating with sheer delight.

I don't understand why they wanted to keep this from me, but I figure Gray wanted to wait until I adjusted before telling me the truth. He's probably scared I'll choose to leave him and pick another male, which is understandable.

No longer will I be some sought-after, rare treasure. I'll just be a woman—nothing special and nothing unordinary. Nobody will fight over me or try to steal me. I won't have to fear being alone with a man who isn't my family, and I'll live to see relationships just like the ones in the books I read.

I think over the possibilities, my jaw growing sore from how hard I'm grinning. This is the most incredible day of my life.

Silas clears his throat, and I throw caution to the wind and slam my mouth down on his. He freezes as our lips make contact, his hands darting to my hips to hold me steady while I press our chests together and force my tongue into his mouth. His grip tightens as I wrap my arms around his neck, my current happiness outweighing the fear and insecurity I have surrounding him.

I want Silas, and I want Gray, and maybe the incubus is right in his claims that I'd be happy as their female.

It takes only a few moments for Silas to return the kiss, a muffled groan slipping from his throat as he slides his hands down my thighs and grabs my ass. His grip is surprisingly hard, and I can't hold back a moan as he rocks me against him.

Silas likes his women to dominate him, but I have minimal knowledge of what that entails.

I slip my fingers up his neck until they're buried deep in his hair. He doesn't react much to it, and with a silent prayer that Gray wasn't messing with me earlier, I curl my fist around the strands and yank his head back.

Given the strength differences between our species, I pull his hair as hard as I can in the hopes it's enough for him. I don't know what the expectation is here, but I assume if he wants his hair pulled, he wants it to hurt.

Silas winces as he exposes his neck, and I take the throaty moan he releases as a good sign as I bring my mouth to his ear.

"Good boy."

Chapter Twenty-Three

SILAS

CHARLIE MOANS AS I squeeze her ass. The noise elicits a response I haven't felt in a long time, and I can't help but groan into her mouth. It's been years since I last felt the touch of a female, and as Charlie grinds herself against me, I can't remember why I decided to hold out in the first place.

Even the fact that she grossly misunderstands the situation with the females isn't enough to pull me away.

She's been on my mind since that infuriating day in Aziel's room. The way she wiggled on his chest and rode his fingers has become the thought I resort to when I'm finishing myself in the shower each night.

Fuck.

My jaw drops as Charlie tugs on my hair again, the skin on my scalp aching under her harsh treatment. She's rougher than she needs to be, but I don't mind. If anything, I want her to pull harder.

Charlie moans and rolls her hips, her breaths deepening as I bring my hand to the front of her pants and slip my fingers into the waistband of her leggings.

Gray was more than eager to share his desire for her to

dominate me earlier, and as much as I love the thought of them forcing me to go down on her, she's not ready for anything of that nature without Gray's help.

She may have had me fooled for a second with her dirty whispers in my ear, but I can smell the nerves oozing out of her now that she's given me the one line she learned from Gray.

Sweet little thing.

Charlie gasps when my fingertips graze her clit, her hips jerking forward. She's already wet for me, her sex slick with arousal. I hold back a smirk as she grunts and shoves her tongue farther into my mouth, her desperation for me evident as she licks my canine.

We aren't even kissing at this point, but I let her continue her dirty exploration as I skip past her clit and slip two fingers into her entrance.

I want her to moan for me as she does with Gray, and I curl my fingers before rocking them back and forth. She splutters, her mouth disconnecting from mine as she leans back and brings our foreheads together.

The action is strangely intimate, but I try not to overthink it. She knows this is just for fun.

Fuck.

I'm quick to remove my hand as her earlier conversation with Gray pops into my mind. She doesn't know this is just for fun. I should've never encouraged her yesterday. She may have a good claim on us, but that doesn't mean this is truly what she wants.

She likes us because it's all she knows. I have no interest in bonding with a purchased female, especially one who will grow to resent us in the future. Her lifespan is short, and there's no way she's accurately comprehending what it will be like to live thousands of years tied to three demons.

We can't bond with somebody who's only got a short twenty-something years of life experience under her belt, especially when most of them were spent in hiding.

Charlie knows nothing of the real world, and her quickness to believe we plan to share our knowledge of the females is proof enough of that.

"Charlie," I mutter, gently pushing her hips away from mine.

My cock screams out in anger at the lack of contact, but I ignore it. Charlie pulls her forehead off mine with a huff, her eyes glassy and unfocused.

"I'm not ready for a female," I say, finding it better to rip the bandage off in one go.

She frowns, her full lips tugging downward in a gesture that has my heart thumping. Gray and Aziel may not be able to think logically when it comes to her, but I'm not going to let myself fall into the same trap.

"I'm not asking to be your female," she retorts.

I hum, but I won't argue with her. Nothing good will come out of hurting Charlie's feelings and embarrassing her further. She's a nice girl, and if things were different, then maybe this would be a relationship I'd consider.

Charlie bites her lip and looks away as the scent of her salty tears reaches my nose. The sudden guilt that accompanies making her cry surprises me, but I shove that emotion aside with the rest of them.

"Don't cry," I say, wiping her cheeks. "You only feel this way because you have no other options."

Her chin wobbles as she tries to hold back her tears, the sight only deepening the painful guilt I feel. I shouldn't have let her climb on my lap in the first place. I knew what would happen the moment she launched herself at me with that wide grin.

Charlie continues to tear up despite my assurances, and unsure what else to do, I grab the back of her head and press her face into my chest. A loud sob bursts from her throat the moment her skin meets the fabric of my shirt, the sound startling.

Where the fuck is Gray?

I know he can hear what's happening, and I wait anxiously for him to come and console Charlie. He's probably purposefully staying back and forcing me to be the one to comfort her.

I'm sure he also heard me telling her about the females, but I will leave that particular heartbreak of truth to him. He's the one who insisted we keep our knowledge a secret, convincing Aziel and me it would be best for Wrath to give them a decades-long advantage before sharing our findings.

Is it cruel? Yes. Does it give us an edge over everybody else? Also yes.

I try to console her. "Don't cry. I'm not saying *no* because I'm not attracted to you, Charlie. I'm very, very old, and you have so much growing left to do."

This doesn't seem to help as she lets out another wet sniffle. I know these tears aren't just for me and are a cumulation of weeks of stress bubbling over at once, but I can't help feeling entirely responsible.

My rejection is acting as the catalyst.

"I'm not a child," she argues.

I hum and scratch the back of her head.

"No, but you are much, much younger than me. Don't let us take advantage of you. Even Gray," I say, shouting the last part to catch his attention.

It seems to do the trick as, seconds later, I hear his approaching footfalls. Nothing gets the bastard moving quicker than a perceived slight. Gray looks pissed as he barrels into the library, his cold gaze landing on me before softening and sliding to the crying human in my lap.

I'm sure I'll get an earful from him later, and I take solace in the fact that he won't say or do anything in front of Charlie. He'll take her upstairs and settle her like a good little male before lecturing me on the importance of building relationships.

My thoughts race as Gray scoops Charlie into his arms and pulls her off my lap. I can't bring myself to meet her eye, and I turn my head away while he carries her out of the room.

I could have handled this situation better.

Her shaky breaths continue to make their way to my ears as Gray takes her upstairs, and I force myself to listen to them in punishment. I don't like being the reason she's upset, even if it was the right thing to do.

Sinking into my chair, my eyes flutter shut as I venture into the fated world for answers. It would be nearly impossible for anybody else to navigate, but I easily slip my consciousness into it.

I can feel my soul brushing against the spirits as I try to hunt down Charlie's fate, and my annoyance grows as they tug at and steer me away. It's risky to try and force them to give me information they aren't looking to give, but I've been a good fate and I've earned some answers.

They won't punish me for one slipup. Others of my kind have done much worse before facing repercussions.

The tugging on my mind and soul grows the harder I search for her, their tight grip making my head ache as I force my way forward.

I want to know Charlie's fate and whether she's to be our female.

I'm already aware our lives are intertwined and she'll be with us until she dies, but I don't know if that death will be of old age or if it'll be with us in the future too far to see.

I groan, my head splitting. I can vaguely feel the wooden armrests beneath my hands cracking as I fight through the pain betraying the fates brings about.

I need to know.

The fates have hidden Charlie well, and I'm willing to bet they're actively moving her around to keep her out of my reach. Fucking assholes.

"Silas."

I ignore the voice as my soul fights against my kind. *Let me see her*. They ignore my demands and yank me back with more vigor. She's close. I can feel it.

"Silas!"

I continue to ignore the voices, not needing the distraction they're sure to bring.

"Silas!"

My eyes snap open as I'm yanked out of my chair and thrown across the room. My body slams into and knocks over a bookcase, and I groan in pain and slump over the top of the pile.

Fuck, that hurt.

My body aches as I roll over to face the two men in the room, my head spinning so much that the two have turned into four.

"What do you think you're doing?" Aziel asks, his face and body unrecognizable behind the thick layer of smeared blood that coats his skin.

I blink up at him, my mind taking a moment to process what's happening. My head lolls to the side as Aziel grabs my shirt and yanks me upward, and I make brief eye contact with a terrified-looking Gray as I'm lifted and dropped in my chair.

The incubus must have summoned Aziel here, his fear forcing the demon to leave the pits and rescue me from the threat of myself.

"He refused to leave!" Gray's quick to inform Aziel. "He's been slumped in that chair for hours looking like a damned fool."

Snitch.

Despite his angered words, Gray still tugs off his shirt and wipes the blood seeping from my eyes and nose. I stare at him as he cleans me, my guilt only amplified by the care he takes to keep me safe.

"What were you looking for?" Aziel asks.

I shrug, not wanting to tell them I was on a selfish hunt to figure out who Charlie is to us. Aziel doesn't seem to like my non-answer, though, and I feel him forcing his way into my mind and searching for the truth himself only seconds later.

I'm too weak to fight him off as usual, and I glare at him as Gray continues his cleaning.

"You're an idiot," Aziel eventually mutters, pulling back.

Gray snorts, agreeing wholeheartedly before turning and bringing the dirty rag to Aziel's chest. He's only smearing the blood around at this point, but Aziel remains still and lets him do his frantic cleaning.

I groan as the incubus finds himself dissatisfied with the absorbency of his shirt and turns to rip mine off my body. He's not gentle as he pulls it over my head and returns to Aziel.

It's not the first time Gray's forced my clothes off so he could clean us with them, and I'm sure it won't be the last. It's crucial to Gray to care for us, and despite how weird we found it when we first met him, we've grown quite accustomed to it over the years.

It makes me wonder what incubi dens are like behind closed doors.

From the outside, it appears their entire life revolves around sex and feeding, but given Gray's desperate need to serve us, I imagine they're licking one another like cats when there are no observers. It would make sense why Asmod's kingdom never had an issue with females. When they love, they do so wholeheartedly and with many.

"That's enough, thank you," Aziel says, gently pushing Gray away when my shirt is rubbed roughly down the front of his face and shoved slightly into his mouth.

We both know the incubus did it intentionally to show his anger about Aziel leaving us for the pits, but neither of us comments on it.

He thrives off these little victories.

Gray holds my ruined shirt to his chest. I have half a mind to take it away before he brings our blood to a mage and tries to make another salve that ties us to him, but as I take in his angered stare, I decide not to do so.

Aziel clears his throat, the noise capturing our attention. I drag my eyes to the Wrath, my frown deepening as I take in his suspicious grin.

"There's somebody I want you to meet."

Chapter Twenty-Four

CHARLOTTE

THE UNMISTAKABLE SOUND of yelling makes its way to my ears, the voices loud and angry. Rubbing my eyes, I sit up and look around. Gray's not here, and I frown as I touch the spot where he usually sleeps.

Cold.

My movements are jerky as I angrily crawl out from underneath the sheets and head to the door. He promised he wouldn't say anything to Silas about what happened tonight, and I should've known better than to trust him to drop it.

I'm humiliated enough, and I don't need him making it worse by trying to defend my honor. I knew better than to launch myself at Silas so desperately, and I can't believe I let my momentary excitement over the female news cloud my judgment.

At least Silas was kind in his rejection.

His words were hard to hear, but he's entitled to his opinion. I understand why he wouldn't want to date a purchased female who's not even a tenth of his age.

I wouldn't be interested, either, if I were in his position.

I chew at my bottom lip as I sneak downstairs, my bare feet

pattering quietly against the floor with each step. The house is a bit scary when it's dark, and I wrap my arms around myself as I navigate the hallways I've grown familiar with these past few weeks.

I wonder if I can convince Gray to get some nightlights.

It sounds like the shouting is coming from Aziel's office, and I tiptoe closer as somebody lets out a frustrated shout.

"You're out of your goddamn mind, and I'm not going to fucking do it," Gray says.

His voice is laced with more anger than I've ever heard from him, the sound of it startling. Gray's quick to worry and be frustrated, but he rarely grows genuinely angry.

There's murmuring I can't quite make out as I continue my slow approach, but the voice is unmistakably Aziel's. My hands grow clammy at the knowledge that he's back, but I push away my fear as I peer through the crack in the door.

"I don't care," Gray snaps. "It's not going to happen!"

My eyes widen as I take in the sight before me, my thoughts racing a million miles a minute. What have I missed?

Gray stands shirtless in the center of the room, his back turned toward me as he faces Aziel's desk. His body's blocking the view of the older demon, but I don't care much about seeing Aziel anyway, so I shift my attention to Silas.

I do a double-take. Silas is already looking at me, leaning against the wall with his arms crossed over his chest. His entire face and neck are covered in smeared blood, and he wipes away a tiny droplet that drips out of his nose before pushing a strand of hair out of his eye.

What happened to him?

I can't help but note he's also shirtless and has a large bloody handprint on his side. Maybe he was the one who went and got Aziel, causing the Wrath to attack. I wouldn't be surprised. Aziel has a concerning tendency to resort to violence.

"You can come in," Silas says, his voice cutting through the arguing between Gray and Aziel.

The room goes dead silent as Gray turns toward me. His face softens, and he opens his arms in a gesture for me to come to him. I gulp, my hand shaking as I push open the door and step inside.

The power in the room is overwhelming, but I do the trick Aziel taught me at the Lust party and breathe in slowly through my nose. It helps slightly and is just enough to keep me from hunching.

Gray wraps his arms around my waist and presses his chest against my back before spinning us toward Aziel.

I stiffen the second my eyes land on him.

He sits behind his desk with a wide grin, but it's hard to notice with all the blood that coats his skin. I have only a second to worry about the stain it will leave on the furniture before sliding my attention to the familiar woman on his lap.

I suck in my cheeks to hide the explosive anger that erupts from me. Of all the women to bring here, he chooses Shay? I haven't seen her since the Lust party, and I was honestly hoping never to lay eyes on her again.

She smirks and waves as I struggle to wrap my brain around what's happening. I was under the impression that Aziel didn't like her, but I suppose I was wrong in that assumption.

"What's going on?" I ask.

Gray scoffs and glues himself to my back.

"I agree with Gray," Silas says to Aziel. "I'm not doing this."

I look to Gray for answers. He refuses to make eye contact, and I scowl before turning back to Aziel. Are they seriously going to ignore me?

I'm not stupid, and I'm fully aware that another woman on Aziel's lap doesn't look good for me. Aziel is the only thing standing in the way of Asmod, and without his claim, I doubt the Lust king will wait long to swoop in and steal me away.

Aziel seems eerily calm as he watches me look for answers.

"I didn't realize you were back," I say to Aziel.

"I just returned tonight," he says, gesturing to the woman in his lap. "This is Shay."

I nod, trying to hide my growing annoyance.

"We've met," I say between clenched teeth. "Or have you forgotten, Aziel, when she tried to kill me?"

There's silence on Aziel's end, and the muscle in his jaw twitches as he looks me head to toe. I cross my arms over my chest to hide my exposed body, unappreciative of his wandering eyes. Gray insists on buying me practically sheer pajamas, and up until now, I loved them.

Shay turns and shoots Aziel a frosty glare before readjusting herself on his lap. I refuse to look in her direction, not wanting to provoke her into attacking me again.

Aziel sucks in a deep breath before shaking his head and straightening his smile. "Yes, well, that was just a misunderstanding." He's speaking slowly, as if addressing a child. "We've decided to take her as our bonded female."

My mind goes blank. Gray was tucking me into bed and whispering sweet assurances into my ear just a few hours ago. I doubt he's planning on bonding with another woman.

"We haven't decided on anything," Gray says. "I don't fucking want her."

I didn't even know Aziel was back, let alone with a female he intends to bond with. I hope my facial expressions and body posture don't show my disappointment. It was stupid to have hoped they'd genuinely consider me. If Silas's painful and humiliating rejection earlier wasn't enough of a sign it'll never happen, then this sure is.

I shouldn't have let Gray's whispered compliments and promises get to me. I knew better.

Silas clears his throat, drawing my attention. He looks stressed as he wipes away another trail of blood leaking from his nose, the slight tremor in his arm shocking.

He and Aziel must have gotten into a fight.

It'd make sense, considering they're both covered in blood. I didn't take Silas as the type of person to resort to physical blows, assuming that was more of a Gray and Aziel thing, but I clearly don't know these men as well as I thought I did.

Silas scans Shay's form, his eyes trailing down her body. I refuse to be hurt by it, and I purse my lips as he then does the same thing to Aziel.

"You're embarrassing yourself," Silas eventually says.

Aziel frowns, his full lips tugging down at the corners before he shrugs and the negative emotion vanishes. "I most definitely am not. I saw Shay in the pits a few days ago and just knew she was the one for us. She was all alone."

I resist the urge to vomit at the sickly sweet voice he uses.

Shay runs her hand down Aziel's arm. "I went there to apologize, but I got lost. Aziel saved my life, and we connected as he taught me how to fight and protect myself in the pits."

Gray practically growls as he rests his chin on my head and holds me tighter. Even Silas takes a step toward me in response to Shay's words. I'm surprised by the reaction, but I don't question it.

I'll take all the support I can get.

Aziel hardly seems to notice or care. "Shay's the perfect female for us. She's strong, intelligent, and high-bred. I'm willing to wait for you two to come to your senses, but let it be known we *will* be bonding with her."

Gray scoffs, and Silas shakes his head.

"We don't want her," Silas repeats. Gray's quick to agree.

Shay straightens up, looking offended. "That's not what you two said when you were taking turns fucking me all those years ago."

I bristle in Gray's arms but do my best to keep my face flat and void of strong emotions. Acting like the unhinged woman Aziel so clearly thinks I am isn't going to get me anywhere. I still need his protection.

Although I doubt it'll take long for word to spread that I'm fair game now that Shay's here. I'm sure she'll be running to give Asmod the good news the moment she's alone.

"I don't see why this is such a big deal." Aziel is the first to speak up. "I've gone through the trouble of finding a female all three of us will enjoy. You should be grateful."

Shay smiles as she looks between Gray and Silas, the cocky glint in her eye infuriating. I may not have a claim on Silas, but Gray is mine.

That's the only thought rushing through my head as I curl my fingers around his forearms. Gray's chest vibrates against my back at the subtle claim, which I take as a good sign.

"I will not enjoy her," Gray argues.

Aziel laughs. "You already have."

I hope they can't hear my racing heart as Gray falls silent. Is there any part of him that's considering this? It's clear Aziel isn't going to change his mind, and I doubt they'll come to any agreement tonight.

No meaningful change has ever happened at the hands of three tired, grumpy old men.

"You're being incredibly transparent, Aziel," Silas says, stepping in. "While I've come to accept that you like to lash out like a child, this is a new low. I will not be taking Shay, so you can either get rid of her or get rid of us."

Aziel appears genuinely shocked for a moment, his eyes widening before narrowing. He turns his attention to Gray for confirmation, an angry snarl spreading across his lips as I feel the incubus's head nod against mine.

"You choose the human over me?" he asks.

Silas scoffs. "In a sad attempt to distance yourself from Charlie, you are choosing Shay over us. We have not shifted our stance. You are the one moving it and expecting us to follow."

Aziel waves an arm toward me. "You overestimate my emotions toward the human. This timing is purely coincidental."

Silas blinks but doesn't respond.

Even I must admit his acceptance of Shay is too coincidental to ignore. I would've never said it myself, but it does seem like he's doing this in a sad attempt to hide his feelings for me.

For being old as dirt, he sure does act like a petulant child at times. I suppose that's the attitude that comes with being a royal and having not been told *no* enough growing up.

I feel bad for the female he ends up with because it won't be me after this. I may have considered it during a moment of temporary weakness, but I'm not interested in a man who is this insecure and scared of his emotions.

Aziel places his fingers underneath Shay's chin and turns her face toward his. She preens underneath the gentle touch before kissing him.

It's disgusting.

Silas looks at me, but I ignore his stare as Gray nudges me toward the door.

"Let's go back to bed," he whispers. "Silas will stay and watch."

My heart drops. "Stay and watch?"

Gray hums, the noise quiet and sad. "To make sure Aziel doesn't do anything stupid and trigger the bond," he clarifies. "I'm sorry Aziel kissed her in front of you. Wraths are the most vengeful of the demons, but this is unexpected even from him."

Does he think I'm upset by this? Admittedly, I am, but I refuse to let it be shown as I laugh and wave the concern away.

"I don't care what Aziel does," I lie.

Gray hums. "You know Silas and I won't let anything happen to you, right?"

I nod, hoping what Silas said to Aziel about not wanting her was true. I doubt Aziel will follow through without their blessing. The man's a dick, but I'm willing to bet he cares more for Gray and Silas than he does Shay.

"When's he leaving again?" I ask instead.

Chapter Twenty-Five

AZIEL

I CAN'T HELP but listen to Gray comfort Charlie while Shay smashes her lips against mine. She's rough as she forces her tongue between my lips and prods at the inside of my mouth, but I let her do what she wants as I focus my attention on Gray's conversation.

The human wasn't nearly as upset as I anticipated, and I'm interested in hearing if that attitude changes when she's alone with Gray. My anger grows when it doesn't, but the pulsating thread of hurt that feeds into me through Gray's bond keeps that emotion in check.

Gray whispered that she was developing feelings for me, stating she's been having dreams about us, but now I know that to be incorrect. I should've known better than to believe him.

He's not one to lie, but it wouldn't be the first time he's stretched the truth to sway my opinion on something.

And to think I almost began to regret bringing Shay here.

It's unfortunate that my desires shifted from managing my kingdom to taking a female so abruptly, and I can't help that Charlie happened to be the female in my presence when that happened. It's purely coincidental.

The pits were supposed to help me get over her, but Charlie's still taking up more space in my mind than I'd care to admit. She's seeping in too far, and I hope Shay will fix that. She fucking better. Otherwise, this entire thing is a waste of time.

Shay whines when I don't return her kiss, and she lowers her lips to my jaw instead. I know she's trying to provoke some physical reaction from me, but she should know she will not get one by now.

Despite my best attempts, I can't seem to get aroused by anything she does. She's arguably an attractive woman, but my mind is still too stuck on Charlie to enjoy Shay.

I hope that will change when I bond with her, though. Shay's the only female Silas and Gray have ever shown any interest in, and I'm willing to tie myself to a woman I don't particularly enjoy if it makes the other two content.

Silas clears his throat and leans against the wall as she brings her attack to my neck. I watch him, surprised by how against this idea he is. He was the one who suggested we consider taking Shay all those years ago. It was I who was against it.

I'm willing to bet if it weren't for Charlie's interference in our lives, he wouldn't have an issue with this. The human's ruining everything.

"Enjoying the show?" I ask.

Silas's staring is getting annoying.

He sucks in a slow, deep breath and shakes his head. "No."

His face pinches as Shay rolls her hips into mine, but I don't stop her. He's in no place to judge me when he's running around playing house with Charlie every time I leave.

I saw her kissing him while I was probing around in his head. The memory practically threw itself at me when I seeped into his mind, its aggressive intrusion signaling that it was weighing heavy on him.

For a brief moment, I was him, and it was *my* hair she was pulling as she ground herself against my thigh. He can sit here and pretend Charlie's nothing more than Gray's annoying female, but I could feel his excitement and hope as she planted her lips on his.

He might not want to admit it, but she has him wrapped around her little finger.

"You and Charlie are getting close," I say, carefully watching his reaction.

Despite his calm facade, his eyes dart toward the door for a quick moment as he listens and scans the house for her. Her timid footfalls as she follows Gray upstairs make their way to my ears, and I find myself momentarily distracted by them.

Gray reeked of her tonight, his pores seeping nothing but her scent. Despite the relief I know I should feel at the knowledge that she's feeding him so well, I find myself clenching my jaw and shaking Shay's mouth away.

"That tends to happen when you live with somebody," Silas says.

I hum. A lot happened while I was in the pits, and I don't like needing to catch up. Gray and Silas are always steady. They're here when I leave and here when I get back, their attitude and beliefs never changing.

Now I feel like I'm interacting with two strangers.

It's all the human's fault. She's different from the other females we typically associate with—soft and weak and, most notably, uninterested in me. Most women practically throw themselves at our feet, but Charlie hardly seems to care about pleasing us. Well, she seems uninterested in pleasing *me*.

I can only imagine the things Gray's been whispering in her ear. It's in his nature to try to create an environment of free-flowing lust, and he's always been eager to have one in this home.

He could have one with Shay if he weren't being so stubborn.

I should've clarified I don't intend to turn back on my word and remove my claim on Charlie. This doesn't have to be a Charlie versus Shay situation. It's simply a Charlie, *then* Shay.

I'm willing to let Gray have the human until she grows old and dies.

"Why are you so against Shay?" I ask.

Silas raises a brow and turns his attention to her. She spins to meet his gaze, her back straightening and head held high as all high-bred females have been taught. They show no weakness and meet the stares of men head-on.

It's a shame she's so shit at fighting. I was disappointed by her inability to defend herself in the pits, and no coaching was helping. She didn't even seem that excited about it, either.

"She's fun, but she's not a woman I'd ever want to bond with," Silas eventually responds. He holds eye contact with her as he speaks. "I want a female I can love, not a selfish, cruel one who serves as only a mediocre fuck."

I hold back a groan as Shay tenses in my lap, and I wrap my arm around her waist to keep her seated. I don't want her picking a fight with Silas.

I can tell he's not in the mood for a friendly spar. He'd kill her. I'm sure the only reason he hasn't done so yet is because he doesn't want to deal with my anger afterward, but there's not much I can do if he's directly challenged.

A challenge is a challenge. It would be a fair kill.

"Why did you bring Shay here?" he asks. "Is this some sad attempt to make Charlie jealous? She'll never care for you if you keep treating her like she's disposable."

I shrug, feigning indifference. "She *is* disposable."

Even if I don't want her to be, she still is. Her entire life is just a tiny blip compared to mine, and she offers no skillsets that would even remotely serve to make her indispensable. She is, in every sense of the word, disposable.

Silas laughs. "Try saying that to Gray."

"What's that supposed to mean?"

"You missed a lot in the time you've been gone," Silas says. "He loves the human and has already begun whispering to her about bonding."

Shay snorts. "He would never."

Silas glances to the side, the action just enough for me to realize this is a sensitive topic for him, too. Has he thought about bonding with Charlie? Why would Gray go to Silas about it before me?

My body warms at the thought of bonding with her, of finally feeling her soft flesh on mine, but I push the idea aside before it gets out of hand. We could never bond with a human. It's not even worth considering or fantasizing about.

While Silas and Gray like to believe we'll pick a bonded mate out of love, the sad truth of the matter is that it will be a political play. I'll do my best to find a female we all care for, but at the end of the day, the one we choose will need to benefit my position.

Shay's uncle is the king of Envy, and her ties to him are strong.

"He'd never suggest we bond with a human," I say before turning toward Shay. "Leave."

She scoffs and crosses her arms over her chest, clearly unhappy with my order. This situation has made her cocky, and I resist the urge to roll my eyes as I grab her jaw. She flinches as my fingers dig into the bone on both sides of her mouth, but she continues to meet my gaze dead on.

"We want a female who obeys us," I spit. "If you can't give that, it seems as if I've made a mistake."

In all honesty, we'll need a female who can hold her own

against us, but I don't trust Shay enough to let her sit here and eavesdrop on this conversation. There will be riots if my people hear we are discussing bonding a human, and Shay loves to gossip.

Her eyes flash with anger before she gives in and leaves. I readjust as her weight is removed from my lap, a relieved sigh slipping from my lips as I fix my pants and stretch my legs.

She's not heavy, but having her on me was sure as fuck uncomfortable.

"I made it clear that Charlie is only temporary when I bought her," I say, continuing the conversation.

What happened while I was gone that Gray decided Charlie would be our bonded mate? I know he wants her to serve all three of us in some capacity, but never as our mate.

My lips flatten into a straight line as I force my mind into Silas's head.

He groans and fights it at first, pushing against me, but I ignore it and enter anyway. I know it's risky entering a fate's mind, but he's keeping things from me and I need to understand what's happening if I'm to fix it.

His thoughts are a maze, and I shut my eyes to focus as I find a memory of Asmod. He and Valentine sit at our dining table discussing my bond with Gray, and I grow still as I hear the insults he spits toward my incubus.

He's lucky I wasn't there.

The conversation shifts to the uproar that bonding with Charlie would cause, and I mentally groan as Silas and Gray fall perfectly for his trick. Nobody would be dumb enough to think we'd bond with the human, and Asmod was sneaky in the way he put the idea in their heads.

I'm sure Gray was already thinking about it, always the optimist, but I can feel in Silas the moment he realized it was an option. The fucking warmth he felt in his chest as the potential settled over him has me reaching up and pinching my nose.

Asmod likes that I'm with Gray, and he only cares that we don't choose a female who will take my affections away from his kingdom. The humans are practically extinct, and bonding with her means I have one less consideration to make in my decisions.

It's less competition for him and his people. He *wants* us to choose her.

"You've got to be kidding me." I groan. "Gray wants to bond with every woman he finds himself in a relationship with. You shouldn't have supported those thoughts."

Gray, even on his best days, is petty and stubborn. If he's gotten it in his head that we should bond with Charlie, it should've been removed immediately and not left to simmer. I suppose it makes sense why he was so against Shay.

He isn't thinking of Charlie as a female who will die in sixty years. In his mind, it *is* Charlie versus Shay.

"You need to tell him it's not going to happen," I order.

Silas surprises me as he kicks off the wall and shakes his head.

"No. If Charlie wants to be our female, I think she deserves the opportunity to fight for it."

"Fight for it?" Is he dumb? "She wouldn't stand a chance against even the weakest demons. They'd snap her neck in milliseconds."

Well, they'd try to. Despite my annoyance toward the human, I have a feeling I wouldn't be able to sit back and let anybody hurt her.

Silas doesn't respond, instead turning his back to me and heading toward the door. My lips curl at the disrespect, but I hold in my instinct to punish him for it.

I can't leave them for the pits and demand they respect me the moment I return. Even I understand it must be earned again.

"Not everything is about physical violence, Aziel."

Silas glances at me as he pulls open the door, his exhaustion apparent even through the blood coating his face. His chest deflates as he lets out a quiet sigh, and with a subtle shake of his head, he leaves.

Chapter Twenty-Six

CHARLOTTE

I STAB AT my eggs while the three demons I've been shackled to continue arguing amongst themselves. There's not one good reason Gray dragged me here for breakfast.

I'm still recovering from Silas's painful rejection, and now I've got to sit here listening to Aziel and Shay cooing at one another like fucking birds. It's nauseating, and I don't understand how Gray and Silas have put up with him for so long.

"Is your plan to sit here and glare at me this entire meal?" Aziel asks.

I glance up from my plate to see whom he's speaking to, my eyes widening as I realize he's talking to *both* Gray and Silas.

Both men sit on either side of me, thanks to Gray, who forced me between them, and they look just as miserable as I feel on the inside. Even Aziel and Shay look stiff and uncomfortable, their backs straight and knuckles white from how hard they hold their forks.

Gray scoffs and readjusts in his chair, his arm brushing mine.

Shay makes eye contact with me in what feels like a challenging gesture. I return the angry stare before thinking better of it and dropping my gaze to the table. These people aren't my family, and I'd be stupid to act cocky. While my mom and dad might have gotten angry and yelled, these demons are quick to blow past all reasonable responses and jump straight into fighting and murder.

I'm smaller and weaker than them, and at the end of the day, I need to be in their good graces if I want to stay alive. Especially if I want Aziel to continue protecting me. I aim to remain as inconspicuous as possible in the hopes they forget I'm even here.

It worked when my parents were arguing, and I hope it works on these men, too.

Silas reaches over me to grab another hash brown, and I hurriedly lean back to avoid bumping into his arm. Besides some very uncomfortable glances, we haven't spoken to one another since his rejection. I'm more than okay with that, though. The last thing I want is to hear him explain in more detail why he doesn't want me. I got the memo last time.

He remains silent as he pulls back and drops one of the larger hash browns on my plate.

"Eat," he orders.

I stare at it, my eyebrows pulling together.

This man's giving me whiplash. I try not to look too annoyed as I shove my fork into the potato heaven. I'm only doing this because I love hash browns and wanted another.

"How domestic," Aziel comments.

I don't respond. Despite what Gray said, I still hope Aziel will leave again soon. It's only a matter of time before he finds himself irrationally angry about something and storms off to the pits. Maybe he'll come back with a better attitude next time.

He doesn't care about me, so I'm not going to care about him.

I want Aziel and his evil demon girlfriend out of here.

Today's original plan was to badger Gray for more

information on the females, but now I fear I won't get the chance. It's hard to get any information out of these men on a good day, and I know I won't get so much as a crumb when they're angry.

Nonetheless, the slight bit I learned from Silas is enough to have me bouncing on my toes. I hope they let me participate in their plan to help. I may not be the most educated person, but I've sure got spirit and am willing to do the work.

I'd try to pull more details from Silas if I hadn't embarrassed myself so much last night. He doesn't seem eager to tease or hold it over my head, though, so hopefully, it'll be forgotten in a few days and we can go back to normal.

The silence in the room is deafening, the only noise the quiet scraping of silverware against plates and the occasional sigh. This is potentially the most uncomfortable, melodramatic meal I've ever had the pleasure of sitting through.

Although maybe now that Gray realizes how awful it is, he won't drag me to another. I'd much rather eat in my room or office.

"This food is surprisingly good," Shay says, breaking the silence. "Do the humans eat this all the time?"

I frown as I realize she's talking to me.

"Some do," I say.

She hums before stabbing an egg and lifting it curiously in the air. The food dangles dangerously before slipping off and landing on her plate with a wet slap. I cringe at the sound.

She laughs. "Well, I can honestly say I'm surprised. I was under the impression you guys ate nothing but trash. Gray and I used to crack jokes about the human slop."

Aziel offers a weak chuckle, but otherwise, her joke receives no response. How am I supposed to respond to that? *Thanks?*

Shay turns and beams at Aziel, visibly happy he found her words funny. It's hard to tell if he actually likes her or if he's doing this in an attempt to hide his slight feelings for me. Although, at this point, I'm no longer confident in my earlier assumption that he has any softness in his heart for me.

And to think I was going to apologize to him.

For all I know, he's already striking up a deal with Asmod or reaching out to the auction houses to get a quote on me. Gray promises he won't do that, but I'm not sure. Aziel hates me for absolutely no reason. I've never done anything to him. He's just angry I exist.

I'm probably worth a pretty penny since I'm still a virgin. I should give in and fuck Gray to spite him. You can sell me, but you sure as hell won't get back most of the money you spent.

"Gray, remember when we were drunk and you licked eggs out of—" Shay starts, but she's interrupted by Gray before she can finish.

"How long do you plan to keep up this little charade?" he asks Aziel.

Aziel frowns, looking confused. "What charade?"

I jump as Gray slams his fists against the table. The tension in this room is unbearable, and I have trouble understanding why Gray even insisted we all eat together in the first place.

I get it's in his nature to want everybody to get along, but that's not going to happen any time soon. I don't care whom Aziel decides to spend his time with, but I refuse to sit around and play house with the woman who started the drama that almost had me killed.

Besides, her constant glances toward Gray and Silas are grating my nerves. I trust Gray isn't going to touch her, and I believe him when he says I'm his only female, but Silas hasn't made those same promises. He's made it clear he doesn't want me, and given what Shay said about him and Gray taking turns with her, I assume he's already fucked her.

If Silas decides to switch sides and agree to bond with Shay, I'm screwed. Gray can't protect me on his own, and I doubt he'd continue to fight for me if everybody starts teaming up against him.

"This is embarrassing for you, Aziel," Silas mutters.

Shay hisses. "What is? The fact that he found a woman who can help lead his people?" Her flirty gaze shifts into one of anger. "Your human will die soon enough, and Aziel and I are willing to wait."

My face flushes. I don't need the constant reminders that my life is nothing compared to theirs, and I hate how they talk so casually about my death. Even Gray doesn't seem to be put off by the topic.

I'm sure your view on death is different when you live for so long, but I'm still uncomfortable with the thought of it. I don't want to die, and they act like I'm expiring tomorrow or something. I've still got a good sixty or seventy years left in me.

Shay makes a good point about just needing to wait, though. Once I'm gone, there isn't anything standing in her way.

My options here were already limited and are even more so now that Aziel's chosen Shay. A small part of me admittedly considered the possibility of becoming the bonded female for the three of them, but Shay's thrown a wrench in those plans. I thought I already had Aziel in the bag and Silas would be the one I had to convince, but now Aziel's out of the picture and Silas is far from interested. I don't have a leg to stand on here.

Not that I want one anymore.

Aziel can shove whatever thoughts he may have ever had of bonding with me far up his ass. He's a dick, and I'd rather live my sad, short life than spend eternity with him. My jaw clenches as I secretly glare at him, angry with how much he makes my blood boil. I need to stop letting him affect me.

"Are you not hungry?" Gray whispers in my ear. "Do you want another hash brown?"

I glance at my full plate, my appetite nonexistent. Gray quietly sighs before pushing a strand of hair behind my ear. The kind action makes me smile, and I look at him from the corner of my eye before forcing a bite of food between my lips.

Gray's a good man, and there's no point dwelling over what he'll do after I die. I may hate it, but at the end of the day, he and Shay had a relationship that will probably be continued once I'm no longer here.

He deserves to be happy when I'm gone.

Gray looks pained as he watches my thoughts flicker across my face. I'm sure it doesn't take a genius to figure out what's happening in my head.

"You're my female," he assures me. "That's not going to change because Shay's here. Aziel doesn't even like her, and I'm sure she'll be gone soon enough." He doesn't even bother to be discreet in his promises.

While I usually appreciate them, now is not the time for him to publicly address my insecurities.

"Thank you, Gray," I say between clenched teeth.

If I could teleport as they do, I'd be long gone. I don't even know where I'd go, but I figure I'll be happy in any place warm and free of the four demons currently staring at me.

Once more, the room is sent into a tense silence. It's painful and makes my skin itch, and I continue mindlessly poking the food on my plate before I push my chair back and jump to my feet. I clear my throat and gesture to the doorway leading to our offices.

"I should get going," I say. "Rock's waiting for me."

Rock doesn't tutor me on the weekends, but I doubt Aziel or Shay know that. I need to leave this room before I lose my mind, though. Nobody comments on my statement, and I turn and run from the room with a relieved sigh.

Gray stands and follows as I make my escape. I'm thankful he doesn't say anything or try to stop me, but that relief is short-lived as his arm wraps around my waist and yanks me into his chest the second we're out of the room. He spins me around and shoves my face into his shirt.

I gasp at the sudden contact, continually surprised by how quickly he moves.

He says nothing as he buries his face in my hair and breathes in my scent, and I instinctively tense before sighing and relaxing. I refuse to let myself get upset and cry, and I bite my bottom lip to distract myself.

"Shay's nothing to us, Charlie," he whispers.

I open my mouth, ready to argue, before deciding it's not worth it. We both know I'm jealous and denying it isn't going to prove otherwise.

"I'm not going to eat with them again," I say, not caring how dramatic it makes me look.

Gray pulls back and scans me, and I force myself to remain strong. I'm not going to change my mind on this.

"Okay," he says. "We'll eat elsewhere from now on."

Happy, I lift on my toes and bring my lips to his. Gray has to duck so I can reach him, and I sigh into his mouth as he wraps his hands around my thighs and lifts me up. I love it when he does that, and I'm sure I have some reaction that gives that away as he chuckles and walks us to his office.

"I like when you get jealous," he says, kicking open his office door. "My tiny human is a protective one."

Gray plops me onto his couch. His movements are gentle, but I still gasp as he cages me against the soft cushion with his arms.

My legs spread to make room for him, and Gray lets a healthy amount of his lust seep out as he slots himself between my thighs.

I've gotten a lot better about remaining in control when I smell it, and I'm proud of myself for the way I breathe it in but don't turn to mush.

Gray trails his fingers up the inside of my thighs, his teasing smile growing as I shiver.

"Aziel's one wrong move away from me smothering him with a pillow while he sleeps," he admits.

I snort, unable to imagine that.

Gray talks a big game, but I know how much Silas and Aziel mean to him. Even when they piss him off, he goes out of his way to ensure they're safe and well cared for. I overheard him asking Silas to check on Aziel several times while the Wrath was off in the pits.

"You're to be my bonded, whether or not they approve," he continues.

His words make me flush, but I don't acknowledge them. This isn't a conversation I'm ready to have, not today. Not when I'm still reeling from Aziel's return and Silas's rejection.

Gray doesn't seem to mind, and I bite back a moan before pushing his wandering hands away. I don't want everybody to hear.

He pouts. "I'm hungry."

"I have something to ask you," I say, changing the subject.

"What is it?"

Gray grabs my waist and slips his fingers underneath my shirt, his touch distracting. Everything he does is distracting. Fucking incubus.

He absentmindedly rubs my sides while I collect my thoughts. "Silas told me yesterday why the Wrath demons have been birthing more females," I say, closely watching his reaction. Gray tilts his head to the side and holds my gaze, but nothing he does looks concerning. "I want to know what I can do to help."

Gray visibly hesitates, worrying his bottom lip between his teeth. After a minute of silence, my nerves begin to grow. What's taking him so long to answer? Is he worried I'm going to try to leave him? I imagine that's why he didn't tell me the truth in the first place.

Fixing the female decline means we have more choices and more freedom. He's scared.

Gray's throat bobs as he gulps, and I decide to push this conversation off a bit longer as I bring my lips to his neck. He sucks in a deep breath, and I trail my mouth to his shoulder before sucking the skin into my mouth.

"I'm happy with you," I assure him.

He groans, and I can't help but gasp as our positions are switched and it's his mouth on my neck. Gray's always teasing me, and I grab the fabric of his shirt as I push him to the side and climb on his lap. He lets me take control, and he beams as I rock myself against his hardening length.

I don't want everybody to hear, but I can be quiet.

Gray gasps. "The females?"

I roll my hips before bringing my lips to his ear. "We can talk about that after. I have an incubus to feed."

Gray moans and grabs my hips, helping to guide my rocking. I'm happy about it, needing the help. This is still new to me, and my motions are slightly jerky.

"You want to feed me, baby? You know what you have to do." Gray's voice is dangerously loud as he slips a hand into my leggings and presses his fingertips to my clit.

Fuck, that feels good. I writhe against him, my moans growing in volume as more of his lust fills my lungs. It doesn't feel like he's holding any of it in, and I force myself not to fall victim to it as I throw my head back and rock forward.

"Fuck my fingers," Gray urges, curling a hand around the

front of my throat. "Show me how you'd ride my cock."

He pauses, waiting for me to confirm I'm okay with this, before squeezing just hard enough to cut off my oxygen. It feels good, but it's nothing compared to the feeling of him sliding two fingers into me.

They're amazing, and I lean back and roll my hips until they glide in and out. I can feel my face turn red as my breaths grow shallow, Gray's tight hold on my neck making it hard to breathe.

I love it, though.

"You look so pretty," he compliments, his voice rough. "I love when you act like the little slut I know you are."

The only noise I can get out is a breathy gasp, and I continue rocking against his fingers while he rubs my clit with his thumb, his touch perfect. Being with an incubus has its benefits, the biggest one being the orgasm I can already feel building.

Gray sucks in a deep breath as it grows, probably feeding.

"Cum."

His teeth are sinking into my neck a second later. He doesn't bite hard enough to break the skin, but it will still leave a mark. *Good*. I want Shay to see it and know he's mine.

Gray is mine.

I bite my bottom lip as an orgasm tumbles through me, my thighs clenching around Gray's hips. He continues to pleasure me, and he doesn't stop until I'm sagging against his chest.

"I want to touch you," I breathe into his ear.

Gray hums, thinking it over, before nodding. I try not to look too shocked as I sit up and make room for him to undo his pants. Is he finally going to let me touch him?

It's about time.

"You can't make me cum," he says. "I'll tell you when I'm close and take over."

I don't love that, but finally getting to touch him keeps me from complaining. Gray shoves his pants and underwear down his thighs, and I gulp as his hard length smacks against his stomach.

It looks the same as it did in my dream, and I meet Gray's eyes before returning my attention to his manhood.

His skin is warm and soft, and I revel in the tiny gasp he lets out as I curl my fingers around him.

"Harder," he instructs. "A little harder."

I tighten my grip.

Gray continues to work his fingers in and out of me, his tempo the same as the one I tentatively stroke him with. His eyes are squeezed shut and his face flushed, both reactions I'm going to take mean this feels good.

"That's so good," Gray says. "It's really good, Charlie."

I tighten my grip and stroke faster. Gray's hips twitch upward, and his swollen lips fall open with a low moan. I love hearing it, his noises a turn-on.

He grunts as I twist my fist around the tip.

"I'm not going to last long," he admits. "Keep rubbing me like that. Just like that."

I nod, so eager to please. He's pleasured me several times, and I'm eager to return the favor. Gray tries to push my hand away after a few seconds so he can take over, and I fight him for a brief moment before letting go.

I want to finish him, but maybe next time.

Gray curls his fingers inside me and rubs my inner walls in a way that has no business feeling as good as it does, and I make eye contact with him as I feel another orgasm building. I've never cum without having my clit touched, but I'm not surprised Gray's the one to change that.

I stiffen at the exact moment he cries out, both of us finding our release at the same time. It feels romantic, and I collapse on him as he feeds.

"Naughty girl," he teases, removing his hand from my leggings.

My laugh is a bit more breathless than I care for it to be, but Gray seems to enjoy it if his answering smile is anything to go by. He relaxes back against the couch and drags me down on top of him, the content smile on his lips warming my heart.

Mine.

Chapter Twenty-Seven

GRAY

I'VE NEVER NOTICED just how short Charlie's legs are. She's an average height for a human female, but demons are naturally taller, so she still seems small. I hold my hand next to the back of her head. Her skull would be easy to palm.

"Come on," I urge, patting her butt and hoping she'll get a move on and walk faster.

When she said she wanted to do one last thing before bed, I thought it'd be quick. I should've known better. Sometimes I think she moves at a snail's pace to piss me off.

"Don't rush me," Charlie snaps, spinning to poke at my chest. I lift my hands in surrender as she continues. "Nobody asked you to follow me around like an oversized poodle all day."

I frown, unsure what a poodle is and whether or not I should be offended. At least she used the word *oversized*. I like that she thinks of me as large.

"I follow you because I like you," I say.

Charlie grins as she spins back around, her scent transforming into one I love to smell. My female is happy.

She doesn't need to know I'm lingering because I fear Shay

hurting her. Aziel seems to think he's got the woman wrapped around his finger and she's going to listen to his every command, but he fails to realize that demons from Envy don't play house with the competition.

Shay is sneaky, and I don't trust her not to hurt Charlie when our backs are turned. If that means following my female around, then so be it. Aziel will be forced to scramble and complete all the work I'm unable to get done, but that's on him.

Plus, this allows me to keep Charlie so distracted that she doesn't think about the females.

I've come to regret the part I played in encouraging Silas and Aziel to keep the information we learned a secret. I'd just returned from dinner with my family and felt wildly insecure after listening to them rant about how Aziel had made a mistake with me.

I thought it'd impress him if I gave additional support to Wrath, and I pushed him to keep the findings a secret. How fucking stupid of me. Charlie's not going to be happy to learn I condemned her entire gender just because I felt self-conscious.

It was only supposed to be for ten years. Just long enough to give Aziel's people a head start in upping their population numbers, but then ten turned to twenty, and twenty turned into fifty. Dozens, if not hundreds of species have gone extinct in that time.

Humans are next in line. They've already lasted longer than anticipated, and they've produced just enough females to keep them afloat.

I have to tell her. She's bound to find out eventually, and I'd rather it be from me. I can't change what's already happened, but I can work to fix it now. We can do what we initially should have done and share the findings. Charlie can spearhead it if it makes her happy.

Charlie continues her slow walking until she reaches the back patio doors, and I eagerly rush to open them for her. Rock told me it's considered polite for human men to open things for their females, and even though he laughed as he shared the information, he seemed to have been telling the truth.

A demon woman would probably punch me in the balls if I tried to open a door for her, but Charlie flushes and nods in thanks.

I grin and flick on the patio light so she can see. We don't spend much time out here, so it's scarcely decorated, and Charlie walks right past the small sitting area and down the few steps that lead into the yard.

It's chilly tonight, and small bumps rise on Charlie's arms as we approach the small garden bed where she planted her human seeds. I'm not surprised to see nothing is growing, but I refrain from commenting as she bends to inspect the soil.

If she had told me what she'd been planning before planting them, I would have purchased human soil for her to use. I'll have to order some for the next planting season.

Charlie groans and sticks her finger into the soil as if it'll give her answers, and I tilt my head to the side in confusion. She's not a very good gardener.

"I'm sorry your plants aren't growing," I say.

"I don't know what I did wrong."

I perk up. If there's anything I'm good at, it's gardening. Silas told me to let her do it herself and not to nitpick, which I've been careful not to do, but I can't contain my excitement as she asks for help.

"Well," I start. "You planted them off-season and in dirt that doesn't contain all the good bits they need to survive. This part of the house also gets a lot of shade, so even if they did have enough nutrients, their growth would be stunted. You're also watering them four times a day, which is way too—" I trail off as I realize she's not listening.

Charlie's body is rigid as she cranes her neck and stares through the library windows. The blinds are lowered, so I can't see anything at my height, but from where she sits, she has a perfect view through the tiny crack left open at the bottom.

I resist the urge to sigh.

Which of the two fuckheads is she staring at? My money's on Silas.

When I sent her after him, I genuinely thought he'd accept. Silas hasn't had sex in years, and it's always been the way to his heart. Get the man to submit, and he's putty in your hands. She did and whispered all the right things, and the scent of his arousal was strong enough for me to know he loved it, but I didn't expect the man's integrity to get in the way.

If my female wants him, who cares how old she is? She may live a short life compared to us, but that doesn't mean she's some child. She's capable of making her own decisions, and I don't appreciate him treating her like she can't.

Crouching, I peer through the window in the direction she's looking. My lips flatten as I finally see what she's staring at, and I gently grab her hip in what I'm hoping is a comforting gesture.

I know Aziel's aware of Charlie's attention on him, and he pointedly avoids looking in our direction as he pushes Shay against the bookcase and slams his body into hers.

Charlie flinches, her breathing shallow as Aziel kisses his way down Shay's neck. The anger and hurt Charlie's body emits is suffocating, and I grab her arm and yank her to her feet before she can see any more. Aziel will stop when he senses our eyes are off him, but Charlie doesn't know that.

Charlie scoffs as I force her to her feet, but I don't care. I'm not going to let her sit here and hurt herself in the name of spite.

"Charlotte! Stop!" I order as she fights against my hold.

She freezes, her eyes turning venomous as she stills. I wince as her lip curls upward, knowing she's unhappy with what I've done. She looks me up and down in what I'm sure is supposed to be a menacing gesture before spitting the demon word for erection and stomping away.

I sink my teeth into my bottom lip as I try to hold back a laugh. I'm sure she was trying to call me a dick or give some insult involving my manhood, but she, unfortunately, missed the mark.

I let out a huff as if my feelings are hurt.

"That's not very nice," I say.

She ignores me as she stomps through the house, and I avoid voicing any praise about how she's finally moving at a reasonable pace. I know she's embarrassed about being caught watching Aziel and is even more so over the fact that I had to practically wrestle her away.

I don't mind, though, and I just wish she hadn't been looking in on something that hurt her feelings. I would've rather she peeked in and saw him jerking off or wandering around with an erection. He does the latter a lot, his forced chastity and 'too cool to masturbate' attitude often leading to tented pants.

Silas loves to watch and lurk, too. It's nothing new in our home, but I know she still feels embarrassed.

I follow closely behind as she storms upstairs and into my bedroom. I'm happy she's still choosing to sleep with me, and I can't help but grin as she enters my closet to grab a shirt to sleep in. She does that a lot, and I fucking love it.

It makes her smell of me, and seeing her frame swallowed by my clothing makes me desperate. I like seeing her in my things more than the slinky pajamas I've bought her.

"Can I shower with you?" I ask.

She glances at me over her shoulder before giving a curt nod. Good. I'd have been offended if she'd said *no*. I don't bother grabbing myself clothing as I head into the bathroom and turn on the water. I can feel her eyes on me as I strip, but I find myself too annoyed with Aziel to tease her about it.

Why was he kissing Shay like that?

I don't understand why he's fighting so hard to keep Charlie at a distance. I know we never anticipated taking a human as our bonded, but times are changing and he needs to get with it. His people will be annoyed, but they'll get over it.

Demon genes are dominant, so it's not like we have to worry about any children coming out human. They'll be just as strong as a full demon.

Aziel's always been weird about keeping his emotions under lock and key, though. He learned from a young age that when he expresses them, they get exploited, but that was hundreds of years ago. Silas and I aren't his father, and we have no intentions of hurting him.

The Wrath has only shown me true softness when I'm in his head, and I know that's only because he believes he's safe as long as things stay in his mind.

He's a fucking idiot.

Charlie grabs my shoulder for stability as she steps into the shower.

I force my body still so she can comfortably use me to adjust. She never would've voluntarily touched me when I first bought her, let alone trust me enough to use me as an anchor. Despite how small the action is, my heart warms whenever she expresses her silent affections.

She trusts me.

We don't speak as we clean ourselves, both of us too lost in thought to joke around as we usually do. I still take this opportunity to admire her naked body, the incubus in me desperate to see her, but I don't try to touch her.

I'm going to crawl into Aziel's bedroom tonight and strangle him. Charlie's trying hard to pretend what's happening isn't affecting her, but I know she's upset. She wants us all for herself, and I'm desperate to give that to her.

I hand her a towel as we step out of the shower, and we dry ourselves off before crawling into bed. Her hair is wet, and I push it out of the way before wrapping my arm around her waist and holding her tight.

"I'm sorry for snapping at you," she says.

I hum and shower her back with kisses.

"You don't need to apologize," I whisper. "You've been through so much these past few months, and I admire your strength. I've done much worse when I'm feeling hurt."

Charlie relaxes, and I stroke my hand down her arm and whisper truthful praises into her ear until she sags and falls asleep. I can't keep lying to her.

I'll tell her about the females tomorrow.

I wait until she's asleep before closing my eyes and letting my mind wander. I intend to infiltrate one very specific body tonight, and I find it rather quickly.

Aziel's mind is warm, and I'm happy to note there are no others in his room. He went to bed alone tonight. Good. He's already asleep, too, which is perfect.

Being a greedy bastard must be exhausting.

This is probably a bad idea, but I don't care as I rush to Charlie and pull her soul from her body. It's dangerous and hard to do, but I'll return her before anything bad happens. We won't be gone for long.

I can feel her confusion as I lead her to Aziel's room, her soul unfamiliar with being removed from her body. My chest warms at the trust she has in me. A soul can't be removed without permission, and she so quickly gave it to me.

I materialize her into a body as we enter Aziel's room. She

looks shocked as she glances at herself and then at Aziel's sleeping form.

"Gray? What's happening?" she asks.

I grab her hand and pull her into my chest. Our forms are not real, but I make it so she can feel me as if I'm a solid object.

"You're sleeping," I say. "I'm going to take you into Aziel's mind."

She frowns before shaking her head and trying to pull away. I tighten my grip, preventing her escape. I know she's scared, but this will benefit her in the long term. I need her to see there's nothing to be afraid of.

Despite her objections, she ultimately lets me sneak her into Aziel's head. It's a bit harder than usual, his body unfamiliar with Charlie and putting up some resistance, but I stroke our bond until he settles and lets us in.

The poor Wrath never stood a chance at keeping me away.

Charlie squeezes my arms as I navigate us into Aziel's dream. I'm willing to bet none of what she's experiencing makes sense, and it probably feels like nothing more than loud sounds and bright blobs of color. Someday, I'll show her how to read a mind when we have more time. Hers is so beautiful.

Finding and latching on to Aziel, I pull all three of us into a new dream. Charlie and I hide in the corner, watching as Aziel sits at the dining table across from a furious Shay. Charlie opens her mouth and begins to speak, but I clamp a hand over it before she can give away our presence.

Aziel's too intelligent not to notice the hushed whispers of another in his mind.

"It's frustrating. Valentine won't stop talking about him," Shay complains, launching into a tirade about Lust. She's always loved my kind. "Honestly, I think Romeo should fuck her and get it over with. It's so embarrassing for her, and I can't believe

Asmod tried to pawn her off on you," she continues, scoffing at the mere thought of Aziel choosing Valentine over her.

Aziel hums, looking terribly bored as he stabs at the food on his plate. Shay doesn't seem to get the hint as she continues complaining, and I have her use her extra-high squeal to annoy him even more. His frustration grows, and I bite back a smile.

I tighten my grip on Charlie and ensure her mouth's covered as I have a dream version of her barrel into the room. Dream Charlie looks annoyed as she stomps toward them and sits at the head of the table. I give her the same attitude she had when I made the real one join us for breakfast this morning, knowing Aziel found it endearing.

Dream Charlie says nothing as she fills her plate and begins to eat. Shay scoffs, eyeing her with contempt. Aziel sits up straighter. The Dream Charlie takes a few bites before giving Aziel her attention. Her lips purse as she looks him up and down, appearing entirely unimpressed.

"How was your day?" she asks, sounding annoyed.

Aziel blinks, taken aback as Dream Charlie takes the initiative to speak to him. Shay glares at them both, her irritation visibly growing. She hates my female, and she's not very good at hiding it.

"It was fine," Aziel eventually says. "How was yours?"

Fuck. He's stuffy even in his dreams. I really should teach him how to better talk to women. He needs help.

Shay slams her fork down. "Oh, fuck off."

Aziel stiffens, his pupils dilating as he glares at Shay. My pulse races as I wait to see his response. I don't know how he will react, but I hope he doesn't disappoint.

Despite the indifference he tries to portray, I know he'd never let my female be harmed.

"This is *her* home more so than yours." Aziel's fists clench under the table as he defends Dream Charlie. "She has every right to sit here and eat."

I'm going to make this interesting.

Aziel jumps out of his seat as Shay turns and lunges for Dream Charlie. Dream Charlie screams and falls out of her chair, her knife and plate clattering to the floor. The entire thing is dramatic, just how I like it, and relief floods my system as Aziel places himself between the two women.

Shay realizes a moment too late, and her nails sink into his chest just as he grabs her throat. Her nails do little to him, but they would've killed Charlie.

The real Charlie stiffens in my arms as Aziel snaps Shay's neck. He's panting and ignores his bleeding chest as he spins toward the Dream Charlie on the floor. I know this is a lot to see, but I think it'll be good for Charlie to know Aziel isn't going to let any harm come to her.

He may be acting like a dick, but that doesn't mean her life is in danger.

Shay falls to the floor with a loud thud, and I have her body disappear as Aziel approaches Dream Charlie. She screams and crawls backward, her face upturned in raw fear.

"Fuck," he groans when, in her frenzy, she accidentally impales her hand on the knife that clattered to the floor.

He's in front of her in a heartbeat, his knees bent as he crouches. Dream Charlie flinches as he grabs her hand and forces her to hold it between them. His lips purse as he inspects the wound, and with a frown, he turns her hand over to ensure it didn't go through her palm.

"Don't touch me," she hisses, pushing at his chest with her uninjured hand.

Aziel grumbles and shouts my name. I'm not going to come.

"Calm down," he orders when she tries to rip her hand away.

"I'm not going to hurt you." His free hand falls to her exposed thigh as he tries to settle her, the action pushing up the summery dress I put her in.

Dream Charlie kicks at his leg, and Aziel shoves her feet underneath his thigh to keep her from hurting herself further. He holds her bloody palm up before pausing, laughing, and making the wound disappear.

It seems he's realized he's in a dream.

I stiffen as I wait to see how far his awareness grows, but I relax when he lifts his thigh to release her feet. He doesn't know this is a dream of my creation.

Dream Charlie giggles, the action his doing, and wraps her now-free legs around his waist.

What? I blink, unsure what to do in a sexual situation for the first time in my life. I intended to keep this dream clean and straightforward, wanting only to give Charlie insight into who Aziel will choose in a fight between her and Shay.

I remove my control of Dream Charlie and let her act on free will as I tug the real Charlie backward. It's time for us to go. Aziel can fuck his Dream Charlie all he wants, but he sure as shit doesn't need to do it in front of the real one.

"Are you wet for me?" Aziel mutters.

I pause, instinctively spinning toward him with a cheesy grin. That's not a comment a man who's encountering a dream woman for the first time says. The Charlie on the floor hums and lifts her hips to give better access. Aziel isn't surprised as she exposes herself to him.

I suck in my cheeks, angry I need to leave.

Has he been dreaming about her so frequently that he's not the least bit suspicious when she shows up and throws herself at him? I'd give anything to stick around and see what he does when he thinks nobody is looking.

I tug at the real Charlie's hand, silently telling her it's time to leave, but she plants her feet firmly into the ground. Does she want to stay? Why?

Aziel slips his hand between the fake Charlie's thighs.

"What about Shay?" the fake Charlie asks. "She'll be upset you're touching me."

Aziel shrugs and hooks his fingers into her underwear. The real Charlie continues to fight me, refusing to leave the dream, and after a second, I drop my head onto hers and give in. My female loves to watch, and I won't deny her this.

Besides, I want to see it, too.

"I don't give a fuck about Shay," Aziel says, shifting onto his knees. "You know that."

I shudder, so pleased with how gently he's touching the fake Charlie. He's going to make love to her, and my Charlie will see every second of it.

This is perfect.

My inner incubus is screaming with joy as Aziel strokes the fake Charlie. The real one clenches her thighs together, and I slide my body behind hers before removing her clothes. I like that this arouses her, and I cover her mouth with a near-silent shush.

She needs to be quiet, and I pull her farther into the shadows so we're better hidden. I don't want to risk Aziel seeing us. He won't be pleased.

I breathe in her and Aziel's arousal, the scent intoxicating. It takes everything in me not to let my lust spill out, and I fight the urge with everything I have. Aziel would recognize it and know I'm here.

Charlie's already panting into my hand, her breath warm against my palm as I trail my other hand down her chest. I lightly graze over her nipples, knowing she likes that, before continuing downward.

Aziel picks up the fake Charlie and bends her over the dining table, and I slide my fingers to the real one's sex.

She's soaked.

"I'm so fucking obsessed with you." Aziel groans, undressing.

I tease Charlie's clit as Aziel strips. He's lean and covered in hard muscle, and I can tell she likes it by the way she shivers. Good. Aziel will be pleased to learn she's appreciative of his bare form.

I'm going to tell him all about this tomorrow. I'm going to rub it in his face that we watched him fuck his Dream Charlie and he missed getting to see the real one writhe in my arms. It's going to piss him off, and I can't wait.

Aziel curls his fist around himself before urging the fake Charlie to spread her legs. Her back is arched, and I'm sure he's loving the view. It's a shame it's not an accurate description.

He's making assumptions about her body, but he's off about many things. The real Charlie has more marks than this one, and her pussy is significantly better than the one he's conjuring.

I will take great pleasure in telling him how wrong he is about that, too.

I circle Charlie's clit before sliding lower.

Aziel groans. "This is mine."

I bite my lip. He wishes.

Charlie pants into my palm as I ease two fingers into her. She rocks against them, focusing on Aziel as he brings himself to the fake Charlie's entrance.

This is the moment of truth, and I hold my breath as Aziel steps forward and guides himself inside. Charlie's walls clench around my fingers as she watches Aziel fuck the copy of her, and I drop my hand from her mouth so I can rub her clit.

Aziel is gentle with his Charlie and works himself in and out of her in slow, easy thrusts. They don't look bad, and I bite back a moan as he reaches around her to touch her clit as I taught him. Good boy.

I'm fucking aching, desperate to feel something, anything, on my cock, but I ignore the urge as I work over the female in my arms. I'll worry about myself after. I finger Charlie at the same pace Aziel's fucking, and I bury my face in her neck as I feed from both her and Aziel.

Their lust tastes so good, and I'm only half paying attention as mine begins to seep out in response. I can't stop it, and I press my hips against Charlie's ass for relief as Aziel's nostrils flare.

The Charlie in my arms is writhing, both her hands plastered over her mouth to stay silent, and I can practically taste her nearing orgasm as Aziel snaps his head in our direction.

He snarls, angrier than I've ever seen him, and he glares at us as he removes his hand from the fake Charlie and slams her chest against the table. Gone is the gentle man he was trying to be.

Both he and Charlie are too close to stop, and I forget trying to hide my moans and lust as I groan and fuck my fingers into her even harder.

Aziel grabs the fake Charlie's ass, his glare deepening as I grin and copy the action with the real one.

Charlie moans, and I return my hand to her clit as Aziel curses and curls his hand into the hair of the fake Charlie. I can just barely make out his cock sliding in and out of her slick entrance, and I can't take my eyes away.

"Look how he's fucking you," I whisper in Charlie's ear.

She grunts, her nails digging into my forearms as she finds her release. Aziel isn't far behind.

Things go silent as they both come down from their high, and Aziel pulls out of his fake Charlie with a grimace.

"Why are you here?" he asks.

I shrug. "I wanted Charlie to see you wouldn't let Shay hurt her."

"And then you thought it would be fun to stick around and watch me?" Aziel asks, disgust thick in his voice. "This doesn't change anything. Shay is my chosen female."

My blood boils, but I don't argue.

Charlie squeezes my hand, and I know this is her silent way of asking to leave. This is a conversation for Aziel and me, and I won't drag my female into our problems. I was the one who brought her here, and I'll be the one who deals with Aziel's anger.

He's always mad at me, anyway, so it's nothing I'm not already familiar with.

I try to move, but I quickly realize my muscles aren't cooperating. Aziel's refusing to let me leave, the man overpowering me. Controlling dreams is supposed to be my specialty, and I fight back my shame at the knowledge that even in this form, he's still stronger.

Aziel's lip curves down as he watches the devastation cross my face, but I hide it quickly.

He releases his hold, and I clear my throat before straightening my spine and pretending everything is okay. I'm good at that.

Charlie seems none the wiser to what just happened between Aziel and me as I take her back to our room. My chest tightens as I return her soul to her body and slide back into my own. Charlie is asleep, and I take a moment to ensure she remains that way before rolling onto my back and staring at the ceiling.

Chapter Twenty-Eight

CHARLOTTE

I PUSH AIR into my cheeks until they're so puffed up that I can feel the skin stretching. I've already finished the worksheets Rock laid out this morning, and boredom is quickly settling in.

"Do you know when Gray will be done with his meeting?" I ask Rock for what feels like the hundredth time.

Rock flips the page in his book and shrugs. His lips purse as I stare, and I see what I assume to be his fingers twitching underneath his shadowy figure.

He's annoyed by me.

"Stop staring at me, Charlotte," he says when I don't let up. "I'm not Gray's keeper. If you want to know his schedule, you should ask him for it in advance."

He makes a good point, and I don't like it. I narrow my eyes, glaring even harder in his direction, before giving in and returning my attention to my desk. The plate of food Gray brought me before rushing off sits untouched, and I use my fork to move the contents around aimlessly. I appreciate his constant need to feed me, but I can't eat nearly as much as he seems to think I should be able to.

Besides, I prefer eating the snacks hidden in the bottom drawer of my desk. Gray keeps it stocked, and he knows what I like.

I resist the urge to sigh as I glance at the clock. I've never thought or cared much about Gray's schedule, but now that he's insisting I hang around Rock whenever he has to step away, I'm more interested than ever.

He only had time to hastily explain that he doesn't trust Shay and is trying to keep me safe when he woke me up and dragged me out of bed this morning. I didn't even get a warning that I would have a babysitter, and I don't understand why I couldn't stay in our room.

My eyes are still puffy with sleep, and I want to remain as hidden as possible. Last night was a moment of weakness, and I don't want to see Aziel.

I don't care about him, and I hope he knows that.

I've already decided to live in intentional blissful ignorance and pretend last night never happened. I didn't watch Aziel fuck a carbon copy of me, and I sure as hell didn't let Gray touch me while it happened.

"I'm going to wait in Gray's office," I decide.

Rock nods and follows me without a word, and I can't help but glance at Aziel's door as I leave my office. Gray didn't tell me what his urgent meeting was about, but I'm willing to bet all three are in there right now.

I hope they're not discussing me.

With a shake of my head, I open Gray's office door and welcome myself inside.

Rock continues reading his book as he finds his way to the couch in the corner of the room and plops down. I'm sure it's not fun being woken up at the crack of dawn to babysit me, and Rock's making his displeasure of it quite known.

I wander around Gray's room and look at all his knickknacks before sitting in the chair behind his desk. I don't usually come in here without him, but his meeting is now in its third hour and I'm bored.

I fish my translator out of my pocket before getting to work snooping through the papers on his desk. He always leaves it so messy, and I've been dying to organize it. How he gets anything done is beyond me.

Rock snorts, drawing my attention.

I shoot him a playful glare. "Something you want to say?"

He makes a show of closing his book and setting it on his lap.

"I didn't realize how much of a snoop you are."

"I'm not snooping. I'm organizing." I'm quick to defend myself. "Besides, don't act like you haven't peeked at their things now and again."

Despite not seeing his face, I can tell he's scowling. Rock's in a mood this morning.

"No," he says. "Unlike you, I have self-restraint. Besides, if you get caught going through Gray's things, he'll probably get you off before shoving more food down your throat. The help doesn't get the same, easy treatment." Rock tilts his head back and runs his thumb across his throat for emphasis.

I shrug. I'm sure Gray wouldn't kill somebody for going through his things. That's dramatic, even for him.

I level my gaze with Rock and lean back in Gray's chair.

"Somebody sounds jealous," I tease.

"Excuse me?"

"If you want Gray to touch your penis, I'm sure he'll be more than happy to oblige. I can even put in a good word for you." I laugh as Rock splutters and fumbles to grab his book.

I'm willing to bet his face would be beet-red if he were a human. I raise my eyebrows as Rock pretends to be so entranced by his book that he can't hear me.

One point for me, zero for Rock.

As I begin translating the papers on Gray's desk, I can't help but wonder about Gray's prior relationships with the staff. I've gathered that almost everybody is attracted to sex demons. I've also concluded that the sex demons have no issues fulfilling those desires.

Has Gray ever been with Rock? The thought has never crossed my mind, but I hope he hasn't. I know sex and intimacy are a necessity of survival for Gray, but it'd be nice not to constantly be surrounded by people who've touched his dick.

"Have you and Gray ever…?" I ask, hesitating and trailing off at the end.

Rock shakes his head. "An incubus of his status would never be with a shadow. We can't give him a satisfying feed, so it'd be pointless." He sets down his book. "It isn't my place to comment on this, but I know our customs are new to you."

Rock pauses and clears his throat, clearly uncomfortable. "Incubi are sought after, especially to the lower demons like me. Giving them away for an evening is a common gift among demons. I respect you enough to treat your offer as the joke I know you intended it to be, but most won't."

I grimace and look away, thoroughly embarrassed. I had no idea.

"Gray's got enough weight with Aziel and Silas backing him that I'm sure he could get out of a promise without too much backlash, but it'd still reflect poorly on the house," Rock continues, each word only furthering my shame.

The silence in the room is deafening as he returns to his book and I return to my translating, both of us pretending this conversation never happened. I'm thankful Rock knew it was only a lighthearted joke.

Gray would kill me if I offered him up and got him stuck in that position.

I glance at the clock again before returning to Gray's papers. What are they talking about? Maybe Aziel is trying to convince them to return me to the auction house.

I trust Gray wouldn't let them do that, but the thought still sends shivers down my spine.

My spirits lift as I continue stacking and organizing Gray's messy desk, the hardwood surface slowly coming into view. Either he will be happy I've taken the time to do this or annoyed I messed with his stuff, but that's a bridge I'll cross when I get to it.

I bend and pull open the drawers beneath his desk to look over the folders within them. My need to type everything into the translator slows me considerably, but thankfully, Gray isn't one for decorative language. He's straight to the point in his notes and labels.

My lips curl as the translator returns the word FEMALES, and I glance at Rock to ensure he isn't looking before grabbing the file. I do my best to remain stealthy as I pull out the papers and translate the headlines.

Gray's been avoiding talking about it, but this is too perfect an opportunity to pass up.

The headlines align closely with what Silas told me the other day, and I let out a sigh of relief before continuing to flip through the stack. The few charts and lists are quick to translate, and each one raises my spirits.

I don't quite understand all the science, but from what I'm seeing, these odds don't look too bad for most species. Some will go extinct, but most will see a full recovery if action is taken soon.

I'm practically bouncing as I resist the urge to squeal. I'll ask Gray to read this to me later so I can hear all the intricate details. I'm sure I'm missing a ton by only getting the headlines.

My excitement grows as I continue my way through the file. There's an extensive timeline filling two pages near the middle, and I place them next to one another so I can view it in its entirety. My lips twitch as I try to make sense of it.

These dates are all in the past? I groan and type them into the translator for clarification, confused when they come out confirming my initial assumption.

"Rock?"

He hums, and seconds later, I hear the hushed rustle of fabric as he approaches.

"What are these dates?" I ask. I must be misreading them.

The demonic language is complicated on its best day.

Rock glances at the paper, and I can practically feel the shift in the air as he enters his tutor mode.

"This is going to be the day, this is going to be the month, and this is going to be the year," he says, sliding his finger to each set of numbers.

I'm stunned, and I hardly listen as he explains the differences in how humans view time and yearly calendars. I don't understand why these dates are so far in the past. Why would somebody create a report and give timelines for something that's already happened?

I flip to the very front of the report. Rock continues his one-sided conversation as I scan the sheet for a date.

There's absolutely no way they've been sitting on this information. They'd never do that. Even Aziel, who's a complete dick in every way, shape, and form, wouldn't do that. There's no way.

I shake my head as I find the report's date listed on the backside of the first page. I type it into the translator to be sure.

They've had this information for fifty-four years.

Rock goes silent and begins to flip through the pages as he notices what I'm doing.

"What the fuck?" he whispers, his voice hushed and full of shock. "I knew they had some information on the females, but I had no idea it was this comprehensive."

At least I'm not the only one who's been left in the dark.

Rock reads aloud at my request, his words barely audible as he does his best to keep the trio in Aziel's office from overhearing. I wring my hands underneath the table as I listen intently to the information he shares, my heart plummeting with each ominously written warning of danger and extinction.

The only warning I have of Gray's return is the sudden gust of wind against my side as Rock hurries back to his spot on the couch. He gives me a sharp glance before burying his face in his book.

Gray busts into his office with a grin so wide his eyes are practically shut. He nods toward Rock, his gaze moving briefly to the book in the shadow's hands.

"Did you borrow that from Silas?" he asks. "He never lets me borrow his books."

Rock grumbles, his 'angry at being forced to babysit' attitude back. "Yes. Some of us are careful with his things."

Gray laughs, and Rock shoots me another sharp look before leaving the room.

I remain silent as Gray turns to me.

"I'm so sorry," he says. "That went on a lot longer than I expected. Are you hungry for lunch?"

I don't move. Gray cocks his head to the side, his eyebrows furrowing as he tries to figure out why I'm so angry. He blinks and steps forward to see what I have laid out on his desk, and I watch recognition spread across his face.

"Charlie, I ca—" he starts, pausing as I hold up my hand to stop him.

I point to the chair opposite his desk. "Sit."

Gray looks scared as he lowers himself into the seat I point to, his expression similar to that of a dog cowering in the corner after being kicked. I don't let up on my glare as I wait for him to get comfortable, my current disgust for him too great to hide.

"When did you find out about the females?" I ask, cutting straight to the point.

I refuse to let him skirt around the subject any longer. A small part of me hopes he'll tell me the report is misprinted and that he hasn't been sitting on this information for decades, but a larger part of me knows that's not going to happen.

I visibly recoil when Gray responds with the year stated on the report, and the last bit of hope I was hanging on to dies. Gray winces at my body's reaction to him, his shoulders rolling forward and chin dropping to his chest in what I assume is supposed to be a display of shame.

"Why?" I ask.

I can't bring myself to meet his eye. Instead, I flip through the report until I reach the page on extinction. Dozens of species were estimated to be extinct in the next fifty years, and I feel an overwhelming sense of grief as I read through them.

This could have been prevented.

I find humans on this list, my kind estimated to go extinct in seventeen years. It's a miracle we're still around, but it's no secret we're hurting. Even if we wanted to, I doubt we'll ever be able to repair what we've lost. The human gene is spread thin, and unless all the other human females and I procreate exclusively with human males, we'll be diluted until there's nothing left.

"It was only supposed to be for ten years, but then we got busy and, I don't know, we just didn't think about it," Gray explains, each word feeling like a knife to my chest. "We never—"

I raise my hand, unable to handle hearing another pathetic justification. There's nothing he can say to make this better.

There's no excuse.

My bottom lip quivers as I read the list of now-extinct species. Gray remains quiet as I make my way through them, his hands running through his hair and messing up the neatly styled strands. He's visibly uncomfortable as I force him to hear the names of all the species he's condemned, but I don't care. He deserves it.

"What was so important that it came before the females?" I ask.

Gray sucks in a sharp breath and glances to the left. I watch with a clenched jaw as he gnaws anxiously at his bottom lip. After a good minute or two of waiting, I realize he doesn't have an answer.

Nothing was stopping them. They just didn't care enough to do anything.

I push back my chair and stand. I need to get out of here.

"You're a selfish prick," I say.

Gray shakes his head and stands, his need to defend himself only worsening my current contempt.

"Charlie," he pleads.

"Millions of people have died because of you!" I cut him off as I grab the report and roughly shove the papers in his direction. "All because you didn't find it worth your time to tell anybody you found the cause for the extension of an entire fucking gender."

I step back as he moves forward. The absolute last thing I want is his hands on me.

"It was only supposed to be for ten years," he repeats.

"Ten *years*?" I let out a dry laugh. "Why the fuck did you decide to wait ten years in the first place?"

"To give the Wraths time to get their numbers up before—"

"You're not even a fucking Wrath!" I scream, losing the last bit of composure I have.

I run my hands through my hair before gripping and tugging

the strands. All this for the fucking Wraths? Is Gray so desperate for Aziel's approval that he happily agreed to let us die out? Is he that fucking pathetic?

"Charlie, I'm sorry," Gray pleads, taking a step forward. I back away. "It's not too late to do something. We can still make it better."

I snort. He can't seriously expect me to believe that. I don't trust Gray as far as I can throw him.

"I promise," Gray continues. "Aziel changed Wrath's laws and built female rehabilitation centers throughout the kingdom. The women are happy, and we've had a boom in female births these last twenty-five years. We can help others do the same."

I shake my head. "I don't believe you."

Gray recoils and turns toward the door just as Aziel and Silas wander in. Both men look confused as they glance between Gray and me, clearly coming to investigate what all the yelling is about.

I glare at all three of them, my blood boiling as I stare at the reason my life is the way it is. They're all monsters. Heartless, selfish monsters.

"Why's the human yelling?" Aziel asks.

"Why am I yelling?" I ask, my sarcasm thick. "I'm yelling because you three are a bunch of selfish pricks."

Aziel blinks, looking shocked at my sudden outburst. Silas mirrors that reaction, and Gray stares at me like a lost puppy. An evil, face-eating, human-murdering puppy.

"It's your fault I was sold," I say, gesturing wildly in their direction. "It's your fault my father's dead and my mother's stuck in some facility. I would have a normal fucking life if it weren't for you three!"

My voice cracks, but I manage to keep my eyes dry and tone level despite my heightened emotions.

Aziel rolls his eyes, his disrespect and disinterest in how his decisions have affected mine and millions of other females' lives making me blind with rage. Before I can think better of it, I grab the paperweight from Gray's desk and chuck it at him.

He steps to the side and watches it sail past his head. My chest heaves as adrenaline rushes through me, my body gearing up for a fight. I shouldn't have done that.

Aziel picks up the paperweight as Gray moves closer. I skirt away from the incubus when he gets too close. Gray frowns at my rejection, his lust slipping out before he collects himself and reels it back in.

I ignore the involuntary clenching of my sex as the pheromones reach my nose.

"I'm disappointed in all of you," I say. "Which should be surprising, considering how low my expectations were in the first place."

"Charlie!" Gray pleads as I grab the doorknob, and I pretend I don't hear him as I rip open the door.

"Go fuck yourself," I add for good measure, wanting to make sure he knows where he currently stands.

The room goes silent as I curse at Gray. I know I'll have to talk to them eventually and probably face punishment for throwing a weight at Aziel's head, but I can't bring myself to think about that.

I storm out of the room.

They casually sat by and watched as the female numbers dwindled. It never occurred to them to share the information even as they saw us subjected to harsher and harsher treatment. Males have grown feral with desperation, and they sat back and let it happen while Wrath flourished.

I've realized their age has made them jaded and callous on specific subjects, especially death, but what they've done here is beyond that. It's monstrous.

They are monstrous.

I can hear Gray following me, but I ignore him. He comes to a halt as I approach my bedroom, and he thankfully doesn't try to enter as I step inside and slam the door shut.

I didn't think to grab anything to entertain myself with, and I regret not taking the female report and translator with me.

I throw myself onto the bed and crawl underneath the covers. My clothing is uncomfortable and itchy, but I don't bother removing it. Hiding beneath the sheets, I curl into a tight ball and try to recall all the information I read.

Even if the demons do decide to help, the damage is irreversible. Many will be able to recover, but most won't. My kind included.

My head aches, and I wipe angrily at my cheeks as I focus on the sound of Gray moving around in his room.

I thought I loved him, but how can I love somebody who hurt so many people? It says a lot about who he is, and that person is not one I want to associate myself with. Behind his pleading eyes and soft gestures is a man who has no problem with mass genocide.

I'm not sure how long I spend in my room, but eventually, I hear a light tapping at my door. There's a quiet squeak as it's pushed open and something is set on my floor. I wait until the latch clicks shut before climbing out from underneath the covers and looking to see what's been left.

I frown, angry at Gray's thoughtfulness when I'm mad. He's left a plate full of sugary snacks and treats, and I shove a brownie down my throat before repeating the action with a chocolate chip cookie.

Fuck him.

"Charlie?" Gray's voice travels from the other side of the door.

Has he been standing outside waiting for me to get out of bed?

"I know I fucked up," he says. "Will you please speak to me?"

I set the plate on the dresser and crawl back into bed without responding. He says my name a few more times before seemingly giving up and going away. I stare at the ceiling and count the tiles.

I knew this was too good to be true. Gray was too good to be true.

Chapter Twenty-Nine

CHARLOTTE

GRAY'S LOOMING SHADOW is the first thing I see when I wake up, and I groan before rolling away. How long has he been standing next to my bed?

I'm not sure I want to know.

"You've been in here for twenty hours now," he says. "Do you want me to tell Rock you aren't coming today?"

I flinch as the weight of his hand is pressed into my hip, and I don't hesitate to reach out and shove it off. I don't want him touching me. Gray's shoes squeak against the floor as he backs away, and I take that as my cue to get up and throw on some clothes.

Gray quietly watches as I step into my closet to get dressed, and he remains a safe distance away as I leave the room and head to my office. He seems to have gotten the hint that I don't want anything to do with him right now. Good.

Silas, Aziel, and Shay are in the dining room eating in tense silence, and all turn to watch as I step inside. Their gazes are heavy and intimidating, but I ignore them as I walk through the room.

Screw them.

I refuse to show any weakness, and I keep my chin held high as I make my way to my office and slam the door shut. Rock's already waiting for me, and he raises his eyebrow as I clutch at my chest. I think I held my breath that entire journey.

"Are you okay?" he asks.

Why does he look so calm?

"Aren't you angry?" I ask.

Rock looks toward the ceiling and lets out a quiet sigh. If I were him, I'd be livid the men I serve kept such vital information from me. He sure seemed frustrated when he was reading the report yesterday.

"I am, but being angry isn't helpful," he says, gesturing for me to sit. "And yelling at them as you did will only get me killed."

My cheeks flush as he acknowledges my freak-out yesterday. I was hoping nobody heard. It's unlike me to raise my voice and yell like that, and I shouldn't have let my anger get the best of me—even if they deserve it.

I don't want to give Aziel any more reason to get rid of me, and throwing heavy iron objects at his head is doing precisely that.

"Although I must say I did get a kick out of listening to you scold them like young children," Rock admits with a laugh. "I'm sure it's been hundreds of years since those males have been put in their places."

My lips threaten to curve into a smile, and I glance at the ground to hide it. It did feel good to yell at them, even if I regret it now.

"Well, they deserved it."

Rock has already laid out my work for me, and I hold back a groan as I scan it. He's placed an ancient history book front and center on my desk, the topic quickly becoming my least favorite. Rock finds it necessary that I learn about the human way of life before the collapse, but I think it's useless information.

Why do I need to learn about a culture that's long gone and will never return?

Pulling open the candy drawer Gray keeps stocked, I grab some sweets and flip to the page I left off on last time.

"I have a test for you to take after you finish this chapter," Rock says.

My lips purse, but I don't argue with him as I force my racing thoughts to settle. Rock scolds me whenever I take too long to read, accusing me of not paying attention.

He's not wrong, but that doesn't mean I'm happy hearing it.

I'm finishing the last question on Rock's test when a quiet knock on my door draws my attention. Rock gets up to see who it is and steps to the side as Silas appears in the doorway. My jaw clenches as I pretend not to notice him and focus on my work.

Both men stand silently and watch until I've completed the assignment, their attention making my hands clammy.

What does Silas want? He's made it clear where his loyalties lie, and I have no interest in engaging with somebody who chose the Wraths at the detriment of millions of others.

Rock grabs my test as I set my pencil down, and I stare at him with pleading eyes as he tucks it into his bag and prepares to leave. I don't want to be left alone with Silas, and Rock is the only thing standing between us right now.

Rock ignores my nonverbal pleas for help and leaves, gently shutting the door behind him.

I glare at Silas as he welcomes himself into my office and sits in the chair opposite my desk. Unlike Gray, he meets my stare head-on and refuses to back down. The defiance only serves to fuel my previously dulled anger.

"I'm sorry," he says.

Refusing to let my shock be shown, I blink slowly and continue staring at the door behind his head.

If I ignore him long enough, he'll go away.

"I understand why you're angry with me," he continues when I don't respond. "It's justified. We dropped the ball here, and it was, unfortunately, a pretty big fucking ball. How can we make it better?"

I resist the urge to roll my eyes. The answer to his question is obvious. "Telling everybody the truth would be a good start."

Silas hums in agreement, seemingly not surprised by my demand. I'm sure he anticipated this would be my request. It's the right thing to do, and they know it.

"We can do that," he says. "And we should have long ago."

"Are you going to tell the whole truth?" I ask. "That you've known about this for decades and kept it a secret?"

I already know what Silas's answer will be. They're going to pretend they just found out and play the role of hero. Revolting.

"Telling people that will cause needless drama."

Pathetic.

I rest my elbows on my desk. Dropping my head into my hands, I let out a pained sigh. Why couldn't they have done the right thing when they had the opportunity? I wonder if they'd even bother entertaining the idea of sharing the information if it weren't for me throwing a fit.

Neither Silas nor Gray seemed particularly eager to tell me the truth of their own volition, and I'm willing to bet they'd still be lying if I hadn't found the report.

Silas clears his throat and rubs the back of his neck, the action oddly human-like.

"I have something for you," he says.

I snort. "Oh, wow. Make a girl mad, then buy her a present. So original."

Silas raises a brow, clearly unamused by my snarky response. I purse my lips before gesturing for him to show me what he got, wanting the present even if I'm mad.

I try to keep any intrigue out of my expression as he pulls two navy blue gems out of his pocket. One is fastened into a necklace, a thin, gold chain looped through a hole carved into the top of the rock, and the other is just the stone.

Silas sets them both on the desk. I hate to admit it, but they're beautiful. The stones are shimmery and full of rich color, and I could just get lost in them.

"I had these made a few days ago, so this isn't a present I purchased just because you're angry with me," Silas says. "Your lack of power makes you helpless—no offense—so I had a mage shove a handful of mine into the stones."

What? I didn't realize that was possible.

"They should be fairly straightforward to use. If you slam one into somebody with enough force, it'll explode. It won't kill me since the power is mine, and it probably won't work on Aziel since he's stronger than me, but it should bring down anybody else." He gestures for me to pick them up.

I tentatively run my finger along the top of both stones. I must admit that's pretty cool.

"Won't it kill me?" I ask.

Silas shakes his head and grabs the stone that is not connected to the chain. He holds it out for me to take. I do so carefully, afraid to set it off.

"I gave the mage some of your blood, and he tied your presence to the stone so it won't affect you." How did Silas get my blood? He continues. "It's a lot of intricate magic I don't understand well enough to explain accurately. This one's for you to test out on me. The other is for you to wear."

He wants me to test it out on him? Under normal circumstances, I'd be nervous about shoving an exploding rock against his chest, but that sounds particularly exciting right now. I stand and walk around my desk with the gem in hand.

Silas squares up, his feet separating so he has a firm stance.

I pull my arm back for momentum before flinging it forward without hesitation. I open my hand mid-thrust so all that's between it and his skin is the gem, and I follow through until my palm slams into the center of his chest.

The stone heats just a second before Silas grunts and falls back, the sudden distance causing the stone to drop to the floor. I glance between it and Silas, noting that the vibrant color has vanished and all that's left is a gray-looking pebble.

Silas's head slams against the floor as he falls, and I watch from above as he flails and grabs the spot where the stone made contact.

I guess it worked.

Silas gives a thumbs-up as if reading my thoughts, a choked breath slipping from his lips as he struggles to regain his composure. His black eyes look darker than usual as he finally pushes himself to his feet.

"Works," he grunts.

I nod, watching wide-eyed as he rips open his shirt to look at the bare skin underneath. There's a visible chunk missing where the rock exploded, and I feel sick as the muscles and ligaments start to repair themselves in front of my eyes.

Silas closes his shirt when I uncontrollably gag, and he grabs the remaining necklace off my desk.

I'm still recovering from seeing his wound as he clasps it around my neck. He's careful not to touch his skin to mine as he puts it on, and I remain stiff until he steps away once more.

"If a certain female tries anything with you, don't hesitate to use it," he says. "She wouldn't hesitate to use it on you. The chain's enchanted so only you can take it off, and it's thin enough that you should be able to break it easily in an emergency." He gives the necklace a firm tug to prove his point.

The metal bites into my neck, and I lean forward to relieve the pressure until he lets go.

"I'm still angry with you," I say.

Silas nods. "This present is unrelated to the argument about the females. I don't expect you to forgive me because I give you something pretty and shiny."

I sink my teeth into my bottom lip, hesitating. "If you don't do the right thing, I'll do it myself. Even if it gets me killed."

This does seem to surprise Silas, and he tilts his head to the side as he looks me over. I refuse to back down. The issue with the females is bigger than me, and I'm willing to do whatever it takes to spread the word.

I don't know how, but I'll figure something out. I'm crafty, and being Aziel's purchased female has to give me some sort of leverage.

Silas reaches for me, his movements slow and calculated, and fixes where the necklace hangs on my neck.

"That's frightening," he finally admits.

I nod, holding my position until he leaves.

Gray is sitting on the ground on the opposite side of the pond, his skin tanned and his body looking annoyingly good. I figured it was only a matter of time before he entered my dreams.

We stare at one another from opposite banks. I'm still angry, and I'll be damned if I let him think I'm going soft.

I'm not sure what his game is with the pond and sunshine, but knowing Gray, he won't be able to resist keeping me guessing for long.

Turning away, I stare at the water and watch my reflection.

There are no fish here, and I dip my toe to test the temperature. It's warm, and I suck in a shaky breath before walking in deeper. Gray watches from his spot on the ground, but I ignore him and splash around with a soft smile.

I've never been in woods before, let alone had the opportunity to wade through a pond.

My clothes disappear as the water reaches my waist, and I continue forward until it's at my shoulders. The water is refreshing, and I flail around before maneuvering myself onto my back.

No words are exchanged as I stare at the sky and float around, but I can practically feel the burn on my skin where Gray's watching. He's probably worried about what I'll do when he tries to make his move, but I promised to feed him, and I'm not going back on my word.

Unlike him, I'm not a liar.

I contemplated asking him to rehome me, but some sick, twisted part of my heart still longs for him. I'm lucky to have been purchased by males who treat me well, and even if the news does get out, I know it will take a while to see change. I don't want to risk being stuck with somebody else in the meantime.

Besides, Aziel's status gives me better opportunities to spread the news. I still don't have a plan, but I'm pretty sure being the female of the king of Wrath gives more weight to my accusations.

Birds chirp as I float around, and I finally give in and glance at Gray. He's still sulking on the ground, his legs tucked against his chest and his chin resting on his kneecaps. I watch as he wraps his arms around his shins with a pout.

What's going on in his head?

I hold eye contact with him, and after a few seconds, he stands and wades into the pond.

I shift so I'm standing instead of lying on my back, and I can feel my face and neck reddening as Gray comes to a halt in front of me, our chests practically touching.

Our height difference means that while the water covers me to my breasts, it only comes to the middle of Gray's stomach, exposing most of his abs and chest. I can't stop eyeing them, my attention captured by a wayward droplet making its way down his body.

"Is this okay?" he asks.

Will he think all is forgiven if I say *yes*? When I don't immediately answer, Gray crouches until everything below his collarbones is submerged.

His hands make contact with my hips seconds later, and I squeak as I'm pulled closer.

"My little female, I can smell just how much you want me."

He nips at my earlobe, his hard length pressing into my lower abdomen. I glance at the water to get a look at it, but the view's obstructed by Gray's hand as he takes hold of himself.

"I'm going to rub your soft pussy against my cock until you cum," he decides. "But I'm not going to cum, even if I want to."

Gray presses his length flat against his stomach before pulling me against it. The position has the entirety of me rubbing against him, and I gulp as he gently begins to rock me back and forth.

"I want to feel your thighs tensing around my waist as you cum, your warm cunt just begging to feel me inside it. I want that, too. I want to be inside you, but I don't deserve it."

He moans, his hips twitching.

His words render me silent.

"Naughty boys don't get to cum, do they, Charlie?" Gray continues.

I know what he's doing, but I can't stop myself from shaking my head. No, they don't.

"Have I been bad, Charlie?" Gray pinches my nipple.

I arch my back and press my chest further into his hand. He smirks, pinching harder until I'm hissing and rocking shamelessly against him.

My legs seem to have a mind of their own as they wrap around his waist. Gray grunts as my heels dig into his butt, his grip on my hips tightening. I can see the vein in his neck pulsing if I look close enough, his blood pumping hard.

"Tell me. Tell me how naughty I've been," he orders. "Tell me I don't deserve to cum. I won't until you give me permission."

I close my eyes as his shaft rubs directly against the most sensitive part of my clit, and I rock my hips in quick, jerky motions as my orgasm slams through me. Gray takes advantage of my distracted state, his lips pressing against mine and his tongue forcing its way into my mouth.

He swallows my moans as I come apart.

"That's it, Charlie," he coos.

Gray's abs flex as I pull away, and I enjoy the hiss he lets out as I disconnect our bodies.

I hate to admit how much I've missed touching him. I've grown accustomed to his warm body next to mine in bed each night, and I've had trouble sleeping now that we're no longer sharing.

"My Charlie," he whispers as I stand on shaky legs and put some much-needed distance between us. "Please. I'm so sorry. I never truly understood the severity of the female declines until I saw it through your eyes, and I'm so ashamed I didn't do anything earlier."

I continue to back away. It's not my responsibility to make him realize how awful his actions were, and no amount of pleading will make me forget he couldn't see that for himself.

He knew his actions were wrong, even if he wants to pretend otherwise.

"Are you full?" I ask, ignoring his apology.

Gray frowns but doesn't answer.

"Are you full?" I repeat.

He looks pained, and I turn so I don't have to see it.

"I'm full."

The sound of splashing water has me walking toward shore, eager to get away before he tries to touch me again. The closer I am to Gray, the harder it is to stay angry.

I want to stay angry.

"Then I don't see a reason for you to be here," I say.

Sand sticks to my feet as I leave the water, but I don't care. I need to get away before I let my feelings get the best of me and do something I regret. If I give Gray an inch, he'll take a mile.

"Charlie," Gray starts, but he pauses when I shake my head.

I turn back toward him, wanting him to see how serious I am.

"You came here to feed, didn't you?" I wince as my voice cracks. "You're full now, so you need to leave. You don't get to use your dream manipulation to force me to hear you out."

Gray's mouth snaps shut, and I cross my arms over my chest as I wait to see whether or not he's going to argue. After a tense moment, he gives a jerky nod and disappears.

I wipe at my cheeks and lie on my back. Sleep's my only peace, and Gray's ruined even that for me tonight.

Chapter Thirty

AZIEL

SHAY COULD TALK to a brick wall for hours without growing bored. She's been trying to discuss the Lust drama for thirty minutes now, and I don't think I can handle much more of it. I tap on the wood of my desk, resisting the urge to turn away from her and return to work.

Shay's cheeks redden as she tucks a piece of hair behind her ear, her heart fluttering loudly in her chest. She rarely, if ever, gets my undivided attention, and it's clear she doesn't know what to do with it. I nod and pretend I'm invested, but my focus is on Charlie and Gray. They're fighting again.

I'm not sure what about, probably something involving the way to save females, and I'm a little surprised with how nasty she's being.

The entire manor echoed with her moans when Gray fed on her last night. I thought that meant all was forgiven, but as Charlie spits her insults, I realize my assumption was wrong.

"You're pathetic," Charlie says, her tone venomous. "No wonder Nicolette chose the den over you."

Gray's response is too quiet for me to hear through the wall.

Shay stutters as I accidentally push out more power than my body naturally emits, my heightened emotions causing more to seep out. I worry she'll recognize it to be a result of the fighting happening just down the hall, but as she uncrosses her legs and the scent of her arousal hits me, I realize she believes it to be caused by her.

I suppose that's good.

I don't want anybody to know how much it affects me when Charlie and Gray fight, the bickering making my stress levels rise.

I force my lips to curl as I lean back in my chair, pretending to be a tempted male. My curse gives me the perfect excuse not to be intimate with Shay, but I still choose to pretend I'm excited. A small part of me worries Shay will hurt Charlie if she discovers how deep my attraction toward the human goes.

Even when she's fighting with Gray, an action I'd expect to provoke my wrath, I still want her.

I wonder if Gray's attachment has forced me to view Charlie, by extension of him, as one of my bonded. I've never felt particularly close to any of his lovers, and I usually end up wanting to kill them more than anything else, but Gray's also never been so invested in one.

Silas claims I'm attracted to Charlie because I like her, but he doesn't know anything.

He admitted he finds her outspoken tendencies to be enticing. Despite her physical weakness, she still screams and yells at us as if she has the strength to back up her words. It's a human trait. The sad things are inclined to ignore power imbalances when they grow comfortable.

All I know is that she wasn't like this when we first got her. She was a bit snarky, sure, but she never raised her voice or so blatantly defied us. Now she's running around snapping at everybody like a fucking banshee.

I both love and hate it.

Most species can't see past the power imbalance. It's a miracle if they can even get a word out around me, choosing to either gape and stare or tuck tail and run away. Then there are the few who do nothing but cry.

I'm not sure what's wrong with humans that they can ignore the part of their brain that screams *danger*. It explains why they were so foolish before the decline, constantly getting themselves into trouble and dying from reckless behavior.

"When will you be ready to bond with me?" Shay asks, pulling me from my thoughts.

I shrug, frowning. "I will not be touching you until Silas and Gray have agreed."

Gray groans and slams Charlie's office door shut. I reach out to him through the bond, wanting to know if he's okay, but he pushes me away and stomps toward the kitchen.

"Don't let Shay near my human," he grumbles as he walks past my open door.

Silas says something from the library, but he's too quiet for me to make out the words. Shay frowns and shifts uncomfortably in her seat, anger and envy mixing heavily into her scent.

Shay's as much of a threat to Charlie as Charlie unknowingly is to her, and I observe Shay carefully as she sucks in a deep breath and cracks her neck. Despite her promises to leave the human alone and wait for her to die of old age, I know she won't pass on an opportunity to end Charlie sooner.

"I want you to stay in Envy until Charlie's reached her time," I decide.

Shay doesn't immediately respond. I'm sure she's thinking hard about her following words, trying to find the ones that will keep her here. Unless Gray or Silas change their minds and ask her to stick around, I don't see the point in her living with us.

She's a threat to Charlie and my relationship with Gray, and it'd be best for her to lie low. Silas and Gray have had feelings for Shay in the past, taking her to their beds and parading her around Wrath, and I'm sure they'll find those emotions again in the future.

I've never been lucky enough to feel that way toward her, but I'm more than willing to give up my need for true female companionship if it means the other two will be happy.

Besides, I'm sure attraction will grow after bonding with her. That's how it worked with Gray. If it weren't for him tying us together, I never would've looked twice at him. Even if he is the son of Asmod, he was too unpredictable and loud for me to find interest.

"I don't understand," Shay finally admits. "Don't you want to get to know me?"

I stare into her eyes as I listen to Silas walk down the hall and turn into his office. He's taken the responsibility of watching over Charlie while Gray's trying to cool down. I've told the incubus I won't let Shay hurt his female, and I'm annoyed he doesn't seem to believe me.

"I do know you," I say, my eyes narrowing as Shay stands and approaches. "We've crossed paths many times, and you've spent ample time at this house during your relationships with my men."

Shay walks around my desk and climbs on my lap. Instinct tells me to push her off, but I remain still. What's she planning? She's not stupid enough to think she can seduce me into bonding with her.

"Sex isn't the only form of intimacy." She grabs my hand and places it on her thigh. "You might care for me more if you put in the effort."

I resist the urge to sigh. I've never been interested in pleasuring a female, Charlie excluded, both because I don't want to tempt myself and because I've never found the thought appealing. I felt arousal at the sight of females before my bond with Gray, but that urge has faded with time.

Wraths are monogamous, and I struggle to find interest now that my body recognizes Gray. I'll have to take a female if I want to further my line, and when I finally accepted Gray and I would have to share, Silas decided to throw himself in the mix and demand he be included, too.

"No." I remove my hand from Shay's thigh and gesture for her to get off.

She doesn't, and I clench my hands into fists as I fight the urge to shove her onto the floor. I can't hurt her if she's to be my bonded. It may be all I want to do now, but I'll regret it someday.

"You touched the human," she snaps.

I don't know where she got that information, but I don't deny it as I turn away and gesture again for her to get off. She tries grabbing my hand again, but I remain firm and keep it by my side.

"You can pretend I'm her," she says, her nails digging into my wrist as she tries to yank my hand back onto her thigh. "Your males don't take me seriously because *you* don't take me seriously. If you touched me, they'd know this is real. Touch me as you did Charlie, and I'll leave."

I bark out a laugh before I can stop myself, finding her desperation funny. I shouldn't expect anything less from an Envy.

"That's what this is all about?" I ask. "You're upset I touched Charlie and not you? Will you also demand the same from Gray and Silas? They've had thousands of lovers, so it may take a while. Or is this request reserved solely for me?"

Shay frowns, finally scampering off my lap. "What is wrong with you? You should be thankful I'm considering your bond," she says, raising her voice. "Most women are terrified of being stuck with you." She laughs and points an accusatory finger in my direction. "No high-bred woman wants to bond with the horrid, infamous Aziel. Silas and Gray are the only good things about you, and women want them to warm their bed while you scamper off in the pits like the fucking monster you are."

I hum, my smile growing as I hear Silas walk to the wall separating our rooms—nosy little fate.

Shay takes a step back as I stand and approach her, her eyes full of fear as I back her into a corner.

"Be careful, Shay," I warn. "You're letting your envy show, and I only have so much patience. We both know every demon woman is salivating over the thought of having me. I'm happy to choose one of them instead."

My wrath urges me to grab her head and rip.

I hate her, and I hate even more how the words she speaks are true. It's not a secret women fear what a bond with me would look like. They're all curious about what Gray and I do behind closed doors. There are rumors that I beat and starve him, and there are even some whispers among the nobility that I take pleasure in raping him.

Even so, women still try to catch our attention. They're willing to settle for me if it means they have unlimited power and two good men to stand by them.

I wonder what they'd say if they knew how frequently Gray defies me and sneaks into my dreams. I'm sure they'd be surprised to learn that when he was plagued with nightmares after we found him in the woods, it was me who sat with him every night until he fell asleep. When he comes home crying because he's been slighted, it's me who brings him food and wipes away his tears.

We were a unit before Charlie came along.

But that's none of their fucking business.

Charlie lets out an annoyed shout just as Shay gulps and disappears—about damn time.

"I'll handle it," I say as Charlie rips open her door and storms into Gray's office.

Silas knocks twice on the wall, acknowledging my words, before heading back to whatever he was doing before Gray summoned him. Gray will chew him out later for entrusting her to me, but that's not my problem.

Charlie rifles through Gray's drawers as I approach his office and slip inside. Her head pops up from behind the wooden desk as I close the door and place my body in front of it.

Her eyes narrow as she stares at me, and as I breathe in, I note the slight tinge of fear she emits. She *should* be scared.

"Need help finding something?" I ask, cocking my head to the side.

She gulps and clenches her jaw, both physical signs of her fear. I'm sure she's looking for the female report, and I mentally pat myself on the back for taking Gray's copy. Charlie's sneakier than she lets on, and I don't trust her to have ownership of something that could easily wage war.

"What're you doing in here?" she asks.

Charlie stands and tugs on her shirt, bringing to my attention the amount of stomach she's showing. It's not like I haven't seen a woman's bare body before, but hers is distracting.

She looks soft and warm, and I hate that I can't touch her.

I refuse to step aside as she tentatively approaches. Her fear grows stronger the closer she gets, but she doesn't back down.

"Excuse me," she says, gesturing to the door I'm blocking.

I step closer. "You're being awfully mean to my incubus."

She backs up as I approach, but I continue forward until I've gotten her trapped. Her eyes fill with tears before one trails down her cheek, and I don't bother hiding my interest as I capture the tear just before it reaches her chin.

She freezes as my fingertip makes contact with her skin.

Intrigued, I pop my finger into my mouth to taste the tear. It's salty and gross, and I smack my tongue until the flavor's gone.

"You have salty tears," I say.

"Let me go," she croaks. "I haven't done anything to you."

Other than throwing a paperweight at my head.

I hum. I should leave her alone. She will tell Gray and Silas I cornered her, only furthering our growing divide. They're going to be disappointed in me.

My body doesn't seem to get the memo to move, though. I saw how she so eagerly threw herself at Silas in the library. She was looking at him with the same expression she's now looking at me, but her scent had less fear and more arousal.

I wonder if that scent would appear if I kissed her as he did.

Gray told me she dreams about us, and I want to know what she fantasizes about when she's alone. She seemed to enjoy watching me in my dream, and her moans grew louder when I finally looked over.

I knew the entire time.

She's not very quiet, and I could hear her loud breathing the moment Gray pulled her into my head. I could smell her arousal the second I touched the fake Charlie Gray had conjured for me, and I could hear him fucking his fingers into her as I found pleasure in the replica.

"This will be our secret," I whisper, touching her belly.

She doesn't push me away, and I trace my fingers over her exposed skin as I've imagined for weeks. Her throat bobs as she gulps, her muscles pulled tight.

My jaw drops as I slide my hand up her chest, oddly nervous as I touch her breast over her shirt. I've never felt a female like this before, and I shift my weight between my legs as my body responds.

I pull my bottom lip between my teeth and run my fingertip over her hard nipple. I like this.

Charlie refuses to meet my eye as I slide my hand back down her chest and belly. I pause once I reach the top of her leggings. Her quiet gasps have me hesitating, worried I've taken my selfish exploration too far, but at the sight of her flushed cheeks, I groan and shove my fingers into her bottoms.

She flinches as my cold hand cups her, and I waste no time shoving two fingers inside. *Fuck.* I let out a silent moan as the overwhelming feeling of her goes straight to my cock.

I want to know how she'll feel sinking onto my shaft. The only women I've had are the dream ones Gray gives me, and they feel no better than my fist.

Charlie feels nothing like my calloused fingers.

My length is painfully hard as I shove my face into the top of her head and sniff her hair, wanting to surround myself with anything that smells of her.

I gently pull my fingers out and ease them back in, copying the motions I've seen thousands of times at the Lust parties I've attended. I'm nervous, and I hope I'm doing this right.

Charlie seems to enjoy it as she grabs my bicep and gasps, her legs spreading to give me more room. She wants me, too.

I'm so lost in her that I don't notice the shift in the air, but I sure realize it as blinding pain spreads from my balls to my throat. The overwhelming need to vomit overtakes me as I rip my hand from her leggings.

Charlie flinches and pulls back her fist.

Did she punch me? In the dick?

Instinctively, I try to take control of my wrath, accustomed to it taking over when threatened, but I'm surprised to feel nothing more than pain and annoyance.

"Don't fucking touch me," Charlie spits, scampering around me and out of Gray's office.

I don't chase after her as she rips it open and hurries down the hallway, her feet slapping loudly against the wooden flooring. I'm sure Silas will hear as she makes her way past the library, and I suck in a sharp breath before sitting on Gray's couch to recover.

She fucking tricked me. That bitch.

Chapter Thirty-One

CHARLOTTE

MY LEGS CARRY me quickly around a corner, and it takes everything in me not to scream when my face smashes into a hard chest.

"Whoa there!" Silas laughs, planting two hands on my hips to stabilize me.

My lungs don't seem to be working, but I'll die before I let anybody know what just happened between Aziel and me. I can't believe I let him trick me into giving in to him for even a second.

"Charlie?"

Silas slides his hands to my shoulders and crouches to my level, and I avoid eye contact and stare at the stairs just over his shoulder. I was so close.

"I'm fine," I blurt out.

My words seem to go in one ear and out the other, and I hold my breath as Silas leans in and brings his face to the top of my head. For fuck's sake. What's with these men and smelling me? It's weird, and I can tell he smells Aziel as his muscles stiffen and he pulls back to look me over more urgently.

His eyes span the length of my body, and I continue to stare at the stairs until he releases me.

"Go to your room," he orders.

I don't need to be told twice, and I round his body before sprinting away. I'm not appreciative of how he commands me to my bedroom like a child, but I was on my way there anyway and I want to avoid Gray until all my arousal has dissipated.

He's drawn to it like a shark is to blood, and the second he sees me, he'll know something's happened.

I'm unsure what Silas thinks he knows, but I'll leave it to Aziel to come up with a lie. The Wrath is better at it than I am. He's had thousands of years to practice and has no morals to hold him back.

Gray's nowhere to be seen, and I sit on my bed and wait for his inevitable arrival.

He's never gone for long, the man still insisting on monitoring my every move even when I make it clear I don't want to be near him. I know he's concerned about me, but he should have been concerned about the thousands of females he's condemned.

I'm no more special than they are.

Not much time passes before my bedroom door is pushed open and Gray's face appears in the doorway. I refuse to let any emotion show as he welcomes himself inside my room and sits in the chair by my door.

"Where'd you go?" I ask.

He doesn't respond.

I probably shouldn't have called him a pathetic male, and I especially shouldn't have said that's probably why his last female chose the other incubi over him. It was too far, and I regretted the words the moment they slipped from my lips.

We both knew I was trying to hurt him. I wanted him to feel the way I did after learning about his betrayal of the females. I suppose I succeeded.

Does he know what happened between Aziel and me? I know he's angry about my cruel words, but I can't tell if part of his anger is also because Silas told him what happened.

I'm sure it doesn't feel great to hear that the female who just heartlessly attacked you allowed the man she claims to hate to touch her.

"Have you spoken to Silas?" I ask, keeping my voice calm.

I don't want to alert him that there's something Silas knows that he doesn't, but I also don't know how to pry without giving myself away.

"Yes."

I suppose that answers my question. He knows.

Gray and I sit in silence until a shadow peeks in and informs us dinner is ready.

"Come," Gray says, standing.

I don't want to eat with everybody, but one look at Gray's pursed lips and tense posture tells me he won't take *no* for an answer. He's beyond pissed. This should be fun.

Aziel and Silas are already at the table, Aziel at the head and Silas in the seat to his left. Gray sits on his right and points for me to take the spot next to him. The air is awkward, and I clear my throat and lower myself into my seat.

"Where's Shay?" I ask.

It's a sad attempt to diffuse the tension.

Silas is the one who answers. "Gone."

That's a relief, but I'm sure she'll be back soon enough. She always is.

Awkward silence stretches over us once more as we serve ourselves the food the shadows have laid out.

Gray and Silas glare at Aziel from across the table, but he ignores them and stares at me instead. I avoid meeting his gaze, choosing instead to prod at my food and pretend I don't notice.

I'm desperate enough for a distraction that I wouldn't hate it if Shay were here.

Anything to get Aziel's black eyes off me.

Even without looking at him, I know he's got an arrogant smirk on his lips. I hope his dick hurts.

Gray probably made me come to dinner to punish me. I'm sure he feels betrayed by what I've done, and he probably wants to see how Aziel and I interact before confronting me about it. I didn't want anybody to know Aziel came onto me, and I especially didn't want them to know that, for a moment, I welcomed it.

Something as shameful as that deserves to be kept quiet.

I peek at Gray before turning to Silas. Both avoid eye contact, and in a fit of desperation, I turn to Aziel. He's the only one who will look at me, and he smirks as we lock eyes.

"Is there anything you'd like to say, Aziel?" Gray finally asks.

I feel the weight of Aziel's gaze leave as he turns toward Gray.

"Is there something I *should* say?" he asks.

"You touched my female."

I sink into my seat. I wonder if they'd notice if I dropped to the ground and crawled away. My guilt grows as I think about how easily I gave in to the Wrath, and I feel shame over how good it felt when he touched me. I hope Silas told Gray I punched Aziel in the balls.

Aziel clicks his tongue against the roof of his mouth. "I thought you wanted to share."

I sink further into my seat.

"Oh, so now you want to bond with Charlie?" Gray retorts, turning the question around on him. "That's why you sent Shay away? Or did she leave when you refused to touch her? I get it, though. I'm sure it's embarrassing being seen with the thousand-year-old virgin."

Aziel stiffens. "I told you I'll wait until Charlie expires, so there's no reason to keep Shay around. Besides, we both know that's not the real reason you're upset. You're scared Charlie's going to leave you. She said it herself—you're a pathetic male, and history does have a way of repeating itself."

"Aziel," Silas warns.

"That's not true," I snap, twisting my sweaty palms in my lap.

I didn't think anybody was listening to Gray's and my argument. I didn't mean what I said, and my heart aches as Aziel repeats my cruel words to hammer the point home. Gray doesn't fight me as I grab his hand under the table, and I hope he understands my touch to be an apology.

I'm angry, so fucking angry, but I still care for him.

Aziel frowns, his gaze lowering to my arm.

I've seen them bicker several times, but they never cut this deep. Gray clenches and unclenches his fist, and I give his hand a tight squeeze.

"Tell me, was it hard watching Mommy laugh at your screams while Daddy beat you?" Gray snarls. "How old were you in that nightmare you always have? The one with the cables. Five? Six?"

The three men are out of their seats before I can register what's happening. It's impossible to keep up with their quick speeds, but from the glimpses I can capture, Gray and Aziel throw punches while Silas tries to pull them apart.

I stand in a panic, unsure of what to do but filled with fear. I've never seen them fight like this, and I grab the rock between my collarbones before changing my mind and snatching up the knife on the table.

"Stop!" I shout, my voice cracking.

My words are ignored altogether, the three lost in their own world as they continue throwing fists. Blood sprays out along the floor before a body's dragged through it and thrown against the far wall. I don't have time to make out who's who before they're back at it again.

Bile rises up my throat as I step away from them. The last thing I need is to get in the middle of three frenzied demons and end up with my brain matter splattered along the table.

My shoes squeak as I spin in search of help, looking hopelessly at the shadows who sneak out of the room.

"Please!" I plead, gesturing to the fighting.

They ignore me and continue filtering out, not wanting to get caught in the middle of this. I don't blame them. My fingers curl around my knife, and I feel so fucking stupid as I bring it to my neck and press the blade against my skin.

"Stop, or I'll hurt myself," I threaten.

At a minimum, I think this will stop Gray and Silas. Hopefully, their stopping will be enough to settle Aziel. It's a sad attempt, but I don't know what else to do and I don't want anybody to die because of my stupid actions.

The fighting continues, and I squeeze my eyes shut before pressing harder and letting the blade sink into my skin. If my words aren't going to affect them, maybe smelling my blood will.

Silence fills the room the moment the blade sinks into my neck. I smile, satisfied, as all three demons turn toward me.

Aziel has Gray pinned against a wall, his knuckles covered in the blood that fills and pours out of Gray's mouth. Silas is halfway between the two, the man shoving his body between them and attempting to force separation.

"Are you finished?" I ask, gasping as the knife is ripped from my hand and I'm pushed against the wall by my neck.

I have just enough time to make out Aziel's crazed expression before his admittedly soft grip on my throat is removed and Silas places himself between us. Gray and Aziel stare at him like they're gearing up for a fight, their bodies low to the ground and eyes flickering between him and me.

I curl my fist around my exploding rock as Silas steps back and crushes me against the wall. I grunt and push at his back, but he doesn't budge. Is this his way of keeping me from moving? I crane my neck and stick my face out from behind his back, feeling slightly claustrophobic.

"You two need to leave," Silas says, wiping at his bloody mouth.

He looks like shit, but so do Aziel and Gray. My stomach roils as I notice a few crooked fingers on Gray's hand.

I could feel the tension building, but I didn't realize it would come to a fight of this magnitude. I thought Gray would give a few snarky remarks and Aziel would punch a wall or something. Why don't they throw iron weights at each other's heads as I do?

It was an excellent way to relieve my anger, and nobody got hurt.

"Charlie, let's go," Gray says, his voice taking on a desperate edge.

Silas steps forward so I'm no longer trapped, but I don't move.

"I'm tired of the fighting," I admit, not caring if saying this makes me look weak.

Aziel scoffs but doesn't leave. He can pretend he doesn't care about anything or anyone all he wants, but the concern in his eye as he looks at Gray's bloody nose tells me otherwise. He cares for Gray more than he lets on, and their fighting isn't healthy.

We need to work together to fix the female issue, and to do that, they need to be in a room together for longer than ten minutes without bickering and fighting like a bunch of children.

"I'm done fighting with him," Gray promises, stepping forward.

Silas shakes his head, stopping him. "Either you two leave and sort out your issues, or I take Charlie away until you're seeing eye to eye."

Aziel gestures wildly in my direction. "Charlie isn't unsafe here."

"Charlie just cut her neck because of you two," Silas points out. "She's hardly eating and sleeps almost seventeen hours a day. Her lips are bloody and cracked from constantly biting them, and she's ripped most of the skin off her fingertips. Both of you need to leave and cool your heads. We'll talk when you return."

Gray hesitates, his eyes lowering to my hands that, until now, I've been doing an excellent job of hiding.

"I'm so sorry," Gray pleads. "I promised I'd take care of you, and I'm doing an awful job at it."

Aziel's gone by the time Gray finishes his sentence, but the incubus hardly seems to notice as he looks me from head to toe. My intentions were never to cause a rift between the men.

"Gray," Silas warns. "Go."

Gray frowns, his eyes darting between Silas and me before his body's gone and I'm stuck staring at an empty, blood-coated room.

"Come on, Charlie," Silas mutters, rounding the corner of my office. His eyes flicker around the dark room before landing on me. "It's time for bed."

I blink my heavy eyelids and straighten my spine before shaking my head. Despite my anger, I want to be here and awake when Gray gets home. His fight with Aziel was hard to watch, and I'm sure he'll be in a state when he returns. I want to show my support, and falling asleep is doing the exact opposite.

Silas leans against the doorway. Nobody's forcing him to stay awake with me, and I've told him many times that he's free to go to bed if he's tired.

"Shay's gone. It's safe to leave me alone," I say, resting my elbows on the desk and dropping my face into my hands.

The last time Silas came in, he turned off the overhead lighting and left me in the dark. I cursed him out as he walked away, but I haven't gotten the energy to get up and turn them back on. It was a transparent attempt to get me to fall asleep, but I won't let him win.

My eyes flutter shut as I give them a moment of rest. Each minute feels as slow as an hour, my mind racing through the possibilities of what Gray and Aziel are doing right now.

I hope they aren't fighting. Silas is one of the strongest demons in existence, and if he struggles to break them apart, I don't think anybody else will be able to.

If they get into it, there'll be nobody to stop them.

"What would happen to Aziel if Gray died?" I ask.

Silas's sigh is loud and full of annoyance, but I don't care. I don't bother looking up as I hear him approaching, too busy resting my eyes.

"Aziel would never kill Gray," he says. "They're bonded."

I hum, not quite content with that response but too tired to pry any deeper. My body jerks upright as the sudden feeling of falling takes over my mind, and I blink sleepily at Silas as he grabs my arms and pulls me out of my chair.

Groaning, I shove at his chest, unhappy with the manhandling.

"Go away," I mutter.

He ignores my order and hoists me over his shoulder before stomping toward the door. I hiss in pain, his shoulder digging into my belly, and shove my hands against his back.

"Put!"

I slam my fist into the base of his spine.

"Me!"

I slam my fist into his kidney.

"Down!"

I slip my fingers into his hair and yank the strands back.

This seems to get his attention as he grunts and throws me farther behind him. I shriek as my face slams into his butt, and I grab blindly at his calves in an attempt to stop his walking. The blood rushing to my head makes me dizzy, and my anger grows each time my face smashes into the back of his thighs.

I have half a mind to grab the rock that dangles in front of my mouth and slam it into his butt, but fear of him dropping or falling on top of me prevents me from doing so.

"Gray will find you when he gets back," Silas says, speaking as if he's not carrying me by my ankles.

I reach hopelessly for the stairwell railing, grunting as my sweaty palm wraps around the wood and catches on the metal that screws it into the wall. Silas comes to a halt, but he doesn't release me.

"I'm going to continue walking in three seconds. You can keep holding that pole and rip open your hand on the metal, or you can let it go and make it upstairs with your skin intact."

Fuck him.

"One."

I huff, tightening my grip.

"Two."

My jaw clenches shut, and I glare at the railing as if it has personally offended me.

"Three."

I release the damn thing and sag against his back. My fingertips dig into his thighs as he carries me upstairs, his movements relaxed and rhythmic. I hate Silas.

"You're not my keeper," I say, knowing he can hear my quiet words.

Silas doesn't respond—not that I expect him to—and

continues forward. I lift my head as I realize he's not leading me down Gray's and my wing, and I search around in a panic as he carries me down his instead.

What's he doing? Silas is out of his mind if he thinks I'll be sleeping with him tonight. My pulse races as he turns into what I assume is his bedroom and drops me on the bed. I flail as I spin and try to orient myself, my brain a bit fuzzy after being upside down for so long.

I look around the room as I kick aside his black sheets and sit on the edge of the bed. Silas flicks on a lamp as I stare at the floor-to-ceiling bookshelves that span the entire back wall of his room.

"This is where I keep the books I don't want Gray or Aziel touching," he explains.

In front of the bookshelves is a dark wooden desk with piles of paperwork cluttering it. The rest of his room is typical, with a giant four-poster bed and matching dresser. There are two doors to the right, one of which I assume is a closet and the other a bathroom.

"What're we doing in here?" I ask.

Instead of answering, Silas turns away and pulls off his shirt. His back muscles flex as he tosses it toward his hamper, the fabric landing smoothly inside despite his halfhearted throw.

"Do you like to sleep in long pajamas or short ones?" he asks, pulling open his drawers.

I clear my throat.

"Short. Why are we in your room?"

I slide off his bed and step toward the door, hoping he won't notice and I can sneak away. As much as I trust and am comfortable around Silas, I don't think sleeping in the same bed with him is the right thing to do right now.

"I don't trust Shay not to hurt you while I'm sleeping," he says, turning and tossing some clothes in my direction.

I fumble to catch them, my cheeks reddening as I realize he's thrown me a pair of boxers and a T-shirt. The fabric is soft, but the thought of wearing his things feels strangely intimate. I don't want to get my feelings hurt by reading into these things.

"I have pajamas in my room," I argue, clutching the items to my chest. "Don't you have another bedroom in your wing? Gray does."

Silas purses his lips before shaking his head.

"No, and we could've gotten your pajamas if you weren't being so damn argumentative. Now I'm mad and tired, so you're going to wear those."

I'm sure my face is as red as a tomato as he reaches for the button of his pants. The unmistakable sound of a zipper being pulled down echoes throughout the room, and I stare at the ceiling as fabric shifts and lands softly on the ground.

"Can't you sleep in Gray's bed?" I ask. "Then I can sleep in mine."

Silas snorts, and I eye his shadow as he walks past me and slips into his bed. "No, Charlie. I'm exhausted, so will you please stop being so fussy? You can stay on your side, and I'll stay on mine."

I shake my head, refusing. "Gray won't like that."

Silas lies on his back, the sheets pulled up to the center of his chest. My attention shifts to the smattering of hair that covers his skin before I can think better of it, and I scowl as a satisfied smirk spreads across his lips.

"We both know Gray will be delighted to hear I've brought you to my room. He could walk in on us fucking and would happily stand by and wait for us to finish," Silas says, sitting up. "Now get in the fucking bed before I tie you to the damn thing. You're acting like a right brat tonight."

My lips purse as I glare at him, and I angrily shove his clothing onto the mattress before yanking off mine. His eyes bore holes into my own as I rip off my shirt and sports bra, his gaze never once dropping below my chin as I throw his shirt on and repeat the action with the bottoms.

"Hamper," he orders as I start to crawl into bed.

I grind my teeth and stomp to the laundry basket. He watches as I throw my clothes inside and walk back over, a satisfied smirk playing on his lips.

"You're a prick," I snap as he continues his wordless gloating.

I'm sure I'll regret my words tomorrow, but I feel nothing close to that right now as I rip back the covers and climb into bed.

Silas rolls over and turns off the bedside lamp as I settle.

I can practically hear my heart beating as we lie beside one another in the dark. My fingers twitch as I fight the urge to wiggle, and the more I resist, the more I want to fidget. Eventually, I can't hold back any longer and start to shift. Silas remains silent as I adjust myself every few seconds, but he lets out a quiet sigh when thirty minutes pass and I don't stop.

"What's bothering you?" he asks, his voice thick with sleep.

I swallow around the lump in my throat and shrug.

There's a rustling as he rolls over. I can't see him in the dark, but I can feel his breath hitting the side of my face. He can probably see clear as day in the dark, and I desperately hope he doesn't notice the wetness on my cheeks.

I feel stupid for crying.

Silas touches my arm, and I don't pull away as he slides his hand over my stomach and curls it around my hip.

"Do you want to know your mother's fate?" he asks.

Seriously? I turn toward him, my eyes desperately trying to adjust. I can't make out anything other than the slope of a nose and what I think is a jawline.

"It might not make you happy, but it's not bad," he warns, his voice oddly warm despite his earlier annoyance with me. "Fates are secret. You can't tell anybody, or it might hurt the balance."

Why would her fate not make me happy? Will he get in trouble for telling me? Silas pulls me closer.

Is he cuddling me because he wants to or because he feels bad for me? I don't like the idea of him touching me out of pity. I move to pull away, but Silas tightens his grip and entwines our legs, making escape near impossible.

This doesn't mean anything. Silas has made his disinterest in me quite clear, and I'm not going to get my hopes up, only to be let down again.

"Tell me," I decide.

Fingers trail over my collarbone, and I forget how to breathe.

"She spends a while in the facility," Silas starts. "I can't tell if you interact because I can't see your fate, but she's not unhappy there. She ends up in another realm. I can't tell which one, but there's a lot of snow and trees." His voice grows quiet, and he clears his throat to wake himself up. "There's a man. He's not human. Elven, maybe. They share the same aura, which can mean many things, but given they are intimate, I'd take that to mean they're bonded. She looks happy."

Silas brushes his lips against my shoulder, and I soften in his grip as hope blossoms within me. She's going to be happy?

"There are chunks of her life I can't see, which I'm taking to mean you're in it," he continues.

"Why can't you see my fate?" I ask, hoping he'll let something spill in his sleepy state.

Silas smacks his lips and curls his arm further around my waist. His fingers slip under my shirt and press against my skin. I try not to react.

"Because I can't see my own. You and I are too close for the fates to let me see it," he explains. "I can't see Gray or Aziel's, either."

I hum. I suppose I should take it as a good sign he can't see it. That means that Gray isn't going to get rid of me.

"I'm tired, Charlie."

"Then go to sleep."

I don't understand why he feels the need to force himself awake.

Silas grunts and releases a deep sigh, his breath warm as it fans over my neck and shoulder. I roll over and press my back against his front, and he seems content with the change as he forms his body around mine.

"You'll stay, right?" he asks. "You won't leave in the middle of the night? I'm a deep sleeper."

I shake my head and let out a silent breath.

Now that I've spent so many nights with Gray, I don't like sleeping alone, and Silas's presence is comforting. I'll probably wake up tomorrow morning and regret this, but that's a problem I'll deal with then. My feelings for Silas haven't changed, and when he holds me so close and whispers such nice things in my ear, I struggle to keep them locked inside.

"I won't leave."

My words are met with a quiet snore.

Chapter Thirty-Two

GRAY

NOISY CHATTER KEEPS my mind from racing as I sit at the bar, nursing my drink. I can feel Aziel's presence to my right, his shoulder only inches from my own, but neither of us takes the initiative to start a conversation.

I'm willing to bet if it weren't for Charlie's scared cries, Aziel would've never agreed to Silas's demand. I sure know I wouldn't have. Even now, knowing we aren't welcome home until we've settled our differences, I still can't bring myself to speak to Aziel.

I thought he cared for me in his own twisted, indifferent way. Loved me, even. These past few months have proven I was wrong in that assumption. Aziel cares only for himself, and there's no room in his cold, dead heart for anybody else.

His end of the bond prods at mine, the first bit of acknowledgment we've had with one another in the hours we've been sitting here, but I ignore it and take a swig of my drink. It burns as it slides down my throat, and I spin to face the room of people.

My eyes fall to the corner where Charlie and I once played pool. She was so nervous, the smell of fear seeping out of her pores the entire time, but I still think she enjoyed it. I sure know I did. It was the best date I've ever been on.

My lips twitch as I remember how she found herself comfortable enough to tease me near the end, spreading her legs and distracting me on my turns. I want to bring her back here. Now that she's welcome to my touch, it would be fun to switch roles and put *her* on edge.

I would whisper naughty things in her ear while she leans over the table and lines up her shot, and I'd slip my hand between her legs while she takes her turn. Maybe I could even bring Silas to block the view of the other patrons as I get her to orgasm in the dark corner, urging her to keep quiet so they don't know.

They will, but they're smart enough to keep their eyes averted. That'd be fun.

Aziel breaks the silence. "Why are you aroused?"

I take my time responding, my eyes lingering on the table before sliding to him. He's facing me and is holding his glass so tightly, I'm surprised it hasn't shattered.

"I took Charlie on a date here," I say, offering no further information.

He knew I took her out for a date once, but he never bothered to ask how it went. I would've happily told him if he'd ever shown interest, but now I don't care to tell him the details.

He doesn't care about me or my life, so why should I burden him with it?

"Pool was a human game," he notes, his voice tapering off at the end.

I nod and finish my drink. Aziel's gaze is heavy as he watches my every movement, but I pretend to be oblivious as I set my now-empty glass on the counter and gesture for the bartender to make me another.

The woman catches my eye, and hers widen before settling

into a smolder. I haven't seen her before. She must be new.

"What can I get you?" she purrs as she comes to a halt on the other side of the counter.

I ignore her advances as I give my order. She leans forward, but I hardly find myself tempted to look at the view she's offering. I won't insult Charlie by admiring other women.

The bartender doesn't seem to sense my disinterest as she trails a finger along my wrist. I pull my arm back with a scowl and turn away. She frowns at my rude actions, and I listen as she snatches my empty glass and walks away.

"That was cold," Aziel says. "You love to flirt."

"Charlie wouldn't like it," I say. His observations are grating. "She's possessive. You'd know that if you bothered to get to know her."

"She said you can't flirt with other women?" Aziel scoffs, his annoyance only furthering mine. "You're an incubus!" His surprise only shows how little he knows about me.

I enjoy flirting, always have, but I enjoy Charlie more. I want to make her happy, and flirting is a small thing to give up to make her feel good. Besides, when I'm not in the constant state of starvation Aziel so enjoyed keeping me in, the desire to seduce isn't nearly as strong.

The bartender returns with my drink, but I wait until she's gone before swiveling toward the bar and grabbing it.

Aziel continues to watch me, and I continue to ignore him.

"Was she excited when you brought her here?" he asks after a long silence. "I'm sure she was surprised to see demons playing pool."

I look at my glass and watch the foam dissipate as the drink settles. The strong scent of the alcohol burns my nose, and I let it filter through me before lifting the cup to my lips. I thought it was only fitting to serve human alcohol here, but each time I come, I forget why. It's not particularly enjoyable.

"She didn't know what pool was," I say. "The human world is different than when we used to frequent it."

Before the auction, it had been eighty years since we'd last visited the humans. They're such a small species, and they never gave us a good reason to visit. They're expected to come to us if we need to do business.

Even when we went to the auction, we did no exploration.

We teleported directly into the building, and neither Silas nor Aziel bothered to step outside before leaving. It wasn't until I went into Charlie's home that I realized how depleted the human world had become.

I'm sure Aziel can hear my pulse racing as I face him.

"I want to show you something," I say, extending my hand.

He glances at my outstretched arm before tightening his grip on his glass. The action has my anger flaring, but I force it down and wiggle my fingers. I know why he's nervous about letting me teleport him, and his lack of belief in my strength is infuriating.

"Tell me where you want to go and I'll bring us there," he suggests.

My jaw snaps shut with a click, and I narrow my eyes until he gives in and places his hand on mine. I grab his fingers harder than necessary as I shut my eyes and visualize our destination.

I can feel my body draining with the energy it takes to move both of us, and I hope Charlie won't be angry with me for using so much of what she gave me during our last feed.

She's still mad, and I don't want to take advantage of what she provides and force her to feed me more than necessary. This is important, though.

The overwhelming smell of mold and dust invades my nostrils as the world materializes around us, and I release Aziel with a pained cough. His hand slips underneath my elbow, silently stabilizing me while I work to collect myself after such a big travel.

Fingertips dig into the muscles of my arm, holding me tightly until I shake Aziel away with a huff. I don't need his help.

"Where are we?" Aziel asks.

I straighten back up and look around, my heart aching at just how rundown Charlie's home has become these past few months. The entire place is covered in a thick layer of dust, and I can hear rats scampering within the walls and underneath the floorboards.

My human would be devastated to see her childhood home like this, and I make a mental note to send some shadows here every few weeks to clean.

Aziel clears his throat and approaches one of the picture frames on the mantle. I skipped these particular ones when I packed all her belongings, unable to bring myself to take them with me.

Aziel steps over the moldy, bug-infested spot on the carpet where her dad once lay, and his throat bobs as he grabs one of the frames.

Charlie is young in it, and its contents break my heart. Raising a child without interaction with the outside world must have been so hard. It's clear from the pictures that her parents tried, their desperation visibly growing with each passing year.

The picture Aziel holds is of Charlie on her sixth birthday, a wide grin spread across her lips as she sits at a table surrounded by giant stuffed animals. They all wear birthday hats and human clothing, probably having been dressed by her parents while she was still in bed.

It hurts to know she's never had a friend. Nonetheless, she shows no longing as she beams at the camera with her arm thrown around one of the toys.

Her mother crouches to her left, holding a cake with six

candles, and her red-rimmed eyes telling me she had been crying just minutes prior.

"Come," I order, turning and walking down the narrow hallway that leads to Charlie's old bedroom.

My palms grow unusually sweaty as I think about where I'm heading, and I unintentionally sink my teeth into my lower lip as we approach the hatch. I avoided this area when I came last time, unable to handle being inside, but Aziel needs to see.

I need to see.

I can sense his worry as he takes in my anxious state, but he remains silent as he follows.

Holding my breath, I kick aside the rug and reach for the handle.

My mind never went to the female report when I came here, but after her accusations about how our selfish hoarding of information resulted in this, I can't get the small room out of my mind. *I did this to her.* Maybe not directly, but if I had done the right thing and spread the news, the humans would've never resorted to such measures.

I can feel my eyes brimming with unwanted tears as I pull open the door and peer into the dark hole. It's pitch-black and swarming with rats I'm sure were here even before the capture.

Aziel sucks in a sharp breath as the scent of Charlie's fear seeps out. Even after months, the smell hasn't diminished. The amount of time she spent here forced the walls to absorb her pain.

I could barely endure the smell when my feelings for her were minimal, but now that she holds my heart, the scent is suffocating. Nonetheless, I step forward and slip inside.

The smell chokes me as I crawl to the corner and sit. Aziel follows, and I gesture for him to close the door.

He hesitates with his hand on the latch. "Why?"

"We deserve to know what we've forced the females to

endure. I want to know how Charlie felt."

"We can smell how she felt."

I glare, and Aziel sighs before following my instructions and closing the door. Immediately, we're thrown into complete darkness, and I frown as my eyes adjust. Charlie's eyesight is not this good. She wouldn't have been able to see.

Aziel cocks his head to the side as I pull off my shirt and tear it into strips. I hand one strip to Aziel before tying the other around my eyes to block my vision. This has the added benefit of hiding my tears, and I wait and listen for Aziel to do the same to himself.

We sit silently for hours, neither of us having the courage to speak as we suffocate on Charlie's overwhelming fear. I don't want to know how long she spent here surrounded by the rats, her little hands fiddling with her clothing as she waited for the Seekers to find her.

The day they took her must've been horrific. She was torn from her family, forced to look at her father's corpse, and shoved into a facility where she was treated no better than cattle.

I went to that facility and purchased her, so excited as she was forced to stand naked on a stage and have her dignity torn away.

I was a dirty male.

I *am* a dirty male.

"I love her," I admit, breaking the silence.

Aziel is quiet for a long minute before he clears his throat and sucks in a shaky breath. I pretend I don't hear it as I wait for him to respond.

"Why?" he asks, his voice lacking the sarcastic tone I've grown accustomed to recently.

"I initially liked her because she was angry and fiery," I admit, my voice no louder than a whisper. "She is, don't get me wrong, but she's so much more than that. Charlie's kind and persistent, always eager to learn. She's got a huge fucking heart and such strong convictions. She's everything we're not."

It feels wrong to shout in here. This is a room for quiet and secrecy. For being hidden. Charlie would've never shouted in here. A rat scampers across my foot, and I let out a choked cry at the sensation. Human pests are disgusting and full of disease. They could have killed her.

"Why don't you want me to be happy?" I eventually spit out, my voice cracking.

Under normal circumstances, I'd be embarrassed by the emotions I'm spilling, but I feel different when I'm in here. I can't think straight when surrounded by so much pain and fear, the scent seeping from the walls and soaking into every one of my pores.

I know it's affecting Aziel, too. This is a common torture method among demons. We're sensitive to these negative emotions, incubi more than the others, but Wraths still struggle with it.

I don't fight against the hands that latch onto my forearms and pull me forward. Aziel's chin rests on my head as he holds me to him, his heart thumping frantically beneath my ear.

"I want you to be happy," he says. "You know I do."

Shaking my head, I move to pull away but am pulled back to his chest.

"No, you don't," I protest. "If you wanted me to be happy, you wouldn't dismiss Charlie so easily. You won't even give her a chance."

Aziel sighs and trails his fingers down my back. I don't like the gentle touch, unfamiliar to receiving them from him. Even when we're at our best, we keep our distance. Aziel's made it clear he doesn't want intimacy from me.

"I'm choosing Shay because I want you to be happy. You and Silas will find comfort with her," Aziel says, still misreading our relationship with Shay. She was a fun fuck, but that's all it ever was.

We tolerated her because she was accessible and willing, and she didn't make us work for it. I would never want her as a bonded, though. She's selfish and vindictive and an all-around bad person.

I tug my blindfold off with a grunt and wait for Aziel to do the same. Why is he so dense?

"I don't want her, and neither does Silas," I say. "We will be happy with Charlie, and I know you care for her, too."

My heart thumps as I cup Aziel's cheeks. He doesn't usually like it when I touch him, finding my actions too intimate, but he doesn't stop me. His eyes bore into mine as I trail my finger down his cheek and across his full lips.

"The Wraths will revolt," he says. "They want a strong ruler."

I sigh and shake my head, still not understanding this logic.

"You have a strong leader in Silas. Most Wraths only take one mate, but you'll have three. Silas is the strong one, I'm the son of Asmod—which makes me good for alliances—and Charlie is for love. They're getting what they want, and if they're upset, they can leave for Greed."

I lean forward and connect my lips with his before he can object.

His mouth is wet, and I can't tell if the tears belong to him or me.

Aziel lets me kiss him, the first one we've ever shared, and I slide my tongue against his before pulling away and trailing my mouth down his neck. His pulse races, and I lick the spot where most demons choose to bite. Someday, he'll let me sink my teeth into him, and this will be the spot that tells the world he's mine.

Fingers curl into the hair at the base of my neck and pull me away.

"I can't put myself before my people," Aziel whispers, the quiet words giving me my answer. "I will not bond with Charlie, but I'll remain true to my word and protect her for as long as she lives. Even if you bond with her and start a family."

I suck in a sharp breath and clear my throat, not enjoying how much of a goodbye this feels like. Aziel and I will always be bonded—that will never change—but that doesn't mean we have to honor it. We don't have to share the same female, even if that's what I want.

"I do love you, Gray, and I'm willing to give you up if that will make you happy."

He runs his hands through my hair before wrapping his arms around me and pulling me close. In the hundred-something years we've known one another, he's never held me like this. There have been the occasional hugs, but never anything so emotional.

Deep inside, I know this is the only time I'll ever experience this, and I remain still and enjoy it while it lasts. We both know I'm going to choose Charlie over him.

I'll tell her about my conversation with Aziel, and we can move forward with bonding. We can have one another without strings attached.

"Thank you," I eventually say.

The light brushing of lips across my temple is the only response I get.

Chapter Thirty-Three

SILAS

MY CALLS CONTINUE to go unanswered, and I pull my phone away from my ear as Gray's voicemail begins to drone on. I can't imagine where he went that he has no cell service, and I hope Aziel didn't convince him to go to the pits again.

The incubus was torn to bits afterward, and he refused to speak for an entire week.

I hang up my phone and set it on my desk with a quiet sigh. I didn't anticipate they'd be gone this long, and I'm starting to grow worried for Charlie. A day or two is nothing to us, but it's practically an eternity for her.

At least, that's how she's acting.

She hasn't spoken to me since I forced her out of my bed and downstairs for breakfast, her anger pouring out in waves. She was even less happy when I made her eat a large portion of her food, my worry for her health turning me into Gray.

I don't know how to feel about my constant desire to watch over her well-being. My nerves twist whenever I catch her doing something unsafe, and a small part of me hopes Aziel will return with the mindset of wanting to pursue Charlie.

I wouldn't be upset.

I've been full of regret about having pushed her away. My assumptions about her age and species were wrong. Charlie's more than proven she's capable of making her own decisions, her near-constant arguing and bickering bringing me hope. I feared she'd never be able to do anything other than submit to us, but that's not true.

It felt nice having her in my arms last night, and I wouldn't mind having her there more often. I'm sure Gray will make a fuss when I tell him I want my own time with her, but he'll adjust. There's no way I'll lie in his bed after the atrocities I've witnessed there, but I imagine we could fix up the unused wing of the house for the three of us to use.

I stand and head toward the library. Charlie's been cooped up in there all day, reading as much as possible about the females.

She would've made a strong leader before the fall of the humans.

Despite her anger toward us for not prioritizing the females, that issue seems to have been momentarily put on the back burner as she focuses her attention and worries on Gray and Aziel.

Peering inside the room, I spot her lying on the couch with a book propped up on her chest. Her thumb rests inside her mouth, her jaw moving as she gnaws at the skin. My lips purse as she peels off a chunk, and a tiny droplet of blood pebbles to the surface.

This is new, and I can't lie and say it doesn't alarm me. Humans are known to gravitate toward self-mutilation, which is especially dangerous when coupled with their weak bodies.

Charlie doesn't sense my approach, and I make no effort to make myself known as I come up from behind and round the couch. Her big eyes dart toward me as I crouch beside her head and grab her wrist.

I tug her finger out of her mouth.

"Are you okay?" I ask, already knowing she's going to lie.

She nods with a weak smile, probably still embarrassed about our night together. Her nerves are visible in both her scent and expressions whenever I'm near. I want to assure her there's no reason to feel uncomfortable, but I'm sure acknowledging what happened will only make it worse.

"Have you heard from Gray?" she asks, setting down her book and propping herself up on her elbows.

I shake my head.

"Not yet, but I'm sure he'll be back soon," I promise.

It took them two days to begin speaking the last time I sent them away and another three before they were calm enough to return home. Aziel's rejection of his bond with Gray drives a wedge between them every few years.

This isn't anything new.

"What if he doesn't come back?" Charlie asks.

I resist the urge to laugh. Gray is stuck to her like glue, and I know he'd never up and leave her. The incubus has many good qualities, and loyalty is at the top of the list.

"That's not going to happen, but you'll be well protected with me if it does," I promise, hoping to help soothe some of her worries. "I'm not going to let anybody hurt you."

Charlie does seem soothed by my words, her heartbeat slowing and her body sagging into the couch. I hate to admit it, but I love how she depends on me.

"This is all my fault." Her cheeks redden as she admits this. "I shouldn't have let Aziel touch me."

I grab her arm as she brings her fingers back to her mouth. I don't let go this time, and I hold her clammy hand within my own as I adjust my crouched position into one that's slightly more comfortable.

Dropping my knees, I sit back on my heels as her lips twitch. She's trying not to smile at her hand in mine.

"Gray was looking for any excuse to blow up on Aziel. It would've happened eventually," I say, leaving out the minor detail that this happens frequently.

I don't want her to think we live in a dysfunctional household. It's far from perfect, but we're generally pretty good, and I don't want to taint her image of Gray. She views him as a solid, forever person in her life, and she'd no doubt be bothered if she knew his short absence isn't rare.

My pulse races as I eye the gem between her collarbones. I'm happy she's wearing the necklace. Charlie watches me closely, her eyes darting between my face and my hand wrapped around hers.

I'm not used to being around females, and I don't know how to comfort her. I understand facts and logic, but feelings aren't based on those. No amount of assurances that Gray will be back is changing the part of her mind that's convinced he's left for good.

I run my thumb along the back of her hand, hoping she finds comfort in the action. Her pulse races instead, the opposite effect of what I'm going for. Maybe I should try something else. I lean forward and pull her into a hug. She follows my lead, thankfully, and crumbles within my arms. There are no tears, which surprises me, but she does release a few shaky breaths.

"Thank you." She buries her face in my chest. I like it. "I needed this."

She shivers as I run my hand down her spine, and I gulp as I feel my body begin to betray me. I like her tiny frame against mine. My arms tighten around her waist, squeezing her until she groans.

Charlie shoves her hands between our torsos and pushes me back so she can look me in the eye. Hers shine with curiosity, and a second later, she licks her lips and glances at my mouth. She wants me to kiss her.

"Do you think Gray is angry I let Aziel touch me?" she asks. "He always says he wants us to be together."

I shake my head. It doesn't take a genius to know what she's trying to understand. She wants to kiss me, and she wants confirmation Gray won't be angry about it.

He won't.

The incubus views us as family, his den, and instinct makes him want to share her.

His urge isn't nearly as strong as it is for the other incubi, and I doubt he'd be happy seeing her with somebody he doesn't consider his family, but it's different with us. He'll enjoy knowing I kept her warm while he was gone.

Charlie's pulse races as I cup her cheek. Her arousal hits me as I stroke her soft skin, and I can't stop myself from leaning in and connecting my lips to hers. *Fuck.*

She tenses as I kiss her, her body stiffening before relaxing into mine. I tighten my arms around her waist and lift, giving me room to slip on the couch beneath her body. Charlie gasps, but she doesn't complain as I set her on my lap.

"Gray isn't going to be upset, but I'm okay with waiting if it makes you feel better," I say. I don't want her to do something because she feels she has to, and I won't be upset if she needs Gray's explicit permission.

Charlie sucks in a sharp breath as I suck her bottom lip between my teeth. My canine nicks her and draws some blood, and I suck the metallic liquid into my mouth before releasing her lip with a pop. Her body's small and warm on mine, and I slip my hands underneath her shirt to feel more.

I hold back a moan as she tentatively leans in and reconnects our lips, her cautious actions a far change from our last kiss. I can't tell which one I liked more.

She took charge last time, but it was all an act. She was trying to do what she thought I wanted, and her dominance wasn't organic.

I've been watching her with Gray, and I see how she's gaining confidence as she grows comfortable with him, but I haven't earned that from her yet.

It's a good thing I'm patient. Mostly.

I drag my hands over her body. It's not fair both Aziel and Gray get to touch her soft flesh while I'm stuck watching. Charlie's going to reek of me when they get home. They'll know she and I were intimate, but they'll have no idea what happened. They decided to fight like two idiots, and this will be their punishment.

Knowing Charlie tends to get spooked easily, I don't rush anything as I explore her mouth. It kills me not to push this, but I don't want to end up with two bruised balls like Aziel.

Charlie's arousal reaches my nose as I run my fingertips down the ridges of her spine, her hips twitching against mine. I moan, loving the smell as my hands flex against her back.

Fuck.

My cock hardens as she slips her fingers into my hair and tugs on the strands. I thought she was doing it for me the first time, but as the smell of her arousal intensifies, I realize this is for her.

She likes to hurt me.

I grunt as she rips my head back and brings her mouth to my throat, her soft lips making contact with the spot where my neck and shoulder meet. This is an intimate spot for demons, where we put our marks, and I release a shaky breath as she licks it.

It's an insult to my future bonded to let another place their mouth here, but I don't make any moves to stop Charlie as she nips the skin.

Gray must kiss her there frequently, a silent promise.

I ache as she latches on and begins to suck, and all caution is thrown to the wind as I push her onto her back and drop to my knees. They make painful contact with the hardwood, but it's easy to ignore as Charlie lifts her hips and lets me yank her pants off and throw her thighs over my shoulders.

I pause and wait for her mind to catch up with our new position. Her sex teases me, wet and swollen, as I stare at her from between her thighs. Charlie's eyes widen when it finally clicks, and I hold back a smirk as I slide my hands up her legs and spread them further.

"Can I taste you?" I breathe. "Please?"

I don't want to be just another male who takes from her. I want her to give it to me.

Charlie blinks and adjusts before nodding. She's wet, but not nearly as much as I want her to be. Demon women can control their arousal, but I like that Charlie can't.

Her body will let me know if I'm not adequately pleasing her.

She clenches in impatience, and I chuckle before leaning in and licking a broad stripe from her entrance to her clit. She tastes better than I imagined, and I hold her twitching hips still before leaning in and repeating the action.

As much as I'd like to take my time and tease her, I don't know how long Aziel and Gray will be gone and I don't want them interrupting us.

Charlie's breath hitches as I wrap my lips around her clit and suck. I flick my tongue over the sensitive nub and shift uncomfortably. My dick aches, but I ignore it. This isn't about me.

Saliva drips down my chin as I work her, my actions taking on a desperate edge as her thighs begin to shake around my head. I tighten my grip on her legs as she slips her hands into my hair and yanks again.

"Fuck," I moan, my cock twitching as she uses my hair to guide my mouth. "Use me, baby."

I stop what I'm doing and let her take the lead, rubbing herself sloppily against my tongue. Unable to hold back, I slip a hand into my pants and touch myself.

I'm aching, and I give my length a tight squeeze as Charlie rides my face. This is precisely what I wanted, and I twist my fist around my tip as she finds what feels best and begins to rock in that specific rhythm.

"Silas! Silas! I—" She chokes, her voice high-pitched and desperate.

My scalp burns as she twists her fingers in my hair, her orgasm too close for her to pay attention to what she's doing to me, but I don't mind. The pain goes straight to my dick, and I frantically stroke it as she stiffens.

I'm so close.

Charlie presses her sex into my mouth as she finds her orgasm, and I eagerly lick her through it as I chase my own release. My eyes roll back as it builds.

"Stop." Charlie gasps, her voice stern despite its breathy nature.

I whine and continue as my fist flies over my length.

I'm so fucking close.

"Silas. *Stop!*" she repeats.

This time I obey, my cock screaming as I release it with a pained groan. My hips jerk forward as I instinctively seek out more friction, and I pull my face out from between Charlie's thighs with a frown.

Her face and neck are red, and she pants as she stares at me with an expression that says I'm not going to like what happens next.

"You can't cum," she orders. "I don't want you to."

My eyes narrow, and I mentally curse her as I sit back on my heels. The corners of her lips twitch at my angry expression, and I don't bother hiding it as I shove my cock into my jeans and zip myself back up.

I hate it, but I already know I'm going to listen to her. She's got me wrapped around her bony little finger, and now she knows it. Fucking tease.

"And why would I listen to you?" I ask.

Charlie's pulse quickens as she sits up and clears her throat. She pushes her shoulders back and clenches her hands into fists by her side, the sudden change in posture worrying me. Before I can ask, she slides off the couch and kneels with me.

I don't move as she leans forward and brings her mouth to my ear. Fear and anxiety seep from her pores, and I place what I hope is a comforting hand on her waist.

"Because you're one of my males, and I said so."

I'm stunned silent for the first time in my life, and I blink at her as she stands. Does she consider me to be her male? I've been thinking of her as mine, but I didn't realize she was returning those emotions. I thought it would take more work than that.

Charlie grabs her clothing with shaky hands, and my nostrils flare as the scent of her shame hits me. What? I try not to look too confused as I take the clothing from her and push her back down on the couch.

"Calm," I say, ignoring how she huffs.

She eyes the wetness around my jaw, and I suck my bottom lip into my mouth to taste her arousal while she watches. I like it.

Charlie's quiet as I straighten out her clothing and grab her leg. I help her into her underwear, my fingers tapping against her thigh to get her to lift so I can slide them up her hips.

She seems embarrassed, so I avert my gaze as I help her dress. What's wrong with her?

There's a quiet shuffling as Gray stands outside the library door, his return unnoticed until now. Good timing. I search for any sound of Aziel, but I can't hear him anywhere in the house.

Still, I'm thankful Gray remains out of sight and gives me time to talk to Charlie. I help her stand and stroke her hair, unsure how to comfort her. She sighs and fists the hem of my shirt as I kiss her temple, both of which I think are positive responses.

"Do you regret calling me your male?" I finally ask, needing to know where these sudden negative emotions are coming from.

She avoids eye contact, and I grab her face in frustration. I keep my grip light as I cup her cheeks and force her to meet my gaze. She still refuses to answer, and I shut my eyes and suck in a deep breath before continuing.

She's been a handful all day, and I don't know why I thought that'd change after touching her.

"I was wrong when I said I couldn't take you as my female, and I'm sorry," I say, rubbing her cheeks with my thumbs. "I'm not a mind reader, and I need you to communicate. Would you like me to go first?"

She nods, sinking her teeth into her bottom lip. I can see the skin caving underneath her sharp teeth, and I nudge her lip until she lets it go. She needs to stop doing that.

"I care for you—a lot—and I want you to be my female. I'd like to know if you called me your male out of lust or because you genuinely feel the same way." I hope being upfront with my emotions will urge her to do the same.

She's as bad as Aziel when it comes to being vulnerable, the female refusing to give anything away unless it's absolutely necessary.

Charlie's eyes widen, her grip on my shirt tightening as she twists her hands around the fabric. She lifts the end of my shirt with a grimace and wipes my jaw, removing the visible traces of her arousal from my mouth.

Damn. I liked it.

"I don't know," she finally admits, her eyes growing wet. I knew the tears were coming. "What would that look like? With you and Gray? I'm his female, too, and I'm scared he'll be upset with this." Her bottom lip wobbles.

Her heart hammers as she glances at the ceiling, the action an apparent attempt to keep tears from falling. I know this must be hard for her, her confusion about Gray's desire and the unanswered questions about how we move forward overwhelming.

"There's a lot to figure out, yes." I chuckle, glancing at the library doors when I hear Gray inch closer. I can practically smell his impatience. "Gray's been standing outside for a few minutes now. He's not angry," I finally admit, hoping to soothe her.

Shock, then horror, and finally excitement flickers across her face as she turns toward the library doors. I try not to be offended by her excitement as I release her and murmur for Gray to come in.

I wanted to talk about our relationship, but she's clearly not ready.

The incubus comes barreling through the door the moment permission slips from my lips, his arms outstretched as he rushes toward us, and I back away as he pulls Charlie into a tight hug. Have I pushed her too quickly? Gray knows her better than I do, and I should've talked to him about how to approach this first.

"I missed you," Gray whispers in her ear. "I'm sorry I was gone for so long. Aziel and I had a lot we needed to work through," he admits, some of his lust leaking out as he feeds on her residual orgasm.

Sometimes, he reminds me of one of those animals you find rooting around in your trash, searching for leftover food. If it's cum, he's there.

I wish I had cum, too, and I wince as I readjust myself.

"Where's Aziel?" I ask.

As much as I want Charlie to have this nice reunion with Gray, I'm concerned at the realization that Aziel isn't back. They always return together, usually drunk and geared up to pull some childish prank on me.

"Aziel's making a detour at Envy," Gray says, rocking back on his heels. "He's setting up a meeting with Levia to discuss the females. We're going to make it right, and no more generations of females will feel the pain you've been forced to endure." His wide eyes are frantic as he cups Charlie's cheeks. "I promise."

Levia? Aziel has a good enough relationship with the king of Envy, but I'm not sure if he'd be the first person I went to with this. Levia lives up to his kingdom's name, and he's notoriously hard to do business with.

Charlie looks cautious as she glances between me and Gray.

I step back, giving her space. I've made my feelings clear, and I don't intend to pressure her to speak about hers. Charlie isn't the type of woman to hide her emotions, even when she tries, and I'm sure it's only a matter of time before she comes to me wanting to talk.

I hope, at least.

Her head snaps in my direction as I put space between us, and I offer a slight smile to show I'm not upset.

Charlie sucks her lips into her mouth, her eyes lingering on me before turning to Gray.

"I don't understand," she says. "Where did you and Aziel go?"

That's a question I'd like an answer to, too.

"We went to your childhood home and sat in your hideaway," Gray says. *Her what*? "Charlie, I can't put into words how sorry I am for what we've done. It was beyond selfish for us to keep the information we learned to ourselves, and we intend to do everything in our power to make up for it."

Charlie looks at a loss for words, and she runs a hand through her hair before taking a seat on the couch. I feel a similar shock, but I can't say I'm disappointed.

I feel horrible about what we did, and I'm eager to make it right.

It won't be easy, but it needs to be done.

* * *

END OF BOOK 1